For all the hacks who seek the truth
and all the flacks who help them.

THE
LOVE
EXPERIMENT

AINSLIE PATON

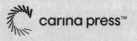

carina press™

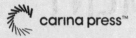 carina press™

ISBN-13: 978-1-335-00623-3

The Love Experiment

Copyright © 2017 by Ainslie Paton

www.CarinaPress.com

Printed in U.S.A.

THE
LOVE
EXPERIMENT

Chapter One

Derelie Honeywell heard the word *cutback* and felt her organs flip inside out and shrivel.

What exactly was a cutback? Back home it was what people did with out-of-control weeds. Was it worse coffee in the breakroom? Could that be a thing? Longer hours for less pay? Was that even possible? Freaking hell. Getting this job had been hard enough, and now it was going to be that much harder to keep it.

It didn't help that the word *cutback* came from the mouth of the paper's biggest bastard. Phil Madden was one of the reasons life in the big city of Chicago was more scary than windy. His once upon a time offensive tackle massiveness was one factor. But it was the reality that as editor-in-chief of the *Courier*, and Derelie's ultimate boss, he muscled over anything that opposed his vision for the paper that made him truly formidable.

Phil got what Phil wanted or you got a different job somewhere else. He was a bastard amongst bastards in an industry that proudly measured that kind of thing.

Less than a year into her new job, Derelie was quietly terrified of him.

She must've made a sound because her cube mate

Eunice elbowed her and she scored a glance from her section editor. "Don't look so scared," Shona whispered. "Every year around now we get the cutback talk."

"You're not a real reporter till you've survived a cutback," Eunice muttered.

Apart from Yogaboy with his man-bun and his perfect lotus position and his effortless vinyasa, there wasn't anything a whole lot more that interested Derelie than surviving a cutback and keeping her job. Said job allowed her to pay the rent on the shoebox she lived in, eat something green regularly, make long calls home, get her teeth straightened and update her wardrobe. But she appreciated Shona's attempt at reassurance.

If there was such a thing as tenure at a newspaper, Shona had it. She was rumored to be doing it with Phil. And since Shona had Tinker Bell proportions to go with her pixie cut, that took some thinking about.

Best not to.

"What does cutback mean exactly?" she whispered back.

Shona used a cupped hand to cover her response, as Phil kept talking. "Hard to tell what it means now. We once had potted plants and a dry-cleaning service, and we used to report on foreign and national news. Now we only cover the state. I remember when we used to have a book reviewer, and a film critic. There were always free books and tickets to shows being handed out. We used to have more editors and photographers too." Shona sighed. "All of that went in cutbacks."

That was not reassuring. Derelie covered lifestyle for the web edition of the paper, which was where any story that didn't belong anywhere else went. Her last story was on the rise of athletic wear as everyday fashion. The one before that was on the benefits of standing desks. Not exactly breaking news.

"Remember, you were hired for the online edition and we all know that's the future of the newsroom," said Shona.

At twenty-eight, with only a slightly shop-soiled degree, another six months of wearing her invisible braces, enough student and credit card debt to qualify for a personal World Bank assistance loan, and the unrequited love of Yogaboy, being considered the future of the newsroom was more of a threat than a reassurance.

This job was her career break, a way to cement her skills base and make a name for herself. She'd do whatever she needed to grip on to it with all ten fingers, all ten toes, and her near perfect bite, because she wasn't going back to small town butt-fuck nowhere until she'd made something more impressive of herself in the city than a decent sun salute and straight teeth.

From the front of the room across the tops of the rabbit warren of cubicles, Phil said, "There'll be a tightening of costs, an increase in the number of syndicated stories and a reduction in the number of pages going to print."

Management speak for "things aren't getting any easier."

"Much thinner and the paper will disappear up our asses," said Dante Spinoza, another beefy bastard who wrote for the sports pages.

"More complaints and I'll have you disappeared up your own ass," Phil fired back.

Derelie's shriveled insides tightened further at that. It was management speak for "if you know what's good for you, shut the hell up."

The only person that didn't apply to was Jackson Haley. Another of the scary bastards. Haley, who was billed as the Heartbeat of the City and the Defender of the People, was a multi-award winning investigative reporter who had his own daily column. His dinkus—which was a thumbnail of his smarmy handsome face—was always part of the masthead on the first page of the paper where he broke the latest big scandal.

He was courted by cops and CEOs, who wanted to be on his good side, and hated by the people and organizations he exposed for unsavory practices. He was well connected and unafraid, despite the fact he'd had death threats, and gossip had it someone once totaled his car with a baseball bat. He was a newsroom legend. He sold papers. He was the only man in the room who could out-bastard Phil without raising a sweat.

Jackson Haley didn't determine whether Derelie kept her job or not; they'd never even bumped elbows in the breakroom, but he was still terrifying in that "I'm utterly fascinated by you, but please don't notice me" way.

Derelie noticed Jackson Haley, though. She couldn't help it. He had lookability. A kind of Old Hollywood glamour with his sweep of dark hair and hard blue eyes that even bracketed behind tortoiseshell-framed glasses were instruments of interrogation. He showed up to work in good suits with starchy white shirts worn without a tie, when most of the other men wore chinos and short-sleeved, soft-collared polo shirts. He shined his shoes and they never had rubber soles. It was as if he was single-handedly trying to bring back the golden age of newspapers, before there was the internet and breaking news sometimes came in one hundred and forty character tweets.

That made him seem like some Clark Kent wannabe.

Clark Kent was a nice guy. Jackson Haley, who everyone called Haley, was a sharp-tongued steamroller, an avenging, all-seeing drone in human form. He'd stalk about the bullpen where the business writers sat with his coat off and his cuffs rolled back, a hands-free earpiece constantly connecting him to whatever secret source his stories came from.

He drank coffee by the gallon and smoked in the alleyway outside the office. She'd never seen him eat. She had seen him bruised, which proved he was no Superman. He never tried to hide the occasional black eye, reddened jaw, or hitch to his stride. Story had it, he boxed in one of those "guys who need to beat other up other guys to feel like real men" clubs.

Cut Jackson Haley and he bled the alphabet. He was journalism royalty. His grandfather was a famous war correspondent and a former editor of the paper.

Derelie knew these things about Jackson Haley because everyone knew them. Heck, the whole city knew them.

Over the top of the kind of rustling silence from a floor full of anxious reporters Jackson Haley said, "No cuts to the city pages," and it wasn't a question. He didn't even look at Phil. His eyes were down on his cell.

Phil's whole frontal lobe collapsed into a frown worthy of an earthquake warning. "We'll continue to produce a quality news service the city can be proud of and I'll do what's necessary to ensure that happens."

Haley laughed. The sound made Derelie flinch. It was the sound of ice cracking. "Are the PR people writing your lines, Phil? They could do with having more actual content, like the words yes or no."

That caused a ripple of nervous humor and made Shona's head whip around to look at Haley.

"I write my own lines, and I don't need to go through you for permission to run this paper," said Phil.

Now there was eye contact between the two men who stood some distance apart, which made for a lot of head turning. Derelie wished for popcorn, job security and fewer visits to the dentist, and she wasn't getting any of those things anytime soon.

"That man has balls the size of Texas," Shona muttered.

If Haley behaved like a man who knew what women were capable of outside of work, who used his good looks and glamour, his fame and professional power to do something as normal as fool around like other men did, Derelie might think Shona had firsthand, closely sourced, eyewitness knowledge of said Texas-sized balls.

But the collective powers of the paper's editors, reporters, fact checkers, photographers and librarians had been unable to muster sufficient evidence that the human headline used his balls for anything as unjournalistic as sex, which had the makings of a tragedy as far as Derelie was concerned.

"Not for permission—for the stories that keep the presses and the dollars rolling in the first place," said the man with the balls in question.

"This is not a debate," said Phil with a savage tug on what little hair he had left.

"No, it's our jobs, our livelihoods and the public good of the city," said everyone's sudden current favorite champion of the worker, using his rumored Texas-sized balls for the good of all.

"Christ, Haley, no one is losing their jobs." Over the collective sigh of relief Phil said, "We'll buy cheaper light bulbs and scratchier crapper paper, so when you're all stumbling around blind with sore asses—" he pointed at Haley "—you can blame that asshole."

Derelie knew working at the *Courier* would enlarge her worldview, but she'd had no idea today's lesson was mostly going to center around sex and waste organs. She snuck a look at Haley. He was oblivious to the stir going on around him, leaning back on a wall with his eyes down on his cell phone screen, too cool for school.

Someone should have the dangerous job of investigating how Jackson Haley looked when he wasn't suited up defending the city, his own face, or the newsroom. Not that she was volunteering, because fascination from afar was safer and the newsroom spin was that Jackson Haley was more into the men he liked to hit than anyone who wore a skirt and heels.

And wasn't that a lifestyle story headline.

Chapter Two

Jack sat at the conference room table for the daily editorial meeting with his cell phone held low on his thigh so he could read email under the table. He'd already pitched his story for the day to Madden, now there was just sports and lifestyle to have their moments to jockey for page position and he was out of here.

He scanned a purloined police report about the hushed-up arrest of a prominent businessman and considered whether it was a story worth pursuing or merely scandal that writing about would only elevate to more importance than it was worth. Deciding it was the latter, he tuned back in as Spinoza talked about a leaked document naming a bunch of sports stars for using banned substances. Some big egos in the sporting world were going to have a bad day once Spin had finished with that story.

For a guy who mostly wrote about tackle counts, Spinoza was right about the *Courier*. If the paper got any thinner, if they employed any more junior reporters to write clickbait about vegetable detoxes or thigh gap, the paper was going to disappear like hundreds of others across the country already had. Not that Jack had any answers. He was an investigative reporter, not a miracle worker who could recast the economics of the newspaper business.

Worse luck.

Potter was the last to pitch. Jack listened to her talk about some university experiment that was supposed to be about finding inner peace or some crap while he prepared for a fast getaway, pushing his chair out and standing. Did everyone know Potter was banging Madden? Madden sure didn't treat her differently than anyone else on the senior editorial team. If anything, he interrogated her pitches that much harder, but this one was seriously hokey.

Jack leaned on the back wall alongside some woman he didn't know, who must've been an intern. *Welcome to the last gasp of serious print journalism, sweetheart.* He listened to Madden grill Potter on her story pitch.

"It's called the Experimental Simulation of Inter-personal Familiarity," Potter said. "It's a famous social psychology study and this year is its twentieth anniversary."

Madden gave her raised brows. "The what?"

"It about accelerated intimacy," said Potter. "I want us to put it to the test."

"What the hell is accelerated intimacy?" said Madden.

"Like what happens between two strangers seated next to each other on a long-haul plane journey," she said.

"I thought that was called free drinks and passing out," Madden dead-panned.

Jack almost squirmed for him when Potter came

back with, "It's about love, Phil," and everyone in the room laughed. Yeah, they all knew Potter and the main man were simulating horizontal accelerated intimacy.

Madden's forehead cratered. "And you want to replicate this experiment?"

"It's a detailed questionnaire and an exercise in sustained eye contact."

Madden sustained an eye-roll, and Jack was glad he'd stuck around for the amusement value. "And why would anyone care?"

"Everyone cares about love, Phil. It's our most basic human interest after food and shelter."

There was some spirited agreement from the section editors, not all of it insincere. Jack didn't bother to stifle a laugh, which scored him a sour look, before Madden barked, "What's the story?"

"It's a series. We pick two people to do the study and they write about their experience and then we follow up and see what happens to them."

"So, if this couple hate the very sight of each other, they'd write about that?"

Potter narrowed her eyes at him. "The study has a high success rate. It's more likely they'll fall for each other." That got a reaction, very sincere disbelief.

"I've got stats." Potter shuffled her notes. "It's been responsible for making friends of enemies, creating lifelong partnerships and lots of marriages."

Madden groaned. "What poor unfortunates do we put through this? A couple of D-grade celebrities?"

Jack's phone buzzed and he looked at the new text. A story lead about an insurance company fraud he'd been waiting on. He needed out of here. He took a couple of steps toward the door.

"That could be fun, but even the D-grades want to be paid. I'm suggesting we match Derelie with one of our male staff members."

"Haley," Madden barked.

"What?" Hand on the door, Jack looked at Madden. "Got a lead."

"Don't leave this room."

"No, whatever this is. No." Jack made a throat cut gesture to go with his response.

"The great Jackson Haley is scared of a lurve experiment." Madden said *love* as if he was a 1970s porn star. *Bow-chicka-bow-wow.* His Marvin Gaye impression was better.

"It's a cute feature." As well as a crass setup, because the couple who got press-ganged into this would have to pretend they liked each other or come across as entitled assholes. "Pick someone else to be cute in it."

"I'm picking you."

Christ, this was payback for pulling Madden up in yesterday's staff meeting. Jack was about to say so when Potter cut in.

"It's, um, it would be better if the couple actually had potential."

Madden wagged a fat finger at Potter. "Enemies to friends, you said."

Potter scrunched her eyes. "That might've been a tiny exaggeration. I was thinking Derelie and Artie Chan."

Jack knew Chan, the guy worked the health beat, got halfway to being a doctor before he turned to reporting. Derelie was no doubt one of the newbies specializing in clickbait, with a freshly minted degree and a huge collection of shoes. Regardless, he had no time for fluff pieces. "Sounds about right to me…" What was Potter's first name again? Why couldn't it just be Harry? "Potter."

"Not to me," said Madden. He wore the same evil grin he sported when he was forced to account for himself with the *Courier*'s owner, and it was directed at Jack. Not good. "You want the feature, Shona, you make it work with Delia and Haley."

"Derelie," Potter corrected.

"No," Jack said, sliding his phone into his pocket and folding his arms across his chest.

"Rhymes with merrily," said Potter.

It rhymed with zero fucking way.

"Touchdown," said Madden. No surprise he'd go for this, it was a score-settler. "Here's the pitch. The *Courier*'s own Jackson Haley, Heartbeat of the City, takes part in a love experiment and we all live happily ever after. It's adorable." The word *adorable* simply didn't belong in the man's mouth. "Readers will eat it up. What do you think, Shona?"

Fuck the love experiment. Jack cracked his knuckles, readying to box his way out of this. He was nobody's happy ending.

"It's only, um, isn't he…" Potter turned from Madden to Jack. "Don't you prefer, aren't you—?"

"What?" Madden barked.

"Gay?" she said.

"What?" said Jack. "No." Where did that come from? A man takes pride in his appearance and he's gay. Did gay men have a monopoly on a decent haircut and suit-wearing now? If that was the case, then yes, he was gay, the gayest of them all.

"No?" asked Potter. Could she possibly sound any less convinced?

"No." Fuck, he should've said yes, that would've ended this since they seemed fixed on the idea of a traditional couple for this shit-show.

"Derelie thought, so I thought. But are you sure, because we could still have you and—"

"Not that it's any of your business." Christ, they'd have him doing this with Artie in a minute. Jesus, he needed a smoke. He'd have to detour by the alley before he hit up his contact about the fraud story.

Madden clapped his paws. "That's it then, you have your story, Shona. Samson—I mean, Haley—and Delilah do the love experiment and we'll make a big splash of it online, lead story, promoted, and it will be good for the clicks. We throw advertising dollars at it too."

Jack sighed. He'd get around this by being unavailable. "My investigation and daily deadlines come first."

"You're being a pussy, Haley," said Spinoza, with undisguised glee.

He hated that phrase. Jack's pussy would give Spin a run for his money.

"It has to be done in the next month," said Madden.

"You're only doing this because of what happened yesterday."

Madden slapped his hand over his heart and rearranged his meathead into an expression of hurt. "I'm shocked you'd think I'd be steamed you challenged my authority in public. You're my star reporter, a living legend. Our readers will want to watch a hard-bitten champion of the fourth estate find true love in a questionnaire with a woman who thought he was gay. Who wouldn't? It's genius."

"Chan is more interesting than me."

"Afraid of a little multiple choice are we, Haley?" said Spin. *Dickhead.*

"It's a little more than a check in a box," said Potter.

Madden tapped the tabletop. "And because you're a good guy, Haley, you get that this paper is struggling, and what makes our owner happy is lots and lots of readers."

Jack closed his eyes and blew out an irritated breath. He was caught against the ropes and his opponent was bigger, meaner and paid his wages.

"And you also get that our lifestyle stories bring us lots of lovely readers, and our advertisers like that. And, Jack, if you fuck with Shona or me on this, I'll spike your next juicy exposé so fast and replace it with, oh, I don't know, some junior school kid's discovery of an ancient civilization using only Google and a crushed Oreo. You got me, Haley?"

"Loud and clear." *Bastard.*

He suffered consecutive back slaps as the room emptied, *yeah, yeah, very funny*, but he focused on Potter. "Give me this questionnaire. I'll get it done today." No time like the present to bury this idea where the sun and a snappy URL would never shine. He'd be so boring they'd spike the story.

Potter gathered her folder of stuff. "It's not that kind of a questionnaire."

"It's online?" That made sense. "Okay, email me the link."

"It's not that kind of questionnaire either."

"What do you mean?"

"It's a discussion based on a set of questions."

Shit. "I can't do this now?"

"No, it'll take a couple of sessions, each addressing ten questions."

He did a quick calc. Not multiple choice. A minute a question and that was generous, ten minutes a session. He could knock this out in thirty minutes. No sweat. His phone was going crazy buzzing in his pocket and he had a deadline to meet. He held his hand out. "I got it."

"No, Haley, you haven't got it."

"Right, right. Derelie-rhymes-with-merrily has to do it too." She could come get her own questionnaire.

"You have to do it with Derelie."

Oh hell.

"You and Derelie have to sit together, face to face, and discuss the questions, all of them, and record your responses and how they make you feel about each other. You need to meet a couple of times, over drinks or dinner. You can expense it."

No freaking way. He didn't have time for that kind of nonsense. "You're jerking me around."

"I'm not." Potter's phone rang and she silenced it. "That's how the experiment works. Plus there's the eye contact exercise."

Fuck that. Thirty minutes, an hour tops, in a bar with a beer and Derelie and he'd have it done. Fact that it'd be next to useless in terms of the happy ending wasn't his problem. Artie "Heartthrob" Chan was on standby.

Potter went for the door. "I've gotta run. Derelie will fill you in." She left Jack standing in the empty room.

He called after her, "Who's Derelie?" but Potter put her phone to her ear and didn't respond.

"I'm Derelie."

Huh. Not alone. It was the woman he'd taken for an intern. "You're Derelie?" This was the woman who thought he was gay, who should've fought harder for Artie.

"I'm Derelie."

"You work here?" She didn't look old enough to drive a car let alone work in a newsroom.

"Seems that way."

"You're not…" Not quite glossy enough around the hair and lips and the shoes to be one of the women who wrote for the fashion pages and read books with Girl in the title in the breakroom, that's what'd thrown him off. "Never mind."

"Wow, and you're not Artie Chan."

Swipe left, baby.

"You thought I was gay. It's the suits, right?" They were easier, he didn't have to think about getting dressed in the morning or get changed if he had to make a sudden appearance on TV.

"It's not the suits."

"Then what? Heck, forget it." Enough time wasted on this. "Show me the goddamn questions."

Chapter Three

Jackson Haley sucked. Like big time, sour lemon, jaw
aching sucked. And it wasn't the suits, it was the ego.
You could probably see it from space. It'd be this great
glowing balloon of overinflated male confidence and
starched master of the universe entitlement—with pin-
stripes.

Derelie liked him better when he was a headline, a
dinkus and a legend she could speculate freely about,
not the real thing standing in front of her, mating his
eyebrows with annoyance.

He hadn't even registered she was in the room, and
then that crack about whether she worked here. What
did he think she was doing at the editorial meeting,
haircuts and shoeshines?

Derelie didn't want to be part of this either. Being
the story was different than writing them. A byline,
maybe a thumbnail of her face, her own dinkus or digital avatar, was all the fame she was looking for, but
Shona hadn't exactly given her a choice, and despite
what Phil had said at the staff meeting about cutbacks
meaning cheaper crapper paper, an email had come in
talking about buyouts and voluntary layoffs.

It was better to be volunteered to endure the human headline than to be involuntarily polishing her resume. She tried an ocean breath and lifting her weight from the earth with her armpit chest open to see if that helped. It didn't.

"I don't have the questionnaire." The world's least likely romantic lead took his eyes off his cell long enough to blink at the ceiling. "Shona will email us the first part when we're together."

"We're together now."

If she let him intimidate her, she'd fail to get this story. If she failed to get the story, she'd fail to make the rent. If she thought about him in his underwear, he'd be less intimidating. "You're not taking this seriously."

"Good observation, cadet. You were listening in journalism school."

Neck to knee underwear made from something ugly and scratchy, like a burlap sugar sack. "I have a name and it's Derelie." Ocean breath. *Jackson Haley, you are going down; you are not going to frighten me out of my job.* "Are you being a jerk because of the gay thing or are you always this way?"

His expression didn't change. "I'm always this way. What's the rest of your name?"

"Honeywell."

"Derelie-verily-sounds-like-merrily Honeywell." He stuck his hand out. "I'm Jackson Haley and we got off on the wrong foot. Call me Haley."

She looked at his outstretched hand suspiciously, took it reluctantly and didn't wince when he squeezed harder than necessary. He was just a man wearing hideous underwear who smelled like cinnamon. "I'm going to call you Jackson, because that's friendlier."

That got a grimace out of him and his eyes went to his cell screen. "Jack, if you must. Only my mother calls me Jackson about once a year, which is quite enough. You're right about Chan making better copy. Go tell Potter I'm a mutinous asshole and we'd be a car crash, tell her I'm not cooperating, and ten to one, Chan will be your man."

He'd rolled with it when she'd called him a jerk, so she went with "You are a mutinous asshole." How was it the world housed so many of them? What sin had she committed that meant she had to get experimentally intimate with one? All the yoga calm she stored up was nothing in the face of this man. Her peaceful warrior was bristling, but better to be infuriated than terrified.

"Start the way you mean to go on, Honeywell," he said with a wry half smile that indicated his burlap sack underwear was lead-lined and nothing she said would get to him. Good to know.

"My name is Derelie. I mean to hold on to my job, so I'm big on doing what Shona and Phil say."

"Look, they want a solid story, full of pathos and emotion, that feel-good, human connective tissue stuff. They want two colleagues who become friends. They want great lines they can turn into promo. They'll want photography. They'd marry us off for readership if they could. We all know I want out of this. But Chan— young, pretty, intelligent, witty, knows how to give a heart massage. Chan will make good copy."

"At least we agree on that."

"We're done here then. See you 'round, Honeywell."

"We're not done, Jack." Shona expected her to get this story done. She'd get it done.

His cell rang and he answered it. He might look like a gentleman, turn heads when he passed, but he had the same manners as the drug dealer who had a corner outside her shoebox. "Haley. Yeah. No. Can you substantiate that? Okay. Two hours." He disconnected. "You're still here."

"I work here, remember. I want to keep working here."

"So you can write about how teal is the new black."

Bastard. "No." Maybe. That story got a lot of clicks. Not her fault teal was the color of the season and people were interested in that. And she didn't get to choose her stories; they were assigned to her, like this one.

"Your last piece was on sexting horror stories." He shivered in mock horror and she flinched, which made what came out of her mouth embarrassing.

"You read my pieces?"

"Don't be ridiculous, Clickbait." He held up his phone. He'd just searched her. "That's not serious journalism, and while I get it has a place in the infotainment age, it's not my thing."

"Asshole." He let loose a deep chuckle, and for some reason that sound, rather than what she'd just unthinkingly said, made her face get hot. He might be an asshole, but he wasn't pretending to be anything else. "I can't go to Shona and tell her I couldn't get you to play ball."

"Why not? It'll be entirely accurate. That's a positive trait in serious reporting, Honeywell."

"Derelie, my name is Derelie." *And did he call me Clickbait?*

"Rhymes with merrily. What kind of a name is that anyway?"

"The one my mother gave me. It does the job of, you know, identifying me."

"From all the other Derelies."

She sighed. "Yes, Jack, from all the other Derelies. I can't go to Shona and admit failure."

"You can—no one is expecting me to cooperate."

"Surprise them."

He muttered the word, "Rookie," to his cell screen.

"I'm not a rookie. I'm not a cadet. I banked four years of reporting experience before I got this job."

"In your hometown farm news sheet."

How did he know that? Fricking Google. She'd written a lot of stories about livestock, and bake sales. She'd had the Little League coach on speed dial. "That's not the point. You think I'm frivolous. It's not like reporting jobs are fresh for the picking. I took what I could get."

"I thought you were too young to be paid to work here, Honeywell. And other than that first impression, I haven't spared two brain cells on you."

He was unreal. "I bet your dinkus brings all the girls to the yard."

Up went his brows till they rode above the frame of his glasses. "Now now, you don't want to stoop to my gutter low standards. But interesting to note you've moved on from gay."

No self-respecting gay man would wear neck-to-knee, lead-lined burlap. And yes, she did want to roll in the gutter with him, if that was the only way to get him to take her seriously. "Spin is right, you're scared of a little questionnaire and some eye contact."

He hit her with a blue blaze of hot as hell eye contact that turned the ligaments in her legs to mush. *Oh shit.* He was a big city reporting god with his own dinkus and she was a small-town mouse clickbait rookie. But that was okay, she didn't need her legs to go anywhere at this precise moment, she just needed not to not fall over and not fail on what would be her first web-print crossover lead story.

"I want to keep my job."

"No one is going to fire you because I screwed with you."

With, he'd said with. That wasn't a proposition. No need to wander on down to HR where voluntary redundancy was the new teal. "They won't fire you."

"Not my job to make you feel secure, honey."

"Honeywell." She shook her head. "I mean Derelie. You're such an ass."

"We established that in the lede. Go get Chan. He's Prince Charming, more your type."

"How would you know what my type was?"

He touched the side of his nose in a gesture of "I know what I'm talking about" and then said dryly, "It's a vague guess, based on the supposition that you thought I was gay and asked for Chan in the first place."

He had her beat. She let go a distressed sigh and flapped her hands. "How did you do it?"

"Do what?"

"Become formidable. You're not that old."

"Compared to you, I'm ancient."

"I'm twenty-eight and you're, what?" He wasn't

going to answer unless she baited the hook with a tire. "Forty?"

"Are you trying to questionnaire me by stealth?"

She grunted. Hadn't thought of that. A missed opportunity. "No, I'm just trying not to lose my job before I've learned everything I can from it. You could teach me." The things she could learn from Jackson Haley would accelerate her competence-building to the nth degree. If she could stand to hang around him. It was a bold ask, and she held her breath waiting for his answer.

"I think you've got a better bead on the season's top colors and the ten best sleep hacks than me, Clickbait."

"You know what I mean." It was worth a try. "And don't call me Clickbait."

"I know you're trying your hardest to get me to play nice."

"But you never do, right? Phil is putting you in your place." She dropped her eyes to the carpet. Sassing Jack in the gutter wasn't winning her any points, and she was out of tactics. "Wow, I've had some bad dates, but I don't think I've ever been set up as anyone's punishment."

He said nothing, his eyes still on his cell. It would be smart to detour by Artie's desk and recruit him before she went to Shona, if she could make her legs work.

"Honeywell, do you smoke? Because if you're going to carry on being pathetic and wanting an audience, I need a cigarette, so we have to relocate this stimulating argument to the alley."

She wrinkled her nose. "I don't smoke. They'll kill you." Now he was trap-setting. But if he was so desperate to get away from her, why hadn't he simply answered a call or walked out? Maybe he had a shred of compassion tucked into those trim gray trousers.

"Do you at least drink? You can't be a respectable member of the profession and not know how to hold your liquor."

She wasn't much of a drinker. To her disappointment, she'd been called a lightweight more times than she cared to recall. She was trying to switch from coffee and make green tea her usual poison, but this was Jackson Haley, Heartbeat of the City, asking her for a drink. Wasn't it?

"I drink." She could fake drinking. Done it a million times.

"Tomorrow night, seven. Donovan's. Tell Potter you convinced me to play ball."

"I did?" With only jellied hamstrings to show for it. This had to be a trick.

"No, Honeywell, I have every intention of getting out of this story, but we can make it look like you tried."

That goddamn big swinging dinkus.

Chapter Four

Jack watched Kelly pour his drink and place it on a coaster in front of him. The bartender didn't linger. She'd long since learned Jack didn't do idle conversation. Five minutes later, a man took the stool beside him, placing an envelope on the bar top between them. The guy ordered a beer and Kelly poured it.

Jack waited. There was every reason to believe this was Henri Costa, his whistleblower inside Keepsafe General Insurance, but he lost nothing in waiting for Henri to declare himself, though he had to make a determined effort not to snatch the envelope, rip it open and dive into the contents.

"You're Jackson Haley?" Henri didn't turn; he spoke to the row of bottles behind the bar. "You look younger than your picture."

The best word to use to describe Henri was *average*. Average height, build, blue suit, white shirt, black shoes. You didn't have to look exceptional to be courageous and Henri Costa had courage, the kind that could get him into a lot of trouble.

"Is Henri Costa your real name?"

Now the man turned with a panicked expression above his five o'clock shadow. "You can't use my name."

"Relax, Costa. I need your information, not your name."

Costa prodded the envelope, pushing it slightly toward Jack. "It's all here. Names, emails, phone transcripts, internal memos, financial records. I can't afford to lose this job, but they shouldn't be allowed to get away with this. It's corruption all the way to the top. They're ruining people's lives."

Jack put his hand on the envelope and slid it in front of him as Costa stood. "I'll take care of it." He'd use Costa's information to start an investigation to verify the insurer was defrauding accident victims out of compensation by paying off doctors to invalidate legitimate claims.

Thousands of privately insured accident victims had discovered their injuries weren't covered because of a criminal loophole in how they were assessed. At a time when they needed help the most, injured people were left without support, often unable to work, with horrendous medical expenses and without hope of putting their lives back together.

Stories like this were what Jack crawled out of bed for. It was how he made sense of his life. He downed his bourbon. He'd get started tonight, and if Henri Costa's information checked out, Jack's story would bring to light the corrupt practices of the insurer, start legal action, topple careers and with luck, provide relief and recompense to the victims.

Costa left his beer untouched. It was on the bar top

still when Honeywell slipped onto his stool. *Shit*, he'd forgotten about her.

She took in his empty glass and the abandoned beer. She glanced at her watch. "Have you been waiting long?"

"Something's come up, Clickbait." He swiveled to face her. "A tip I have to follow through on."

"Now?"

"I didn't buy that beer for you." He signaled Kelly as he stood. "I've got an account, get yourself something on me."

"Jack." She swiveled, just as he stepped into the gap between their stools. Her knees bumped his thighs. He almost touched her shoulder to steady himself. Her face colored and her mouth shaped an O. "Sorry, ah, I."

He said almost the same words, dropping the Costa envelope. He'd gotten a nose full of floral perfume while she'd come too damn close to kneeing him in the groin. He bent to snatch up Henri Costa's evidence and she moved too, and he scored an elbow to his ear. It knocked his glasses askew. When he straightened up, she had her hand clapped over her mouth, but it wasn't enough of a barrier to stop her laughter spilling over.

He adjusted his glasses. "Yeah, very funny, the defender of the people needs defense against a woman who wrote about feminist art activism today."

"'Knitting in the City.' You read my story."

Curiosity had gotten the better of him. He read a dozen papers every morning and subscribed to more national, international and special interest news services than he could list, but he'd specifically looked for her story this morning because she'd surprised him.

She clasped her hands at her chest and fluttered her eyes. "Aw, Dinkus, you care."

Dinkus. "At least it wasn't 'Movie Heroes in Extremely Tight Pants,'" which was the actual lead story for the *Courier* in terms of eyeballs that day.

"If you read that story I'll have to rethink my stance on your sexuality."

"I stopped at the headline."

She grinned. "I won't call you Dinkus if you don't call me Clickbait."

He'd intimidated her for all of five minutes yesterday, and she'd held her own admirably. There was something farm-fresh and freckled about Honeywell, with her auburn hair and her pale, otherworldly eyes, and for a moment he wanted to tell her to get out of this industry before it turned her humor to hardness and disappointed her.

"Sorry about the assault," she said, with a shrug more reminiscent of a schoolgirl than an ace reporter.

"I've had worse."

"I've heard you do a fight club thing." She gestured to her eyes. He had no idea what color they were—washed out, ethereal. "How do you manage with glasses?"

"Contacts."

"But you don't wear them during the day."

He almost responded. Almost fell into the back and forth of a discussion with her like he'd done yesterday. She had such an open, easy manner, a good skill for a reporter to use to get people to open up. But he had the Costa envelope and a night of reviewing its contents in front of him, and she made him feel ancient, eight years between her twenty-eight and his thirty-six. And love, even a watered-down, highly stylized infotainment for the masses version, wasn't an experiment he was signing up for. Better to hit it and quit it before he wasted any more time.

"See you 'round, Honeywell. You'll do great with Chan."

"Hold on, Haley. We have a date." He'd stepped away, but she spoke loudly. "If what's in your envelope is going to become invisible if you don't look at it tonight, then by all means, dump me."

He turned in time to see her tip her chin up to the ceiling, then she leveled her eyes at him, less schoolgirl than grade school teacher. No man in his right mind would dump this woman without further investigation. But this was work and she was a huge distraction and he hadn't been interested in dating for so long now, he wouldn't know how to start. It was better that way for all concerned. Married to the job was fine with him. It had the occasional perk of attracting the right kind of female attention and that worked—no complications.

"Is it?" she said.

"Is it what?" He had no idea what she'd said, only that the tone was not to be messed with.

She quirked her head to the side and pointed at his hand. "Does that envelope you've got a death grip on contain proof of alien life?"

Now that would be a story he'd like to write. "Proof of something equally important, I hope."

"And you have to look at it right now?"

"I told you, this love experiment, it's not for me."

"Gotta say, if Artie Chan wasn't going off on a medical conference junket, I'd agree with you. Might've been the one doing the standing up. You forgot about asking me here, didn't you?"

No point pretending otherwise. "Don't take it personally, Click—Honeywell. You're enterprising, you'll work this out."

"Before or after we explain to Phil what we're doing here together?" She waved over Jack's head and then dropped her voice to a confidential hush. "He didn't know I existed before yesterday." She laughed, making her stool swing side to side in a tiny arc. "Look at me, coming up in the world."

She was something this Derelie Honeywell. She made him smile, though the bite of Madden's hand on his shoulder put a stop to that.

"Is that what I think it is?" Madden's eyes went to the envelope.

"Yeah. I'm about to go—"

"You've done your lovemaking experiment then?" Madden switched his gaze to Honeywell.

"Making good progress," she said, making Jack raise a brow at her. She didn't falter under Madden's glare. She'd just lied for him. Farm fresh gave good urban savvy.

"Good to hear, because Haley…" Madden squeezed Jack's shoulder. "I don't see this love story happen, that fraud story—" he nodded toward the Costa envelope "—you're hoping is your Pulitzer gets buried on page fifty to give your son-of-a-bitch father something new to complain about."

"You won't do that." For all the clicks and ratings guerilla knitting, weird animals from the deep, gruesome murders and appalling bridezilla stories got, the *Courier*'s reputation as a serious newspaper still mattered.

Madden laughed. "Trying me would make my year, Haley." He let go of Jack and left them, going into the adjoining restaurant, where he met a woman who wasn't Potter. Man was a dog, because that white woman didn't look like his sister, nor was she adjusting her neckline like she was a source of any story except a bedtime one.

"Your father is a son of a bitch?"

That's what Honeywell went with? She followed up with, "Phil and Shona aren't exclusive," and rounded out with, "If I didn't want this job, I'd like to see you go up against Phil." And what do you know, urban savvy with a side of reckless endangerment.

Honeywell was almost eye-to-eye with him, sitting cross-legged on the stool. Jack took in the fact she had legs for the first time since she'd almost done him some damage. She had damn fine legs.

"Go on, get out of here. I won us some time," she said.

Jack was back on his stool before he realized what he was doing. The envelope would wait for the half hour it took to show the woman some respect. He wouldn't demean her by calling her Clickbait anymore. Also, he needed to eat, so it wasn't Honeywell who was making him stay.

"They make a good burger here," he said.

"Make mine with extra cheese and a side of fries."

Interesting. He'd half expected her to turn up her nose at a burger or ask for it to be free of all the things that made it great. Women lived on kale, as far as he could make out.

"I can't resist a good burger and I can't get a read on you, Jackson Haley. You smoke and drink and throw punches. You eat badly and dress well. You're passionate about reporting, and you haven't tried to come on to me, which, given the setup would almost be understandable."

He signaled Kelly and ordered. He wouldn't know how to come on to Honeywell. He should know. But he hadn't had to worry about that kind of thing. It'd been on tap. Now it seemed like a terrible gap in his capability set. "And you surprised me, Honeywell. You lied to Madden."

She shrugged. "You're still here, and if you check your phone, Shona has emailed us both the first set of questions. I'd call that progress."

"The paper is pimping us out and you're comfortable with that?"

"We don't have to become lifelong friends." Her eyes went to her hands in her lap. "I get that's not going to happen. All we have to do is meet a couple of times and record how the questions and answers makes us feel."

He checked his phone. Goddamn lifestyle reporting. It was taking over the news business. "Chan is really away on a conference?"

"He really is. It's in Hawaii. He's taking vacation time."

"Would you lie to me, Honeywell?"

She looked at him with a frown. He put his cell down to watch as she considered that. Those eyes were the palest blue on a color chart, right before you hit gray. They should make her seem icy. "I might if I thought it would help. If I thought you'd buy it. Getting you to do the story looks good for me."

They stared at each other. Nothing cold about her, a smile that could start an adventure and a complete lack of posturing. "How am I supposed to trust you now you've admitted that?" But oddly, he did trust her, her answer was so damn honest.

"You don't need to trust me. I can't hurt you. Whatever this power play between you and Phil is about, it's got nothing to do with me. I don't think either of you care about me one way or another."

She made him sound like a chump. "You're making it difficult for me to dump you and this ridiculous story, Honeywell."

"I am?"

"You know it."

"Oh no I don't. You're all business and power to the people, Jackson Haley, and I'm all 'look at Jesus's face in a piece of toast' and 'here's a python that ate a goat.'"

She said that so matter-of-factly he nearly choked on his laughter, shocking the Jesus toast out of Kelly, pulling a beer behind the bar.

"Swear to God, Haley, you've been coming to my bar for years and I've never seen you laugh like you meant it. Didn't know you had it in you." Kelly cocked a thumb at Honeywell. "Who is she?"

She was a woman who'd gotten in his goddamn way and was about to complicate it.

Chapter Five

Derelie had skipped yoga and the chance to see Yogaboy do his sinuous sun salute to prop up a bar with Jackson Haley. And he'd forgotten all about her. It was bad enough Ernest was forgetting her. Ernest wasn't competent with a calendar. Maybe Jack wasn't either. But then she'd almost taken out Jack's manhood with her knees and his eyesight with her elbow, so perhaps that was the problem.

She'd liked how his eyes had gone wide and he'd grunted in surprise when her knees grazed his thighs, almost reaching for her and dropping his precious envelope. Another few inches higher, she'd have been able to verify if his balls were Texas-sized. They'd said sorry at the same time.

And then he'd stayed and suggested the best burger she'd eaten in years. It was a burger to make all future salads taste like grass clippings. She wondered if he'd notice if she undid the button at the back of her pencil skirt.

He was a man trained to notice things. But he was selective. And at the moment, he wasn't being a bastard.

Not that she cared. Jackson Haley was a high-profile

assignment not a potential assignation. She wanted Yo-gaboy to notice her. Over the months they'd shared the same class cycle she'd shuffled her mat closer to his to give him a fair chance of catching her eyes. But he was so focused in his practice, he'd never once turned his man-bun her way; she'd only ever seen his tattoos side-ways and upside down. It was a crime against hotness.

Jackson Haley's notice, outside of what he could teach her about the newspaper business, was a little too unsettling to consider, although he did show traits of being human, and under the gruff stuff there was a sense of fun. She hadn't had to think about him in burlap undies since the food arrived, but he'd just read the first question from the study, and his brows veed under his glasses, so feeling tentatively secure was probably a mistake.

"'Given the choice of all people in the world, dead or alive, whom would you want as a dinner guest?'" He looked at her right on cue to see her lick mayo off her finger. "Goddamn ridiculous, pseudo-intellectual dinner party question."

She licked another finger, because he was riled up and wasn't paying any attention to her, which meant she could eat her fries and undo her button. She tried not to even sweat around Yogaboy, because according to her yoga instructor, sweat was her fat crying for re-lease. So unattractive. But that whole "keep yourself nice in front of the boy you like" wasn't a factor with Jack. He noticed her in the way he'd notice a roadblock before he drove over it.

"I can't believe this is a university-designed study. A load of bullshit."

"At least they got the right use of whom," she said, when the look he shot her way had that "explain yourself right now" quality. "I'd invite a dead person for sure. Think of the interview opportunities from any of the great figures of history. I'd invite Jesus and ask him why he thought people keep seeing his face in their burnt toast."

He blinked hard, as if what she'd said had come at him like a punch. "That's your answer?"

She took a fry from the basket and waved it at him. "Why not?" He wasn't going to do this for real—what did it matter what she said? She'd have to come clean with Shona in the morning and completely fail to recall Phil sitting a dozen yoga mats away in the restaurant part of the bar with a glamorous blonde woman in a shirt at least a size too small. That was one of her lessons about the city, more people, more politics, more secrets to keep.

"'Question two. Would you like to be famous and what for?'" Jack held a hand up to stop her responding. "You'll be famous for your Jesus dinner party and for solving the mystery of why he chooses to communicate through bread."

She took another fry. Might as well go the whole hog, they were on him, and he could slaughter the whole ten questions in this first batch by himself if he wanted.

"'Question three. Before making a phone call, do you rehearse what you're going to say?'" Amusing how he could make his made-for-radio voice positively creak with disdain. He put his cell on the bar top. "I would rather let Madden strip me naked and flog me raw in the middle of the office than bother with this tripe."

Holy hamburger. Way to make a girl's mouth dry. Under Jack's burlap underwear he'd have muscle, she could tell from the width of his shoulders, how his body narrowed to a slim waist, from the strong wrists and shift of muscle in his forearm where his sleeves were cuffed back. He had that ropy vein thing she liked. Jack twisting under a lash—would he cry out or be all stoic and heroic? Yeah, he'd be all hard jaw, straining neck muscles and edgy breathing.

"Christ, Honeywell, you like the idea of blood being spilled."

"Um." Sprung. Baggy burlap undies. Whatever she'd let show on her face was replaced by a swipe of paper napkin. What was the question? "I do rehearse important calls, especially because it's so easy to hang up on me. I try to get it all out in the first few seconds. Bet that doesn't happen to you. Bet you just say, 'Haley—'" she did her best imitation of his clipped way of speaking "—and whoever you called starts blabbing."

The fact that he tried not to smile and failed was the best. "Some people won't take my call at all. Particularly anyone I've helped bankrupt, send to jail, or generally fucked with."

"Does that mean you do rehearse?"

"It means I have to be sneaky about how I get to people."

One last try at getting some of the Haley journalism magic to rub off on her. "Would you teach me the tricks?"

"Stick with the knitting, Honeywell. You don't want

to go annoying the kind of people I annoy. They play rough."

Which was only slightly less insulting than what he'd said yesterday. "Meaning you don't think I can write hard news like you. That's so sexist."

"It's not sexist. I can name a dozen great reporters who happen to be women. It's about experience and not getting death threats."

He might've had a point there, a slim point, like a fine darning needle. "Is that why you do the fight club thing?"

"I'm more likely to need a lawyer than to throw a punch if someone decides to come after me." She remembered hearing he was the *Courier*'s most sued reporter. "It's getting late and—"

"You have aliens to investigate."

"I do."

"One more for the heck of it." They both knew this wasn't going anywhere. Despite not knowing how to take Jack Hayley since his dreadful underwear made him less terrifying, and the idea of him naked and gritting his teeth made her indigestion twist into an altogether more pleasant sensation, she didn't give him time to walk away. She opened her email. He wasn't someone she could trust—he'd ditch her, embarrass her, make her feel young and stupid without trying, but he'd stopped calling her Clickbait and she could stealth learn from him.

"'Question four. When did you last sing to yourself or someone else and what was the song?'"

"That's not a real question." He leaned across and lifted her phone out of her hand.

"Hey!" she groused. He adjusted his glasses and read the question and handed the cell back. It was the real question. "I guess you don't sing."

"Nope."

"Not even in the shower?"

"Nope."

"Singing in the shower is too frivolous for the human headline. The great defender of the city does not hum."

"I think you like the idea of me belting out show tunes, like I'm a terrible gay cliché. Don't write clichés, Honeywell."

The only reasonable response was a salute, which he didn't catch because he'd looked away. Probably just as well, it wouldn't be smart to get too comfortable with sassing him. "I sing. Badly. To myself. I don't have anyone else to sing to."

His head snapped around. "Did you add that last bit so I'd feel sorry for little single you?"

Crappity crap. "Oh hell no. I was just—wait, yes, I'm single, this is a love experiment. It's supposed to be done by two single people. And you don't need to feel sorry for me. I'm doing fine." Which was absolutely true, most of the time.

"And you assumed I was single, like you surmised I was gay."

She frowned. She'd bought into the office gossip, which suggested he was gay and a player. Rookie mistake. But he seemed so undateable. The oddest combination of unapproachable and compelling. This wasn't going to work, since all they could do was snipe at each other.

"Yeah, this is stupid." Jack was never supposed to be part of the story anyway. She'd have to give up the idea of landing him like he was a whale. "I'm going to talk to Shona."

"I like how you're thinking."

"You'll just have the thing where Phil will bury your alien proof story and you won't win a Pulitzer to shove up your son-of-a-bitch father's ass." It wasn't like that was a death threat, so he'd cope.

She wasn't ready for his reaction. Jack slammed his hand on the bar top and laughed. Hard enough to make the bartender look across at them with an amused expression. Derelie waved her off. It was late and they didn't need anything, and as soon as Jack stopped cackling, he'd be out the door and off into the night, and she'd never see him again except across the top of cubicles and computer screens. She'd say Jack, he'd say Honeywell—if he didn't revert to calling her Clickbait again—and that was that.

She sighed. Jackson Haley was the most interesting person to happen to her since she moved to the city and took the job at the *Courier* eight months ago, even if he wasn't the slightest bit interested in her outside of how quickly he could dump her. Unlike Yogaboy, at least Jack knew she existed.

As predicted, he pocketed his cell and collected his precious envelope, signaled to the bartender and pushed off his stool. "See you 'round, Honeywell."

He didn't wait for a response, just slipped his suit coat on and left. She sipped the last of her ice water and headed for the ladies', peed, soaped her hands, tidied her hair and put her invisible aligner back in. She had a finger to her mouth, fiddling it into place, when she came back into the bar and found him standing there. He gave her the kind of look that made her freeze in place, teeth clamping on her finger.

"How did you get here?" he said.

She gave the aligner one last shove and took her finger away. It was a trick question. Donovan's was around the corner from the office. "Walked, but Red Line from home."

"Take a cab."

"I—ah." Despite a free dinner, a cab home would blow her budget for the week. Dental was expensive.

"I have an account, this is a work expense, like the meal."

"You're going to drop me home on your way?" She wasn't sure how she felt about Jack knowing where she lived. Better if they dropped him off first.

"No. I'm going back to the office."

"You're going to pay for my cab ride home?"

He clucked his tongue in exasperation. "That's what I just said, didn't I?"

She grinned at him. "It's kind of like you singing to me."

He closed his eyes, poked his fingers under the rim of his glasses and rubbed at them. "It's nothing like that."

She didn't want to be his unlooked-for obligation. "I go home in the dark by myself all the time, and this is not a date."

He'd half turned away before he said, "Suit yourself."

She put her hand on his arm. A free ride home was

a free ride home, and sadly this was the closest to a date she'd had since arriving in the city. "I'd love a cab ride home."

They went outside and walked to the corner where cabs usually lurked. He didn't look at her. The office was in the other direction, but he stood there, watching the flow of traffic, saying nothing, giving off chill factor number two-hundred and thirty-seven.

"You don't have to wait with me." He didn't respond. "Jack, you don't have to wait with me."

"Yeah, I do."

"I'm perfectly capable of getting a cab by myself." And really, she'd had enough of him for the night. Brushing elbows in the breakroom would be enough Haley in her life after this.

"Not if you want me to pay for it."

"Oh." That.

He took a soft pouch from his pocket. Lifted a homemade pre-rolled cigarette from it and put it in his mouth, but he didn't light it. The smell of almonds, cinnamon and spicy honey hit her.

"What kind of tobacco is that?"

He said, "Clove," with his lips still wrapped around the cigarette and no eye contact.

To think she'd thought she could drop the burlap and finagle a mentor, that he wasn't so intimidating; wrong, so very wrong. He'd seemed different in the bar. Now he was as remote and surly as a dull stone pillar. He took a few steps away and lit that cigarette, kept the hand holding it and his face turned away, but the sweet sultry scent of it was strong.

The longer they waited, the more uncomfortable

she felt. Did he not feel that too? What would it cost him to chat about something, anything? They'd really needed the near unmanning, the food and the experiment questions to connect at all.

He was scanning the traffic for a cab, and when he turned his head her way she said, "For what in your life do you feel the most grateful?" It was question number five.

His arm shot out and he stepped toward the curb. "For this damn cab pulling up."

Well, hell. Way to make a girl feel like punishment.

He opened the cab door, spoke to the driver across the seat and handed her a voucher. She didn't look at him, just took the slip of paper. He was a bastard, and for a little while she'd forgotten that. *Stupid.* Inside the *Courier,* anyone known as a bastard had a reputation for being tough and efficient, for knocking down doors, breaking hearts and taking numbers, and never writing with clichés. The word was a compliment.

There was a print newspaper definition for a non-standard width for a column of text known as a bastard measure. That was Jackson Haley. Non-standard, not a good fit with those around him, and she'd do well to remember that.

She got in the cab, reached for the door to close it and found he had a hold of it still. "What did you last sing to yourself, Honeywell?"

She yanked on the door. That morning she'd murdered Beck's "Guess I'm Doing Fine" but there was no way she was telling him that.

Chapter Six

Honeywell's cab pulled out and Jack changed his mind about going to the office, ditched his cigarette, and hailed the one behind it. He gave the driver directions to the church and called Barney.

"Haley," Barney said over the customary din of a dozen or more men shouting and cheering.

"Can I get in the pit?"

"Now? No. Twenty-four hours' notice and you know it."

"I'm ten minutes away."

"I don't care if you're on the fucking moon without a spaceship. Twenty-four hours."

Jack ground his teeth. He hated calling in favors, but he hated himself more tonight. Honeywell was fine with the whole experiment gone bust, but the look on her face when she worked out he wasn't a nice guy under the bastard carved a hole in him he needed to fill or he wouldn't be able to concentrate on the contents of Henri Costa's envelope. He didn't understand why that mattered to him, but it did, and it was a distraction he needed rid of.

"Barney, I'm calling in a marker."

"Fucker." Barney disconnected, but he'd get a fight.

Inside the old garage that housed the Church of St. Longinus of the Cocked Fist, Jack pulled his gear from his locker and changed his suit for cutoff sweatpants and gym boots, and swapped his glasses out for contacts. The envelope made him hesitate. It was the only thing of irreplaceable value in his possession, but then it would be meaningless to anyone else.

He had a half hour wait for the bout Barney had arranged for him. Time to warm up, glove up. The current bout was bare knuckle. It'd been going for a while, both men bloody and unsteady on their feet—one of Barney's refs would call it soon enough.

Jack stood above the fighting pit and watched the two men take out whatever anger the day had inspired on each other. Better than the wife, the kids, someone in the wrong place at the wrong time at work, themselves. He liked the madness of bare knuckles, but he couldn't work with busted hands, needed them for the keyboard, so tape and gloves it was.

He also didn't have any martial arts expertise to his name. He could box and he could brawl, but he couldn't land a kick. His opponent, gloved and standing on the other side of the pit, could. This was going to be interesting.

"Best I could do, short notice," Barney said. "Ryan knows this is a straight boxing match, but I wouldn't be surprised if he forgets. If he lands a shin on you, he'll be disqualified. You'll win, but you won't care 'cause you'll be in the heart of hell. You still in?"

Jack nodded. He knew tonight's doctor on call was

McGill. If he ended up with broken ribs, he'd have decent care.

"Need to hear you say it, Haley," said Barney.

That was why the Church of the Cocked Fist— illegal, ill-advised, badly kept secret—thrived. Father Francis Barney ran it in the deserted industrial garage like he'd once run a prep school, before he'd quit the priesthood in disgust over the Church's cover-up of child abuse. Jack would always have a marker with Barney because the other man would never forget he'd written the story when no one else would.

"I'm in."

"Why?"

"I'm on a big story. Need to settle my head." In the pit, one of the fighters was down and not getting up. His name was Khan, a lawyer Jack often used on background. He'd be explaining a broken nose in the office tomorrow.

"You're always on a big story."

"This one is—"

"As important to you as all the others. Why did you need this tonight? You're not going in that pit till I know."

If he said something vague, Barney would cancel the fight. If he said he was worried about what was going on at the *Courier*, the newest round of cuts and layoffs, Barney would tell him to grow a pair. Half the men in this place had lost their jobs and worse.

Beneath him they were clearing the space set aside for the fights, a once-deep cement well where mechanics had walked around under hoisted vehicles they were fixing. "I've forgotten how to be with people."

"What people?"

"People who aren't men."

"You want to get in the pit and have that Australian bastard who's at least five pounds heavier than you beat you up over a woman?"

Over a woman with ethereal eyes, rusty curls she failed to tame, teeth she was trying to straighten and a way of handling him that made him laugh. Over a woman who'd tried hard to connect with him as a colleague and a human being despite the fact he was dismissive and he made her nervous. She'd come armed with a patented method of getting that connection to happen and he'd ridiculed her experiment questions. He'd barely stopped short of calling the work she did frivolous, and that was going to bother him until he had something else more urgent to think about.

Women didn't usually bother him past a certain point. He liked it that way. On the occasion he bothered them, the fact that it was one and done was in unmissable headline type. But for some reason with Honeywell he was annoyed with himself for being an unreliable source. He couldn't even get colleague right with her, and that said something about his character he wanted to erase with his fists.

"A woman at work. She deserved better from me."

"Reason enough." Barney signaled to the head ref, another ex-priest, and slapped Jack across the back. "Go learn tolerance and kindness, my son."

Tolerance and kindness. Two of those soft skills Jack mostly lived without. Odd to think he might find them while dodging fists and being on the lookout for feet meant to stay on the ground.

He took the ladder into the pit and touched gloves with Ryan, at least five pounds heavier and two inches taller than Jack's six two. "Try not to break my jaw."

"Glass jaw, eh? Got it. If I forget and kick you, I'm sorry, mate."

"Don't fucking forget."

Ryan grinned. "I fucked up at work." He was a broker, which meant he lost someone's money; hopefully he could make it back.

"I fucked up at being human."

"Right, let's fucking get to it then, mate. What am I teaching you?"

"Tolerance and kindness," he said repeating Barney's lesson. Maybe if Ryan could teach him those attributes, he could fuck up less.

Ryan laughed and pointed his worn glove at his chest. "Patience and fortitude. Aim high."

They separated. Ryan stalked him, let Jack bounce around and take his measure. That was a kindness, probably the last one he'd see for the next little while.

When they connected, Jack aimed high, showing Ryan how patient he could be by laying a set of uppercuts to Ryan's jaw and forehead. Ryan responded by pounding the need for tolerance into Jack's ribs until he was breathless from it and disengaged to come at the other fighter with a new approach.

Time shifted, collapsed into sweat and muscle strain, into reflex, skill, judgment and luck. The first three rounds were exploratory, a test of each other's intentions. Ryan's punches stung like guilt and Jack was distracted trying to anticipate the moment the man forgot he was boxing and kicked out like Ultimate Fighting's Nate Diaz. It unbalanced him, made him hyper alert, and he loved it. No time for anything but adrenaline, anticipation, attack and response. It was the one thing that cleared his head, reset his expectations, let him focus. In this, unlike in the rest of his life, it didn't matter whether he was matched fairly, if he won or lost—it only mattered that he survived.

The next three rounds were brutal. A fist to the temple made Jack see Tweety Birds. He still recognized the moment Ryan understood his disorientation, but no amount of shaking his head prepared him for the onslaught. All he could do was curl forward and protect his gut until the ref pulled them apart, but somehow it was Ryan spitting in the blood bucket.

They went on, attack, retreat, Ryan occasionally rocking back on a foot as if to ready for a kick, Jack pummeling him while he was mid-motion. After a while they both dragged their feet but were evenly matched—this could go on all night unless one of them went down, Ryan broke the rules or someone called it.

Forty minutes after they'd descended into the pit, Jack spent a few seconds on one knee on the mat letting the ref get almost through the count before he stood. Ryan had more stamina—he'd learned his lesson and Jack was done, reduced to an autopilot haze of defend and withdraw as Ryan came at him, until a wild punch split his brow and needed styptic to stop the bleeding.

They went one more round after that, getting mouthy, taunting each other to take a dive. Ryan sprayed bloody spittle at him. "Do yourself a kindness, Jack—take a fall."

"Fuck off." He got a solitary hit to Ryan's shoulder,

could feel it slide off before it did much damage. His own body had taken all he could tolerate. When Ryan opened the cut on his brow again, the ref called it.

They held each other up on the way to the showers. McGill put a stitch in Jack's brow. Ryan's jaw turned a sick shade of purple. "Feel better?" he asked from the adjacent rubdown table.

Jack felt smoothed out, felt ready. "Feeling groovy."

"Who won?"

They both laughed. St. Longinus was the near-blind Roman soldier who'd stabbed Jesus in his side while he was on the cross. Longinus recovered his sight before converting, was arrested for his faith and tortured, losing his teeth and tongue but still miraculously continuing to preach. In the Church of St. Longinus of the Cocked Fist, everyone who entered the pit and came out laughing was a winner.

All Jack needed now was sleep and the contents of Costa's envelope. But later, at home in bed, with an icepack on his shoulder, feeling bruised and stiff, the touch he remembered most was the brush of Honeywell's knees on his thighs. Seeing her put her finger in her mouth to touch her aligner had made him imagine her doing that under different circumstances, not the one that had him scowling at her inside Donovan's, practically blowing smoke in her face on the street, and shoving her into a cab he had no business expensing.

He'd like to feel Honeywell's knees across his thighs, her ass in his hands, her breath on his face. He'd like to feel her laugh ripple through her when their bodies were pressed together hip to lip, and look into those eerie eyes while he thrust inside her.

He must have a touch of concussion. He didn't even know how to talk to her with the aid of a questionnaire expressly designed for the purpose of creating intimacy, and here he was sore and cut and still capable of getting hard and annoyed about his self-imposed social impotence.

He should've let Ryan knock him out, because he was clearly delirious and needed his brain reset.

Next morning the pain in his body was a leveler. He chugged water and chewed ibuprofen, working at home for a few hours on the contents of the Costa envelope and got into the office early afternoon. He'd barely made it to his desk when Potter appeared.

"Did you win?"

"The other guy did." He'd had a text from Ryan, checking up on him. Nice gesture. The guy had Jack on points in the fight as well as in basic decency.

Potter leaned on the top of his cubicle wall. "I've got a proposition for you."

"Can hardly contain my excitement."

"I'll do the love experiment story with you instead of Derelie."

"No." He turned his back on her to face his screen. Potter was a solid reporter and a good operator. They'd been colleagues for years. Didn't mean he was going to play nice.

"You know Phil wants it to happen."

"I know Phil has an agenda, and since you sold the story to him you can unsell it just as easily."

"It's a good story. Marketing likes it a lot. A couple of big advertisers jumped on board."

"Awesome."

"When do you want to meet?"

"When I said awesome, I meant fuck off, Potter. Honeywell would've told you I'm out. I thought about giving her nothing worth writing about, but she's a nice person." Better that he thought of her that way, farm-fresh, wholesome, apple pie and cream. "She showed me the error of my ways, so I'm out."

"Phil wants you in."

He spun his chair to face Potter. "You want our esteemed editor-in-chief to want me in, and you want to do this instead of Honeywell because she told you lover-boy was with some other woman last night. This is another get back strategy."

Potter folded her arms across her chest. "Phil and me, we're not… That's got nothing to do with it."

Yeah, guessed that in one. Honeywell didn't have subterfuge in her repertoire and Potter wasn't above playing politics. "Don't care."

"Haley."

"On a deadline, Potter." He spun back to his screen.

"Got a responsibility to the paper, Haley."

"To my part of the paper, the part that…" He faltered. Once upon a time he could've said the part that sells papers; now that wasn't so clear. Readers seemed to want Jesus toast and goat-eating pythons and fifteen sexy wash-and-go hairstyles for summer more than ever before.

"You were saying?"

"It's not Honeywell's fault." He didn't want his resistance to be construed as her failure. He turned his chair to face Potter again.

"I should've realized you two wouldn't click. She's

not your type. She's too, I don't know, guileless. Great girl, solid writer, enthusiastic, does excellent work, but you know, not from here."

He was being played. He could smell it over the liniment he was liberally coated with. "Go away, Potter."

"We need the first story by the end of next week."

He turned back to his keyboard.

"What if you'd died last night? Huh, Haley, what would you most regret not having told someone?"

That was one of those fucking questions from the study. "No regrets." Only nervous intensity, buried in rampant workaholism and a deep-seated feeling of misplaced shame. The entire reason he went to the Church of the Cocked Fist.

"Haley."

"Fuck off."

Well, maybe one regret, but not even with his tongue still in his head would he preach it.

Chapter Seven

Jackson Haley showed up for work with two strips of white tape over his brow. Did he walk into a door, or get into a fight on the way back to the office last night? Maybe it was an extreme paper cut from his alien existence envelope. He had a bruise on his jaw and a scrape on his neck and a five o'clock shadow at one fifteen, and Derelie had no business noticing all these things as she watched him argue with Shona all the way across the room in the gap between cubicles.

She had no business telling Shona about Phil either. It just slipped out between "Haley won't do the love experiment" and "I've axed two paragraphs from the how not to play safe using emojis in the office" story.

She badly needed to work on her honesty, rein that sucker back to a more acceptable three wise monkeys in the urban jungle level. That was the hardest part about the city, having to transform herself into someone new; someone slimmer, with straighter teeth, who had a good wardrobe full of nice corporate clothing and knew how to stand all day in heels, ate green things, drank without getting drunk, got enough sleep, and knew how to play office politics.

There'd been no office politics at the *Orderly Daily Mail*. There'd barely been an office to speak of—it was more of an abandoned shop-front full of old desks. Nor were there many colleagues to have politics with. There was Dan, who wrote sports, and Albert, who wrote general news, and the lead reporter was Maisy Brownlow, who wrote "The Downlow with Brownlow" and had done so for thirty-five years. There was nothing hip about Maisy's reports on what the mayor was up to.

Derelie badly wanted to know what happened to Jack's brow. Didn't she have a responsibility to find out? What if he was jumped on the way back to the office and lay comatose on the street for hours while she was bubble bathing in an attempt to stop her brain from exploding?

Getting jumped was the kind of thing that happened in the city. That's what yoga, with its lift your heart's energy, marry your pulse to the movement, open your armpit chest and find your *Drishti* focal point in ocean breathing, was supposed to help with; the sense that the city was a foreign place with different rules, that the world was moving too fast and she didn't have a firm foothold on it.

Breathe the negative forces of the day out through your pores, suck the energy of the cosmos in through the soles of your feet. Leave the earth and enter the limbic system. That's what she was supposed to do. She wasn't entirely sure if entering her limbic system was a good thing. It was the news desk for emotions like fear, pleasure, anger, as well as drives for hunger, sex, dominance, care of offspring, which might account for her obsession with Yogaboy and how the sight of him in child pose made her offspring-making bits squirmy.

Mostly she staggered through the class, trying to find length, soften her knees, breathe through her armpit chest and not dump her weight on the earth until the part where you got to lie like a dead thing on the floor to feel as light as a filament of air. She always kept her face turned toward Yogaboy. He always closed his eyes. He was just like Chicago, mysterious, complex and confident. She was sure he never worried about getting on the wrong train and ending up in the wrong neighborhood where unspeakably awful things might happen to you. There was no wrong neighborhood for him. He fit.

She didn't need to know what happened to Jackson Haley. Who cared what bounced off his thick head? He was a bastard despite the meal and the cab home, if only because he'd already written her off as out of her depth and not worthy of his notice. Screw him and the good neighborhood he no doubt lived in and the hackneyed expense account he rode in on.

Shona came back to her cubicle with a scowl. Derelie made herself not ask, and got on with her current story headlined "Six Common Laundry Mistakes." Jack's story today was headlined "Secret Pact Explodes Cartel." No wonder he thought she was a waste of his time—she was common as laundry detergent while he got to blow things up.

An hour later, he almost exploded her 3:00 p.m. energy crash, only-two-calories soup packet pick-me-up. His email said, Thursday night, 7:00 p.m. Elaine's. Meet you there.

She googled Elaine's. A swanky reservation-only restaurant. He must mean this for someone else. How to respond? She could stoop to his level and be just as clipped and weird or channel her inner harmony. She popped her aligner off and sipped the tomato soup, then typed, I think you meant this for someone else. Also, what happened to your head?

It took a while, but then she got, Can you do it or not? No mention of his head injury. Was this his ungracious way of agreeing to the experiment after all? Shona had intended to force his hand and Elaine's looked amazing—it would be a legitimate expense account meal. Crazy not to go, even if it meant missing yoga. May absence make Yogaboy's heart reach to the sky, while his shoulders traveled to the earth points of his very squeezable ass.

A city life adventure. I can do it. See you there.

Her life had been more like a series of carefully thought through decisions that'd left her bored and frustrated, because she was born in a small town where nothing much happened except economic hardship, but those days were over. Now she was a reporter for the *Courier* and the editor-in-chief knew her name and the Heartbeat of the City, the Defender of the People Jack Haley was going to answer some questions.

Shit, she had nothing to wear.

Jack would wear a suit. Even her best outfit wasn't Elaine's-ready. Elaine's had chandeliers. But her deadlines for the day were met, and though she should be researching for tomorrow, online shopping looked a lot like research and express delivery was even better for you than properly aligned chakras, besides everyone did it. The mailroom was constantly complaining about personal deliveries.

A day later, she was sitting in a booth at Elaine's in her new Cooper Street Can't Get Enough wrap dress in Barely Plum, waiting for Jack to stand her up. The restaurant was impossibly classy, the dress was a keeper, but the colleague was a late-ass, rat-faced piece of work who'd probably dumped her again.

She'd nervously chewed through two breadsticks and waited an agonizing thirty minutes before he swept in, the wind in his hair and the tape off his brow. He stood at the maître d' station and took in the room, definitely looking for someone who wasn't Derelie, because he answered her wave with a nod, but made no move to come to the booth. When he did come, pocketing his earpiece and doffing his suit coat, she could see he'd had that brow stitched.

"What happened?" She pointed to her own brow.

"I thought you knew I boxed."

He'd put her in a cab and instead of returning to the office, he'd gone out to get smacked in the face. Okay then. "How do you want to do this? We can go back and forth or do a complete set and then swap, whatever you prefer. Do you mind if I take notes?"

He blinked twice, then closed his eyes on an outbreath that was all exasperation. "We're not here for that."

"We're not?"

"I thought you… Hell. I'm on a stakeout and I—"

"What, like a cop?"

"Same idea without the weapons."

"Then what am I doing here?"

"You're backup. I can't sit in a restaurant like this for hours on my own without it looking suspicious."

"I'm, what, a fake date?" She'd bought the dress for herself, for Elaine's, it wasn't a date dress. If she'd thought this was a date, she'd have gotten the Betty Basic Black dress that showed she owned kneecaps. If she'd thought this was a date, she'd have swallowed her aligner instead of simply leaving it at home.

"A decoy."

Ah, that made sense, and way to go, coming up in the world. A decoy was at least one step up from a punishment.

"But I didn't explain myself and so you thought— and you look—ah shit, Honeywell."

"What?" No blush. Not even the hint of one. Such a pro. She looked down at herself. "This old thing? Who are we staking out?" Oh god, she was in a new dress, at Elaine's, on a freaking stakeout. *Take that, career, breathe that in and let it blow sky high through your limbic system.*

"Bob Bix. A man who won't take my call, and hopefully a few of his buddies."

That's who Jack had been looking for. "But he's not here?"

"Not yet. But I had a tip-off he'd be here tonight."

"What do we do if he comes?"

"We eat. I watch. You go home. I go back to the office."

She laughed. "No, really, what do we do?"

He pushed his hand through his hair. "The veal is good."

"You're not joking."

"Nope."

This whole time she'd been leaning forward, her ribs pressed into the table in expectation of learning stakeout procedure. She dropped into the padded seat back. "What do we do if he doesn't come?"

"We skip dessert."

Stakeouts seemed way more exciting in the movies. Jack's eyes were down on the menu. "Why me?"

He put the embossed folder down. "You ask too many questions."

Now *that* was a joke. It scrunched at the corners of Jack's eyes and tipped at the edges of his lips. A good reporter found a different way to ask the same question until it was answered. But this was Jackson Haley, and she'd exhausted her bravado passing off the new dress as old, feeling like she'd been stood up and chomping the breadsticks.

With nothing else to do, they ordered and then Jack got engrossed by his cell under the table and Derelie thought about the questions. She had the first set memorized. They couldn't very well sit here all night in silence.

"Do you have a secret hunch about how you'll die?"

His chin shot up. "I box. I don't have a death wish."

He looked down again. End of discussion. It wasn't the best question to start with. Morbid much?

"What would be your perfect day?"

Up came his head again. "Oh, fuck no, Honeywell, we're not doing this."

"We have to talk about something."

His expression said, do we? "I told Shona to take a hike with this."

That accounted for the flounce and the immense

amount of chocolate eaten in the last day and a half and confirmed Derelie's wise monkey decision to play it on the Maisy Brownlow with Shona. Now she wouldn't have to admit she'd gotten the whole Elaine's thing upside down.

"I'm back to, why me?"

"You're doing me a favor. Can't you simply enjoy the meal?"

Arrogant dinkus. "Look, I'm not some desperado who needs to be taken out for a good feed."

"You said you wanted to learn the tricks." He looked up. The smashed brow didn't take anything away from him being a handsome late-ass, rat-faced piece of work. "This is a trick."

Right, this was Jackson Haley playing the mentor. He was so bad at it. "I understand now."

He went back to whatever he was doing on his cell. Derelie studied her nails. She'd tried shellac for the first time. Her hands looked like they belonged to someone else. Stakeouts were boring.

"Can I ask another question?"

He closed his eyes, and he didn't look up. "As long as it's not from the idiotic experiment."

No point asking about his most treasured memory. "Why is it important to see these people having a meal together?"

That got his interest. They were sitting opposite each other in a horseshoe-shaped booth. She'd sat facing the door so she could see him come in, which meant the bulk of the restaurant was behind her.

"Slide over," he said, indicating the center of the

semi-circular seat. She eased closer and now had a better view of the main seating area as well as the door.

He quarter-turned to her and pitched his voice low. "I need to prove the CEO of Keepsafe personally knows a couple of doctors who are helping him rob legitimately insured people of their injury payouts."

"Seeing them share a meal is proof."

He nodded. "It doesn't prove they're in it together to commit a crime, but proving they know each other well enough to share an expensive meal is a good start."

"Disappointing if they don't show."

"It was a good tip-off, I think they'll show. By bringing you, I can pass this off as a coincidence. I'm just here to share a meal with a friend."

He could've bought a real friend or any of the team on the business pages for that. There was activity at the door. "What does this guy we're spying on look like?"

"Bix is in his sixties, tall, thin, bald, wears a hearing aid."

"We have contact." Jack smiled, and Derelie was so distracted by it she almost missed the fact that Bix was on his way over. "Close contact."

"Jackson Haley." Bix approached their table. "Ouch." He touched his own brow. "Glad to see they pay the Defender of the City enough to eat at Elaine's. I trust you didn't get that bump in the service of the *Courier.*"

Jack went to stand with a hand out to shake, but Bix motioned him to stay seated. He had narrow, squinty eyes, and they drilled into Derelie. "And who is this?"

"Robert, this is Honey." Jack cut himself off abruptly enough Bix frowned. Derelie saved him by sliding closer, mashing his suit coat between them to rest her head on his shoulder.

"It's my birthday," she said, prompted by the cake topped with sparklers being delivered to a table across the room.

"Well, isn't that lovely? Happy birthday, Honey. You show your girl a good time now, Haley."

Derelie grinned at Mr. Bob "Probably Going to be Consulting Lawyers About a Story in the *Courier* Soon" Bix, and inspired by a racing pulse and utter wickedness kissed Jack's cheek.

Up close he smelled of sweet, spicy cinnamon. Under the table he made a grab for her thigh, the muscles in his side going hard. He turned his face and his eyes were open wide behind their frames, brows lifted above them. He had an unforgiving grip on her leg. She licked her lips. All her boldness deserted her.

"Better make a good show of it," he muttered, and kissed her on the mouth.

It was so quick she might've dreamed it. He was already back in his own personal space, wishing Mr. Bob "Fooled by a Kiss" Bix a good evening before she could process it. The first kiss of her new city life and it'd happened with a difficult, intimidating man she wasn't sure she liked despite his attempt to show her some tricks.

"You started it," he said, when Bix was safely on the other side of the restaurant.

A difficult, intimidating, argumentative man. Not much she could say to that, other than, are you five years old? It seemed redundant asking him what roles love and affection played in his life, question nine. Wild guess, not much of a one.

She moved around the seat to her own place, reached for her water glass and sipped. She couldn't tell how annoyed Jack was, his expression gave nothing away. "I'm sorry if I overstepped. He looked suspicious and I got carried away."

"I'm not mad." Jack smiled, all the way to his stitched brow. "That was inspired, Honeywell."

Man had an awfully nice smile on his handsome rat-face. The kind that made you want to see it again and again and forgive his terrible choice of underwear and that he thought of you as a decoy and had no use for love and affection.

Damn.

Further lack of discussion was forestalled by the arrival of the meal. Fish for Derelie, steak for Jack. His meal looked better. But never mind post-choice dissonance, the food was a-maze-ing. For a girl used to eating at cheap diners, or alone in her shoebox, this might as well have been a special occasion.

"It's not really my birthday."

Jack's attention was over her shoulder, on the other men taking seats at Bix's table. "I didn't think it was."

This was almost a conversation. She could ask him question ten, which was "If you could change anything about the way you were raised, what would it be?" because she didn't think he'd cope with question eleven, which was, "In four minutes, tell your partner your life story in as much detail as possible."

She went with "What got you into investigative reporting?"

He went with "What got you into writing junk listicles?"

The movement was involuntary. She wiped her mouth with her fingertips. Now she knew exactly how she felt about that kiss. Why did she keep forgetting Jackson Haley was nothing more than the thrill of the chase and the headlines he wrote? He kept telling her, so it wasn't as if he was dazzling the good sense out of her. She had a weird thing for him and she needed to slap her own face. She wanted to track down one of those buses with his Defender of the City face plastered on it and draw horns and a pointed goatee on it.

"Fuck. Sorry, Honeywell." He rubbed at his neck. "I'm a sad excuse for a dinner date."

No debate about that.

"It's not like I was ever conned or ripped off and have a stake in avenging myself against the world. I had a privileged upbringing. This is how I choose to make use of it. And you're doing your job, so I have no reason to be such an asshole. You're helping me out and without what you did, I don't know if Bix and friends would be quite so relaxed. They're on a third bottle of wine, they really do think I'm off the clock."

She ate a few green beans, cooked so they tasted like something bad for you—absolutely delicious.

"What do you want to write?" he said.

If this wasn't a new dress kind of place, she'd ask for a piece of bread to soak up the rest of the yum sauce on her plate.

Jack laughed. "Touché, Honeywell. I wouldn't talk to me either."

She looked up; he was focused on her with those

dark blue, glass-barricaded eyes. He'd asked a question. She'd read that clove cigarettes could numb your tongue, but—Jackson Haley, living dinkus, had asked her a question. "Do you really want to know?"

"You've already worked out I'm no good with chit-chat. I'm interested."

It wasn't flattering. So why was there an odd flutter in her chest? Too weird. "Words matter. Maybe now more than ever. All we've got to influence people with is words. They're still powerful, they still make a difference."

Oh God, now her face got hot. She sounded like a naïve college kid, high on her own self-importance.

"Go on."

She looked at her plate. "I know the traditional newspaper business is dying, but journalism isn't, and it's not all listicles and celebrity updates, it can't be. I want to learn everything I can about being a reporter, about using words to influence people, so I have options in the future." She lifted her eyes to his face, better to know if he was going to mock her before he did it. "I know to you that will sound lacking in ambition, but I come from a town where there's very little choice about what work you do, and if you want to do anything important, you have to wait till the person already doing it dies or moves away. This is my chance to build a career with work I enjoy and I'm not going to mess it up."

He sipped his water—no wine for them—but kept his eyes on her. "They're teaching computers how to do what we do."

She'd read about it. Computer programs that could

create written content, could write entire books made from popular tropes and plotlines.

"Terrifies me," he said. "The *Courier* is already using computer-generated content in business and sports."

"My parents thought I was making a bad decision moving here, taking this job. Thought it was too risky, that I should try for something safer." But she'd already had years of safe decisions and they'd led to stagnation professionally and a string of relationships so lacking in spark it was no wonder she lusted after a man-bun and got tense around the human headline.

"Hard to know what would be safe from change."

The family farm was safe. It was three generations of corn, and a life of juggling a bank overdraft. "If I have to go home, I want to know I tried to make the most of my life."

Jack was silent, probably stunned by her lack of sophistication. His study of her was unnerving. She flapped a hand at him. "What?"

"If you could wake up tomorrow having gained any one quality or ability, what would it be?"

Hah, so he'd read the questions. That was number twelve. "You really want to know?"

"Entirely for my own amusement."

"Does it hurt?" She smoothed her own eyebrow.

He scrunched his face. "I've had a headache for two days. You're stalling."

"I'd like to feel like I'm worthy. Like I'm tough enough to make it on my own. Like no one can stop me, get in my way. I want to feel powerful and in control and in charge of my own destiny." She wanted to be professionally as tough and skilled as Jack.

"And you don't feel like that now?"

She felt small and confused and uncertain. She'd never felt less like she fitted in or more lost and lonely. Her chest felt tight. She shook her head.

He raised his glass to her. "Could've fooled me, Honeywell."

Chapter Eight

Jack had lost count of the number of times he'd upset this woman. He'd tried to make conversation, even used a question from the ridiculous experiment, and managed to do it again. Ordering dessert wasn't going to make things right, but it gave him something to do while Honeywell composed herself like he'd had to after she'd pulled that stunt kissing him and he'd made the whole thing one hundred times more awkward by kissing her back.

Jesus Christ. He'd kissed her lips. Maybe worse, he'd had a death grip on her thigh that would probably bruise, all four fingers rucking her dress between her legs. He didn't know how to bring that up, to apologize, without making things even more impossible.

And now she sat across from him thinking she wasn't worthy, and everything he'd shown her to date reinforced that view. He was a useless human being. If he could wake up tomorrow having gained any one new skill—question twelve—it would be the ability to consider the feelings of others before he opened his mouth.

She ordered the chocolate spaghetti with strawberries and green tea. He chose the North Carolina pecan cake and coffee. When the plates arrived they both coveted each other's order and swapped.

Meanwhile, Bob Bix and his cronies were tucking into soufflés and moving on to dessert wine. If Jack wasn't distracted by how quiet Honeywell was, he'd be writing paragraphs in his head.

She kept her eerie eyes down on her plate, so he could look at her without being caught out. Her complexion wasn't milk and roses, and it wasn't bought at Macy's and troweled on. She'd seen a lot of sunshine in her life, a lot of weather, and it had given her freckles, given her skin a kind of depth that didn't come from hours in front of a mirror. There was something about her hands that told him she was more than he understood as well. A fine white scar ran across the last three knuckles of her left hand, short nails, polished a bright pink she kept touching as if she wasn't sure of the texture or the color. Those hands had done more than worry a keyboard.

She wore no jewelry, no bobbing earrings or jangling bracelets, nothing that flashed or glittered. Her watch was serviceable, a nothing brand. Those absences were remarkable. He'd lay a bet on her hair being wildly curly when it wasn't styled. And another on the fact she hadn't worn heels all her adult life.

He'd say she was playacting at being the kind of grown-up woman who painted her nails, but it wasn't like she wobbled in her shoes or chose awful lipstick or wore too much perfume, and the dress was a knockout, a fabric that had felt silky under his hand.

Whatever those observations added up to, it was enough to make his skin go tight with feeling. It was a bad idea to feel anything for Honeywell. He kept sex out of the work equation. He should never have invited her here, decoy or not; she was a distraction he needed to dispense with, guilt he needed to find another way to deal with.

Fists were good for that, but he'd already tried to have the sense of her beaten out of him and he couldn't do that again for a few weeks. Tired beyond thought was good. If he was going to stay ahead of Bix and the Keepsafe fraud story, he had a long few weeks of work ahead.

She sipped at her green tea and he realized they'd been silent for some time. "You don't seem brittle to me, Honeywell."

She closed her mouth around a forkful of cake and double blinked. Brittle, what kind of a word was that to use? He made it sound like he'd considered her readiness to shatter and found it, to his imminent satisfaction. What a bastard of a thing to say.

"I mean, I'm sure you'll make it."

She rubbed her lips together. It was a very quick kiss and he hadn't caught the flavor of her, but then he had no right to that—he could barely make conversation with her. What he'd just said was the equivalent of patting her on the head like a good dog.

He dropped his eyes to a safer place than her lips, a new message on his cell, and she said, "Keep digging." She was blurry when he looked at her over the top of his glasses, but he didn't miss the cheeky smile. "Every time you open your mouth you dig a bigger hole."

"That appears to be the case."

She made an open-handed flourish. "Can write like a god, but can't make small talk with his decoy date."

"See, you're not brittle at all."

She pushed her plate away. "I'm too well fed to be brittle."

"You look like you're in good shape." Oh shit, was there no end to his shoveling. Good shape, like she was a boxer. One, what the hell was he doing commenting on her figure, two, she was fucking gorgeous, and three, shut the fuck up.

"You are a crack up, Jackson Haley. This is the best fake birthday date I've ever been on."

It was also over. Robert Bix was on the move. Jack's need to hear him say the names of the other two men he'd dined with to confirm they were Michael Whelan and Manny Noakes had him on his feet, credit card in hand. While the other men were dithering over their coats, he paid up and hustled Honeywell outside, seconds before Bix came through the door with his guests. He'd wanted to find a place to stand where he would still hear but not be seen, but there was no time. He put his hands to Honeywell's shoulders and backed her into the restaurant's glass wall.

She made a sharp sound of surprise and her hands went to his chest. He managed to stop her smacking her head on the black glass before he brought their foreheads together. Her peppermint breath puffed across his mouth and she twined her hands around his neck.

"Not brittle at all," she said.

There was that floral scent, there were those curvy hips he'd tried not to notice. She felt good in his arms despite the fact he'd bumped his brow and knocked his glasses askew.

Two feet from them Bix said, "Ah, Michael, next meal is on you," and Michael—possibly Whelan—said, "No, no, it's on Manny."

Jack adjusted his glasses while Manny—possibly Noakes—agreed. "Are they paying any attention to us?" Derelie's eyes were wide pools of opalescent wonder, centered on his face. He could only see his suspects as shadows on the glass wall. "Honeywell."

She turned her head sharply toward Bix and friends. "No. They're drunk. What should I do?"

"Pretend this is not making your skin crawl."

She shook her head, but he didn't have time to interpret that. Bix was on his phone to his car service. "Pick up for Michael Whelan," he said, and gave what Jack prayed was Whelan's home address. Bix did the same for Manny—most definitely Noakes—of a very fashionable address by the lake. Jack had double confirmation, full names and addresses, which Bix knew without prompting after more alcohol than was sensible for a man of his age.

These men knew each other well enough to be colluding, just as Henri Costa's information suggested. They were scum and Jack would expose them. But right now he needed to avoid the same fate.

He shifted closer to Derelie, one hand to the wall behind her, the other to her cheek. He brought his forehead to hers so they were sheltered in each other. Her eyes went to his mouth and her chest rose with short, quick breaths, and all the blood in his brain took a fast train south. He was vaguely aware of a car pulling up, men's voices, but the whoosh of his own heart was louder than the city.

"Are you going to kiss me?" she whispered.

"No."

"Oh."

He thought her earlier head shake might have meant he was going to need to explain how he'd ended up mauling her in the name of a story to Madden or some flunky in HR. Her "oh" left no room for misunderstanding, it simply dripped with disappointment and landed in his gut like a barrage of fists.

He kissed Honeywell, being as gentle as he knew how, touching his lips to hers as softly as possible. He meant it to be brief, playacting, something she was prepared for because she'd sensed it, because of what happened earlier, but now he caught her flavor and one of her hands brushed over the nape of his neck and into his hair and *that*, that did things to his body, revved his engine in the same way as preparing to enter the pit did. But no, this was different, this was a liquid heat that spread right through him, loosening his muscles from his bones.

Nothing hurt anymore, not the bruises on his ribs, not the strain in his shoulder and forearm. Jesus Christ, she was like sunshine. She was warm and pliant and molded to him as if she was cast for his weight and height, as if she was specially fitted to his physical form and the carnal desires he spent most of his time ignoring. He wasn't capable of ignoring them now.

He took that kiss and lit it on fire, angling his head to connect with her better, increasing the pressure and slapping the wall in triumph when she opened her mouth to his on a helpless groan. The first tentative touch of her tongue was a new shock, but he was nothing if not a guy who could roll with the punches. He dragged her hips a little closer and they both groaned. She'd feel how hard he was. She didn't care, this was sudden and out of order, he felt fingernails in the side of his neck and the inside of her knee against his thigh. That dress had a split, he could get his hand under her thigh, and when he did, she clamped down on his bottom lip with a satisfied hiss.

It was the blare of a car horn close by that brought him back, the laughter of people spilling from Elaine's that made him pull away from Derelie's lips. She was lost to the moment still, body pressed to the glass, fingers pressed to the back of his neck, eyes closed, lips wet and parted, and he was in a world of hurt beyond anything Madden could stir for him.

He broke contact altogether and stepped back. "I'll get you a cab."

He dragged his eyes away from her blissed-out expression and made for the curb. She didn't follow, which gave him a chance to settle his head. No way that should've happened. That was all kinds of workplace inappropriate and personally compromising.

He flagged a cab, but let another couple take it. He had to talk to Derelie and it wasn't a conversation he wanted to have in the office.

When he turned to check on her, it was to see her straighten her dress, smooth her hands over her hair, nervous gestures and no attempt to meet his eyes. He went back to her side. "We got them. Thank you.

Couldn't have done it without you. I'll make sure Potter knows what a help you were."

"Help." She looked down at her shoes.

"I wouldn't have gotten what I needed without you, Honeywell. It worked out swell."

"Swell." She put her fingers over her lips. She looked dazed. Maybe she'd banged her head.

He leaned closer and ducked his chin to look more closely at her. "Are you all right?"

Quick shake of her head. "No. No." Then her eyes snapped up and she shoved him. "You kissed me." She wasn't dazed, she was pissed off.

"You asked me to."

"You said no."

"I lied."

She flapped her arms. "Why would you do that?"

He lied again. "I'm on a story. You do what you have to do."

"Kissing me like your blood was on fire was what you had to do?"

"For the story." For the story, because what else was there? She was farm-fresh and he was busy and bad news for her.

"Well, now it's my turn."

"It doesn't work like that." Goddamn, he needed a smoke. "There are no turns."

"Isn't that the trick you just showed me? Do what you have to do for the story."

He turned to look at the flow of traffic for a cab, using his body to signal the argument was over as well as his words. "Honeywell, we're done here. Time to go home."

She grabbed his arm. "We're not done. It's my turn. I'm doing what I have to do for the story."

"What story are you talking about?" And then it hit him. "Ah no, no chance."

"You took advantage of me. You have to do the love experiment now."

He pulled his arm free of her grip. "This is work. You knew I was using you, and you could have left the restaurant anytime if you didn't like it, and anyway I don't go around feeling up colleagues. You started it, with the whole girlfriend, birthday, cuddle up shtick."

"My family is famous for dying in their sleep."

"What?"

"Two sets of grandparents went to sleep, never woke up. That's how I think I'm going to die, question seven. You're doing this with me so I make Shona happy, so she makes Phil happy, so I don't get volunteered for a layoff."

She really thought that could happen. "I'm not. You won't. I'll square it with Madden."

"I thought this was a mistake, that you'd sent this invitation to the wrong person and then I bought this dress because—"

"It wasn't a date." That's what he needed her to get. This didn't mean anything. It was all for his story because that was all it could be. "You said it was old."

"I lied."

He let the air filling his chest go. He could've brought Potter. Or Berkelow. Hell, he could've had dinner with Spinoza or Barney. "This was for my story."

"I know that now, but I didn't have anything good enough to wear to a restaurant like this and how was

I supposed to tell you that, you great heaving din-kus? I've never eaten in a restaurant so fancy and you could've brought anyone as your decoy, but you brought me. The only reason you have to talk to me is the love experiment, so I thought—"

"Oh fuck." He'd walked straight into this, because he'd felt guilty about treating her poorly.

"So you're doing it. Question seven. Do you have a secret hunch about how you'll die?"

He did now. It'd be from acute embarrassment the day the *Courier* ran this story.

Chapter Nine

Jack wasn't happy. But he was sitting opposite Derelie in a café chair with a coffee and a scowl, and that was a victory she'd paid for in a loss of brain function from the oxygen he'd deprived her of while putting his tongue in her mouth last night.

And making her like it.

Dammit, she'd liked it. She'd liked how convinced she'd been he was going to kiss her, how insistent he'd been he wasn't going to, and how it felt to be lied to when he took such exquisite care in betraying himself.

She'd never been kissed like that before. Confident but gentle, twisting into a lustful claiming that had her glad she had a wall at her back because the world and its expectations got slippery. *Masterful* was the word for it. His kiss had driven every thought from her head and made the city fall quiet. She didn't get that kind of easy peace from yoga and it made her sad attempts at meditation look like frantic multitasking.

That wasn't to say he used his lips to put her to sleep, *oh good golly no*. He used them to convince her body it was beautiful, to convince her brain they'd kiss forever and never need any additional substance to live on but each other's breath.

He was a professional level liar, kiss-deep.

And just as well she'd caught him out because there was no way he'd be sitting there, sipping coffee and reading his phone screen to avoid her if she hadn't.

"We should start from the beginning and I'll take notes." She had to get this done and not screw up and not let him think that last night had affected her. She could be a professional liar too, if that's what it took to succeed.

He didn't look up from his phone. "In the beginning there was journalism and it functioned to keep people informed, and civilization was fairer, better, for being open to examination."

"Are you lecturing me?" He was most certainly pontificating over his coffee cup.

He looked up. "Could I get away with that instead of this?"

"No." She flipped her steno pad open and looked at the printed list of questions.

"Wait."

She'd never wished she wore glasses more, because the idea of looking over them at him in a kind of authoritarian way was exceptionally appealing. She felt left out of the serious gesture game.

"You're clear about last night?" There it was, grave eyes behind not-to-be-messed-with glasses.

"By clear you mean I'm clear that you kissed me and you liked it, but it was all for the story and it meant nothing to you."

"Right. It was for the story."

"But you did like it?"

He made an exasperated gesture with one hand. "It had to be authentic. Move on, Honeywell."

Authentic my boot. If he'd been acting she'd have to admit she knew nothing about men and their swelling body parts. "I'm checking because I wouldn't want to get the facts screwed up. Facts are important in reporting. Facts get you to the truth."

He resettled in his chair, a movement that made her think he might leave. "Never let a fact get in the way of a good story. Quit pushing your luck."

She'd push it exactly enough to get through this Q&A. She cleared her throat and pretended she had glasses to raise her eyes over. "'Question one. Given the choice of anyone living or dead, whom would you want as a dinner guest?' I'm sticking with Jesus and the whole 'is there really a heaven slash hell' thing. Also, I want to get a take on the idea of miracles—do they exist, what are the ten best. There's also sainthood. What's the ideal way to become a saint?"

"You know you made that sound like clickbait."

Oh, not good. It was one thing to write list-style stories, she'd had to adjust to that—listicles didn't feature in the *Orderly Daily Mail*, unless they were a list of stock and grain prices—but it was another thing entirely to go around talking like them.

"Answer the question, Haley."

"I don't do dinner guests. I can't think of anything worse than having to make conversation with a stranger."

"That can't be your answer." And it sure didn't explain why he'd invited her to Elaine's last night.

"Why not?"

"You're Jackson Haley. You'd want the scoop, the downlow, the exposé. You'd want Jeff Bezos or Bill Gates or that investment guy who plays the ukulele or the Tesla guy who wants to go to space. You can't dodge the question."

"I didn't dodge it. I've interviewed those people." She grunted in annoyance. Of course he had. She should've picked dead people. "I didn't converse with them. I asked questions. They gave answers. They talked. I listened. I gave you an answer. It's not my fault you don't like it."

He was playing with her, but there wasn't much she could do about it. He'd played with her last night as well and she'd been happy to be his toy, but now she'd happily brain him with her empty cup. "'Question two. Would you like to be famous? In what way?'"

"What's question three?"

"What's wrong with question two?" A bus belching smoke pulled up at the corner with Haley's face, sans devil's horns, on its side. No way.

He pointed to the bus. "There you go?"

She wouldn't have put it past him to sneakily plan that. "But do you like it? I don't want to be famous, it seems like a lot of trouble."

"There are worse things."

She wrote on her pad and recited, "'Jackson Haley gets a hard-on from having his face plastered on the city's buses and he likes it. He doesn't do idle conversation.'" But since he did get scoops, he had to have a talent for asking the right question and hearing what got said between the lines.

She didn't get a ghost of a grin; she got, "Okay, Jesus Toast, get on with it. This can't take all morning."

"Question three, I know this one. You don't rehearse phone calls and I do. Do you rehearse for your radio and TV spots?"

"I have an idea what I'm going to talk about. I know how I want the segment to go. I don't practice my speech in front of a mirror, if that's what this question is getting at."

The big dinkus didn't have to rehearse because he was supremely confident and his head was big enough to put on the side of a bus. "'Question four. What would constitute your perfect day?'"

She gritted her teeth against him saying "not having to do a love experiment" and he said, "Not having to do a love experiment."

"Oh, puhleeze. I knew you were going to say that."

"We must be highly compatible then. Hurrah, the experiment works. Can we stop now?"

"No. Because all I have down is that you're a fame hog who doesn't like people and is so sure of himself he doesn't rehearse."

"And that's a bad thing? What's your perfect day?"

She looked away from his infuriatingly superior expression. God help the businesspeople he interviewed, alive or dead, if he was this rigid and forbidding on the job. They'd surely tell him all their secrets and turn over all their cash if he looked at them so sternly and used that particular do as you're told voice.

It didn't help that his face was still bruised, the cut above his eye red and irritated, and that she wanted the Jack of last night back, the one who looked disheveled and on edge after they'd kissed. The one who for about five minutes might have worshipped her, who caressed her face and held her body as if he knew she felt out of place, was starved for affection, and he was the only man capable of making her feel good.

"It wouldn't be in Chicago." The city was seductive but it was also untrustworthy. It lulled you into believing you needed a nice dress for a good restaurant when you were simply set dressing for a play you didn't understand. "It would be somewhere quiet. No, not quiet, just with less industrial noise. Not this clanging and whirring that never stops."

She looked up at a patch of blue sky between the buildings, and the long shadows of other buildings, the unforgiving harshness of so much concrete and glass. "I could take birdsong, the sound of the wind in the trees, and the smell of fresh air—it's much sweeter than you think. It's a rush."

She looked at Haley, wondering if someone born here could possibly understand how alien this built environment was to her. "The air here smells like diesel and grime, underarms and old shoes. I'd want sunshine that's fierce and not filtered between buildings and hardly warms you. That would be a start. Then I'd want endless velvet skies at night and a million stars. And I'd want close friends around me." She wanted Ernest and his mad enthusiasm and sloppy kisses. She missed him so terribly. "Laughter, good food, and I'd feel at ease, just happy to be. That's a perfect day."

He probably thought her lacking in imagination, and now that she'd had that thought, she realized she was.

She could've wished for anything and she'd wished for nothing more than home. She should go for a do-over.

"Which tells me you hate the city, you're lonely as fuck and unhappy besides."

"That's not true." She didn't hate it; it was her future. It was just taking a little bit of time to acclimatize. "I didn't say that."

"You love the city, the sound and smell of industry, the clamor of millions of strangers who'll never care about you sharing your space. You love the visual and physical pollution, the lack of sunlight and green things and stars, they're your jam. I see."

Jackson Haley, covert grade listener.

She waved a hand in the direction of Lake Michigan. "I like all the water. I do love the city." Another gesture toward the river. "It's exciting. It's where I want to be."

"Aha. What's question five?"

He said "aha" like you'd humor a child. He didn't think she was a child when he'd had his hand up her skirt. "You didn't answer question three."

"My perfect day would be too unsuitable to print for readers."

She squeezed her pen and the top popped off the end. "I think I hate you."

"You think? Try harder. It's a stupid question. A day you wake up breathing and it doesn't hurt is a good day."

"Are you always this chipper or is this a perfect day?" She didn't wait for a response. "'Question five. When did you last sing for yourself or someone else and what was the song?' I'll start. I sang a Taylor Swift song this morning in the shower."

"Because you knew you'd be answering this question."

She couldn't stop her mouth twisting. She was such a dimwit about not cheating the questionnaire when he had no intention of treating it with any respect. "You don't sing. I remember."

"What Taylor Swift song?"

"As if you care. Do you even know who she is?"

"Now who's being childish?"

He'd asked her this question that first night he'd put her in a cab. Last night, he'd put her in a cab without saying a word except to the driver. "'Shake It Off.'"

"Is that a song?"

"You're lucky it wasn't 'Bad Blood.'"

He grunted, but it was a sound cut with humor. "Question six, Honeywell." He gave her a near-blinding grin. "I feel we're making progress."

Progress was a dog with a limp chasing its tail. Jackson Haley smiling was bastard measure, slay 'em in the aisles, and damn the cliché. "'Question six. If you were able to live to the age of ninety and retain either the mind or body of a thirty-year-old for the last sixty years of your life, which would you choose?'"

"I have no idea. You go first."

"It's a tough question. I used to play this game with a friend called Would You Rather. Would you rather lose a leg or an arm, or would you rather live on an island all alone without power or running water, or in a luxury hotel but be bedridden with an incurable disease."

"Did you not have cable and video games in this fresh smelling, growing things place where you grew up?"

"Of course I did. Didn't you ever play made-up games?"

"Only as an adult and only ones not suitable for discussing with a colleague or the paper's readers. Answer the question."

"I'd rather keep my mind."

"I want to be dead before I'm ninety."

"That's not the question."

"That's my answer."

When progress bit its own ragged tail, it hurt, and to think they had to do this twice more before she could write the final story. "'Question seven. Do you have a secret hunch about how you will die?'"

It was too easy, it was a closed question, he'd say no. Note to whoever wrote this, closed questions were junk.

He said, "No. And you're planning on dying in your sleep at a ripe old age, in the great family tradition."

Industrial espionage grade listening. She'd said that to him on the street last night. "Was that a cliché?"

He dismissed that with a quirk of his head. "Question eight. I can smell the end of this, it's sweet, a rush."

"Don't mock me. And this is only part one."

He closed his eyes, and slumped back in his chair. "Dear God."

"'Question eight. Name three things we appear to have in common.'"

He snapped them out. "Profession, place of employment, this ridiculous experiment."

That about covered it. How the heck was she going to write this up? "You're not being helpful."

"Cute that you actually thought I might be."

How could he kiss so warmly but be so stubbornly difficult to get along with? "Curmudgeon," she muttered. Not a word she'd use to describe anyone else she'd ever met.

"Never use a ten dollar word where a two dollar one will do, Honeywell."

The only good thing about last night's ravishing was that Jackson Dinkus Haley no longer intimidated her. He exasperated her, but he'd groaned into her skin and he'd cradled her head and he'd chased her tongue, and some of his forbidding nature, his aloof dominance, had dissolved in her mouth at about the same time as bruises from his fingers blossomed on her thigh. She was free to imagine him wearing standard tighty whities.

"Why did you agree to come?" She swept her arm out to indicate her notebook, the café.

"You guilted me into it."

And now she wasn't proud of it. "Guilted isn't a word."

"Language is a living thing. Did you have any trouble understanding what I meant?"

Ignoring that. "Question nine." It was a disastrous question. "'For what in your life do you feel the most grateful?'" He'd say for the fact this questionnaire is nearly done. "I'm grateful for the chance to be in the city."

He eyed her speculatively. "What went wrong with your hometown life?"

"That's not one of the questions?"

"No, but I'm interested. You left the sun and the birds and the bees for concrete and steel, swapped stars for neon for a reason."

"I was bored. I wanted more."

"How's that working for you?"

She made a rude gesture under the table, but kept her voice level. "Fine, thanks. I'm grateful for my move to the city. What are you grateful for?"

"That I can do what I do, that I can write about injustice and inequality and if not change things for the better, at least bring what's rotten into the light."

It was the first honest, straightforward piece of information he'd given about himself. It said a lot about Jackson Haley the reporter and something about Jackson Haley the man, but it was hard to marry that with the Jackson Haley who'd kissed her legs into noodles last night and was sarcastic and unsympathetic now.

"Question ten. Two to go."

"Hallelujah."

"'If you could change anything about the way you were raised, what would it be?'"

He frowned and looked away. "You go first."

"I wouldn't change anything. I had a great childhood. I love my family. I've been very fortunate."

He grunted. "Two more questions, you said." He looked at his watch. "I wouldn't change anything either."

"But your father is a son of a bitch." He blinked in surprise and then rubbed his eyes under his glasses. "Phil said it."

"My father is a brilliant and difficult bastard who does not approve of what I do."

She heard the bold type and underlining on the word *not*. Truly? What kind of parent wouldn't be proud of the work Jack did? "I can't imagine that."

"What's the next question?"

"What did your father want you to do instead?"

"Follow him into a respectable profession, his profession. Not become a hack."

Like pulling teeth. A cliché, but it didn't count if she didn't say it out loud. "Which is?"

"He's a surgeon. He saves lives. I only scribble about vulgar things like money and power. He'd have more respect for me if I made serious money or ran for office. He once did an interview with the *Courier* on an unrelated story where he described me as a radical experiment in parenting gone wrong. He'd said it to get at my mother after she asked for a divorce."

"Your own dad?" Appalling. Derelie's father would rather cut his own arm off than say anything so hurtful.

"My mother is not much better. Also a surgeon." Jack rubbed his eyes again. "I need a smoke." He glared at her. "I barely saw my parents. They liked work more than they liked each other or me. I suspect they secretly hated each other from the day they married. My granddad raised me, and stop looking at me like that."

She rearranged her features into an expression different from whatever it was that'd irritated him. "I'm not judging."

"You're weepy-eyed, Honeywell."

"Am not." It was the smog, made her eyes watery. She was allergic to urbanization.

"You'll only go and look it up, so I might as well tell you. He was my mother's father. He survived reporting on a bunch of wars and conflicts, but had a heart attack in Walmart when I was fourteen. My parents never divorced but keep separate lives. They live to detest each other. I have no idea why and I don't care."

"You don't really have a home, do you?" His life had been a war zone. He had no perfect place to go back to.

"Cardboard box under the expressway." He tapped the tabletop with the edge of his cell. "You think this ridiculous experiment has uncovered some fundamental clue to my character and we're bonding over my not particularly unique childhood."

She compressed her lips lest they tell him anything at all about what she thought and give him ammunition to use. That she'd like to kick his parents, congratulate his granddad, cook him a meal, and despite Jack being a prize jerk, have him back her into a wall again as soon as possible.

His phone rang. He swiped it off the table and answered it. "Haley."

He kept his eyes on her while he listened. She refused to fidget. They had two questions to go, but the chance of him agreeing to spend four minutes telling her his life story before he nominated the quality or ability he wanted to magically gain overnight was about as good as her chance of writing something Shona would agree to run. She was doomed.

"Got it. I'll check. I'll be there," he said, already standing. He quit the call. "This is urgent."

"Five more minutes and we'll be done." But he had to write up his part of the story too.

"I'm done now."

"One minute. 'If you could wake up tomorrow having gained one quality or ability, what would it be?'"

She braced for a predictable offhand comment about

his ability to be free of ridiculous experiments, and he said, "Patience and kindness."

That was two things, but they were like shiny nuggets of golden goodness, and she was so pleased to have them she gave him a free pass.

What would you rather, be patronized by Jack Haley while learning that he'd had a difficult childhood, or feel his heart thud too fast under your hand while he made love to your mouth?

She was going to need the discipline of a good dozen sun salutes before she knew the answer to that.

Chapter Ten

Gerry Roscoe studied Jack across the forest of paper and the two computers on his desk. He was one of the good guys. As the *Courier*'s senior legal counsel, he'd saved Jack's hide on multiple occasions. He was the reason Jack was never troubled with legal fees and could go after crooked players without fearing for his own financial security.

"The story needs to be as tight as a practicing drunk, otherwise Bix will come after you and the paper for everything he can." Roscoe transferred his attention to Madden, who sat on Jack's right. "I don't need to remind you that being sued makes our new owner a very nervous man."

"But you're reminding me anyway," said Madden, as unpleasantly as possible.

It made Jack wonder if that was how he'd come across with Honeywell, as if he resented the very implication of her. Because he did resent her, from the paprika sprinkle of freckles across her cheeks that she didn't cover with makeup, to the fact that she'd utterly lost her hesitancy with him and had stopped worrying about offending him. She was lonely and hated the city and he was half in love with how hard she tried to hide that and ashamed with himself for how he'd acted with her.

He should never have touched her. It was conduct unbecoming. The ridiculous kiss in front of Bix was reprehensible enough. It was inept, for one thing. She'd surprised him with her kittenish playacting and she'd saved the moment, but he'd kissed her as if he was afraid of catching girl germs. But on the street, on the street, when he could feel Bix's downfall coming together, he'd kissed her like he was a sick man and she was the medicine that would restore him to life. She'd tasted like hot rain on a sultry night, lit with fireflies and perfumed with orange blossom and the promise of an endless blue-sky morning.

He could tell himself it was all for the story until he traded in his creaking body at sixty to retain his brain till he turned ninety, and it would never be less than a lie.

"I'm reminding you," said Roscoe, "because on top of the current suit from Sungold Investments, we don't need another. If you're going after Keepsake and Bob Bix, Jack, be very clear you have the story and there's nothing remotely libelous about your accusations."

"I'll have more than accusations. I'll have proof Bix and his associates are deliberately defrauding people out of their insurance payouts," he said.

"You said that about Sungold and they're coming after you for criminal libel and emotional distress."

"They were crooks stealing from pension funds." That reminded Jack he had an unanswered email from

Roscoe requesting additional background notes on the case in progress.

Roscoe checked one of his screens when it pinged. "America's retirees thank you, Jack. Florida rejoices. They were crooks, but they exploited a loophole, and while you got the regulator to stomp all over them, they're coming at us for damages to their good name. I signed off on the Sungold exposé and I'd do it again, but the legal fees the *Courier* spends to keep you out of trouble and the paper in business are not insignificant, and given the current climate of cutbacks—"

"We get you, Gerry." Madden snipped the lecture about newspaper economics short and stood. Jack followed him upright.

They all knew the situation had changed in the last few years. It wasn't that Jack was more or less aggressive in going after corruption, or the level of legal action had increased, it was that costs all round had gone up while advertising revenue had fallen, and legal fees were clearly something the accountants felt should be cut. Better that than reporters, and so many of them had already been trimmed away like excess fat.

"Make sure you do, Phil. I heard the *Clarion* was going digital-only."

"It'll never happen to the *Courier*," Madden said. "Digital is an important part of our strategy, but the print edition is our heartland."

Roscoe arrowed in on Jack. "If ever there was a time for you to tread carefully, this is it."

"Are you suggesting we don't go after Bix?" It would be the first time management had actively interfered with one of his investigations.

Roscoe sighed. "Fellas, I hate this as much as you do. If what you've told me about Bix and what's happening at Keepsafe is true, I'd like to see the guy stripped of his assets and jailed for the rest of his life. I'd like to see you make that happen, Jack. All I'm saying is our owner is exceptionally cost-focused, and if the price of reporting the truth includes another tangled long-running legal expense, right now it could be bad for all of us."

"You're saying don't get sued," said Madden.

"I'm saying do your job, bring the bastards to account, but not until your story is a thousand percent watertight."

"You know it doesn't work like that, Gerry," said Madden. "Big corps and rich assholes use the law to punish us for messing with their scams, making their investors run for cover and their kids get beat up in school. They don't like it when they're forced to explain themselves, and they blame us for being the pricks that ruined their perfect little worlds, even when we have the truth locked down tighter than a convent during a bacchanal."

Roscoe pushed into his chair back. "The way it works when I call you into my office, Phil, is that I talk about how the law works and you listen so we keep the lights on around here as long as possible. When I want to know how to sack a quarterback, I'll ask your advice."

"Shit." Madden banged his hand against the side of a four drawer file cabinet. A pile of folders resting on top of it pitched to the floor, and Jack bent to pick them up.

"We're on the same team, fellas," said Roscoe.

"Yeah, yeah," said Madden. "But I want it to be a winning team and a team that wins backs their star players and takes calculated risks. They don't pussy out."

"So don't pussy out," said Roscoe.

"No intention of it," said Jack. When it came to bringing down Bix and holding Keepsafe's management accountable to all the injured policyholders they'd duped. But chickening out was exactly what he was going to do where it came to Honeywell. He needed her safely writing her clickbait pieces while he was doing his thing on opposite sides of the office. "And stop using that expression, it's as bad as man-up. It's offensive to women, and cats."

He caught up with Madden in the elevator well, impatiently poking at the down arrow. "Don't screw this up," he said, and poked the up arrow. "I want the paper trail, all the gory details, use whatever resources you need. Get the art department in to make graphics, tell them to do the whole interactive thing, and use that forensic accountant woman. Get photos, video too."

Jack checked his cell—dozens of messages. Most he'd never return. They were from flacks trying to drum up coverage for clients, or defend them from something Jack had already written. Phil was describing what Jack normally did on a big story, the only difference being he didn't usually go after video. He could've used a camera last night. Would've stopped him taking advantage of Honeywell. Footage of Bix, Whelan and Noakes at the restaurant would've made them look stunningly complicit. He'd have to talk to Henri Costa again, put some junior reporters on the case to interview the victims and keep a watch on Bix's movements.

"I'm on it. All I need is the time to connect the pieces."

The up elevator arrived and they both watched its doors open. There was no hijacking it for their own floor. It was packed with people holding sandwich bags and drinks. Someone had takeout Chinese and Jack's stomach rumbled. No one made eye contact.

Madden lurched forward and poked at the lit down arrow again, just as another of the elevators in the bank signaled its arrival with a *bing* and a light indicating it was going down. "And don't even think about blowing off that love experiment story. I want it to run right before the Keepsafe story."

Jack stepped into the elevator and pressed the button for their floor. "Enlighten me as to how the two are connected. One is a puff piece and the other is the newspaper business."

Madden stepped into the elevator car. "Eyeballs, Jack. Gives us a chance to get the city talking about you, so more punters buy the paper the day the exposé drops."

"That's preposterous."

"It's marketing."

"You've already got my face plastered all over the place. I can't buy groceries without someone wanting to take a selfie or tell me how I got it all wrong on page one. Women in the cereal aisle at my market hand me business cards with their sexual preferences and availability printed on them. Printed, full color with photos. It's enough. It's too much. I'm not doing the—"

"You're doing it. Because I'm doing everything I

can to make sure the *Courier* isn't going to become a digital-only edition. And it'd better be brilliant. You'd better be ready to fall on your knees for, er, one of Shona's team." Madden waved at his face. "The one with the dead fish eyes, what's her name again?"

"Honeywell. And she doesn't have—"

"Delia, rhymes with Ophelia, that's it."

"Derelie." Rhymes with necessarily, extraordinarily. Like her eyes. Jack avoided looking into them because they were so clear he could see right through to her brave, tender heart.

"Yes, Derelie." The elevator door opened on their floor. "Do one of those fantasy date things like on those TV dating games." Madden stepped out. Jack should've too, but he wanted to put his hands around Madden's neck and squeeze. "Don't spare the horses. Romance the fuck out of her."

Madden turned back when he realized Jack hadn't followed. He said, "Get video," as the doors closed.

Jack needed food. He needed a smoke. He did not need to spend time romancing Derelie Honeywell and have it immortalized on video. He needed a plan to convince her to drop out.

He went for his cell, pulled up his calendar and searched for the next open night at St. Longinus. He sent an email to add his name to the list of sinners, in the hope he'd be selected for a fight.

He was going to need it for absolution, because what he was about to do to Derelie would be unforgivable.

Chapter Eleven

Shona wanted to know how the love experiment was going and Derelie wasn't sure what to tell her. For the millionth time she looked wistfully in the direction of Artie Chan's empty cubicle. There was no more inspiration there than in her notepad.

The walking dinkus had given her nothing she could use. If she had to write the story today it would be a commentary on meeting people in the city, how different it was from where she'd grown up, where you talked to strangers and made friends with passersby and even your enemies were polite and didn't make you want to poison their coffee.

Her face got hot when she thought about how dismissive Jack was, right down to when he talked about his own messed up family life. But he was angry too, and if she had to guess why, it wasn't about old wounds, it was about having opened himself up to her, because he'd shut down just as quickly.

The Defender of the City could dish it out, but wasn't any good at taking it. He hadn't been able to take her scrutiny or get past his own ego to answer a few simple questions. How would telling her the last song he'd sung damage his credibility? And yet he'd remembered the things she'd told him and he'd drawn her out despite her attempt to guard her own responses.

She hit Return on Shona's email and typed: We've done part one, two more to go, plus the staring contest. The thought of that made her squirm. But Jack is very uncooperat—delete—busy. I'm not sure when I'll be able to pin him down for the rest. He was the one doing the pinning so far. Making progress. I'll keep you informed.

She'd no sooner hit Send than Shona appeared behind her. "Phil really wants this story, so if you're having trouble getting Jack to play ball, let me know."

It would probably be smart to throw herself at Shona's mercy and admit Jack was being impossible and there was little chance she'd ever get the kind of heart-warming human interest story they were after.

The first twelve questions were a warm-up. In the next set, he'd have to open up and tell her about his hopes, dreams, memories and achievements. There was a question about his relationship with his mother. This was so not happening.

But there was another email in her inbox about the voluntary layoffs, so now was not the time to admit defeat, especially if Shona was going to bring it to Phil's attention. Shona was very keen on getting Phil's attention, and whose fault was that? Derelie should never have mentioned the whole "saw Phil with another woman in a too-small shirt" thing because she'd lit a fire under Shona's red-soled stilettos that Shona wanted to quench by poking out Phil's eyes.

Office politics Chicago-style was like rolling in

barbed wire. Office politics back home was more of the "it's your turn to unjam the copier, make the coffee, cover the funeral" variety. There was no eye poking, no brooding sabotage of other people's objectives. And yes, she was Pollyanna, and it was time to grow up and realize the rest of the world didn't work like Orderly, home of the white squirrel, not red or gray like everywhere else. It was time to toughen up, embrace the ambiguity, sharpen her elbows and keep going after what she wanted.

And right now, that was Jackson Haley. On a plate. In a purely professional way.

If everyone knew he was being difficult, and she managed to rise above that challenge without having to resort to using the chain of command to pull off the story, that had to mean her job was safe, it had to. Because once Jack knew she'd complained, she would well and truly cook her goose with him. Cliché or not. He'd have no respect for her if she tattled.

"No trouble. He's actually more bark than bite."

Shona picked up the picture of Ernest from her desktop. "This dog is more bark than bite. But if you think you can get Jack Haley to play dead and the story is good, I'll do what I can to see about getting you promoted."

Derelie'd get Haley to sit up and beg if it meant more job security and more money. *Heel, Dinkus.*

She left Jack alone for the rest of the day, worked on two other stories, "Five Weight Loss Tips You Can Break" and "Ten Everyday Indulgences That Are Good for You," and made it to yoga on time to claim her place near Yogaboy.

He sat on his mat in full lotus pose with his legs crossed, feet turned up on the opposite thighs, elegant wrists resting on his knees, with his eyes closed, and a serene expression, his body a perfect example of both physical and mental health.

Didn't matter how many classes she took, how much extra practice she did, Derelie would never be that flexible. Her hips and abductors were too tight. Her bound angle pose looked more like a poised frog with her knees sticking up too close to her shoulders instead of lying parallel to the floor. She aspired to a half lotus, but today was not the day to try it out. It might be the day to get Yogaboy to notice her. But he'd have to open his eyes to do that.

An hour later, her shavanasa was a true corpse pose. She was exhausted and wondered if anyone would stop her lying on the floor for the rest of the night. She turned her head to see if she was alone, and her eyes collided with Yogaboy's.

"Namaste," he said, bringing his hands together prayer-style as he came to his feet.

"Namaste," she replied, too shocked to move. She lay there as he rolled his mat and walked off, a sweaty mess on the first occasion of being noticed.

Once he'd moved past her, she sat. She had to get out of the way of the people taking the next class. Yogaboy had a lovely deep voice, a tan and wicked, knowing green eyes. He was the opposite of every man she'd ever lusted after and everyone she'd slept with. She'd never touched a tattoo on a man's skin, she'd never dated one who had longer hair than she did, or who looked like serenity was a life goal.

Her two long-term partners had been boys she'd gone to school with who'd known her since her tomboy days of climbing trees, skipping stones, and stealing fruit from McDowell's orchard. In both cases they'd gone from swimming in the river to kissing in the shallows to rolling in the hay.

No wonder she had a problem with clichés—she was one.

Her one serious hookup had been with a much older man, a harvester salesman who'd thought she was amusing, called her beautiful, bought her dinner, treated her to a hotel out of town and allowed her to be mysterious for once. He didn't know how she got the scar on her hip, so she told him she'd been thrown by a horse. It made her sound more glamorous. Everyone else in town knew she'd been drunk and careless and caught it on a barbed wire fence she'd thought it was a good idea to climb. If you needed stiches in Orderly, it was the kind of thing that got around.

She knew a lot more about sex after her salesman had passed through, but not what it would be like to have sex with a man who could put his ankles behind his head, and it seemed like an important part of her education to find out.

This was what she'd moved to the city for, to expand her horizons, to live a bigger life. She'd expected to feel like a fish out of water, but it was about time she got comfortable with being wet.

Maybe Yogaboy could give her a private lesson. Maybe if she could master yoga and meditation, she could find that calm centered place where she heard birds chirp, not sirens wail. Maybe he kissed like he'd discovered treasure and wanted it all to himself.

She rolled her mat up and went to collect her bag. That treasure thing was all Jackson Haley. *Bastard*. What was he doing interfering in her fixation with Yogaboy? He'd made it perfectly clear kissing her was a tactical one-off, which was worse than calling it a mistake. If he'd called it a mistake, she could imagine he'd been overcome and that given the right conditions—night, a stakeout, a love experiment—he might be overcome again.

But that would mean he was a go with the flow kind of guy, and nothing about Jack said *relaxed*. He was deliberate and rigid and controlling, from the suits to the way he wore his hair, and the contained way he comported himself. Which was absolutely the best thing to know about him. It meant she could focus on using him to advance her career while she concentrated on trying to get a name from Yogaboy before she tried for an orgasm.

Next morning, her ego got a considerable boost when she learned her story on celebrity pets and their famous parents was the most read. Seeing it displayed online under the heading *Most Read Articles: Today's Top Five* was a thrill that had her smiling inanely at her screen. She looked for Jackson Haley's story of the day and fist pumped when his story didn't appear on the list.

It did lead the business top five, but she'd effectively out eyeballed the human headline. She took a screenshot of the list with the intention of printing it out and pinning it up by her bed as motivation for those mornings when getting out from under the sheets was hard work.

An hour later, her story had dipped to number four and by lunchtime it was gone from the list. *Shoot.* Consigned to the recesses of a URL wasteland, but she had the proof it had briefly shone and the determination to make it happen again. With Jack's existing fame, imagine how long the love experiment story might rate, long enough to make her feel like floating instead of treading water.

That meant not accepting any excuses from Jack about getting together again. Except he wasn't anywhere to be found, and he didn't answer either his phone or his email. The next day, she tracked him to his cubicle. He sat with his back toward her, with his earpiece in. He was editing a story on his screen. She didn't know if he was listening to a call, so she coughed.

He didn't quit what he was doing. Didn't spin around to face her. He kept tapping away, eyes on his words.

"Jack, it's—"

"No."

"Derelie." The earpiece was a ruse.

"No."

He was cutting straight to the chase, she might as well too. "You do."

"No."

"We need to—"

"No."

"But you—"

"I didn't."

She made a Muppet sound, very Oscar the Grouch. "What do I have to do to—"

He swung around. She got to look down at him, but

that didn't make up for what a bad dog he was being. Shame she wasn't holding a rolled up copy of today's print edition.

"Look, Rookie, I don't have time for experiments. You're going to have to spike that story."

Rookie. That was worse than being called Clickbait. "But you—we—ah."

He spun back to his keyboard. "Scoot back to your celebrity pets and listicles and let the real reporters do their stuff."

Her mouth opened, but no sound came out. Her eyes probably looked like they were on stalks. She'd kissed this man's condescending mouth.

"Jack, can you check this lede for me?" One of the business writers, Annie Berkelow, stopped beside Derelie. "Hi, who are you?"

It took time to get her jaw to work. She got out, "De." And Jack said, "Works for the blogsite." *Blog-site*. No one called it that. She wrote for the electronic edition of the paper, but so did Jack and Annie, it's just that their stories also went in the print edition.

"Oh," said Annie, and put a page in front of Jack. She wore a black pants suit with lace-up shoes and her short hair was stylishly tousled. Her dinkus was more glamorous and made her look older. Jack made an edit to the page and handed it back. Annie said, "Ah, that's better, thanks," and left.

Jack didn't turn around, so he couldn't see how red Derelie's face was. He wouldn't see her furled fists or the tension in her neck. He pressed a button on his earpiece and said, "Haley," and she knew it wouldn't matter how long she stood there, he was going to ignore her. But there had to be something wrong with the connection between her mental faculties and her legs, because she was standing there when Annie came back a few seconds later.

"Still here?" Annie said. She put a data stick in front of Jack. "He's busy. You need to get out of his way so he can do this. It's the biggest story we've had all year. It's prize-winning stuff."

"He had time for you."

"He always has time for me."

Jack put his hand to his ear and disconnected the call. He swung around to face them. "Is that the Shenker case study?" he said to Annie.

"Yeah."

"Thanks." He looked directly at Annie. "I'm going for a smoke." He rummaged on his desk for his tobacco.

"I'll come with you. Getting coffee," said Annie.

Jack stood, pocketing his cell. Annie led off. Jack stepped around Derelie and she turned toward him, still stupid enough to expect he'd acknowledge her. All she got was the sound of him answering his cell, "Haley," and a sick feeling in the pit of her stomach.

"Now that was brutal. And I'm a single guy who writes for the sports pages—if I can see that was brutal, I'm not sure how you're still standing."

Derelie looked up past the chinos and untucked polo shirt into the craggy face of Dante Spinoza. "Jack," she said, because she was still part Muppet and was having trouble talking and moving at the same time. He'd never exactly been warm and forthcoming, but he hadn't treated her like dirt either.

"Being an asshole. Classic. I could give a play by play of that and it would still be brutal."

"Is he always that way?"

"No, that was something new. Did he get you pregnant or something?"

"*What?*" Total Muppet flail.

Spin made a quiet down gesture with both hands. "Joking. Bad joke. Really bad. I'm sorry about that. You're Derelie, rhymes with happily."

"Merrily," she muttered.

"Jack's supposed to do some story with you for the online edition, right?" She nodded. Spin rubbed his jaw, which sported ample stubble. "Find a way to do it without him."

"How am I supposed to do that?"

"I don't know, but that was cold. That was Jack giving it to you old school. He's not going to come around. He has bigger fish to fry and he's top dog around here. You can't win this one."

"Cliché."

"What?"

"Bigger fish. Top dog."

"Sports, remember? We're all about the cliché."

"I don't want to be a cliché. I need to write this story."

"Can't you improvise?"

"What do you mean by improvise?" *Please don't mean make it up.*

"Write a different story."

Oh. "I don't think that's going to work." That wasn't what Phil expected.

"What are you thinking?"

"What do you care?"

Spin looked offended. "Just because I write about tackle counts and sack stats doesn't mean I don't have a heart. What are you doing after work?"

"Are you asking me out?"

He was older. His nose had been broken more than once. Not that older and a little rugged was a problem. Think harvester salesman with a sporty city flavor.

His shoulders went back. "Do you want to go out with me?" He sounded as surprised as she had.

He probably couldn't cross his ankles behind his head. "Uh." She probably should know when someone was hitting on her.

"You're right." He rubbed his big hands together. It was hard to imagine how he fitted them on a keyboard. "Let's keep this professional. Jack is running the team through the big exposé he's working on. You should come and listen in. He's brushing you off because he's a rude bastard and he's on a big story and they kind of take over your life."

Like her little story was doing.

"Don't imagine that was the first time he told you he wasn't on your team," Spin said.

"He didn't have to be so rude." He'd looked through her like she was part of the city, made of glass, nothing but sidewalk to be trodden over. It was a long way from kissing her, even if there was now zero doubt in her mind that it really had been just about the story for him. She might as well go and see how his investigation was coming along. It would be instructive.

Hours later, she tracked Jack down to a meeting room that had been turned into what looked like a scene from a police procedural drama. There were two whiteboards covered with what looked like evidence. One had photographs, and she could identify Bix, Whelan and Noakes. The other had a scrawled headline that said *Money Trail*. Nothing she'd ever written had this amount of research and preparation. It was awe-inspiring.

The room was packed, with faces she only vaguely knew and some she didn't. No one in this room wrote for the website only. She had to hover in the doorway, which was just as well because she felt out of place. The other business writers sat around a table. Phil leaned up against a wall with another man who wore a suit. Jack stood at the front of the room.

"Everyone here is sworn to confidentiality," said Phil. He pointed to the man beside him. "This is Gerry Roscoe. He's the Courier Group's legal counsel." He aimed his attention to the doorway. "No tourists. Get out."

Four people standing in front of Derelie pushed past her to scramble away. She caught Jack's eyes, but his flickered off before he could make her feel like glass again.

"Honeywell can stay. She helped me on a reconnaissance mission."

Was she hearing things? She glanced at Phil, but he was focused on Jack, so she stayed and for the next ten minutes listened as Jack outlined the evidence against Keepsafe and the role played by Bix. He didn't acknowledge her again, but she forgot to be angry with him as the depth of his investigation unfolded. It made the stories she wrote seem insubstantial and pointless, forgettable, vacuous entertainment rather than news. Jack's reluctance to spend time on the love experiment was framed in a whole new light.

"He's going to smash this. Bring the whole thing down."

She tipped her head up to see Spin standing behind her. "I get why he brushed me off now."

"Get out, Spinoza!" yelled Phil.

Spin blew Phil a kiss. "Love you too," he said, and backed off to laughter, but only far enough that he was out of Phil's line of sight. He put his finger to his lips in a shhh gesture and motioned to Derelie to turn around so she didn't give him away.

She tuned back in to Jack, who was now talking about the victims. He motioned to Annie and she recounted a story about the Shenkers, injured in a car accident and denied their insurance, forced to sell their home and move to a trailer park to pay for medical care.

"Questions," said Jack, then answered questions about Bix's professional background and how they'd pieced together the money trail.

"What if your whistleblower is lying?" Derelie said, before she stopped to think that everyone would look at her.

Everyone looked at her, including Jack.

"This is not 'Ten Best Looks for Summer,'" he said, and there was a rumble of laughter, which he acknowledged with a smile. "We vet all our sources."

Not even the barn-like presence of Spinoza blocking the corridor stopped Derelie from fleeing the scene of the crime as if she were the one Jack was intending to expose.

Chapter Twelve

Too many people wanted to talk to him, including Roscoe, so it took forever for Jack to get clear of the conference room, and when he did it was to run into Spinoza.

Spin stood there, stance wide, arms folded, a bad-smell look on his face. "You feeling good about that?"

"Would feel better if you got out of my way."

"You're not going back to your desk."

It wasn't a question and the man blocked his way to anywhere. "I didn't mean it to be like that."

Spin shook his head. "That's what they said about the Cubs."

"What do you want?"

"Me? Nothin'." He let Jack shove past, but only because it was clear he was headed for the web team. "Good decision, friend," Spin said.

As if Jack needed Spinoza as his conscience. This was exactly what he'd wanted. Honeywell had opened herself to a couple of cheap shots and he'd taken them. He didn't have to think about it. She was soft, fresh and defenseless, and he'd used her weaknesses against her with no more effort than rolling a cigarette. His participation in the love experiment was over, if only because he'd seen her face and he'd left her cut up and bleeding.

No victory in the ring had ever felt so small and worthless. No scoop he'd missed had made him feel like such a low, unconscionable shit.

He had difficulty locating Honeywell's desk. There was a midline in the office, hard news on one side, all the rest on the other. He had to cross over to where they talked about eyeballs instead of circulation, where they considered things like unique visitor counts, search engine optimization and bounce rates, where statistical algorithms ruled in place of a reporter's second sense for a killer hook.

Over on this side of the office they didn't write the news so much as curate it, and though he knew it was the future of journalism, he didn't like it, for all its keyword-dependent, page view hit, search engine referred conversion rates. It wasn't reporting—it was repackaging. It wasn't what people needed to hear about, it was what would distract, engage or amuse them.

Crossing the midline made him feel like a dinosaur lumbering to certain extinction.

Lost in the confusing layout of cubicles, he gave up and called her name. Expecting her head to pop up over the low walls and big screens, he was annoyed when he had to call again. But then, if their positions were reversed, he'd have made her work for it too.

"Derelie Honeywell!"

He got back, "She's not here."

Well, fuck. Most of the workstations on this side were empty. No one over here worked to a print deadline. She'd probably gone home for the day. He turned to trek back to his own desk when he spotted her coming into the main office area from the service corridor. That was where the breakroom and bathrooms where. God, if he'd made her cry in the ladies', he'd need someone to lay him out for the count.

She saw him. She hesitated for a second, taking a step to the side as if to avoid him, but then she lifted her chin and walked straight for him. If she'd been crying there was no evidence of it, but there was a balled-up tissue in her hand and he didn't like the symbolism of that.

"I came to say I'm sorry."

She mashed her ruby lips together and frowned, head tilted to the side. "For what?"

"For that." He gestured in the direction of the conference room. "There was no need for me to say what I did."

"But I asked a stupid question."

"It wasn't stupid. You couldn't have known."

"But I knew everyone else there has been through that kind of rodeo before and I should've held my question, not wasted time."

That was one way to interpret it. "You're not upset about what I said?"

She shrugged a shoulder and looked away. "I deserved it."

"No, you didn't." He had to quell the urge to shake her. He didn't like this meek acceptance, this lack of fire. It was as if he'd doused her in doubt and she'd sucked it all up till it infused her. He preferred her when she was mouthy. "I was a prick. Twice in one day."

"No, no, I get it. No need to feel bad. I was pestering you and I knew you were only humoring me.

I should've taken the hint. It's not like I didn't know you were on a big story. I should've respected that."

"I was an asshole." He'd deliberately belittled her. Why wasn't she accepting his apology?

"It's okay." She waved a hand. "I'll work something out with Shona. I'll explain to Phil."

"No, you won't." Madden would mince her up. "I'll make the time for it."

"I'd really rather you didn't. We're not ever going to be… It's, um, fine, really, it's just a silly story, and I didn't understand the context, but I see the big picture now. I see it from your point of view, so I get it. Thank you for putting up with me. There's no need to apologize, and look, I have to go. I can make a late class if I go now."

He didn't know what to say. He stepped aside to let her pass, let her go to her desk, collect her things and leave the building thinking she was the one at fault, she was the one on the sharp end of a lesson she deserved.

Back at his own cubicle, he checked his messages. There was work to do but he couldn't focus, kept seeing Honeywell's eyes swallow her face when he'd ignored her by his desk, and then how she'd flinched when he'd humiliated her in the conference room.

Bundling up the folders on his desk, the random Post-it note scrawls he needed to follow up on, along with a couple of data sticks, he headed out. He ate a quick diner meal and endured a berating from another customer for the fact his story on unfair bank charges didn't go far enough without doing anything to cut short the exchange for once.

He made it to church, changed, and was looking for an assistant when he found Barney.

"Saw your name on the wild card list. It's too soon for you to have another fight."

Trust an ex-priest to have ethical standards. "I'm fine."

Barney poked a thumb at Jack's brow, over the healing split from the bout with Ryan and Jack didn't dodge away. "It's not going to reopen?" Jack was a quick healer and grateful for it. That was the answer to question nine. "Why are you here so soon again?"

"I want to fight. If I wanted confession, would you turn me away?"

"I don't do confession."

Barney struck, drove his fist into Jack's ribs, knocking his breath out on a hard grunt and making his torso curl into the unexpected pain. He had to stop himself begging for another hit.

"Satisfied?" He ground the word out, watching Barney's timeworn face for the verdict.

"You're off the list."

"No, I need this."

"Why?"

"Same reason as last time."

"Not good enough."

"I hurt someone today. I meant to do it. It was wrong, and when I tried to apologize it was only to realize what a good job I did at screwing with them. I made her think it was her fault and that I was entitled to treat her like shit."

"You want to be punished?"

Barney was too clever. If Jack answered yes, he'd end up on the bench all night with that as his lesson in patience, tolerance and expecting the world to work in the order he wanted it to. "I just want to fucking hit someone."

"I'll think about it."

And there it was, he was benched anyway. Learning humility, the old-fashioned way. Barney was a demonic genius. Jack watched fight after fight, and as the night wore on, he knew it would be smart to go home and work, but he kept feeling the moment Honeywell sidestepped, then gathered her courage and faced him, turned his apology back on him and fucking floored him with it.

She wasn't defenseless. Whether she appreciated it or not, she'd swiped the ground out from under him. If he went home without exorcising some of that sting, he'd want to drink until he passed out. If Barney didn't let him in the ring, he knew he could find a fight at a late-opening bar or a dealer's street corner, but that option was a risk his career couldn't afford, so he sat on, stewing over the words he should have used to treat Honeywell as a colleague, as a person he liked for her ability to take a hit and get back up again; to shake it off where he percolated.

It was almost midnight when Barney motioned him over. Paired him with a man he'd never seen before. The guy was bigger, heavier than Jack, but he looked nervous, glancing eye contact, couldn't stand still, his movements more involuntary than any kind of adrenaline rush.

"Alvarez, Haley. Haley, Alvarez." They touched knuckles. Barney clamped a hand on Alvarez's shoulder and it seemed to settle him. "What's your lesson, son?"

"Courage," said Alvarez, eyes on his hands. Something Honeywell had by the container load.

"Haley?"

He'd had all night to think about it, but it wasn't easy. Humility didn't quite cover it.

"Jack?" Barney prodded with an amused twist to his fat lips.

"Generosity," Jack said, knowing the perverse logic of this would mean the only way to win tonight would be to orchestrate it so Alvarez's courage was tested, but didn't fail. Barney did nothing to hide his laughter, not caring that it spooked Alvarez.

They gloved up. The church was virtually emptied out by the time they entered the pit. Alvarez looked like he'd rather run into a wall and knock himself out than take a swing at Jack.

"I'm here to get hit tonight," Jack said by way of encouragement. He opened his arms wide. Generous to his own detriment. "Go for it."

Alvarez took a step back and dropped his hands. "I'm not going to hit someone who won't hit back."

Jack should've known it wouldn't be that easy. The only way to win tonight was to hit Alvarez hard enough to wake his courage. Jack took two steps forward and gut-punched Alvarez hard enough to make the man stagger. His own stomach flipped as the moment felt too much like what he'd done to Honeywell. It was enough to prove to Alvarez that Jack wasn't messing around.

They traded punches, went four rounds, with Jack landing more hits, but having to work to avoid letting too many of Alvarez's haymakers land. The guy had a colossal reach and he wasn't tiring. The longer they went at each other, the more focused Alvarez got, the more punches Jack landed, the more eager to strike Alvarez was. There wasn't going to be a knockdown here, they'd both be staggering before Barney called them off unless Jack forced things.

"Who'd you fail, Alvarez. Who'd you let down?" he taunted, dancing out of reach.

Alvarez came after him, forcing Jack to keep backing up. "Shut up."

"Your wife. Your kids?"

Jack defended his face as Alvarez's pummeled him. "Not married."

They were up in each other's space. "Did you fuck up with your girlfriend?" Alvarez let out a grunt and Jack shoved him away. There it was. "What did you do?"

"Nothing. I did nothing."

Alvarez came at Jack. He got the words "That's not why you're here" out before he took a jab to the hip.

They tussled again. Alvarez was enraged now. He stopped being careful. "She has problems." He landed a blow on the same hip. That was going to bruise.

"What kind of problems?"

"Depression."

He came at Jack hard and made him hurt. This was why Alvarez was here. "You walked out on her."

"Her problems aren't mine."

"Nope, so why are you here?" The game was to make him say it. You didn't get absolution until you said the words. The words were the power, not the punches, it was always the words that described the action; the thing you did that made you hate yourself that much more.

Alvarez dropped his hands, his shoulders slumped. "Because I love her and I'm a fucking shit for abandoning her."

Jack could take any shot he liked, but his arms were heavy and his body hurt and this fight was over, at least for Alvarez. "Go back and make it up to her."

"She won't take me back. Says she can't trust me."

"If that's all it takes to push you away, you don't love her. She doesn't love you if she won't give you a second chance. Fix it or move on."

"I know it," Alvarez said.

They were done. They touched gloves.

"If all you two ladies are going to do is waltz, get out of the pit so I can go home," Barney called from the upper railing.

Both of them were unsteady and slimy with sweat. Jack could drink a river of water. He went to the ladder and hauled himself out of the pit.

"I'm not coming back," Alvarez said. He had trouble getting his feet to the rungs. "Barney told me you're a regular. How much do you hate yourself to do this more than once?"

"It's not about that for me." He'd have given Alvarez a hand up, but with gloves still on that was impossible.

"Then what makes you do this? I hated every minute of it."

"Frustration."

Alvarez made the top of the ladder. He waved a glove at Jack. "I made you bleed because you're frustrated? It has to be more than that."

No one part of his body hurt more, but his brow must've reopened. He'd feel it later. Generosity was helping Alvarez to his revelation, but it didn't help Jack feel any better about what he'd done to Honeywell.

"I'm not that deep," he said as Alvarez stepped up beside him and the assistant attended to Jack's laces. He recognized that as the kind of answer he'd given Honeywell's questions. Flippant, careless, and guarded as fuck. He and Alvarez had smacked each other near senseless, which was exactly what Jack had wanted. The man deserved a more accurate response.

And so did Honeywell.

One at a time.

"This fixes something in me. It takes the noise out of my brain. Gives me a quiet space. I'm more focused on the big picture for having had everything narrow to the question of how not to get hit too hard, how to stay on my feet. A fight is like renewal. It helps me forgive myself for what I screw up and to start over again clean."

Alvarez's mouth hung open. Then he shook his head. "That's what drinking is for." He flexed his freed hands. "Or sex. You just need to get laid more."

Jack laughed, then closed the eye under his torn brow, prodding at it carefully. Now it hurt. "Tried that." That was his go-to before he found Barney and the Church of the Cocked Fist. It'd only made life more complicated. "This is easier."

Alvarez laughed. "You're doin' it wrong."

He was sorry Alvarez wouldn't be back, hoped he had the courage to fix things with his woman or move on if that's what was best for them both.

He borrowed some of that courage for himself, showered, patched himself up, taped his brow, it would heal, and went home to fix things with Derelie.

his son and Shona could say she'd do work. Haylie would have to make it the best format Hatrex ever produced to make up for the exec that called it genius.

And she never needed to cross paths with Jack again. Her first impression of him, and yep, no the bottom all along... pompous idiot. She hadn't asked the boss team into a corner—the begrudging part. The mean Jack's company was the team play—to being the boss called him for no other lost in...

Chapter Thirteen

Derelie breathed into her rib balloons and stretched her earlobes to her shoulders. She massaged her wrist creases and balanced—in a wobbling way—in the place between neutral and enlivened. She flowed as if swimming with no effort in water. She'd made the late yoga class, and she didn't do anything dumb like spending her not-going-to-happen bonus on clothing and shoes she didn't need.

She pulled herself together to try harder, sweat more, stretch farther, hold her poses steadier despite trembling limbs. It was a distraction from feeling so incredibly redneck for not understanding which way was up with Jackson Haley.

She should've seen the politics for what they were. Phil getting back at Jack, Jack doing his best to derail that, Shona using it as an excuse to side with Phil then try to make Phil jealous. Derelie had been the pig-in-the-middle of a game she didn't have the city slick to understand. But she understood it now. And she'd manage it. Artie Chan was due back in a few days. She'd re-pitch the story to Shona and do the love experiment with Artie. Jack could walk free, Phil would get his story and Shona could say she'd delivered. Derelie would have to make it the best human interest story possible to make up for the star attraction going missing.

And she never needed to cross paths with Jack again. Her first impression of him had been on the button all along. Not the gay part—he hadn't kissed like he wasn't into women—the intimidating part. Beneath Jack's contempt was the ideal place to shelter.

She almost called home for the third time this week, just to hear Mom's voice, catch up on the gossip, ask about Dad and Ernest, and receive all the news of his porch-sitting, back-of-the-truck-riding, varmint-chasing days, as if he was a person and not a tan and white hound. But Mom would hear it in her voice, her moment of crushing homesickness, and she didn't have the stones left to act the part of "I heart Chicago," and that felt like a kind of failure in itself.

She slept badly, woke with sore muscles and made it to the office early and then resisted using that first quiet hour before the newsroom filled up to cruise shopping sites for ego-boosting purchases. It was almost research. She'd heard the other girls talking about CC creams and she didn't know what they were and whether she was supposed to be using one. Would a CC cream have helped her understand how to deal with Jack? She got as far as learning that CC stood for color correction, discounted its effect on office politics and switched to email.

And her morning imploded.

Jack had written her an email. Not one of his terse instructions. It filled a whole screen and she'd have to scroll. He'd sent it at three in the morning. It had the subject heading An Experiment in Generosity. She took an ocean breath and read on.

My name is Jackson Haley and I'm a professional question asker. It's the way I understand the world, earn my living and define my life.

I was recently volunteered to take part in a love experiment, a questionnaire proven to promote intimacy between strangers. My partner in questionnaire hell is a colleague who works for a different part of the paper. Her name is Derelie, it rhymes with merrily. We'd never met before we were press-ganged into the experiment.

We've agreed to meet and answer thirty-six questions about our families, our hopes, fears, aspirations and thoughts on a range of topics from most desired dinner guest to last earworm, and to record our feelings and impressions about each other. The idea is we'll go from strangers to, well, not strangers.

My name is Jackson Haley, I'm a professional question asker, and I've discovered I hate being asked questions.

Derelie rocked back in her chair. How the irony burned.

Partly it's the personal nature of the questions themselves, but mostly it's having to open myself up to the scrutiny of a person I've only just met. I would rather repeatedly smack my head against a wall until I passed out.

Unfortunately, I've made Derelie wish that's what I'd done.

She made a choking sound. That was funny.

I was awful. A-triple-plus obnoxious. I dodged, ducked, weaved, disputed, belittled, distracted and minimized, just like a CEO caught with his hand in the till, and all in the face of Derelie's consistent generosity, her unfailing good humor.

This was Jackson Haley not only writing up the first part of the experiment, he was admitting he was a bastard and apologizing—again, but this time in writing, and it was nothing like the apology he'd made last night, the one that made her want to run and hide.

A person with my advantages, privilege and position should be generous. I told Derelie the qualities I needed more of were patience and kindness, now I'm adding generosity to that. I'd be a better person if I was generous like Derelie. She's also brave and intrepid and I was slow to recognize those qualities in her because I couldn't see past my own walled-off reticence.

This was Jackson Haley telling her she was brave. *Wow*. That he admired her. His words did odd things to the back of her throat, made it tight, made her eyes scratchy.

Derelie and I are both reporters, so that should've been a good start to getting to know each other, but ungenerous person that I am, I was more focused on what made us different than what we might share.

I write hard news about the business community and the power brokers who run our city. She writes the kind of stories that everyone would rather read, softer news, stories that entertain and lift people's moods. She's a new recruit to the city and I was born here, have its hustle and grit in my veins. It was arrogant of me to think who I am and what I do is more important than who she is and what she does, and worse, to make her think I judged her inadequate.

I'm writing while the city sleeps and I'm slightly drunk on exhaustion, tired enough to see my own behavior as regrettable and make regret seem foolish. I'm sending Derelie these thoughts before I sober up on daylight. There isn't any reason for her to give me another chance on the remainder of the questions. She owes me nothing.

I owe her my honesty.

She looked away from her screen. Why would Jack write this? He hadn't copied anyone else, unless blindly, so this was meant for her eyes only, or it was a trick, something new he was teaching her about office politics. She could close the email now, never finish reading it, delete it, and there'd be nothing he could say because she didn't owe him anything—that he had right.

She closed the email. Her heart was beating too fast for a person doing nothing more physical than sitting. Jackson Haley confused her. She rearranged the items on her desk: paperclip, big foldback clip, little foldback clip, framed Ernest photo, yellow Post-it notepad, red pen, "Orderly, Home of the White Squirrel" coffee mug. He'd made her look like more of a fool yesterday. He did owe her honest answers.

She opened Jack's email. She could forward it to every desktop at the *Courier*, he'd given her that power and it wasn't like that was an accident. She picked up the big foldback clip and opened and shut its wings while she read on.

The last song I had stuck in my head was the Oscar Mayer wiener jingle. I can almost hear Derelie laugh.

She dropped the clip and grinned at her screen. That was a whole lot more embarrassing than the Taylor Swift song she'd had in hers.

My grandfather was born in Weiner, Arkansas. He used to sing that wiener jingle to annoy me. He's been dead a long time and I still miss him trying to rile me up. I didn't tell Derelie that, because I was mortified by the sorry state of my earworm, which haunts me every year around my grandfather's birthday. I should've realized she'd laugh with me, not at me.

When we talked about fame, what I should have told Derelie is that the fame I do have sometimes scares me. I'd much rather go unnoticed, but you can't do the work I do and not have something of a public presence. That public presence aids my work. That means I have to be tolerant of people expressing their opinions about what I write and talk about. It's only fair; they have to listen to me. But if I had a choice, I'd be less of a public figure and still be able to do the work I love. I understand completely why Derelie said fame wasn't something she valued.

I'm a little jealous that Derelie has a secret hunch about how she's going to die and I don't, although it's clear now that my structural integrity can be dinged by a string of personal questions, so I'm not as hardy as I thought I was. I can only hope it's as peaceful as her hunch she'll die in her sleep. Given that I'm demanding on my bones, I think the question as to what I'd want to keep from my thirty-year-old body into my nineties had better be my brain, so far it's in good condition if you discount how wrongheaded I was over a certain love experiment.

One of the more probing questions was about whether I'd want to change something about how I was raised. I dodged that one hard enough to pull a muscle. I'd want to hang on to my grandparents longer, particularly my jingle-singing granddad, who is my all-time favorite person. Of all the people in the world who I'd want to have over for dinner, it's not someone I want to interview or get to know, it's Pops.

There was another question about gratitude. Feeling grateful is one of those mindfulness activities that I'm hardwired to side-eye, but on reflection gratitude is like generosity, it's a recognition that I have been luckier than most people in everything I have and do. I'm grateful for the circumstances in which I was born, to relative privilege and security that many people will never know.

Hmm, that was more like it. Now she was learning about who Jack was behind his dinkus.

The experiment has a question about what Derelie and I have in common. Because I was in deep jerk mode I picked the most obvious things, our profession and place of employment. I took the easy way out. The hard way out is to admit that I don't know what we have in common other than our work in broad terms, but I have the sense that we both look for quiet spaces in our lives to help make sense of all the noise. It would be interesting to confirm that suspicion.

That leaves a few questions, but I'm going to answer them in a bundle.

My most perfect day would be the one where Derelie agrees to do the love experiment with me, knowing I'm on board, no side-eyeing, no being a superior twerp. I would treat the experiment respectfully. We'd escape the office and the incessant deadlines, ringing phones and pinging messages, and find a patch of sun. Maybe we could picnic somewhere there are birds chirping and a breeze in the trees, far from the sound of traffic and constant interruptions. I'll tell her as much about me as she wants to know in four minutes or less. I'd want the same from her.

Our first twelve questions didn't make friends of two strangers. They gave Derelie a headache, and me a huge serving of avoidance that says more about my insecurities than I ever imagined. I can't help but wonder what answering twenty-four more questions might tell me about myself, but if Derelie is willing to try it, I'm all in.

She slumped back in her chair. Deny. Delete. Forward all. Reply.

Those were her options. Every one of them put power into her hands. Jack was taking a risk she didn't use his wiener jingle earworm, his acknowledgment he'd carried on like a turd, to embarrass him. She read it again. It was publish-ready. Though the words sounded nothing like the Jackson Haley stories that appeared in the paper. He never injected himself into his news stories, never wrote *I*. He reported straight without the sense of being part of the story.

Jack might have been tired and regretting what had happened between them, but this wasn't an emotional kneejerk, it was deliberately done. He admitted to sabotaging the experiment, he called out his own insecurities. He said *wiener*, and everyone knew that little jingle was about being loved, and she knew Jackson Haley was a kid who'd never had much love. He might scoff at lifestyle stories, but he knew how to write one.

She could add her own words and offer this to Shona as part one of their love experiment.

She stood. She had to talk to Jack, to make sure she was reading between the lines properly. Maybe there was some subtlety she simply didn't understand. Maybe he was just showing off the versatility of his writing and this was another way to embarrass her despite the fact he'd called himself a superior twerp. For all she knew it was some sneaky kind of humblebrag trap she'd fallen prey to.

She pushed her chair back and stood, the feeling she was being set up in some way wrapping itself around her lungs.

"Hey, where's the fire?"

She looked at her cubicle mate Eunice. Ugh. "Sorry?"

If Eunice, who wrote about arts and culture, and was the definition of focused, noticed anything Derelie did, it had to mean she'd done it violently.

"You stood up so quick you made me dizzy. Did you get laid off or something?"

Hell. "No." They exchanged glances across the low cube wall. "Has it started?"

"Heard two people, Lopez in science and some nerd in tech," Eunice said.

"That's bad."

"Lopez is ancient. Great editor. Once upon a time we had rows and rows of them. You'll get used to it."

Derelie would get used to it. It wasn't like it was optional.

She sat back down again. She'd reply to Jack's email. After five minutes with the wiener jingle in her head, staring at the space she was supposed to type in, she gave up and went to the breakroom to get coffee. It helped. Back in front of her screen she typed: "Jack"; she no longer wrote Dear in her email correspondence after she'd noticed no one else did.

I read your email and it's too good to be true. I smell a—cliché.

Backspace, backspace, backspace.

I read your email and I have questions.

That worked better, but it was cold. Back, back, back, back.

I read your email. Thank you. I appreciate the effort you went to.

That had the benefit of being true, even if she was still suspicious.

Now I have the wiener song stuck in my head, so maybe this was an elaborate plot to drive me crazy.

That also had the benefit of being true. Shit, the dumb jingle, over and over.

I'm wondering if you meant me to sub your story. It would work for the lifestyle section, but I'm unsure if that was your intention. It would be great if you could let me know what you were thinking.

She took her hands off the keyboard. That would do it. Professional, not too cold, not too warm. Just the right heat in the porridge for Goldilocks facing the big bear.

And then like Goldilocks she waited. She filed two stories, attended an editorial meeting, went out to grab a sandwich with Eunice and waited for Jack to respond. She deliberately avoided his side of the office because she didn't want to face him. Maybe they could simply do everything by correspondence, intimacy at email distance. It would be improvising like Spinoza had suggested. She liked that idea, but by the late afternoon when Shona had asked for an update and Jack hadn't responded, she called him, couldn't leave a message because his inbox was full and went in search of him, tight jaw, fidgety hands, pulse skipping. He wasn't at his desk and his PC was dark.

Just because he wasn't there didn't mean he wasn't

watching his messages. She went back to her desk and pinged him on Courier Messenger.

I thought you didn't do clichés.

That was designed to get his attention, especially because he really hadn't.

Nothing.

She gave it an hour and sauntered casually to the business writer's bullpen. His cubicle was still unoccupied. While she was not so casually staring at his pristine desk, not a single photograph, a female voice said, "He's not in."

She looked around for the owner of the voice. "Do you expect him?"

The top of Annie's head appeared above her cube wall and then she stood. "Working from home. What do you want? You know he's on this major story, right?"

"Er. Ah." She wanted to make a rude gesture in Annie's face. She wanted Jack's home address, because what if he didn't respond? Worse, what if this was a test and she was supposed to sub his piece to Shona or not sub his piece to Shona? She couldn't wait around for days for find out. It was Friday and she'd be twisted into pretzel pose if she had to wait all weekend.

Annie's eyes flashed white and she continued stuffing folders in a messenger bag, which she balanced on top of the cube wall while she answered her phone. The bag was addressed to Jackson Haley.

Derelie almost snatched it and ran. But she was a responsible adult, and that was master-class level stalking and Annie would probably crash tackle her if she tried it. The proper thing to do would be to liberate the parcel from the front desk before the messenger service took it—just because she grew up in crime-free Hicksville didn't mean she lacked a conniving instinct—which is exactly what she did.

An hour later, she buzzed Jack's apartment, lowered her voice and mumbled the word "messenger" into his intercom, let herself into his building, up three flights of stairs and knocked on his front door.

He answered it barefoot, without his glasses, wearing a pair of almost threadbare blue jeans, a jaw full of stubble, and skin. A lot of skin. This was the man she'd once imagined in neck-to-knee underwear made out of a burlap sugar sack.

"Jesus jeans." He didn't have a shirt on, and the word "ripped" applied to both his pants and his chest.

"Honeywell." He frowned at her. "Did you think I always wore a suit?"

"I mean they're holy." She pointed at his legs. "Your jeans have holes." Slashed and torn across his thighs, both knees blown out. "Jesus jeans." Jesus, she'd looked at his wiener. She'd looked at all of him and she didn't want to stop.

"What's the matter with you? What are you doing here?" Abruptly he abandoned his hold on the door to scoop a fast-moving mass off the floor.

She jumped back. "That." A cat, Jackson Haley was virtually naked and had a huge scruffy cat wriggling under his arm.

"If she gets out, she'll end up on a neighbor's bed."

"That's yours?" It didn't seem possible he'd own a cat, or look so out of office attractive. He had the kind of muscles that bulged, that whole ripple thing from his chest to his...*gulp, eyes up*. He had purple bruises on his side and a black eye, a cut over his nose and his brow was taped again.

"Her name is Martha. What are you doing here?"

Martha's front paws paddled, and she said, "Marah."

"What happened to you?" Derelie gestured at Jack's face. "You didn't answer my messages."

Jack repositioned Martha in his arms. Marmalade, black and white. She was the biggest cat Derelie had ever seen. Mane like a lion, paws like a dog, green eyes that sized her up and knew her for the stalker she was.

"You're in my building because I didn't answer your messages?" Jack's voice was low and amused. She thrust the messenger bag at him and he said, "You deliver mail in your spare time?"

"No, it's. Yes. No. There was a cliché. You're a crazy cat person." She shook the bag. She needed him to take the bag, because in all likelihood she was in possession of stolen property, because she certainly wasn't in possession of her wits. "This is yours."

He hip-checked the door to push it open and stepped aside. "You'd better come in."

She stood on the doorstep and looked past the near-naked, battered, bruised, cat-cradling man into his apartment. Most of what she could see was desk and couch. The couch was being used as a filing system. As was a good deal of the floor. The desk had two screens, two keyboards and was littered with office type junk. There was an ironing board, also being used as a work surface, a small chewed blue mouse dangling from it by a string, and a television, on a news channel with the sound down. Suit-wearing, pristine-cubicle-dwelling Jackson Haley couldn't possibly live here in this mess.

"This is where you live?"

"No, this is where I stash my kidnap victims."

After what she'd learned today about the wiener-jingle-singing, not-afraid-to-out-himself-as-a-jerk, wanted-to-take-her-on a-picnic, positively-hunky-without-a-shirt, cat-owning Jackson Haley, that didn't sound too far-fetched.

Chapter Fourteen

Maybe it was Martha. Was Honeywell scared of cats? That might explain why she stood on Jack's doorstep with her mouth open but no sound coming out. It failed to explain what she was doing here with his messenger bag in the first place.

"She won't bite."

"You have a cat."

"If it helps, think of her as a dog."

"I can come in?"

He couldn't open the door wider. He couldn't hold Martha, the door and the messenger bag at the same time. Martha was a two-arms kind of cat when she wanted out. "You can throw the bag in here if you'd prefer. Try not to knock anything over."

Honeywell stepped inside and he closed the door. "Do you want me to put Martha in another room?"

She took in the space he used as an extension of his newsroom office. "Do they all look like this?"

"If I'd known you were coming I'd have moved."

"Oh." She laughed, showing signs of life again. "Why Martha?"

"For Martha Gellhorn. One of our greatest war correspondents. Covered every international conflict from the Spanish Civil War to the invasion of Panama. That's sixty years of reporting. Pops had a huge crush on her."

"She married Hemingway and kicked him to the curb." Honeywell struck a pose. "Gellhorn said, 'Why should I be a footnote to somebody else's life?'" She put the bag on the ironing board and gestured to Martha. "I always like that line. I have a hound called Ernest."

He'd thought about this woman half the night. He'd traded punches for penance for the way he'd treated her. Then he'd sent her his act of contrition in the hope it would make a difference, and now she stood in the middle of his organized chaos like a shaft of unexpected sunlight, wearing a green dress that made her eyes look stormy, reaching her arms out to him. She not only knew about Martha Gellhorn, she'd named her dog after Hemingway. Honeywell was nobody's footnote. She was a front-page headline all on her own.

For a moment he forgot he was holding Martha. He remembered the taste of Honeywell's lips, the little sounds she'd made as she'd kissed him back.

What the hell is she doing here? He took a couple of steps toward her and flipped Martha so he held her on her back with her feet up and her furry belly exposed and her tail flopped over his arm. Martha said, "Merrow," and Honeywell laughed because it sounded so much like hello. She put her hand to Martha's broad head and scratched between her ears. The cat's purr kicked up between them.

"She's lovely."

"She knows it too." Unlike the woman in front of him, who had no idea the effect she had on him. Honeywell's hand was so close to his pec he could imagine her placing it there, stroking his skin.

"Here." He put the cat in her arms, and Honeywell laughed when Martha said, "Foof," then he snatched up a zippered sweatshirt and shoved his arms into it. He should move things, tidy up, create room for her to sit, but he didn't want her here.

He pointed to the messenger bag. "How come you have this?"

She looked up from Martha, who waved a paw in the air for more pats and said, "Marah, marah."

"You were ignoring me."

Oh sweetheart, how I tried.

"You didn't read my email."

"I read it." She rubbed her chin on the top of Martha's head and the cat said, "Yip," making Honeywell smile. "I didn't know what you wanted me to do with it."

"It was my apology for the way I've treated you since the beginning."

Martha squirmed. Honeywell looked equally uncomfortable. "That's all?"

He'd messed this up. Thought it was obvious. He took Martha out of Honeywell's arms and put her on the floor. "What did you think?"

"That it was a test."

"Of what?" They watched Martha saunter over to a row of folders on the floor, select one—Sophia Arrugia, head injury—and sit on it. "And what cliché? There was no cliché."

"That was just to get your attention."

He played with the zipper on the jacket. It only went up part of the way before it jammed—there was too much of his chest on display. He tried to work the snag out, but made it worse. Now it wouldn't go up or down.

"You've got my attention." She'd gotten it the first time she'd smack-talked him, called him an asshole, back when he'd thought she was an intern, a cadet, too farm-fresh and pretty to get herself dirty with him.

"It's the way you wrote it. First person, feature style. You didn't use any swear words or long paragraphs or ten dollar words. But you outed yourself. I'm not sure what you wanted me to do with it."

"I gave it to you to even things up between us. You were generous in what you told me and I was a—"

"Superior twerp. I read it. More than once."

"I didn't expect you to do anything with it. I wasn't sure you'd read it." That was a lie. He knew she'd read it. He'd written it with an eye to what she might choose to do with it out of spite, knowing he'd have to live with it. "And I'm sorry I didn't respond to your messages. I was—" he looked at his folder system "—busy."

"Is this the Keepsafe story?"

"This is one hundred and ten cases of fraudulently denied claims that we know about so far." Martha stood, circled, chose another folder, circled and then sat. "Martha is now sitting on the Yang file. Amelia Yang, crashed through an embankment. She broke her jaw, nose, brow and both arms. She lost the sight in one eye. Her insurance claim was rejected." Honeywell looked at him aghast. "A simple but terrible accident."

Many of them were.

She tapped a file on the ironing board. "Oscar Hernandez, went through his windshield," he said. She tapped another. "Abdul Yemani, got his hand caught in an extruding machine, lost his fingers."

"Is there a file for the Shenkers?"

He picked up the messenger bag and opened it. The first file he pulled out had *Shenker* handwritten across it.

"You know all of these. All one hundred and ten of them."

He nodded. "I'm scared to move them. I know that doesn't make sense." She was still looking at him as if she suspected he'd lost his mind. "This is what I do."

"You're amazing."

Not what he'd expected her to say. The way her voice, breathy with an edge of cheerleader, licked up against his body as if it had a physical presence was unnerving. "Come on, not every room looks like this."

He took her through to the kitchen, which he didn't use as a workspace but wasn't exactly guest ready. There were dishes soaking in the sink and a full basket of clean washing to put away on a chair. The liniment and tape he'd used to treat his bumps and bruises from the fight were still on the counter. Did the place smell? He didn't smoke inside, but maybe everything smelled like the cloves he was immune to. He cleared a pile of newspapers and magazines off the other chair for her to sit.

"It rarely looks much better than this." He couldn't remember the last time he'd cleaned up. "I don't invite people around."

She looked at the chair and then out toward the front door. "I should go."

She should definitely go. "I'm sorry, I didn't mean

it like that." He pulled the chair out for her. "You stole my messenger bag."

She moved around him to sit. "You want to take me out for a picnic. You want to do the love experiment."

"I owe you the love experiment, and not to make me out a hero or anything, Madden wants it."

"You really sing the—"

He clapped his hand over her mouth. "Don't say it." Her eyes went wide and under his palm, her lips and cheeks lifted into a smile. He shouldn't have touched her. He wanted to replace his hand with his lips, wrap his arms around her and keep her hostage.

He dropped his hand and stepped away. "That damn jingle." He looked at Martha, who'd sloped into the kitchen to supervise. Any Jackson Haley investigative reporter magic he'd ever had with Honeywell was about as useful as the cold sludge in his sink. "It's like a groove worn in my head."

"It's about being loved."

"It's about meat."

She sat with a laugh, her back to him. "It's not meat where I come from."

"Where do you come from?" He rummaged in the clothes basket, stripped the busted jacket off and put a T-shirt on.

"Orderly, Illinois. Population ten thousand. Corn country. Home of the white squirrel. That's where my family is. I'm the youngest of four. Three brothers, all married. I have two nieces and two nephews and I Skype with my dog. Sometimes I'm so homesick I could cry." She covered her face with her hands. "I shouldn't have said that. You'll think I'm a failure."

He shouldn't want to pull her into his arms and make a new home for her. "I sign up over and over again to let men hit me so I can hit them back because I have trouble dealing with my life."

She looked up. "Oh."

"Which one of us is handling things better?"

"When you put it like that, coming from a town called Orderly and Skyping Ernest doesn't make me sound like such a loser."

"I've never been homesick, but I don't think that makes you a failure." That was probably a lie too. He'd never had a stable home to be homesick for, and what was missing a grandfather who'd been out of his life for a decade plus, if not homesickness.

"I'm not sure about yoga. I'm no good at it. I hate the whole spirituality through contortion thing. Last night my teacher said, 'Smile inwardly.' What can that possibly mean?"

He knew exactly what it meant. It had nothing to do with yoga. It meant you were utterly delighted with someone and terrifically confused by the phenomenon. That your insides lit up, your blood thrummed and your heart tripped and you felt lighter and smarter and better than you had a natural right to feel, but you couldn't afford to show any of that turmoil to the woman with incredible pale eyes who was sometimes homesick sitting opposite you in your untidy kitchen. All you could do was smile inwardly.

"I hate wieners," he said.

She closed her eyes when she laughed. She was beautiful. She wasn't glossy like most of the women he knew. She wasn't suited up for success like Berkelow or styled to perfection like Potter. She wore color instead of black. She stood out as different and he loved that. Her hair didn't want to be sleek, her freckles showed. Her ears were unadorned and there was no other jewelry. He didn't care that she wore an aligner, but he knew she didn't want others to be aware of it and that she didn't wear it now for that reason.

"Why don't you quit yoga?"

"I don't like to quit. And it's good for me. Why don't you quit letting men hit you?"

"I don't like to quit, and it's good for me."

Her eyebrows danced up and down. "How is it good for you? You split your..." She pointed at his head. "And you're badly bruised. Also, you are something without a shirt on, Jack Haley. You have ripples. Why are you single?"

He pointed into the other room, hoped his stubble hid the heat in his face. "I'm busy."

"That's not a reason."

"Martha gets jealous."

Honeywell's expression shifted from stern to charmed. "I made you blush."

He was a thirty-six-year-old man who had his own column, regular radio and TV appearances, social media feeds that trended and his face plastered all over public transit, and he had no cool with this woman, none at all. "Why are you single?"

"I haven't met anyone here yet. It's not easy being new. Everyone I've met socially is a couple already or not my type, or a girl, and kissing girls is not my thing. I think Spinoza almost asked me out."

"You think? It's not like he's a subtle guy. Don't go out with Spinoza."

"Why not? Is he married?"

All that light and heat inside him screamed "go out with me," until he refocused on why that was a bad idea. They were colleagues, strangers. They'd done a portion of an intimacy experiment and mostly been at odds with each other, which was entirely his fault. He didn't want to go out with her, he didn't want to go out with anyone. He wanted to have sex with her. Starting tonight and not letting up till Monday morning when they both had to be at work again. It'd been a while and everything about her stirred him up.

He wanted to take her apart slowly and bring her home loud. Except that was one of the worst ideas he'd ever had. It was throwing open the door and letting complication have a party in his life and he hated parties, he always left early.

"He's not married." *He's not right for you.*

"He'd put you to sleep with sports trivia."

"And you wouldn't put me to sleep with insurance fraud case studies?"

He'd trade her a story for the revelation of a body part. A victim's name for a kiss, and he wouldn't let her sleep until they were both sated. *Fuuuck.* He had to shut that down. "Can I get you a drink?"

He poured juice and then realized he should send her home or feed her. "Do you eat pasta?" If he was lucky she'd say she was on a diet and didn't eat carbs.

"I love pasta."

"I'm no gourmet, but it'll be edible if you'd like to stay." Ninety percent of him hoped she'd leave. The other ten was hand-feeding her ravioli and licking the taste of Prego from her lips.

She tapped her feet on the floor, a little dance. "I'd love to stay."

He should've let Martha escape, snatched that bag out of Honeywell's hands and slammed the door on her. Instead he let the stagnant water out of the sink and rewashed the dishes, opened a bottle of wine, set the table, and filled Martha's bowl, all the while wondering who he was when he was with Derelie Honeywell and not trying to avoid the pleasure of it.

"Did you want to be a boxer when you were a kid?" she asked, as he salted the pot of water on the burner.

"Did you want to be a ballerina?"

She snorted.

Oh hell. "I'm sorry. I've spent my life being the one who asks the questions. It's a reflex." The reflex of a sexist asshole, or a guy who felt like he had something to prove. "I promise to pull my punches. No, I wanted to be a soldier who drove a tank, fought fires and wrote comic books."

"Does that mean you can draw?"

"I thought I could. By the time I was about ten I wanted to be a reporter like Pops. My parents wanted me to go into medicine and they've never forgiven me for not making the most of my brain."

"So professionally you're living your dream?"

He nodded. "I'm not sure how long it's going to last. True investigative reporting is expensive because it's time consuming, and we're in the age where crowd-sourcing on Twitter and Facebook is considered an investigation, where pop culture is more important than hard news and actual facts no longer matter. We even have the issue of fake news, alternative facts. Reporters like me are fast becoming extinct."

Replaced by reporters like Honeywell, who were content creators whose job was to reflect the post-truth world, entertain it, not examine or question it too deeply.

"How does that make you feel?"

Like he was under attack and Honeywell was making him admit it. He came around the counter to pour the wine. He had no other skills and he'd made so many enemies there was no easy way to cross over from hack to flack and take a PR job. It also made him angry. What kind of world was it going to be if there was no force powerful enough to pressure wrongdoers to account? It'd be a world where men like Bob Bix never need fear exposure.

"It makes me frustrated, despairing."

"Which makes you want to hit things."

That about covered it.

She looked down at her lap. "If you had a crystal ball, what would you want to know about your future?"

"For farm-fresh, you own some devious, woman." It was Honeywell's turn to blush. She had her cell in her lap. "This is a love experiment sneak attack."

"Oh look, Martha is cleaning herself," she said, pointing at the cat, who stopped in the act of licking her butt and stared at them. *Charming.*

"Okay, let's do it then." He went back to the stovetop. "If I had a crystal ball, I'd want to know what the world is like when we've forgotten the value of looking at things critically. I'd want to know how I'm going to keep making a living." He waved a plastic stirrer at her. "And you?"

"I'd want to know a whole bunch of silly things like how long Ernest is going to live and how my parents are going to age and whether the farm can remain viable."

"Nothing silly there."

"I'd want to know if I fall in love, if I marry, if I have kids."

"What would make you think you won't?"

"I'm twenty-eight and I've had two steady boyfriends and a couple of lovers, but I've never been in love and not everyone gets what they want." She shrugged. "On the one hand, why should I be so lucky to get what I want? And on the other, I'm not so special that I'm not like most people, and most people do the marriage and kids thing. It's like yoga, mysterious, unfathomable, but I'm still trying."

The ten percent of him that wanted to kiss her also wanted to assure her she'd get the lover, the family she wanted and admit that he'd wondered about those things for himself on nights when he wasn't too tired and days that were made for families—the holidays, the Thanksgivings and Labor Days.

The other ninety percent of him understood he was largely a bystander in his own life. He asked questions and formed opinions on events outside of himself and he liked it that way. He cooked the pasta and tried to remain objectively, professionally distant, which was much harder to do barefoot in his own kitchen with Honeywell's eyes on him than it was when he was suited up Jackson Haley, a living version of his byline.

"The question you asked me earlier, the one about whether I was doing what I dreamed of doing, what's your answer to that?" he asked.

"My version of your tank-driving, firefighting, soldier comic book writer was Dr. Doolittle. I wanted to fix animals by whispering to them. I wanted them to follow me around and be the only one who could understand what they said. But I wasn't a fan of actual sick animals and got bored with cones and bandages and the amount of time it takes to fix bones, so that was a bust. I never seriously considered becoming a vet. I thought I'd like to write stories and here I am doing that. It was the most unlikely thing for a girl from Orderly to want to do."

He dished the pasta into bowls, hearty servings for both of them, and placed them on the table with a salad that was mostly various types of lettuce and tomato that was past its best. It wasn't a picnic, but it would do.

"This looks great," she said with a gorgeous smile that had the impact of an uppercut, and he lost his place in the conversation, returning to his corner and the safety of a question.

"What's up next?"

"A load of questions I never thought I'd get you to answer."

"I promise to behave." If she kept smiling at him he'd likely do anything she asked, except move the one hundred and ten folders—because that would screw with his internal filing system—and touch her again, because that would screw with his animal instincts; that would make him want what he shouldn't have.

"What's the greatest accomplishment of your life?"

He grimaced, and that hurt his face. "You go first."

She delayed by trying the pasta. He'd likely over-cooked it, but she tucked in. "So far, it's moving to the city. I was comfortable in Orderly, but I wasn't going to learn anything new, meet anyone new, and I wanted more." She pointed her fork at him. "Quit stalling."

"Being able to help people who've been wronged get justice, or at the bare minimum have their stories heard."

"I thought you'd say having your own dinkus."

"You like to live dangerously."

She looked at her plate. "Only with you, apparently."

Shit. Not convenient he felt the same about living dangerously with her? He should take Honeywell's plate away and bundle her out the door immediately with a stern warning to lose his address. "You got another question for me?"

"Do you still call me Honeywell in your head?"

He stalled with a mouthful. She was Honeywell because that's what he did. He used surnames. It kept things professional. He used her surname because it was supposed to stop him from thinking about her as a person he might care about more than he should. He'd had to scrub her surname from last night's email and replace it with her first.

"Do you have a problem with that?"

"No, Jack. I only wondered."

It would be useful if he could step down the aggression. "Do you call me asshole in yours?"

"Sometimes I think of you as Dinkus. I used to imagine you wore very ugly underwear."

That was a new one. He'd been called all the crude,

insulting, anatomically violent, unprintable names there were, but as far as he knew, no one imagined his underwear, which was ordinary, and most of it was in the basket he'd shoved in the corner.

She went on. "Because you were intimidating and being afraid of you wasn't going to get me my story."

"Are you afraid of me now?" He'd wanted to get out of doing the love experiment, and he'd own up to intimidating her, but he didn't like what that said about him. He was often awkward with people socially, with women particularly, and he'd been especially wrong-footed with Honeywell because she came with the pressure of having to show he could be more than his headlines.

She picked up her wineglass and looked at him over the top of it. "About as much as you're afraid of me."

He should be examining his conscience. He'd made a colleague feel vulnerable, deliberately. Intimidation was a tactic he used to get information he needed. He used it in the fighting pit as well. Intimidate your opponent and they'd be on edge, more likely to make a mistake, let slip the words you needed to bring them undone, lower their guard. Intimidate a woman, outside of some bedroom game she was in on—that wasn't the kind of man he wanted to be. But then Honeywell was a colleague and she didn't ask to be treated differently from anyone else.

This was fucked up. What he had on his conscience was a vision of Honeywell's dress on his floor, and that intimidated the shit out of him.

"The next two questions are about friendship," she said. "What does friendship mean to you?"

Talking about friendship was at least five grades smarter than thinking about sex with Honeywell, than wondering if she was thinking about it with him. "It was easier to have friends when I didn't have a dinkus."

"But you have friends?"

He almost laughed at the worried edge she put on that. He had old friends, married with kids, with busy lives. He could say he didn't have time for friends or he needed to make time to reconnect, or people sought him out for friendship of one kind or another but always with an aim to what benefits would accrue to themselves. Both answers made him look pathetic.

"I need to work on the friendship thing." Still a pitiful answer, but it was honest.

"Me too," she said. "At least I don't have to worry that people want to be my friend for what I can do for them."

If he lurched across the table and grabbed her, backed her up against the wall and kissed her till her knees knocked, that would be aggressive. It wouldn't make them friends, and that was the best outcome for this experiment.

"What do you value most in a friendship?"

He needed to move, so he picked up their empty plates and took them to the sink. "That feeling where you don't need to explain yourself but at the same time a good friend holds you accountable to your own truths."

"Oh, that's good. My hometown friends tried to talk me out of coming here. Said I'd hate it, said I'd come slithering back. It hurt. It's like they expect me to fail and they'll be happy when I do. I realized it was because they thought I was judging them, but I'm not. I just wanted something different than living in the same town my whole life."

"Friendship, it's overrated."

"Maybe for you. I miss having close friends. I have colleagues and acquaintances, and I'm on nodding terms with the dealer who hangs on my street corner; he's stopped trying to sell me crack. There's a man I like at yoga and Spinoza likes me."

"Stay away from Spinoza." He came back to the table. He didn't like the idea of her living close to a dealer or having the attention of the man at yoga.

She laughed. "What's your most treasured memory?"

Kissing you against the glass wall of Elaine's. "Time with my Pops. He made everything an adventure, and I was the hero of all of them."

"I had this one weekend." The way she said it made him pay more attention. *Please don't let this be a memory about losing her virginity.* "I guess you'd call it a one-night stand, except it went on for three nights."

Oh fuck me. Friends should be able to talk about this kind of thing, but he didn't want to be that kind of a friend. He was scum. He wanted to be the kind of friend who saw her naked and desperate.

Often.

"And that's when I knew I had to get out of Orderly."

He made a sound of relief and covered it with a cough. He couldn't have stood there and listened to her talk about having sex without damage to his intestinal fortitude, and damn the cliché.

"What's your most terrible memory?"

Without hesitation, it was Pops's death. The funeral. His own rage at having been left alone and the way his parents hadn't known what to do with his grief and alternatively disciplined and distanced themselves from him.

"The scoops I couldn't get. The leads that went to other reporters at other papers and networks, or fell apart for lack of evidence."

"Not buying it. Too general. You think I can't take hearing that losing your Pops was the worst thing that ever happened to you?" She narrowed her eyes to a ferocious parody squint. "I'm tougher than I look."

"I think this experiment is evil." And the woman had a bead on him he found uncomfortable, which was why he didn't want to do this in the first place. Self-examination outside Barney's church was designed to make him twitch. "I'm not talking to you about grief."

"Why not?"

Because that was something he kept locked up tight. It was an old scar, long healed and flexible enough he didn't need to consider it as he moved through the world. Talking about it would only needlessly irritate it.

"Scaredy cat."

"Taunting me won't get you what you want." Unless she wanted to take this up close and very personal, and then it might unwrap her.

"How do you know what I want?"

It couldn't be the same thing he did and didn't want. Complication. Step it back. "Can I get you anything else?"

"You can answer the question and I can be the kind of friend who doesn't judge."

"You don't want to be my friend, Honeywell."

"My name is Derelie, and there's only one thing I want more than being your friend tonight."

It was a trap to ask what that might be. He let the silence between them grow. He knew how to use it to force others to show their hands.

She stood abruptly, startling Martha, who was sprawled on the floor like a rug needing a good vacuuming. "There you go, that's intimidating, that thing you do where you don't talk. It's not friendly. I should go."

"I felt abandoned." She went quiet. "On the day of the funeral I stole a car. All I was good for was crashing into a fence. I think I wanted to die too."

She returned to her seat at the table. "Were you hurt?"

"Bruised, scratched up, a touch of concussion."

"It's your pattern."

"I'm not following."

"You said it earlier. You put yourself into a position where you're going to get hurt to deal with the world."

First instinct was to protest, but she'd turned his own words against him. Astonishing. Second instinct, default question. "What's your most terrible memory?"

"You're just going to skip right over that revelation."

"That's what I was planning, yes."

"All right then. My most terrible memory is the night my dad had a heart attack. We didn't know if he'd make it. I've never been so frightened or so relieved. He has a pacemaker now and nothing stops him. I'm sorry about your Pops." She looked away to Martha, who was snoozing. "I don't want to ask you the next question."

"It must be a doozy. Hit me. I use pain to deal with the world."

"How close and warm is your family? Do you feel your childhood was happier than most other people's?"

Ah. Like ripping off tape and taking the top layer of skin with it. He hated this. He hated feeling that he owed her his answer and the shock of vulnerability that came with it.

"We didn't touch in my family. We weren't the average definition of loving. We didn't spend time together. Work, the hospital was the priority for my parents, prestige and money too. But I had everything I needed. I had a home and food and an enviable education. I didn't turn to a life of crime. I don't drink to excess or do drugs, other than over-the-counter painkillers. I came out of it fine. My childhood wasn't traditionally happy, but it wasn't tragic either and it's a long time ago."

"I would die without touch." She stopped, her face flushed. "We were always hugged and kissed and squashed and sat on laps and pushed around and chased, tickled till we wet ourselves, brushed and scrubbed and smoothed. That's my whole childhood." She put her hand over his where it lay on the table. "It makes me so sad you didn't have that."

What would it mean if he flipped his hand over? If he tangled her fingers in his? If he wanted touch now like he wanted the next inflation of his lungs?

"I don't want to ask the next question either."

He slid his hand out from under hers. "Pain, remember?"

"How do you feel about your relationship with your mother?"

He had an obligatory and grudging relationship with his mother, but how to tell her that? "I messed up my mother's career. That's not a guess. She told me. She couldn't work through part of her pregnancy because it was difficult, and then she took a leave of absence for six months and was penalized by the hospital system for that. She's never gone so far as to say she wished she didn't have me, but that's the territory we flirt with. To both my parents I was an inconvenience on my way to being a disappointment. My parents aren't a factor in my life. They're people who should never have had children."

She stood. Martha opened one eye, but didn't otherwise stir, not even when Honeywell stepped over her on her way around the table. He pushed his chair out to stand, but she put a hand to his shoulder.

"I'm not going to tell you how great my mom is. She was the opposite to your mom. Us kids were made to feel like we were her universe." She put pressure on his shoulder until he opened his body to her and then she was in his lap, her arms around his back, her face tucked into his neck. When he didn't immediately move to touch her, she said, "If you don't hold me I'm going to be very embarrassed."

What choice did he have? He banded his arms around her, shifted their bodies so her hip rested on his belly, and they were chest to chest. He bit down on a groan. She was soft and smelled like soap and fruity shampoo. He shouldn't have her in his arms again. It was where he wanted her, but it made him feel vulnerable.

"If you knew that in a year you'd die suddenly,

would you change the way you're living now?" she said, without lifting her head.

He wanted to touch her hair, take it out of the band that held it, but he kept still, enjoying her weight and warmth. This was what he'd change. He'd add this—a strong, willing woman he admired. Someone to share a meal with at night, to share a bed with.

He breathed her in. Not a colleague, not a rookie he was charged with teaching, not an experiment, not a friend. "I'd want this in my life. I'd want not to be so alone." To stop being a bystander, to make himself a life outside work.

The admission went so deep it might've stopped his heart.

"Me too."

Her voice hitched with emotion. She meant she'd want touch, comfort. "You'd go home to your family."

She lifted her face, and they were eye to eye. "I'd go home, but I'd want more."

Now he touched her hair, smoothing his hand from her temple to the knot of it at the back of her head. "What would be more?"

She rested her head into his hand with a satisfied sigh. It was the only answer he was going to get, and he liked it too much. He stretched a hand out to reach for her cell. They had two questions left in this set.

He had to clear his throat to get his voice in gear. "We're supposed to share five positive characteristics about each other."

"I'll start." He felt her fingers at the back of his neck, playing in the short hair there. "You care about people." What she was doing with her hand sent shivers down his back. "You're honorable." She brought her other hand to his chest, rested it over his heart. "You use your skills for good." She had to be able to feel it trying to leap into her palm. "You write like you can change the world." She brought her face close, brushed her nose on his. He quit breathing and closed his eyes. "You kiss like you can stop time." And it did stop when her lips glanced across his; a whisper, a phantom ache, and then she started the clock again. "Tell me five positive things about me."

She made him hungry, greedy, wishing he had a different life, longing for a place to retreat to when things got tough. He was jealous of her sense of adventure. His was scuffed and tattered, but hers might be enough for both of them if he could find a way to tell her he was nothing without the work he feared the world no longer valued. He was interviews and story outlines, headlines and paragraphs. He was facts and figures and the impact they had on people, but without those things he was a hollow person, living in an unkempt apartment with an untidy cat, with bad housekeeping habits and poor coping skills.

He'd end up punched into one too many concussions, or smoke himself into bad health. He'd end up pointless and bitter and alone and bitter all over again. He'd question everything but a future where he was a different man with a woman who loved him, who he could worship in return, because it was too much to believe he could have that from twenty-four questions.

But Derelie sat on his lap, her eyes full of trust, and he had enough honor not to question that.

Chapter Fifteen

Jack's heart pumped strongly under Derelie's resting palm, his arm at her back held her securely. He wanted her body close, but he'd hesitated on the question and he wasn't a hesitant man. He looked younger and less authoritative without his glasses. He looked curiously uncertain for a supremely confident man.

"You can say I'm brave." He'd said that before, but she regretted prompting him, regretted the impulsive decision that landed her in his lap and the way both of those things made her feel small and soft and needy. And still she wanted to kiss him, forget about the questions and the emotions they shook loose, and simply feel the heat and strength of him; concrete and steel to her sunshine and birdsong.

And he wasn't taking the prompt.

She pressed her feet to the floor and made to stand, a lump of hope turned rancid in her throat, only to feel his arm tighten around her.

"Five things are not enough." His voice was pitched so low it curled inside her. "Five things puts a limit on you. You're not five positive things. You're five hundred, five thousand."

She drew back a little because Jack sounded angry, and since she'd barged in and made herself at home in every sense of the word, he had a right to be.

"I want things from you, Derelie Honeywell." He brushed the back of his knuckles gently over her cheek. "I want them and I shouldn't. You make me feel things I'd forgotten about, remember things I'd locked away. You, not the idiot experiment—you. I'm answering the questions because of you. Because of your generosity, your honesty. Because you have a clear heart and a strong mind and a tenacity that impresses me."

Oh, it wasn't anger, it was fire. It crackled across his skin and flickered in his eyes. She'd never wanted to be so close to a blaze so intense, so willing to be consumed by passion without care for the consequences. There was nothing careful about wanting to be with Jack. It was hot coals, no shoes, a tightrope walk without a net.

"I want your mouth on mine because you astonish me. I want your hands on me because you delight me. I want to hear your voice because you inspire me. I want to smile at you because I'm no longer afraid it might hurt either of us to show you what you make me feel."

She put her lips to his ear. Jack made her feel reckless and free. "Do it."

He crushed her to his chest, his mouth on her neck. "I don't know what the questions mean anymore, but the answers fucking terrify me."

The question was how to keep her sanity while Jack's kisses were restrained and tentative, at her jaw and her cheek and her brow, while his hands stroked, held, explored and her blood sizzled. Her breathing got noisy and her own hands busy, burrowing into his short hair and gripping his arm. She wanted his lips but he wouldn't take them. Wouldn't let her mouth near his.

There was only one more question in this set. What roles do love and affection have in your life? She already knew Jack's answer—he'd had very little love and was wary about affection.

"Please," she whimpered against his throat. He'd kissed her before; his hesitancy now was infuriating and it made her fingers into claws. She'd been loved deeply platonically and grown to adulthood fueled by affection. She'd had sex, great, good, boring, bad, but she'd never felt need like this. She burned for it. "Please, Jack." She would be nothing but ash if he failed to answer.

She was incendiary when he did.

He caught her jaw in his hand and they locked eyes. His had gone dark, in their bed of bruises, and then with a groan that shook through him he brought their lips together.

Kiss followed kiss followed kiss. Thorough and sweeping and possessive. Jack's lips could be soft and addictive or hard and cruel. He didn't censor, he got lost. He gave her his emotions without guarding them, and she reflected them back without judgment. Her tongue to encourage him, her hands to praise him, the echo of her pulse in her breath and her core, ground into his stomach and hips. But there would be more.

Derelie scrambled to exchange sidesaddle for sitting astride Jack's lap without losing contact. He grunted in disapproval when she moved, but woke quickly to the possibilities of closer contact, opening his arms to give her room, but damn this dress, the skirt was too narrow to allow her to settle over his thighs.

He broke the kiss, hands to her waist. "No." He stood, backing her up. "This can't happen."

What was he talking about? "It's happened before." It'd happened with less buildup than this.

"That wasn't real. This isn't real." He took his hands off her and put distance between them. "It's the voo-doo from that experiment."

"You said you wanted me. Was that a lie?" He turned his face away. Her own had gone past flaming and entered nuclear meltdown. Any minute now her features were going to slide down her chin and pool on her chest. "Did you make out with me for the story?" What a complete cad.

"I made out with you because I meant everything I said, because I want you, Derelie Honeywell, but we're being manipulated."

"You think a game of Twenty Questions made us want to kiss." The questions were probing, they forced confessions and the whole setup demanded honesty, but could a question and answer session have that kind of power?

"I don't know, but I think we need to take a breath to find out." He moved about restlessly, putting his back to her. "And that wasn't just kissing." He groaned and turned to face her. "There are a dozen reasons why it's a bad idea that I want you to stay for the weekend."

He didn't say the night. And it was more than kiss-ing. It was more than a game of questions and answers. "Is this about work? Because no one has to know."

"It's about us. My behavior toward you has been

unacceptable." He shook his head as if even his own formality appalled him. "I took advantage of you once before. I'm not doing it again."

"I'm choosing this. It's not like you're forcing me."

"Like I didn't force you outside Elaine's?"

She could've kneed him in the groin outside Elaine's. She'd been more annoyed when he stopped kissing her and shoved her in a cab. "I'm not some backwater innocent. If I want a one-night stand with you, I get to decide that for myself."

"Do you sleep with the man from yoga?"

"That's none of your business."

"You're right. Ask me why I invited you to Elaine's."

"You told me." It wasn't flattering. "You needed a decoy."

"And I could've invited anyone, but I invited you. You thought it was a date."

She mashed her lips together. She didn't like him guessing she'd gotten that wrong. "You said it was to show me how a stakeout worked."

"I felt guilty about how I'd treated you. Guilt and attraction, that's a lethal combination punch. Now ask me why I kissed you that night."

"It was for the story. So you didn't get caught out spying on Bix."

"It was because I wanted you."

It wasn't for the story. He'd lied. "Are you telling the truth now?"

"I needed cover, sure, but I didn't need to put my hand up your dress or my tongue in your mouth."

Oh. It was kind of a date then. The new Cooper Street Can't Get Enough dress didn't go to waste.

"You came through that door tonight and you looked at me as if you'd never seen me before. We don't know each other. I've behaved like a bastard and this experiment started something, but I want to be sure that when I take you to bed it's not the experiment I'm fucking. I want you to know it too."

He wasn't lying now. And she wasn't imagining he had it as bad for her as she had it for him.

"The look on your face, Honeywell." His softened into a smile. "Derelie."

Jackson Haley saying her first name shouldn't make her feel made from beating wings.

"I want to take you on a picnic. I want to finish the last set of questions. When we're done, if you still want me, nothing will stop me making you feel good, not being colleagues, not the story, not knowing you could do better than me."

Not a cad. Not a bastard. There was some kind of unexpected chivalry at work here.

"What now? We talk about the weather?"

"You go home. Do some down dog. Make sure you don't want that other guy you sweat with instead of me."

"That other guy can put his ankles behind his head."

Jack laughed. "The question is, does he make you want to put yours behind his head?"

If her tongue got any dryer, she'd have to make a grab for Martha's water bowl.

"Tomorrow, lunchtime, I'll pick you up and take you out in the sunshine. I'll see what I can do about birds."

"You could've thrown me out because I'm a thief, but you're throwing me out because you don't want to kiss me anymore." She tried to summon resentment, but it was squeezed out by amusement.

He stepped into her space, put his hand to her face and brushed his lips on hers, making it all better. "Go home, Derelie, before we do something we might regret. There's time for that tomorrow night when at least we can pretend to have given this our full consideration."

The fact he was using her first name was enough of a softener, the rest of it didn't hurt either. She bent to say goodbye to Martha, got a "Marah, yip" in response, collected her cell and purse, and met Jack at the front door.

"You don't know where I live."

He pointed at his chest. "Investigative reporter."

"You're going to hack into the employee database to find me?"

"No." He handed her a Sharpie and a pad. "I was going to ask."

She tried not to laugh as she wrote her address down. "Do I need to bring anything?"

"Just that last set of questions."

He stood very close. They were toe to toe. She touched a finger to his brow. "Does it hurt?"

"Had worse."

She didn't want to leave. "How about this?" She trailed her finger lightly around his shadowy eye socket.

"It's just a black eye."

She put her hand to his side over his T-shirt where she knew his skin was branded with a rainbow of color. "And this?" He didn't answer, but he did kiss her, his hands going to her shoulders just as a heavy weight landed on her feet.

She broke the kiss and looked down to see Martha lying over their toes. "Merrow."

"She'll do anything to escape," Jack said.

"Marah."

This pussy was a cock-blocker.

Jack bent and picked the cat up, placing her over his shoulder while he opened the door. Martha made a disgruntled noise that sounded a lot like she'd said, "Noooo" and flicked her tail against Jake's torso.

"Go before she decides to dig in," he said, then winced as she obviously did.

Derelie had arrived at Jack's place a thief looking to steal up on the truth, but she left with more than she'd bargained for. All her hushed outrage and cautious awe was recast as a hum of anticipation that woke her with enthusiasm next morning and floated her through the early yoga class.

She separated her spine anchors and tucked her butt bones with more ease than normal or maybe it was less anxiety about getting it right. She didn't even think about looking around for Yogaboy. They were on the same weekday schedule, but on weekends it varied, and in any case, she was far more interested in putting her ankles behind Jack's head and prone to spontaneous bursts of smiling thinking about that. Only a few hours and twelve questions before she'd get the chance to try.

While she was rolling up her mat she felt a tap on her shoulder. "*Namaste*," he said. She really should've come up with a better name for Yogaboy. He wasn't a boy, for a start. He was in some ways ageless as well as being like a muscly rubber band.

"Hi," she said, because *namaste* sounded wrong in her mouth.

"You enjoyed your practice this morning," he said.

"Yes, it was a good class." Whatever she'd seen in his exotic appearance, and island of calm manner, so different to any of the men back home, was thoroughly muted by twenty-four questions and their unimaginable answers, and having been kissed silly last night by a man she desired more than was sensible.

She made a move to go and he put his hand on her arm, a touch so light and quick it might not have happened at all. "I'd like to have sex with you."

Now, this wasn't a Spinoza-type of proposition—there was no mistaking it for what it was. Something she'd have been seriously all over, if it wasn't so blunt and there was no Jack.

"Why?" It was out of her mouth before she realized she didn't care what his response was.

"I like your ass."

Gosh. "That's not very, um, spiritual."

"Screw spiritual. We'll get chai first, then we'll fuck." She laughed.

He looked confused. "You don't like chai?"

"I don't like you." He'd spoiled the fantasy of himself altogether now.

"But we have a connection."

The only connection they had was situational. "I've been coming here for months, putting my mat beside yours, and we only made eye contact once that whole time."

He looked at the ceiling. "If I made eye contact with every novice, I'd never have a moment to myself." Gross. He wasn't an island of calm, he was river sand in your bikini bottoms. "But I just chose you."

"Like I'm a fun fair prize? An oversize stuffed bear?"

"Exactly. You get me."

She got him all right. She tucked her mat more firmly under her arm. "Go away."

"I'm only doing this once." He plucked at one of his long dreads. It was brown near his head but bleached blonde at the tip. "I won't ask you again."

"Thank God for that."

He made small circles with his hands, describing his confusion. "You're rejecting me?"

With bells on it. "I don't think we're a match."

He looked her up and down, and his appraisal wasn't kind. "You should try Pilates. You have no natural flexibility. You'll never be any good at yoga."

Or a passive aggressive shithead either. She almost said, "How do you like my ass now?" but stopped when she realized they had an audience of students for the next class. She was very conscious of eyes on that ass as she headed for the locker room, but an hour later having shoved it into cargo pants she was self-conscious in a new way.

Jack buzzed her apartment on time. He had an Uber car waiting and a file archive box in his arms. "Are we going to work?" He wore respectable jeans, a nice T-shirt, his glasses and a cap. He looked her right in the eyes, and it was more disconcerting than Yogaboy's full body assessment because she wasn't sure how to read it.

"I don't own a picnic basket."

He was just as bruised, but he'd shaved. "When was the last time you went on a picnic?" She wanted to touch him so badly.

"If I tell you never you're going to feel sorry for me." He opened the car door and she climbed in. He piled in after her, putting the box between them, and gave the driver the address of some park she'd never heard of.

"Is the answer never?"

"Only if that's going to unfairly prejudice you toward me."

"You want me to feel sorry for you?"

He sighed playfully. "I'm giving way to the inevitable."

If the inevitable was a bed and a night together, she was giving it all away.

Where they were going was a good half-hour drive and took Derelie through parts of the city she'd not seen before. That might well be a metaphor for what they were doing, seeing each other in a new way, outside of work. The remainder of the questionnaire felt like it might be a map to where they'd end up.

They found a pond and a tree for shade and Jack had a blanket in that box and the sun was out and there were no long shadows and no concrete echoes. It didn't smell like home, there were certainly no white squirrels, they weren't sitting on the back of a pickup, there was no Ernest, all excited to be out, and there were lots of other people around, but it was a solid effort.

Jack paused in the process of unpacking the picnic

and looked up. "I ordered birds." He'd been to a deli and brought sandwiches, cheese and crackers, bottled water and soda. He had a couple of apples and a bunch of grapes and two slices of lemon meringue pie.

"For a guy who's never been on a picnic, you did good."

"Is this the part where you reconsider sitting in my lap last night?"

"Nope." She considered that part of the night an outstanding achievement.

"You're sure?" She hadn't sighted a smile yet. She craved a smile.

"I broke up with Yogaboy this morning." She had a sudden vision of ankles over shoulders—her ankles, Jack's broad shoulders.

"I'm pleased to hear it."

That was his signal to jump on her, or at least touch her with some sense of his intention to keep touching her, but he stayed on the other side of the blanket with the box between them. Yogaboy was obnoxiously forward, but Jack was the picture of reticence. Had she imagined his heart thudding into her palm for a second time?

"You want me to sign a waiver or something?" She held her hand up. "I, Derelie Honeywell, give full consent to Jackson Haley to ravage my body for the purposes of sexy times. I do solemnly promise not to kiss and tell." She said it in jest, but the look on his face told her he wasn't sharing the joke. "What?"

"Aside from everything else that's happened between us—theft, lies and we haven't gotten to the videotape part—I've been burned before," he said.

Video. "You think I'd cause you trouble."

"I hope so."

"I wouldn't—oh." That was more like it. "I really want to kiss you."

"That's definitely in the plan."

"Video?"

"Questions first, video later. And that ravaging you wanted, I believe it can be arranged." But still no smile. He was dressed like weekend Jack, but his manner was all office.

"Who burned you?"

"It's not so much who as what."

Ah, he was talking about the downside of his slice of fame. "I've seen behind the curtain, Jack, and I still like what's there."

He gave her a slow perusal she met with one of her own. Weekend Jack was all about the arms and shoulders and the way his T-shirt fell against his body and the fact she knew he wasn't office-soft from too much sitting.

"Twelve questions before you can make that assessment," he said.

All right then. Still going to want to trace that raised vein that started near his wrist and charted territory all the way to his elbow.

She pulled a printout of the questions from her pocket. "We each have to make three true 'we' statements, like 'We're both happy to be in the park.'"

She frowned at the paper. The question implied they understood each other. Odd how that made her uncertain.

"I'll start. We're both a little nervous with each other." She looked at him for confirmation.

"That's not going to get you ravaged."

But it was true, and he wasn't protesting it. "We both enjoyed kissing last night."

"Much better."

"We're both looking forward to tonight."

"My turn." He reached over the box and took the page from her hand, but he didn't spare it a glance. "We're a crash course in chemical attraction. We're lab rats let loose and juiced up on conversation. We're as ill-advised as we're inevitable."

Gulp.

"We're staying at opposite ends of this blanket because all I want to do is get my hands on you, taste you, smell that fruit in your hair, hear the way you lose your breath and feel your body grinding up on mine."

And she'd wondered if he was having second thoughts.

Chapter Sixteen

It was possible Jack had frightened Derelie off. He needed to lighten up. They were on a picnic for God's sake, and picnics were meant to be easy. Children went on picnics; how hard could it be? But he'd been wound up since he'd talked Derelie out of his apartment last night and seeing her sitting cross-legged opposite him with expectation in her eyes was making it hard to keep his distance.

He needed the distance, or he would definitely come on too intense. "What I said about what I want with you, was that too much?"

She tipped her head to the side and a hunk of bright curls fell over her shoulder. He knew that hair would be unruly. "It was especially perfect."

There was hope for him yet. This he didn't want to wreck. He looked at the page. "'Complete this sentence. I wish I had someone with whom I could share, dot, dot, dot.'"

"I wish I had someone with whom I could share how I felt about the city without being told to come home," she said, eyes down on the blanket.

"You're stuck pretending everything is fantastic."

She nodded. "My family and friends mean well, but they don't understand why I want to live in a place I can barely afford and work in a job that's not secure."

When she said things like that he didn't feel like they were worlds apart, that he was too jaded and she was too romantic. "I wish I had someone with whom I could share the feelings that make me want to chase a black eye."

"Would it help?"

"I'd like to try it." For the first time ever. Derelie wriggled about, changing her posture. He knew what she wanted because he wanted it too. "Stay on your side."

"Move the box."

"If I move the box we're done with the questions."

"We can extemporize."

"By which you mean make it up."

"I thought a ten dollar word might win you over."

She didn't need to win him over. He was so far over any line that should be drawn between them, and still he wanted to protect this unexpected thing they had from needless regrets because it felt precious.

"No you didn't. You're being a brat, hoping I'll do something about that." She stuck her tongue out at him. *Oh Christ.* He felt that in his body in places not suitable for picnics in public places.

He checked the page for the next question. "'If you were going to become a close friend with your partner'—that would be me, in this example—'share what would be important for them to know.'"

"I have an IUD, barely used, and a clean bill of health I'm not afraid to get dirty."

He groaned and looked away to where a couple of kids were trying to get a kite to fly. "Friend, the question says *friend*. Do you go around discussing birth control with all your friends?"

"Only the ones I want to jump."

"You won't wear your aligner—" he pointed at her mouth "—in front of me, but you'll tell me that." He tried to stare her into behaving. She wasn't embarrassed; she was delighted he was. "How did we get to the place where you're not treating this seriously?"

"I'm treating it very seriously."

"Give me the real answer to that question."

She laughed and rolled to her back. "Payback is a bitch. I don't care if that's a cliché."

He took an apple from the box and crushed it against his teeth, biting down on the tart, crisp flesh with a degree of savagery no piece of fruit required. He wanted to crawl over Derelie, pin her down and eat her laughter. He managed to poke her with his foot to remind her he was waiting without further damage to his tenuous equilibrium.

She looked over at him. "What else is important for you to know? How about I'm strong, I'm ambitious and I'm banking on myself to succeed?"

Great answer. No false modesty and no bragging. And an IUD. *This woman.*

He stuck to the question because it had self-preservation qualities. "I want you to know I don't have a bad temper. I can get a little intense. I intimidated you, and I'm not proud of it, but I'd never hurt you physically. The violence in the boxing is a separate thing from everyday me. It's hard to explain, but I'd never bring that to you."

She sat up, the smile stripped from her face. "I never thought that."

"Look at me." He didn't look like the kind of man she'd want to video-call home with. "You had to wonder."

She gave him direct, unwavering eye contact. "I don't see you as a violent man, Jack. You intimidated me professionally, but I never felt physically threatened and we wouldn't be here if I had."

He closed his eyes. His lenses were tinted, so the relief he felt at that would be hidden from her. How many more goddamn questions were there before he could have her in his arms?

He took another bite of apple and rolled his neck, hearing it pop as some of the tension he'd been holding on to let go. "I haven't been tested for a while." There'd been no need. "If we like what happens between us, I'll get checked out."

"We are so going to like it."

She grinned at him, and the muscles in his shoulders went slack. He referred to the page for next question. "'Tell your partner what you like about them. Be very honest. Say the things you might not say to someone you've just met.'"

"I like that you're more than my first impression."

"You thought I was gay and something strange about underwear."

She laughed. "And that you had balls the size of Texas, not speaking literally, of course." She glanced at his crotch and blushed. "I like that you have this Jackson Haley professional thing going on and you care about your work, but that you're not all ego and bluster. You're the real deal. Walking competence porn. I like that I make you nervous."

On the whole, people didn't make him nervous. But the more he got to know Derelie the more that feeling surfaced. "How is that attractive?" He liked that she knew it wasn't the questions exactly that had him on edge, it was what she made of the answers.

"Are you kidding? You like me, Jack. It's the highest compliment you can pay me."

He groaned. "I've created a monster."

"Cliché."

"Exactly my point." He wagged the half-eaten apple at her.

"I like the way you kiss. I like that so much, and the way you held me and got a little needy with me. Oh man, I like that."

He'd been desperately needy with her. And heroically restrained. "There are kids in this park."

"I like the way you play it so smooth and unemotional but underneath you're a man who craves softness, a way to be gentle without being judged. I like you for Martha and for your messy apartment and your Jesus jeans and your forearms and the fact you know the details of a hundred and ten case studies. If it's not obvious, Jackson Haley, I am so, so into you it's going to be mortifying if we don't happen."

He didn't like her, he was infatuated with her, enchanted, captivated. Was it the enhanced intimacy of the experiment or had she drugged him? "How much do you hate my cigarettes?"

"They make you smell sweet. I like the way they tasted when we kissed."

Game over. He took the clove packet out of the box and rolled a smoke. Held it away from her while he let the comfort of habit knock the last of his anxiety out.

"I like the way you're not WYSIWYG." What you saw wasn't what you got with her. "You look all stereotypical butter wouldn't melt, apple pie wholesome, farm fresh and ridiculously candy sweet. But you're more. You're resilient and quick-witted and a fast study. You have this determination that shines like a light under your skin. Much as it makes me uneasy—fuck, near terrifies me—I like the way you see through me, and it doesn't scare you off. You turn me on, make me want. If you're under any illusion I've got any cool left when it comes to you, I'm going to be a shocking disappointment."

She gave him a look he wanted to interpret as "you couldn't disappoint me if you tried," and that worried him, because there was a dump truck load of ways he could.

"We're supposed to share an embarrassing moment," he said, flapping the page at her.

"You embarrassed me for real that day at the briefing. Everyone looked at me. I felt like the biggest idiot. I was worried Phil would think I'm not a good fit and voluntarily lay me off."

Fuck. He knew all that. He wore it in the black eye and the cut brow and the bruising. "Did I make you cry?"

"You made me go hide in the bathroom because I wanted to cry, but then you made me hate you enough

I held it together. I shouldn't have asked that question, it was dumb, but you were the one with the power and you used it to ridicule me."

"It's one of the most embarrassing moments of my life too. That's the entire reason I look like this." He lifted the side of his shirt. The bruise above his hip was a purple stain, tender to touch, irritated by the waistband of his jeans. "I can help with Madden if it becomes an issue."

"I don't want your help, Jack. I can fix it myself."

Entirely what he deserved. He took another bite of the apple. He wasn't going to be allowed the luxury of acting the big man and saving her. She would save herself.

He checked the page—too many questions left. "We're supposed to share what we dislike about each other."

She pushed hair away from her face. "I don't like it when you pull that Jackson Haley, Human Dinkus crap in front of me. When you look at me as if we live in different worlds and mine is inferior."

"Defense mechanism," he offered flatly. It went with the way she challenged his masculinity.

"Well, stop it."

He liked the heat of command in her voice. "I dislike the fact you're going to complicate my life, Derelie Honeywell."

"Suck it up, you big dinkus."

"Next question. 'When did you last cry?'"

"I cried on the phone to my mom, about three months after I got here. I hated everything about the city and I'd been saying how great it was and I was so caught in that lie. I didn't know if I could cut it at the *Courier* and everyone wanted me to give up and come home and I didn't want to let on that's what I wanted most in the world."

He'd forgotten to tell her how much he liked her generosity. "I don't remember the last time I cried, Derelie. But that's because I fight instead. By that logic, the last time I cried was two nights ago after I'd humiliated you. I did it in front of a man I'd never met whose name was Alvarez. He cried too. Different reasons, but we both were pissed off with ourselves and wanted to do better."

She came up on her knees. "I don't like the fighting thing, Jack. It scares me, even though I know it's not directed at me."

"Sometimes it scares me too, but I promise you the setup is safe and the man running the show knows what he's doing. He almost didn't let me fight."

She knee-walked a little closer. "What's next?"

Jack looked at the page. The questions ran together. There was one about dying and last regrets, another about what you'd save after people and pets if your house was on fire, and a whole question devoted to sharing a problem. He picked that one as the last question he was going to honor. "We're supposed to share a problem we've got and give advice. Do you want to start?"

She looked away, played with a corner of the blanket. In the quiet, he could hear kids yelling about a kite, and in the distance the hum that was the city.

"I want a promotion. I want more money. I want more job security. I'm not sure how to get them. It's not merit alone. That's how I might've gone about it before, but that's my hometown girl naivety. You need to be more than good at your job to do well at the *Courier*. But it's not like I'm gonna sleep with Phil to get ahead."

His heart dodged that punch, but it collected him anyway. "You can't sleep with me to get ahead either." He'd had those veiled offers. Trading sex for favors wasn't on his to-do list.

"That's the problem. That's what people will think, won't they?"

"Let's take a step back and break it down." He was almost out of apple. He could be detached and clinical about this. "You want better conditions at work and you want to sleep with me."

"I want dirty, filthy, depraved sex with you."

He shouldn't like those words out of her plush lips so much, like how they feathered over his body and made his skin goose-bump. "And the two things could be seen as linked. Easy to unlink them."

"Not so easy for me, not after thirty-six questions, not now."

"I walk away. We finish this story and we're done. Phil gets what he wants. You get to shine." He was a liar, a cheat and a hypocrite.

She pouted. "That's win-lose. I want win-win."

"Greedy." Gorgeously so.

"Why not? The whole reason I'm in the city is greed. Greed for more in my life, more everything." She shot him a heated look. "More you."

His detachment was down to apple core. "How do you think you're going to solve the problem?"

"I thought you were supposed to advise me."

"I'm the problem."

"I thought we could finish the story, give Phil what he wants and have this thing as well."

"What's this thing mean to you?" They were starting a new page—he needed it to be one they agreed on.

"Sex, Jack. Rip-roaring, sheet-soaking, mind-bending, ankles-behind-heads sex."

That was a page in a whole new book of erotic delights. "We can keep it quiet, but do you want to sneak around? The whole Madden-Potter thing is supposed to be secret, but it's common knowledge."

"I hate that, all the gossip, and it makes it look like Shona gets favors."

"Madden is harder on her than anyone."

"But I don't work for you, so it's not the same."

"To summarize, you want a scorching fling with me."

"Fling," she laughed. "I want whatever comes after all these questions. I want what comes of this physical tug between us, and I don't know that we need to name it anything except good while it lasts."

"We're done." He tossed the apple core into the file box.

"We didn't talk about your problem."

He crumpled the page and it followed the apple core. Then he moved the box and shuffled closer to her, took her shoulders and held her while he looked into her pale eyes. "My problem is that this is a public place."

"Have we done all the questions?"

Neither of them had taken a note, but he wouldn't forget anything she'd said. "We can extemporize the rest."

"Make it up as we go along." Her smile was as wide as the sky. "You used the ten dollar word."

"We deserve it."

It was a million dollar kiss. Sweeter for the delay, for the relief he felt, for the knowledge that she wasn't misty eyed about him, wasn't on the Jackson Haley ride for any purpose other than their mutual pleasure.

Derelie wound her arm around his neck and removed his cap and glasses. "You won't need these for a while; I plan on being all you see."

A perfect prescription. He took them both down to the blanket and all they did for some time was explore each other's mouths, share breath, touch with slow certainty. He kept his hips away from her, PG for the park, and in the growing glow they became together, he heard chirps, tweets and trills. He lifted his head to make sure they were real.

They had to be because she heard them too. She squeezed his arm. "All we need now is stars. There are no stars in the city. I miss them."

The stars were all inside her, but he didn't have the words to tell her that yet. "All we need now is food, because you've made me lightheaded."

They ate, they bickered and he couldn't get enough of that because it proved they didn't need a questionnaire to be friends, to be more. They traded kisses, he got more handsy than he should've but her twitchy, excited responses were intoxicating, and then both of them dozed in the fading heat, bodies twisted into each other. Later there was only one question remaining.

"My place or yours?" he said.

"Mine is tiny and yours has Martha."

"I want you to stay."

"I packed my toothbrush."

He ditched the box. He called a car to take them back to his place, stopping at his local market so he could pick up something to cook for dinner. Inside the store they separated, Jack going to the fresh food aisle and Derelie, wearing his cap, disappearing down junk food alley.

It happened while he was selecting chicken breasts.

"You're Jackson Haley."

The woman was someone he vaguely knew on sight. Too much sunshine and Derelie in his head to place her. He wanted to brush her off anyway. "From Monday to Friday."

The woman laughed. "I love what you do, the whole champion of the city thing, and it looks like you cook too. That's too good to be true. You don't remember me? I'm Bridie. I'm on-air at WBBM after you. I've tried to catch your eye before. Can't believe I've run into you here. What happened to your face? I hope you have someone to kiss it better."

Ah, that was it. The radio station. Bridie was an attractive woman, a well-respected broadcaster, and once upon a lonely Saturday he'd have considered starting something with her. He focused on the chicken.

"I know this is none of my business, but if you feel like company…"

He heard the dot dot dot she didn't say. The way she put her hand on his arm said everything else. *Untimely vaguely predatory behavior.* "I'm with a friend."

"Oh, I'm sorry." She let go his arm, gracious about rejection. "Maybe another time. I really dig what you do." And there it was, the phone number and her name on the back of a store receipt. He took it from her as she moved off because it was more of a scene not to. He was shoving it into his pocket when Derelie rounded the deli counter with a basket load of snacks.

"I got—oh, sorry, did I interrupt?"

"No," he said, not sparing Bridie a glance. "You like chicken?"

"Better than wieners."

He dropped the packet he was holding and made a grab for Derelie, backed her into the deli counter and tried to look threatening while he kissed her. "Don't say that word. Don't even think it."

"Too late. It's in your head isn't it?"

He spent the walk home trying not to let that jingle take over his brain, even though Derelie hummed it. And while he cooked it was there, a silly little song that reminded him of laughter, of being loved, of the best part of growing up. Why it'd stuck so thoroughly he didn't know—advertising jingle writers were demonically clever—and the memories he'd attached to the little ditty were happy ones.

They ate chicken and salad in his hastily cleaned up kitchen, with Martha watching them from the floor flicking her tail. They finished up with ice cream that Derelie had chosen, and he couldn't remember a Saturday he'd enjoyed more, but he realized he'd stopped trying to have a life outside of work and wondered what that meant, knowing it was about to change.

He watched her lick the back of her spoon. His fascination with her mouth knew no end. *I like you, Derelie Honeywell. I like you in your cargo pants and your hair all full of the wind. I like you sitting opposite me in the kitchen I felt duty bound to clean up. I like the fact that we're going to take what we did last night and today in the park and do it all again but this time skin to skin. I like the fact you have an IUD and that you're not scared of me and that you brought your toothbrush. I hope you didn't bother with PJs. I'd like you in my T-shirts.*

He didn't say any of that because it didn't seem necessary. That experiment had acted like a fast-forward button, shooting them past the initial awkwardness of discovery into the excitement of consummation.

"Do you want anything else to eat?"

She patted her stomach. "I'm full. I'll help you clean up."

"It can wait."

"The way you're looking at me could boil water, Jack."

"You don't like it."

"I really, really like it. But I ate too much, so can you back off the smolder so I don't end up with indigestion? That would be so unsexy."

He laughed. The way he was about her, everything she said and did was sexy, except the mention of wieners. That made him want to tickle her till she cried for mercy. They washed up and he took her through to the living room. He'd cleaned it up too.

"What happened to your filing system?"

"It was all digital anyway. It was just a way for me to process the pieces of the story like a jigsaw puzzle. We could fool around some more." He pointed at the couch. Which Martha promptly jumped onto and lay down full length over both cushions.

"We'd be putting Martha out," she said.

"We could go to the bedroom." They stood in his

living room, indecisive and deliciously awkward, both of them looking at Martha. This never happened to him. He'd never cared enough to feel like what he said next to a woman he was taking to bed made a difference. He never intended them to be around long enough for it to matter.

Derelie gave him the sauciest possible grin. Prego had nothing on her. "That might be nice."

"If we go in there we're staying put a while."

She shrugged. "I guess I can cope."

He'd wanted to swat her wiener-jingle-humming butt the whole way home. He did it now, with his arms around her, less a swat than a hand clamped down on her ass so she knew what he wanted, and there were no misunderstandings. "Give me ten minutes to tidy up in there."

She pulled on his neck to bring their faces close. "You know, the hottest thing about this whole day is that you weren't so sure we'd end up there that you didn't clean up the bedroom first."

"That's what you find hot? My domestic incompetence?"

She responded by grabbing his ass. "Go on then. Martha and I will have girl time."

When he moved, Martha got up to follow, so he shut the bedroom door on her. She wasn't the girl sharing his bed tonight. He shoved clothes in drawers. Sprayed the room with air freshener. Closed the closet doors and changed the sheets. He turned a side table light on and drew the curtains. He felt the same kind of energy he associated with waiting for a big story to break.

But once he got back to the living room, it was as

if he'd misread it all and someone else had broken the story.

Derelie was gone and so was Martha, and on the floor was a foldback clip wrapped around a wad of business cards and slips of paper he'd collected and kept because Roscoe had said it might be useful to have the names and addresses of people who approached him in public if he was ever threatened again.

He was threatened now.

Chapter Seventeen

The thought of Jack making his bedroom presentable
was an unaccountable thrill. It was just a man making
his bed. It shouldn't have made Derelie feel so efferves-
cent, but she was the glass of soda she'd drunk at dinner, bubbling and fizzing and set to explode if shaken.

She wanted that shaking so badly.

"How do you do it, Martha? Hang out with such a
sexy beast and keep your calm. I'm ridiculous. I just
want to kiss him all over and never stop." She laughed
as Martha turned away from the closed bedroom door
after head-butting it a few times. "Yeah, if I didn't
know he was coming back I'd do that too."

The cat skirted by as if Derelie took up an unneces-
sarily large amount of space and Martha was offended
by that, and jumped onto Jack's considerably tidier
desk. "Are you allowed on there?"

Martha picked her way over the pile of folders and
wove between the two computer screens, then pushed
some items around to make room to curl up. Two of
those items she simply tipped off the desk, a box of
tissues and a foldback clip holding a stack of business
cards and notes.

"So that's the way it is then." Derelie picked up the tissues, but when she put her hand to the foldback clip she recoiled. The first card in the stack had a picture of a naked woman, tastefully silhouetted, on it, with a phone number and the words *Jane F, available for no strings sex*. The next card showed a woman in a red corset—her name was apparently Heidi, and she liked uncomplicated arrangements.

She dropped the clip to the ground. That woman in the market had handed Jack something he'd put in his pocket. Derelie had had his cap on, pulled down low and thought she'd mistaken it, but no, the other woman propositioned Jack, and so had the owner of every card or note in this stack. Why would he keep them? Why would she want to be part of the stack?

She was such an idiot. He'd never said why he was single other than being busy. This was how he'd been busy. She didn't need her heart broken this way.

It took two seconds to collect her purse and her overnight bag and fling Jack's front door open. Let him figure out what went wrong, he was the investigative reporter.

She'd have gotten away with her swift exit too, but Martha was a slick ninja and slipped out the door and bounded onto the landing before Derelie could react.

"No, Martha. Be a good girl and go back inside so I can avoid making a huge mistake. Big scary things live out here, like falling for the wrong men, like thinking you're smarter than you really are, and trusting an experiment."

Martha gave her paw a cursory lick and looked at Derelie. There was only the width of the corridor separating them. She could do this—grab Martha, shove her inside and take off. Derelie put her bag down. If ever she'd wanted to be an animal whisperer, this was the moment.

"Come on, Martha, you don't want to be out here. It's noisy and smelly and there are too many people and not enough trees, and you can't see the stars at night. That's not the kind of world you want to live in." She took a step toward the cat, another. "Good girl."

She ducked down and reached out and got her hands to Martha's shoulders, but she didn't hold tight enough or Martha was made of liquid silver; all she got was a handful of loose fur.

"Shit." Martha took off down the stairs and Derelie couldn't simply let her go. Three flights down, there the slinky ninja was, grooming her tail. If she'd stuck with the Dr. Doolittle ambition this wouldn't be a problem. Instead she had to think she was a match for Jackson Fucking Dinkus Haley.

"Here, kitty. Come on, Martha. You're not meant to be out here."

Martha took that instruction to mean bolt. Derelie didn't catch up with her until she hit the bottom landing. Martha was standing with her front paws on the glass door that led to the street. If someone came in, she'd make her escape, but she was also well placed for Derelie to grab her.

She picked Martha up under the front legs and flipped her like Jack did so the cat landed in her arms like a baby with her tail over Derelie's arm. She gave up her bid for freedom and lay there like a big warm fur loaf of bread.

"You're trouble, just like your owner."

She knew Jack was on the stairs behind her, he'd made a racket. "Come take her, Jack. I'm going home." She didn't turn around; he'd have to come to her.

"I can explain."

"Cliché."

"Sometimes a cliché is the shortcut you need. 'I love you' is a cliché."

Like nothing in a tough yoga pose or moving to the city, that made her body go tense. But this was Jack who picked up women in markets—he was just making a point and being a dick.

"Please, don't go." He stepped up beside her and fastened a collar with a lead attached to it around Martha's neck. Martha looked at him adoringly and Derelie dumped the cat in his arms.

"In the market, that woman you saw propositioned me," he said. "It happens more than I'd like. Sometimes it's women, occasionally men who hit on me, and honestly, that's the easy part. Sometimes people approach to abuse me because they don't like something I wrote or said on radio or TV, or just don't like me, the way I look or talk or breathe."

Oh God, that was awful. "Why?" She knew why he got propositioned. He was *GQ* in his suit, an adventure catalog in his jeans and boots and shirtless, well, stop the clock. But why did people think they had the right to abuse him?

"It goes with the job. Will you come back upstairs?"

"No, I'm going to sulk here for a while." It might be possible she'd overreacted.

Jack backed up and sat on the steps, putting Martha between his feet.

Derelie sat beside him and poked Martha in her large rump, earning a tail flick. "She doesn't look like she's got fast in her repertoire." Martha's ears flattened as if she wasn't sure of the compliment.

"And I look like I've got player in mine."

"A little. I should've guessed."

"I haven't taken up with someone who propositioned me in a long time. It was fun before the death threats started. Before I quit owning a car because it kept getting vandalized. I only keep that stuff because the lawyers suggested I should."

"Are you extemporizing?" It would be easy to make it up, tell her anything.

"I've had four credible death threats. That's over and above the number of suits people bring against me. We once had to evacuate the *Courier* because of a suspicious parcel."

"Suspicious how?"

"There was a phone call to the news desk insisting we print a retraction on one of my stories or we'd be mailed anthrax. It turned out to be cornstarch, but it made everyone jumpy."

She looked at him for the first time since sitting. "That's so weird, Jack."

"It's not normal, but I've gotten used to it."

"I kind of freaked out."

"I wouldn't say that."

She bumped her shoulder against his. "I'm so full of feeling about you and we got here so quickly. I thought I was okay with a hookup, but I'm not sure I can be an-

other woman you sleep with in a long line of uncomplicated entanglements."

"There's no line. There's just you."

"I don't know what to trust."

"That makes me want to—"

"Hit something?"

He turned his head to look at her, mouth drawn
down. "Cry, Derelie. I want you to trust me. This is
only going to work if you do." She leaned her head on
his shoulder and his arm circled her waist. "Come upstairs, we can talk more."

"I need more sulk time."

"Mind if I wait with you? I feel a little sulky myself."

They sat in silence a while and then Martha yawned.
"Do you walk Martha on that lead?" The thought of
Jack with Martha on a leash out on the street was al-
most enough to push the sulks away.

He scratched behind Martha's ear and she gave a
yip of approval. "No. But she's such an escape artist,
on occasions when I need the apartment door opened
for more than a second it's useful to put her in this and
slip it around something heavy. She's so busy trying
to get out of it she's distracted. I used to close her in
one of the other rooms, but she throws herself against
the door so hard I worry she's going to hurt herself or
bust through."

"Jackson Haley, mad cat person."

"As long as it's not Derelie Honeywell, mad at Jack
Haley."

"I'm thinking about it."

"What's worrying you most?"

"I'm confused about whether we'd even be here

without the experiment. I'm catching up to where you were last night."

"I've moved on. Now I see the experiment as a little like what would've happened if we'd been two single travelers who met up somewhere foreign. The only Americans we'd have turned to each other, shared the experience, hung out."

"And then gone our separate ways. Me to a wilderness somewhere—" she thought a moment "—like Australia, you to a big city like London."

"I've already seen London, but I've never been to Australia."

She swiveled on the step so she faced him instead of the street. "The point is we'd be a vacation romance."

"And if it was good, what's wrong with that?"

"That's my problem. I can't decide if we're an experimental romance or more."

"And it's important to you to know that before you come upstairs?"

"I think so. I thought I was okay about a one-night stand with you. I'd like to be built that way, but I'm not."

"And?"

"And you are."

"I was. Ask me why that's changed?"

"I'm not asking you because I'm not judging you. I'm a small-town girl, I'm not a prude."

"I don't want a one-night thing with you, Derelie. I already know too much about you to think one night is going to be enough. I can't promise the whole annual calendar, but I know I want to be with you till we run this thing out."

Oh, man. That's what she'd needed to hear. "I

wrecked the mood." She'd been so sure what she wanted with Jack and all it took was a reminder that he'd had a full life before she came along to make her wobbly.

"Blame Martha."

They should've gone straight from question whatever to bed. Do not pass go. Do not let the cat out. "My bag is upstairs." That made leaving more awkward.

"No, it's behind us. I didn't want you to feel pressured."

She turned to look and at the top of the landing was her gym bag. He'd made it easy for her to choose.

"Whatever you want to do, Derelie."

She wanted him to keep saying her name, the joy of hearing it instead of Honeywell hadn't yet gotten old. Who was she kidding, the stack of cards was a shock; the reason he kept them was worse. They hadn't talked about this. The experiment was defective if it didn't uncover threats to someone's life.

"You'd be the first person I've slept with who's had death threats."

"Please don't make it your special thing to hunt down others."

"How scary was it?"

"I was glad I already knew how to defend myself. I've been attacked in the street. I was shot in the thigh with a dart gun outside the office once." He rubbed a place on his leg. "That hurt. And it ruined a good suit."

Good Lord. "I knew you'd had death threats because it's something everyone at the *Courier* knows about you, but I never thought about the practicalities." It seemed like an abstract thing, like a car accident, a robbery, something terrible that happened to somebody else. "You got shot."

"Dart gun."

"But it could've been—"

"But it wasn't. The more we rely on social media, the more threats of harm and exposure are tossed around. I've been doxxed. I've been the subject of rumor campaigns. It goes with the dinkus. It's the part of being famous I could do without."

"I understand that better now." Threatened. Attacked. Shot. People came up to Jack on the street and online with the intention of hurting him. "But you didn't quit."

"They win if I quit. I keep logs and records of everything because you don't know what could turn out to be important. It's such a habit I don't even think about it."

"Did they get the person who shot you?"

"No. It was crowded, peak hour. No clear suspect."

"You took something from that woman in the market."

"Her name and number. She wasn't dangerous. I vaguely know her from the radio station. She was a straight up proposition."

"But you chose me."

"Over a woman hitting on me in the meat section? I'd choose you every day. That's not even a question, Derelie."

She leaned into him. "I'll come upstairs."

He leaned back. "We can watch a movie if you want."

"Can we not watch it and neck?"

"You know, all those things I said about you, I forgot to mention that I love how generous you are."

"You're the one who cooked, cleaned and provided for us."

"That generosity is inside you. It's the way you are, the way you give yourself to others." He turned her face to his. "I think it's the sexiest thing. I'm going to have a smoke while you think about what you want to do." He handed her Martha's lead and went outside. He stood in the pool of light from a street lamp and rolled a cigarette, lit it and took a drag.

Derelie watched his chest expand on the inhale and his head tip back as the hit of the smoke filled his lungs. What would Jack look like beneath her in bed? Would his body arch, would his chin tip up as their bodies came together? So what if they only had the weekend, so what if he'd been a player and they were just an experiment-fueled fling? That was the most obvious outcome anyway. She was annoyed with herself for these second thoughts.

She was standing with Martha in her arms when Jack came back inside. He picked up her bag and they went upstairs to his apartment. It should've been awkward, the mood all messed up, but Jack made coffee, and he smelled so sweet from the cigarette and by the time they sat together on his couch Derelie was as turned on as she'd ever been.

"I don't want to watch a movie."

He shuffled closer, mug in one hand, the other arm going over her shoulder. "What do you want to do?"

Bathe in his tolerance for her last-minute nerves. "I want to do you."

He closed his eyes and smiled. She used the moment to take his glasses off, urge him to put the mug down, and the next moment to kiss him, and the next to slide up on his chest and lean into him, and then all the moments bled together into a bliss of kisses.

It'd been like this with the salesman. Forbidden, unexpected and thrilling, and Derelie had known wild physical pleasure that left her aching for more. She had that feeling now with Jack, but unlike her probably married salesman with whom she never exchanged names and had no illusions about, she knew so much about Jack and none of it dimmed the head rush.

The man kissing her, holding her, and wrapping her tight against him had integrity and honor and a way with his tongue that was making it hard to keep still. "Please, Jack."

"Whatever you want."

"I want to sweat in your clean sheets."

He disentangled them and stood, gave her his hand and led her through to the bedroom. When Martha followed he looked at the cat and said, "You have to stay outside tonight."

Martha scooted straight under the bed.

He looked at Derelie. "I can coax her out, but she'll throw herself against the door until I let her in again. Can you handle me making love to you with my cat under the bed?"

The way Jack looked at her, the near pleading in his voice made her shiver. "It's a sacrifice, but I think I can manage."

He took his shirt off.

The sacrifice was making her overheated and dizzy. But oh, that bruise went on and on. She'd seen it in the park, but now she realized it went down below the

waistband of his jeans. The jeans he unbuttoned, un-
zipped and eased off his hips as he toed off his shoes.

Already shoeless, she stood on the bare boards of
his bedroom floor in a haze of lust and concern. "Are
you sure we should?"

He stood in his stretchy boxer briefs, unbearably
sexy and clearly aroused, and tapped a finger against
the purple horror on his hip. "As long as you don't knee
me there it'll be fine. You're overdressed."

She looked down at herself. She was overexcited
and her hands shook.

"I'd like to help with that." She looked up and he
must have seen the whirl of emotion rolling through
her. He put a hand to her face. "Who gave you those
eyes, Derelie Honeywell?"

"My mom. All us kids have them. Spooky eyes. I
used to get called that at school. We all did."

He smiled so fully it transferred to her and she
smiled too. It chased her fear about getting naked with
him away.

"I think they're beautiful. I think you're beautiful."

He put his hands to the hem of her shirt and dragged
it up till she lifted her arms and he drew it over her
head. As if that was some kind of special feat, it earned
her an openmouthed kiss that took her breath away. He
worked on her pants button and the zipper and then his
hands were inside her cargoes and spread over her butt,
bringing her body into contact with his.

His skin was hot and she sizzled with the connection, with the press of his erection. It was a cold shock
when he stepped away to drop her pants. That left her

standing in her best underwear, grateful for the investment in something that was cute as well as functional.

He climbed into the middle of his big bed and patted the space beside him. "We have all night, we have the whole of Sunday, come spend it with me."

Was she out of her mind for hesitating? The most incredible specimen of a man was laid out before her, offering himself up for her consumption. After all her talk about wanting wild hot sex, that he knew she needed this first time to be gentle and slow almost made her sob. She knelt on the bed and crawled to him, going lip to lip before she lowered herself into his arms.

There was that silken heat again; it made her moan. It made Jack tighten his grip on her. These bedroom kisses were different from the picnic kisses, from the chair in the kitchen kisses, and the backed-up-against-a-restaurant-wall kisses. They weren't about learning, nothing teasing, or shocking; they were about possession, they were about destruction.

"Your mouth. I can't get enough of your mouth," he said, demonstrating that.

She liked her mouth the way Jack used it. She liked her body the way he alternatively swept his hands across it and gripped, stroked and held. She liked his body, its lean hardness, its economical construction, that he was bigger than her, coarser, but that her smaller hands moving on his skin had an effect on him.

She made him wince once when she pressed on his side, and once when she bumped his brow. *Bang, bang. Two strikes and you're out.*

"Oh my God, I'm sorry."

"It's nothing." He tapped his lips with a finger. "Come back here."

To more kisses that wiped out her higher intelligence and switched on her carnal autopilot. She flicked her bra halfway across the room, she wriggled out of her underpants and lost them off the side of the bed. When they crashed together again there were no fabric barriers.

Now his hands traveled over skin unseen before, over the rise of her breasts and the peaks of her nipples, over the globes of her butt and between her legs.

"Fuck, you're hot, sweetheart."

"You're not too bad yourself."

He laughed. Apart from that odd moment in the market and the near tragedy on the stairs, he'd smiled and laughed a lot since he decided they were finished with the questions.

A smile on Jack Haley's face, not the one used on the side of buses and billboards, not the one in his dinkus that was more of a knowing smirk, made him look almost boyish; the tank-driving, firefighting, comic-book-writing soldier still in him was adorable.

He rubbed a thumb over the slightly raised scar on her hip. "What happened here?"

"Tequila." That earned her a sweep of his tongue there. "Memory loss." That got his lips hot on her skin. "And a belief I was good at climbing fences." That made him laugh then lick up her body, nips of his teeth and swirls of his tongue till he took her mouth.

"Please make me come, Jack."

"Over and over," he said, rolling them so he balanced on top of her. She nearly passed out at the way he looked strong enough to take on the world, at the way he looked at *her,* eyes dark and intense, inside the bruising which was already losing color.

"Let me have you," he said, with a kiss targeted at her throat, with a hand kneading her breast. "Let me make you feel good."

She offered herself up with a groan of agreement, with her back arched and her hands reaching, not to stop him but to urge him on. But the urge was in both of them, tidal, magnetic, clicking them together, slicking them closer. He used his mouth to touch her places that unlocked her muscles and laid waste to her bones and drilled a hole in her head, letting in such light and wonder she was scared to open her eyes.

With his fingers inside her, he made her ache and tremble and rock her hips. With his mouth, he made her gasp and lose her mind. But it was all so quick she came down to a surge of disappointment.

"Jack."

"Just getting warmed up."

"I'm so hot I think I boiled over." She felt flushed top to toe.

He dropped his head to her stomach. "Do you want me to stop?"

"Don't you dare."

He dared a lot. He dared with teeth and pinches and the soothing flat of his tongue. He dared to move her limbs to where he wanted them, to mold them around his body. He dared to simulate the sex they'd have, sliding his cock along her slit, his body shaking with the pleasure of that.

"Jaaack."

She almost turned inside out when he pulled away, deprived of his heat and his mastery. But the short absence—while he opened a drawer, drew on a condom—only made her greedier. "You get those tests. You get them so you never have to leave me to suit up again."

He grinned. "Yes, Boss."

She laughed and flopped back on the bed. She was so strung out, her emotions were chopped into strands. She felt outraged to lose him to the mechanics of protection; she felt grateful to have him stretch over her again. Anticipation was a whip and desire was its sting, and the ricochet of feeling made her toes curl and her back arch.

It felt like a threat when he entered her. Like he'd opened up a secret place inside that only he could, like he'd unlocked the core of her and burned the map so no one else would ever discover it.

"So good, Derelie."

But it was a held breath, not yet anything but a tinge of fear, until he kissed her, cloves and cinnamon and coffee and sex and that was the lubricant, mouth to mouth on her anxiety.

And when he moved, it was relief and tension all wound together and straining. He eased farther inside, stretching her, jerking back to do it again.

"So good, Jack." That ease became a raw dance of power and motion, a slap of flesh, the song of lovers, a spiraling uncoiling of pressure so vast and unplumbed the pinnacle was unreachable.

"Let me have you."

She let go, a gush of heat and wet, a release, a white-out, a loss of control that made her shudder. He let go too, shouting incoherently through his own orgasm, his body tense like a wire snapping to collapse against her a moment before he fell to her side.

There was only unsteady loud breathing after that, sweat soaking into cotton and limbs glued comfortably together, and a cat with a wide-eyed WTF expression, staring in at them from the next room.

"Are you okay?"

She was floating, drifting, unmade, remade. "I'm wonderful."

"You are." He pulled away again. She heard water running, a flush, a drawer opening and closing. He spoke to Martha. He came back with a warm wet cloth, which she used, and slid alongside her and pulled the covers over them. She found herself bundled into his arms, awash with exhaustion.

"Sugar overload," she said. He kissed her behind the ear. "I didn't get a turn to touch you."

"Stick around and take advantage of me later."

She fully intended to. "I don't want to sleep."

"This isn't done, Derelie. Not near done." Fatigue made his voice thick and treacly, made what he said all the weightier.

He was almost asleep already, so she let the comfort of his arm over her hip carry her into dreams, until their body heat woke her in a sweat some time later. He'd turned the lamp out and it was dark in the room. She needed to stretch out, she needed the bathroom, but she didn't want to risk waking Jack.

She could've woken the dead when she shrieked. Within touching distance two slits of light glinted.

Jack was out of bed and had the light on in seconds.

Martha sat on the sheet in sphinx pose and stared at Derelie with her pointy ears pinned back. Derelie's heart thudded in her ears. "Oh my God, cat, you gave me a fright."

"Martha." Jack clapped his hands, but Martha simply transferred her yellow eyes from Derelie to him, turned her ears around and sphinxed some more. He stalked around the bed and picked her up, holding her away from his body, her back legs and orange-and-white banded raccoon tail dangling. "You're not supposed to scare the guests, especially the pretty ones I want to keep. Under the bed or out."

They seemed to reach an understanding. Jack put Martha down and she disappeared from view. He looked down at Derelie, gloriously naked and utterly at ease with that. "Do you need anything?"

She glanced at the clock on his side table. Three in the morning. She'd lost track altogether of how long they'd slept. "I need the bathroom and I need you."

He stepped aside to let her out of the bed, but his eyes didn't leave her body.

"You're going to make me self-conscious if you watch me walk out there."

"Do I look like I care?" He sat on the bed and cataloged her body.

There was zero doubt in her head he liked what he saw. That confidence boost got her to the bathroom, where she found a fresh towel on the closed toilet lid. She peed, washed up and cleaned her teeth. It wasn't the middle of the night anymore. Ding ding, it was round two.

"My turn," she said, coming back into the bedroom, super conscious of the way her breasts swayed and swelled with her breath.

Jack rolled to his back and held the covers up. "Have at me, sweetheart."

"How much control are you prepared to give up for me?"

"How much control do you want?"

"All of it."

He raised an eyebrow. "What's my lesson?"

"Your lesson?"

"When I fight it's always about redemption in one form or another. It's always about working out my feelings for something that doesn't sit right. When I fought after doing wrong by you, I was trying to learn humility and to be as generous as you are."

"You fought because you didn't like what happened between us?" She frowned, uncertain, unhappy about that. She crawled onto the bed. What did he need from her? Sex, it was in his eyes and the gravelly nature of his voice. It was in the response of his body. What else? What was Jack Haley missing in his life?

"Your lesson is love."

He grinned and made a grab for her. He thought she was joking, making a point like he had on the stairs—*I love you is a cliché*. She pushed him off. "No, my lesson, my control."

He dropped his hands, he still didn't get it, but not every lesson took first time. She'd love Jack with her whole self and she'd worry later about why she wanted that so much more than the purely sexual experience.

He was going to make it easy for her—he was hard,

and on the top of the bedside table was the square of a condom wrapper. He was going to make it difficult, because she wanted to go slow but her body was ready for fast. She knelt at his side to avoid the temptation and took his jaw in her hands.

"Your eye looks better." She traced the outline of the yellowing bruise with her finger and he closed both eyes. She shifted forward to string kisses along the unbroken brow and then more gently across the one that'd been split.

"I can smell you, us," he said, a hand caressing her hip. She stiffened, a good-girl response. "I love the way you smell."

She parted her knees, a better response, and watched his chest rise on a deep inhale. He made her feel like a femme fatale out of a sexy movie. She took her kisses to his jaw and his throat and her hands to his chest, stroking thick muscle and the light fur he had over his pécs. He groaned and brought a knee up when she trailed a hand down his chest and sternum and rested it on his stomach.

Jack hissed but not from pain, she hoped, when she flickered her tongue inside his belly button and then put her lips gently, gently to the bruise that extended from just under his ribs to the middle of his hipbone. She leaned over him, pressed her breasts against his side, her hair trailing across his chest and her closed hand over his erection.

"Derelie," he said in warning, and it caused a fluttery thrill to settle in her abdomen. "Where are you going with this?"

"Only nice places. Trust me."

"Trust you. You do know trust isn't high on my capabilities list."

Of course it wasn't. His parents weren't there for him, he spent his days writing about the way people were taken advantage of, and there was a puckered divot in his thigh from where he'd been shot with a dart gun. She played her fingers over that divot and then her lips.

"Hey, all the action is back up here."

"Love means having to wait."

"Love sucks."

She laughed. "Not yet it doesn't."

His hands came off the bed and she shook her head, stopping him from grabbing her. He groaned like he was in pain. "Not the feet, okay? I don't like having my feet touched."

"Not the feet," she replied, glad he'd given her that guidance.

She examined his knees and his shins, she moved to straddle his legs, and other than that one time she'd wrapped her hand around him, she avoided touching his cock. She would. She wanted to see his eyes go half-mast, she wanted to feel his hands on her unable to help himself.

The first touch of her tongue to the inside of his thigh and he lifted his head and shoulders off the bed. "You are torturing me, you know that."

Not intentionally—slow gave her time to adjust to him, to his smell, to his body, to the things he liked. She shoved him back on the bed and nuzzled his cock.

"Jesus Christ."

After that, unspoken words growled in his chest

when she touched her tongue to the crown of his penis. They spilled out, unintelligible when she closed her lips around it. She took as much of him inside her mouth as possible and used her hand to hold him. She let it get sloppy and mostly remembered to keep her teeth sheathed. This wasn't her favorite thing to do, but she wanted to do it for Jack.

She was ready to swallow him, but he stopped her with a hand in her hair and a whimpered plea.

"No, not that way. I want to be inside you."

She wanted that too. A lesson learned.

She could almost imagine calling it love.

Chapter Eighteen

Sleep after great sex was sublime. Waking to find the giver of the great sex in your arms and having no inclination to want her out of your bed, your apartment or your life was positively uplifting.

Jack usually found religion and release in the fighting pit and point size of a headline, but the curve of Derelie's hip nestled against his side was spiritually profound. It was early, and he could hear the wind whistling around the side of his building and rain splatting on the window. He had no desire to move.

If not for a stolen parcel and Martha's bid for freedom, he'd be lying here alone, contemplating more sleep, a long workout and time at his desk. And they almost didn't get here. Derelie's retreat had shocked him, but once he caught up to her on the stairs, he couldn't help but sympathize.

He was a rough choice for a lover, out of practice, out of favor with the whole dating scene. If he hurt her, it would be accidental and he had to hope she'd give him recovery time, because he wanted to keep this sparkling new thing she brought into his life, and not kill it cold with his traditional offhanded discourtesy designed to keep people at a distance.

It might not be as easy to change as he wanted it to be. It was a new experiment and he wasn't sure of the questions.

He should get up and make her breakfast. He'd need to deal with the antithesis of romance, which was Martha's litter tray. He needed a shower, a smoke, to check his messages. Things to do. A woman to have under him. He'd prioritize the latter. He knew he'd wake Derelie when playing with a strand of her hair wasn't enough. He put a hand to her flank and curled it around her ass, brought his own body up hard against her. She came awake with a gasp and a shudder and that shouldn't have excited him.

Everything about her excited him.

He rolled her so he could take her mouth, a taste of her before she was falsely minty. "Good morning."

"No." Grumble. "It can't be."

Not a morning person then, a delicious new discovery. "You can sleep some more." When he'd finished with her. He liked her tasting of them.

She could've swatted his roving hands away, but she pressed into them instead. "Am I dreaming?" She hadn't opened her eyes yet.

"If you want to be."

"I'm in the Defender of the City, the great Jackson Haley's bed."

He squeezed her delectable ass. "Knock it off."

There they were, those light, bright eyes, offset by her dark brows and hair and the natural ruby pink of her lips. "Good morning." She stretched, and he used her movement to press more of their bodies together.

"How good do you want it to be?"

"That sounds like a challenge. I don't do challenges before midday on Sundays."

"Shame." He already had his hand to her pussy, his fingers teasing her opening. She moved to give him better access and he took it, making her grab his wrist. He stopped. "Are you sore?"

"No. Maybe." She moaned. "I like it." She let a breath out. "Go slow." She let go of his wrist and twisted to give him her mouth, and there was nothing shameful about what they did.

He woke her fully with the tips of his fingers, with the length of them, tapping, curling, with the press of the heel of his hand. Pressure on the places that made her jerk against him, made her toss her head, buck her hips. He got a hint of desperation with nails in his forearm and a heady rush of satisfaction when her body rattled in his arms.

His own forbearance was considerably frayed by the time he turned her over and entered her from behind. He was the desperate one now, up on his knees, hands on her waist, pleasure rippling up his spine and pain sparking from the bruising on his hip as he slammed them together.

"Goddamn, Derelie."

"Don't stop, don't stop, don't stop."

Outside the wind and rain became a storm; inside, lightning lit him up, electric volts of energy and Derelie's chant sending him over. A final thrust to take her with him, then he brought them both down to the bed, where he kissed her out the other side of that shared whirlwind and she sighed her contentment into his mouth.

He resented having to leave the bed. Came back to find her smiling at him with her eyes closed and her arms out. Sticky and sweaty, beautiful. "I need to pee, but I don't want to get up."

And his version of delightful.

He couldn't be madder about her. "It's a dilemma."

He dove into her arms. No cool, no cool at all. "Ten minute snuggle and then I'll make you breakfast." *Snuggle.* He buried his face in her neck. One night with her and he'd morphed into a man who used the word *snuggle.*

"Fifteen minute snuggle, and we shower and I cook you breakfast. It's my turn. How do you like your eggs?"

"Any way you want to serve them. I can't remember the last time anyone cooked for me."

"I can't remember ever having been pounded so hard." He lifted his head to look into her face and she laughed at his distraught expression. "It's a good thing. Please do it again."

He brought her lips to his. An array of unusual emotions felt very close to the surface of his skin. It was a distressing feeling, and the only way he could deal with it was to keep moving. If he slowed down to examine things it might wreck him.

He hadn't thought it would be like this. Told himself it was all a manipulation. Didn't know she'd ignite such craving. Yeah, he wanted her in his bed and more. He wanted her at his table and on that old blanket he'd used for the picnic. He wanted all the questions and all the answers with her, but he didn't have a decent up-to-date guideline for what happened with a girlfriend and that's where this was going.

He wasn't entirely sure he was boyfriend material. But this was a pay grade above fling and a bank vault of gold more valuable than a casual hookup.

"I'm going down on you in the shower," she said.

Oh fuck.

"You're trying to screw with me."

"Is it working?"

"I'm an old man. And I'm hurt." He groaned at the image of her on her knees. "You could do me permanent damage." She snorted like a roll-in-the-mud farm animal. "Little heathen."

She was a saint in the shower. She made the cramped space work, though he might've put a fist through the tiles trying to hold back. A champion way to ease into a Sunday. Later, damp, and with a heavy pleasure buzz, he watched her navigate his kitchen, producing poached eggs and thick sliced toast, roasted tomatoes and mushrooms.

"I've worked out what your comment about video means." She nibbled her toast. He'd used his under the eggs. "For the story. We need visuals."

"Fake visuals." She wore his T-shirt and he liked that, the familiarity of it. She had great legs. "For the story we're colleagues who got to know each other better after a rocky start, not lovers."

She looked down at herself. "Staged as a coach. I should feel bad about that, but I don't. You don't have to out yourself." Yeah, he did. "We need stills too." She took another bite of toast. "What would you normally do on a Sunday?"

"Sleep, work out, spend time at my desk, catch up

on reading, file any story due for Monday I've not finished. You?"

"Sleep, clean my place, shop, curl up with a book and talk to my family, lie about going to church."

Both of them passing through Sundays alone. "Is there anything you need to do today?"

"Apart from call home, no."

He had an idea what they could do for the day. It included taking her to church so she didn't have to lie so blackly to her mom. St. Longinus wasn't open on Sundays. No fighting on the Sabbath, but Jack knew how to get inside. In the Uber car, he called Barney.

"Haley, what jail and how much is the bail?"

"Funny man." He gave Derelie's hand a squeeze. "I have a friend with me I'd like to show the church."

"A friend. That friend wouldn't happen to be a woman?"

"She would happen to be."

"The woman you fucked up with."

"That very woman." Who was grinning at him.

"This is progress. I like it. Key to the side door is under the big flowerpot growing a fine crop of dead twigs. I'll be over there myself in about fifteen minutes, so don't get up to anything you wouldn't want an old priest to see."

Jack struggled to think what the old priest hadn't already seen. He found the pot, one of several to fit the description, got the key and opened up.

Derelie stepped inside and twirled around, stirring up dust motes in the weak light from the open door. "This is where you fight?"

It was a large cavernous space once used to house

a row of city buses waiting mechanical checks. Now it housed lockers, gym equipment, rubdown tables, and the pit itself.

"I feel like I'm in something out of *Fight Club*." That'd been Barney's inspiration. "Are you really Jackson Haley?"

"One and the same."

"I'm not sure you are."

He let her walk away so he could watch her move, but called after her. "What does that mean?"

"It means I think there are two Jack Haleys and the one I took a shower with, ate eggs with, is the whole one." Her voice had resonance, bouncing off the hard surfaces of the place.

"And the other one?" His sounded bemused.

She turned to face him, let him catch up the distance between them. She'd practically sat in his lap in the car on the way over and he wanted her close again. "He's a good man, works hard, but he's got a hole in his soul that needs patching."

Goddamn experiment. "Enough psychobabble analysis." He took her hand and led her over to the pit.

"You fight down there?"

The pit bore no resemblance to how it was once used by mechanics. The walls were lined with heavy padding, bright blue in the gloom. He'd left the main lights off and it still managed to look like something greasy and mysterious went on down there.

"Official amateur boxing rules, proper equipment, with the exception of walls for ropes, referees who know their stuff and a manager who doesn't take any shit from anyone and governs this place like it's a kingdom. He's a despot. His name is Barney and you'll meet him later."

"Please don't ever ask me to come watch you get hit. I'd hate that."

"No spectators. It's not about that." It was confession, two men and their failings hashing it out.

"What about women?"

"Twice a month there's a night for women. Not as many women want to get punched in the face as men. That just proves they're smarter." He crowded Derelie into the barricade around the top of the pit with the intention of sampling her lips.

"You're not just brawling. You wanted me to see this wasn't totally irresponsible."

He answered her with a hand to the back of her head and a soft kiss to banish the demons. There were a lot to banish, and it wasn't until the big overhead lights came on they surfaced.

"There'll be no kissing in my gym unless it's at the hand of a glove."

He pulled away from Derelie but kept her hand. "That cantankerous bastard is Barney."

Barney tossed and caught an orange. "And who might this be?"

"I'm Derelie Honeywell. You're the man who let Jack get cut up and bruised."

"An avenging angel is she, Haley?" That thought had crossed Jack's mind already today. "He gets himself knocked about. If he trained harder it wouldn't happen."

She looked at Barney and then slapped Jack on the arm. "Oh."

"Satisfied?" Barney demanded. He tossed the orange to Derelie.

"I think so." She caught it. "You're not really a big grouch, are you?"

"He is," Jack said, same time as Barney said, "I am."

"Take your vitamin C." Barney wagged a finger at Derelie. "And Jack, I got a feeling you've got something you want me to do for you."

He handed Barney his camera. "A favor. Some shots of us. It's for the paper."

Barney closed his hand around the camera. It was smaller than the orange. "This tiny thing is a camera?" He lifted the pocket-sized digital to his eye.

"Use the screen."

"Aye. Technology."

It would be a miracle if Barney could get a single decent shot—he still used an old clamshell phone—but selfies wouldn't cut it for the paper and Jack couldn't think of anyone else to ask. He pulled Derelie in to him and they posed, standing side by side. He remembered to smile. The shot wouldn't do, but it was a start.

"Candid, Barney. Surprise us."

"Got better things to do than to sneak around after you two." He grumbled, but he took the camera while Jack took Derelie down into the pit. He lost the sense of where Barney was after that as they shared the orange and she tested out the slightly sprung floor, bounced off the sides of the wall, and then shaped up to him.

"Show me how to throw a punch."

He could have the debate about why she didn't need to learn to throw a punch, that there were better forms of self-defense, but none of that let him cage her in his body to step her through how to make a fist, how to deliver a punch, how to keep her guard up. He was a fraud, but this got him close to her and made her laugh and soon they were shaping up to each other, fake shadow boxing.

"I like the idea of the women's fight nights," she said, bopping around him like something with batteries included. She'd already tried to *Karate Kid* him, complete with cartoon sound effects that showed off her inner Miss Piggy.

He spun to keep an eye on her. "No you don't."

"I could punch my frustrations away."

Flail was more like it. "Isn't that what yoga is for?"

"Doing yoga is something else to cross off my list of done in the city accomplishments. I also thought it might bring me peace." She stopped moving. "I kind of hate it and I'm not good at it, and don't think I ever will be. Not that yoga is competitive, just that I am."

"You looked very peaceful this morning in my bed."

"Hi-yah!" She leaped at him and he caught her in a hug. "I was."

"We could just keep doing that to take care of your peace-keeping needs."

She wound her arms around his neck. "Do you mean that?"

"I mean it."

"And you'll teach me how to box properly?"

"No. Someone who knows how to teach you how to box will. I can show you the basics, but you need to join a gym and get some experience because this is the underground amateur league here and you're not ready for this."

"But I could be."

He could see the way the idea engaged her. "You could be." He wasn't sure he liked it. He'd find her a good trainer.

"One, two," she said, a mini Rocky, giving herself the giggles and no longer afraid of what he did when he came here.

He found Barney while Derelie waited outside for their Uber. "Thanks for letting me give her the tour."

"What's with the two of you?"

"We work together, writing a story together, and last night we slept together."

"Complicated."

"I'd have said so, but that's not what I'm feeling."

"Don't want to see you back here too soon then unless it's to train." Barney handed over the camera. "Got shit on there. Sorry, photography is not my thing."

Jack was going to have to remember to make it his. He'd last used this camera when Martha was a kitten, but taking pictures of Derelie, especially when she was unaware she was being watched, wasn't going to be a hardship.

She waited on the street, eyes on the road, hands in the pockets of her jacket. A visit to St. Longinus had never made him horny before, but watching Derelie gave him ideas.

"What's next?" she said, when he circled his arms around her from behind.

The ease of it, touching her, having her lean into him, it had a strange effect, like there was some part of him missing and unexpectedly found. What had she said, a hole in his soul. "Afternoon nap."

Her head dropped back to his chest. "It's not afternoon."

He didn't want to share her with the world. "You have a problem with that? We'll go out to dinner tonight."

"I'd like that."

"I'd like it if you stayed over again." Maybe if he could hold on to her she'd patch that hole.

"Planning ahead, Jack."

That made him smile. "I'm an organized kind of guy." At work at least.

"I don't want to wear out my welcome." She turned to face him, but avoided his eyes.

"I don't think that's possible."

She went up on her toes and whispered in his ear. "Do you know how hard that's going to get you pounded?"

She said the most wonderful things.

Between his sheets she was more than wonder. She was the saint, the angel, the sinner. Apple pie meets sex fiend; farm fresh gets filthy. Whatever lesson she was teaching, he was her star student.

He sat on the edge of the bed, Derelie in his lap, her legs crossed behind his back, hands on his shoulders. His were under her ass, helping her grind against him. He was hyped and she was incredibly wet by the time she lowered herself over him. He almost lost it, had to grit his teeth a moment to pull it back, fingers biting into her, hard enough to bruise.

"Oh, Jack. Oh."

The outline of shyness she'd had in bed, the humor she'd used to deflect attention from being naked was gone, and in its place a determination to chase a high that wracked him like disease. He was fatally afflicted with her.

She lifted herself and dropped on him, and both of them hissed. Her thigh scraped his bruise but he didn't feel it. Again, again. She was getting herself off, curling her body into the deep ache of penetration, the hot stab and slide. He gave her his knuckles for extra friction and her body trembled.

"More," she said, open mouth on his neck. "I need more."

He cradled her with one arm and leaned back on the other for leverage. He'd use the bed, the floor and his body. He almost took Martha's head off when she tried to come in the bedroom, kicking the door shut in her face to an outraged yowl, because nothing was going to stop this.

Derelie grasped him tighter, both of them grunting as his thrusts intensified. Outside, Martha pawed against the door in almost the same thumping rhythm as Jack's heart. Derelie's grunts became gasps as she flexed her hips faster, catching him in her slippery heat, drawing everything in him to a pinpoint of purity.

She came with her teeth in his shoulder. That bite connecting all the shards of sharpness and electric lights of pain and pleasure in his body and shattering them. He fell back to the bed and took Derelie with him, sucking in air, spine gone slack and limbs heavy.

"What's that noise?" she said, before licking the shell of his ear.

He used a hand on her head to keep their faces close. "Martha." Pawing at the door.

Derelie laughed. "How long can she keep that up?"

"She sleeps sixteen hours a day, so about eight at a guess. It's not like she's got anything else more pressing to do."

Abruptly the racket stopped. They both said, "Ah," and it started again.

"Is it me?" Derelie said. "Is she jealous?"

"It's doors."

She put her teeth to his earlobe. "How to put a lover in her place."

He put his lover in the middle of the bed and got up to let his cat in. He had no memory of being so contented. With Martha under the bed and Derelie dozing in it, he checked his messages. Nothing urgent, but after two days not on top of them they'd started to pile up. He'd need to start early Monday.

He also checked the camera. The priest was a dirty rotten scoundrel. Shot after shot of him with Derelie. Each one made him look like a stranger. Barely recognizable. Barney had captured him smiling, laughing, and Derelie looked like a storybook Christmas morning. There were shots of them mock boxing. Shots of him showing her how to make a fist and deliver a punch. One shot of them right before a kiss, faces close, bodies aligned hip to chest. His head was bent to her, her chin tipped up. The smile she wore was filled with all the joy he'd never had and he looked like he'd kill to keep it.

He sent Barney a text. Lying is a sin.

He got back, So is lust, but I'm giving you absolution.

He understood why. They looked like the lesson took; they looked like a couple in love.

Chapter Nineteen

Seeing Jack's Church of the Cocked Fist filled a gap in Derelie's knowledge the experiment hadn't. He wasn't a reckless hothead in his off hours. The gym might have been the most unorthodox church in the world, but it was clean and well organized and Barney had ex-priest stamped all over him even though Jack hadn't volunteered that information.

She could see the satisfaction in punching something. It was hard and cold and clean, had a straightforwardness that appealed to her. No doubt that's what appealed to Jack. It was skilled yet uncomplicated.

The afternoon nap was anything but hard and cold. They knew each other now. The fear of the unknown gave way to the thrill of being together. They were getting good at pleasing each other. Jack was addicted to her mouth and she was addicted to his hands and how they could make her body alternatively tremble and give way to sheer purring pleasure.

Move over, Martha, you'll have to share.

She purred again when they went out to eat, the moment Jack reached for her hand as they walked to his local steakhouse. "I never thought Jackson Haley would be a holding hands kind of guy."

He wrinkled his nose, bumping his glasses higher. "It's a new one on me."

She stopped walking. "Is it too much? Me. Us. All of this too soon?"

"Not for me."

An unembroidered answer. "We're doing this." She swung their joined hands like she was five years old and he put up with it. "At work?"

"That makes you nervous."

"I can't help it. I know people will think I'm trying to get ahead by sleeping with the paper's biggest dinkus."

He failed to retain his air of seriousness and laughed. "One of the reasons I never got involved with people at work. It's fraught."

"So we keep it out of the office."

"At least until we see if we stick."

"And if we don't? I don't own a dart gun, but I do know how to shoot."

"Jesus, Derelie." He stopped walking and yanked on her arm till she turned to faced him.

"I'm joking. I'm joking."

Another yank and their bodies were grazing. The expression on his face was somewhere between "you're playing with fire" and "burn, baby, burn." It made her breath catch.

"Are you going to kiss me?"

"You just threatened to shoot me if we broke up."

She gave a one-shouldered shrug. "It'll only be a flesh wound." Never in a million years had she guessed she'd be able to mess with Jackson Haley like this. That he clearly loved being messed with was the biggest thrill.

He gave her the kind of look that could've steamed up his glasses. "A flesh wound." He squeezed her hand. "I'm good with that." He didn't kiss her, and that should've been so frustrating, but whatever showed on her face made him laugh again.

Jack's local was badly lit and a little shabby, and not in a chic way. It was the kind of place he could go without needing to worry he was going to be hit on, and the food was great. The sudden silence that hit during the meal was uncomfortable. Too soon to make assault jokes?

"What if this is some kind of accelerated learning process and we're actually done?" she said, toying with her salad.

"Meaning?"

"It might've taken weeks, months to get through all the questions. We did it in a couple of hours all put together." And then they had each other forty-two different ways to the moon and back. "What if we're already over each other?"

"Because we've been quiet for the length of time it takes to eat a steak?" he said, putting his knife and fork down in the proper order on his empty plate. She hadn't been able to finish everything on hers. Typical taking on more than she could chew. "I don't think we're done."

"When was your last actual long-term relationship?"

"That's a question I'm glad you didn't ask before I introduced you to my clean sheets."

Uh-oh.

"College."

"That's—"

"A long time ago. Casual is the new black, but I don't want to be casual with you. I'm not saying that's going to be easy. My experience with devotion is woefully limited."

Never be the first to break a barrier. Those that come second get it easier. She was sure she'd read that somewhere. "But Martha loves you."

"Martha loves anyone who feeds her."

"Some people have no respect."

He leaned toward her, his hand on her knee under the table. "Come home and let me disrespect you some more."

It was a date, but she had a call to make first. She sat on Jack's sofa with FaceTime open while he worked at his desk, sorting through email and clicking through the key headlines of rival media.

"Mom, hi."

"Hi, baby. You look pretty tonight." Must be the post-orgasmic glow, because she was windblown and a little chafed. "Where are you?"

"I'm at a friend's place. How is everyone?"

Mom made a silly face on the word *friend* and then updated her on the drama with the Denvers's haunted barn and Eli Varga's twins, but Derelie's attention was on Jack. She wanted to swing her handset around so Mom could see him, barefoot with Martha asleep on his lap, his attention on the messages flying at him on his screen. She wanted to say, *I met this guy at work and we didn't like each other at first, but oh, Mom, he's the greatest and he doesn't even know how great he is and I'm so happy we found each other and I'm so scared it's not real, and if it's not real it's going to break my heart and I don't know what to do about that.*

But she didn't say any of that. She didn't mention Jack at all.

On her tiny screen Mom was walking. "You want to see Ernie? Here he is." And there was Ernest, head on his paws, sprawled on the kitchen floor waiting for his bowl to be filled.

"Ernie! Hello, my boy. How's my big boy? Have you been a good dog?"

Mom's face reappeared. "He's been digging holes in the strawberry patch again."

"Ernest." The screen showed Ernest now had his eyes closed.

Mom said, "He knows it's you, honey. He's just distracted. He was wagging his tail a moment ago."

He was definitely forgetting her and that hurt a surprising amount. "I gotta go. Love you, Mom. Tell Dad I love him. Talk later." She disconnected and went to Jack, slid her arms around his neck. She felt his laughter before she heard it. "What? You've never talked to Martha on the phone?"

"Marah," Martha said, and jumped from Jack's lap.

He tipped his chin up and looked at her. "I like you, Derelie Honeywell."

"I know, you changed the sheets for me twice." Plus, he'd shown her who he was outside the parameters of his dinkus, when he wasn't being his thoroughly professional self.

He pulled her into his lap. "I'm going to be behind tomorrow."

"I'm sorry." He was warm and solid and hers for at least another night.

He took his glasses off and brushed his nose over her cheek—"I'm not"—and then along her jaw. "You know you can wear your aligner in front of me."

"Nope, you're good underwear and best behavior."

"I'm not interested in you for your underwear, and if your best behavior is the threat of a flesh wound, what else have you got hidden I haven't experimented on or kissed out of you?"

What she kept a lid on was the audacious hope that she'd found a home in the city with Jack. It was too soon to think that way. "You can't have all my secrets."

But he could if he tried hard enough. Jack took her to bed, and because she was sore, it was his tongue and mouth that agitated then soothed her. She almost told him what was in her heart; birdsong and sweet air, fresh air and stars, but the real world came rushing back in the morning. She had to hustle to get home and changed and into the office, and though she made it on time she was already late.

"Drama," said Eunice in greeting.

"What happened?"

Eunice peered over the cube walls. "Shouting match between Phil and Shona."

Oh no.

"Didn't sound good. She's a smart girl, did a dumb thing. Sleeping with the boss. How is that ever going to work out well?"

Derelie chewed her lip. "Some people must meet their partners at work."

"Sure, sure, but it's the power dynamic that's the problem, and the nepotism, and the gossip, and it's just painful for everyone else. That's why it's against office policy."

Derelie started. "I didn't know there was an actual policy against it."

"Microscopic print. Not that anyone pays any attention to it. Why, you got your eye on someone?"

"Ah, no, not at all." The first lie. She had an urge to run to the bathroom and see what her lying face looked like.

"Oh hey, how is that love experiment story with Haley going?" Eunice snickered. "Tell me he's got no conversation other than work and I'll bring you coffee, the good stuff."

"Ah, he's, ah. We've, um. Oh. He's, er."

The right answer if she didn't want to start down the path of becoming Shona was "Haley is a total bore." She'd get a free coffee. She'd get a free pass. She felt like a coward, even though this was what they'd agreed on.

Eunice gave her double thumbs-up. "That bad. Excellent."

She had to repeat the update to Shona at the section editorial meeting, explaining they'd almost completed the questionnaire, and she was ready to write the story.

"Get visuals," Shona said. "Loved up couple stuff."

It reminded her to check if there was anything worth using on Jack's camera. He'd had a waitress at the steakhouse take a shot of them. It was a classic couple having dinner shot. Nothing in it to suggest they'd rubbed their private parts almost raw before sitting down to steaks, and held hands like they wanted to meld fingerprints.

She spent the morning studiously not looking over at the business bullpen, ran errands at lunch and got back to find an email from Jack.

Hi. It was his typical clipped style; she shouldn't read anything into it, he was different in person. Working late. She had a yoga class to get to anyway, not like she'd expected the weekend to continue. Martha's food is in the top cupboard if you want to meet me at home. She likes the sashimi broth. I like you in my bed.

She could've high-fived her screen. She wanted to meet him at home. She'd even had practice at getting into his place without letting Martha out. You had to be quick and quiet and use your legs as a blocking device. It was possible you'd lose skin.

She typed back. I'd love to feed Martha. See you at your place.

It would mean getting up early and going back to hers again to change, unless she brought a change of clothing. Was it too soon to ask if she could have a hanger in his wardrobe, park a spare toothbrush by his sink? She didn't have any time to think about it because her afternoon went sideways.

She got a call from Phil's assistant. Be in his office in five minutes.

Phil's office. The last time she'd seen Phil, he'd listened as Jack pointed out how much she had to learn about the news business. Phil's office. The only reason she'd have to go to Phil's office was to say hello to sequential morning lie-ins and an unemployment line. There was no Shona to check with and she wasn't even sure where Phil's office was. Eunice—calm, collected, seen it all—babbled when Derelie asked for directions.

"Derelie, take a seat," Phil said, when she found him. That was thoughtful. He wasn't going to make her stand up while he voluntarily laid her off.

"You've been with us almost a year. You do good work. I hear you got that bastard Haley to cooperate on the love story. I want to see it."

Annoying that this was happening exactly when the city was a whole lot more attractive because it had Jack in it.

"Shona Potter is taking voluntary." Phil coughed in place of finishing the sentence. "I'm promoting you to section editor."

Would she have enough time to write the story before Phil made her pack up her desk? She'd have to ask Jack—"Pardon?"

"You don't want the job?"

"Me? There are others—" More qualified. What the heck happened to Shona?

"Yes, there are. Do you want the job? Because the person who had it gave it up."

So Shona quit with a buyout. "I want it." What did she just agree to?

Phil turned to his screen. "HR will fill you in on the role and salary details. Got it?"

"I—"

"Got or not, Derelie?"

"Got it."

"Okay. Get out."

Amazing how your legs could leg it without the active participation of your brain. She made it to the doorway before Phil said, "Derelie. You have talent. You'll get used to me."

"I thought after that day with Jack you'd think—"

"He was being an asshole. That's what I thought. Also, don't fuck anyone. Not even Artie Chan."

"What?"

"You like him. Everyone likes him. Don't fuck him. But if you have to fuck him, keep it a secret."

"Okay." She agreed to keep any fucking of Artie Chan a secret. She still had a job. A better job that would pay more. She almost fist pumped. She'd come in here wanting to barf.

"Get out."

When she got back to her cube it was to the raised eyes of her section colleagues. Shona's desk had already been cleared.

"Hello, boss," said Eunice. "Don't mess this up."

Chapter Twenty

It was possible Jack was more nervous than Derelie was. Her first senior editorial meeting. Her first time sitting in the seat Potter normally occupied. They'd celebrated her promotion with a late meal, a long session of lovemaking that didn't leave much time for talking through the issues.

And the current issue was how unprepared she was for this. The daily editorial meeting was a shark tank. Madden was the whale shark and everyone else was the fish food he fed on, with two exceptions: himself and Spinoza. It wasn't a gender thing; it was the economics. Sports sold papers. So did Jack's stories. Until they moved to subscriptions on the website, that part of the business wasn't an authority at the table. Yet. The day was coming, but until it arrived, Derelie was plankton.

Today, Spin had another player scandal. There was a heavy dose of city politics, a story on low-cost housing, another on extreme weather events, and one on a major archeological find that came about because a professor got out of his car to take a piss. There was also a feature on driverless cars and what happens if you got hit by one.

Health had the most amusing story for the day about a man who'd farted during an operation and got badly burned when his gas ignited a laser being used in the surgery. The truth was stranger than fiction and they'd had a good laugh, but Derelie flinched when Madden called her name.

"We have a work-life balance story about bringing your pet to work and there's a start-up that gives staff stay in bed days, headline is 'In Bed with The Boss'—we've got a video interview for that one."

"And the lovey dovey experiment?" Madden asked.

"I still have to do my part," Jack said before Derelie could try to take the rap for him.

Madden looked at Derelie. "Stand over him till he does it." He looked at Jack. "Your Keepsafe story doesn't run until after the love story, and what's going on with Keepsafe?"

Not good things. "Someone is getting to the victims. Paying them off. Getting them to withdraw their co-operation." The story had started to blow up over the weekend. While Jack was goofing off with Derelie, ten of the victims, including the Shenkers, were visited by a lawyer from Keepsafe who explained there'd been a mistake and offered them generous compensation. They signed non-disclosure agreements. They'd been paid to shut up.

"Is it over?" said Madden.

Jack had no idea what was behind the story softening. He was scrambling to find out if someone at Keepsafe knew about his investigation and was moving to shut the story down.

"No." They had enough still to make a case, unless victims continued to drop out.

"Move up on it like it was hot for you, Jack," said Madden, and closed the meeting.

Jack was almost out of the room when Derelie said, "Please don't do that."

"Do what?" He'd been careful not to show anything of their out of office relationship, remembering to call her Honeywell. He needed to get back to his desk; instead he was replaying the first time they'd stood in this room, an odd couple thrown together to satisfy Madden's desire to keep Jack in his place. He'd never have guessed what they'd become to each other, thirty-six questions later.

"Speak for me," she said.

"I didn't."

"You did. I get that I'm the most junior person here. I get that I don't rank and I have to earn my place, but you speaking up for me doesn't help."

He didn't have time to debate this. "Fine." If he'd had his eye on the ball over the weekend instead of experimenting with love, maybe his own story wouldn't be sliding sideways.

"Don't get mad at me."

He was angry with himself. If the walls weren't glass, he'd kiss Derelie's downturned lips into a happier shape. It wasn't her fault he was tense. "I'm sorry. I was worried for you. I can't help it. I'll do better."

"You mean that?"

"I want to take every punch for you, especially against Madden, but that's not what you need from me. You have to make your own mistakes."

"Wow." He realized how anxious she'd been when her body softened. "I'm really falling for you, Jackson Haley."

A quick glance to check the corridor outside was clear and he put his hand to her face. He needed to touch her like he needed the cigarettes he was addicted to. "I'm already on my knees, Derelie Honeywell."

The smile she gave him was worth the risk of exposure.

Next stop, Henri Costa. They met halfway across town, in a dingy bar in a rough neighborhood. It was difficult to know what rattled Henri more, the surroundings he'd chosen, Jack's impatience, or the fact the story was unraveling. While Jack was in the editorial meeting, fifteen more victims had made contact to say they'd had their cases overturned and received a payout worth more than they were due.

"I don't know why this is happening. The guy driving this is Kaspersky, he's a big wheel on the Keepsafe legal team," Henri said. He didn't make eye contact, as if he thought not looking at Jack might protect him. "I can't imagine him making house calls." But Kaspersky had personally visited eight of the people who'd been denied their coverage. "I've asked around, but I'm an accounting manager, there's only so much I can nose about in claims and legal, before people wonder what the hell I'm doing. I've already had pushback. They'll destroy me if they find out I've been leaking information to you."

"They can destroy you anyway, Henri, and all of this will have been for nothing if it turns out this isn't fraud, but some system error."

"But you have evidence of payments to the doctors, Whelan and Noakes. Isn't that paper trail enough?"

"Not if we can't point to a deliberate attempt to defraud people legitimately entitled to a payout."

"I don't think I can do this anymore."

"Did someone get to you too, Henri?"

Henri slumped over the bar, his forehead inches from the dull wooden surface. "It's unrelated. My supervisor gave me a warning. If I don't shape up, I'll be out of a job."

"Who is your supervisor friends with?"

"No, it's not like that. I've been distracted and I..." Henri sat upright and looked at Jack. "His daughter and Kaspersky's daughter are on the same softball team. He's always jawboning about it."

Henri would've run out into the street with his head on fire had Jack not stopped him. "They know," Henri said, trying to dodge around Jack. "I can't talk to you."

"You can't panic either. You're a whistleblower and you're protected by the law. But not if you've gotten this wrong. If this isn't fraud—" Jack's story would collapse, but for Henri the impact would be personal "—you're in a difficult place."

"They'll come after me for theft and trading company secrets. I could go to jail."

They spent the next hour talking through the additional information Henri could provide without tipping off his suspicious supervisor. If he could provide the names of additional doctors linked to higher than average denial of claims and Jack could connect them to Bix, they were back in business.

It was a big if. Henri was scared, but having come

this far, he had a lot to lose. Meanwhile, Jack needed to prove that Kaspersky's home visits weren't random, while Berkelow and some of the other business writers were tracking down other victims and writing up new case studies.

It was late again when he made it home. He stood outside his apartment door, and checked his cell one last time. Derelie had messaged him hours ago, but he'd not seen her text till well after she'd have made alternative plans for the night, and that shouldn't have been disappointing. He had no juice left for company, and it wasn't like they had expectations of each other aside from keeping the fact they were lovers secret.

He eased his key into the lock and got into position to open the door and slip inside without letting Martha out. The *click click* of the lock retracting wasn't followed by a merrow of outrage. His shins weren't head-butted when he slid inside. His desk lamp was lit and there was no righteous starving cat flicking her tail at him to deal with the empty bowl situation.

What was unreasonable disappointment became irrational chest-tightening when he stood in the doorway of the bedroom. Martha wasn't furious with him for being late, she wasn't crying from hunger, she was curled on the bed, her large rump backed into Derelie's stomach.

Both his girls were sleeping. He leaned on the door-jamb and took them in. Martha might well have been drooling, she looked so content, a large ball of fluff, tail tucked around her like a blanket, face buried in her paws, only one pointy ear indicating which end was up.

Under the covers, Derelie looked equally serene,

her lovely face relaxed, her hair spun out on the pillow behind her in a chocolate-red swirl. She was curled on her side, with one hand under the pillow. He could see a bare shoulder. He could see a different kind of future in the shape of her, one where neither of them were alone, one where his world was the other way up and he wasn't just a bystander anymore.

How the heck was he going to manage not to fuck that vision up?

Martha must've sensed him and woke, pushing her paws out, arching and rolling on her back. "Merrow, yip." She gave Jack a look that said, "this is what happens when you leave me, sucker," and yawned to punctuate her couldn't-give-a-shit-about-him attitude.

"Hey." Derelie opened her eyes. She caught Martha's yawn and came up on her elbow. She'd worn her underwear to bed; he saw the shadow of a nipple through creamy lace. "I hope you don't mind that I stayed over." Her sleep saturated voice, low and crackly, hit his ears and communicated with the rest of his body parts that weren't already alert to possibilities. "I didn't hear back from you and I knew you were busy." She rubbed Martha's belly, and the cat brought her paws up under her chin and stretched her neck out, the position for chin scratch *now*. "I was going to feed her and go, but I really wanted to see you."

Whatever exhaustion he'd trailed home was now an insistent buzz of desire. "You appear to have stolen my cat," he said, with zero attempt to sound remotely concerned about that.

Derelie tickled under Martha's chin. "We're besties now."

"She's five years old. I've fed her every night of her life. You've fed her twice." That's what he liked about cats. No sentimentality, merciless self-interest. You knew exactly where you stood with them.

"Are you jealous, you big dinkus?"

"That my damn cat is close to you and has your hands on her? Hell yeah."

Martha's purring was deep-throated approval, a vibrating hurr sound, as Derelie caressed her. She flexed one paw in her ecstasy, opening out her pink jelly bean toes and showing scimitar claws he'd had to trim when she was a kitten but she'd never used on furniture and only occasionally on skin.

"You're not annoyed that I stayed over?"

"I'm annoyed I didn't answer your text. I love that you stayed over."

"Are you going to keep standing over there being all broodingly attractive?"

Not if she kept looking at him like what she had planned was going to be worth going without sleep. "I need to clean up." He rubbed his jaw, whiskers, and the grit of the city was all over him and he didn't want to infect her with the stench of his failure of a day.

Under the bedclothes Derelie's hand moved, over her hip, dipping down as she bent her elbow. "Hurry."

"Christ, woman." Was she doing what he thought she was doing?

She dropped on the pillow to her back and groaned. "I was having a sexy dream before you woke me up."

"You were having a sexy dream in my bed, without me." He pushed off the doorjamb, dumped his suit coat, walked on something soft that squeaked and looked down. "You bought her a toy." It was purple with green feathers, vaguely dragon-like.

"Not me. I'm a dog person."

"You're catnip." He put his knee to the bed, looming over Martha and Derelie. "Are you wet?"

Derelie closed her eyes. "Hmm."

He poked Martha in the hip. "Get your own." Martha scarpered under his arm and off the bed, and the toy squeaked. He put a hand to Derelie's face, slipped it into her hair. She smiled up at him. "This one is mine."

And she was his, without discussion, without question.

The rest of the week became a race to uncover and interview more victims and the agonizing wait for Henri Costa to report in. Jack's own clean bill of health report was an anticlimax. Every night, he staggered home to find Derelie curled up in his bed with Martha, her clothes for the morning hanging on the back of the bedroom door. She was the reason he bothered to come home, didn't go begging to Barney for a fight. Every night they'd turn to each other, seeking comfort. Mornings were for waking early and finding pleasure in each other's lips and hands and bodies.

Derelie had her head down too. Working extra hours, adapting Potter's editorial calendar, adding her own content and learning to manage her lifestyle team and the politics of the editorial meetings. Madden didn't go easy on her. He was smarting after Potter's defection to one of the new media content companies, and Derelie was a soft target. But Jack held it together in the morning editorial meeting without coming to her defense because she was right about having to do that for herself.

By the weekend, it was no clearer if he had a viable exposé on Keepsafe. All he wanted to do was clear his head of the frustration of weeks of work that might turn out to go nowhere. Spending the weekend uninterrupted with Derelie was the perfect antidote.

He kicked it off by surprising her with a ticket to take a yoga class under the sky dome at the planetarium. It was yoga and stars, even if they weren't real ones. He'd wanted it to feel like a reward for the week she'd had and the amount of waiting around for him she'd done. It didn't work out like that. The reward was all his. She virtually jumped him in the café where he'd waited with the day's papers and his email and social feeds.

She hugged him from behind his chair. "That was awesome."

Hands up to run over her forearms. "I'm glad you liked it." It'd been worth the favor he owed to get her a ticket.

"It was this incredible sensory experience. Total dark room but lit from above with constellations, so unexpected and beautiful."

Like the woman whose hand he brought to his lips, whose company he craved.

She ducked around him to meet his eyes. "And sold out months in advance."

Sometimes there were benefits to being the Defender of the City. And there was delight in playing tourist, showing Derelie his Chicago, including fried plantain sandwiches, and helping her move more of her stuff to his place. If she never had to see the dealer on the corner, it would be too soon for him.

There were benefits to being part of the congregation of the Church of the Cocked Fist, not only for access to its members in their professional capacities, but in knowing about a key under a certain flowerpot. On Sunday, he snuck Derelie into the old garage where they committed sacrilege in the pit, trading practice punches for kisses and body blocks for near-naked wrestling.

Without Barney lurking with a camera, they didn't need to be restrained. Jack let Derelie pin him on the floor, hold him down with her knees aligned along his hips and her hand in his hair. "I win," she crowed, snatching at his shoulders when he dug his heels into the floor and bucked. He was the planet's happiest loser.

"What do you want for your prize?" The hand at his zipper gave him his answer. "Here?"

She took his glasses off and placed them on the floor behind his head. "Don't pretend that's not why we came." She got the zipper down and her hand on him. There was no pretending when a woman did that to you.

"Padded walls." It was exactly why he'd brought her here.

She made her eyes roll back and forth. "Like an insane asylum in a scary movie."

Insane about her. "Are you still scared about us?" Whether she knew it or not, she was the one in control here. He was holding on to her with everything he had, but if she bucked him off it would be what he deserved.

She ran her knuckles lightly over him, added her lips and teeth at his throat. "You don't scare me, Jackson Haley."

"I want to worship you against the wall." Did that shock her?

"I've wanted that since dinner at Elaine's."

He groaned, because that was his motivation too. Knowing a woman wanted you to fuck her against a wall lent him superhuman strength. He got them off the floor in a clinch, backed her up against the padding and kissed her till her knees went soft. Clothing was a goddamn nuisance, not needing a rubber was inspiration. Wrapping her legs around his hips, easing her down on him was divinity.

"Ah, Jack."

He had to still, the sensation of their fit too intense. Her back and head were protected. He didn't have to worry about hurting her when he slammed into her, and he would. "Okay?"

"So good."

He took her mouth, tangled tongues, feeling her in the follicles of his hair and the soles of his feet. She moaned, loud in his ears, ringing in the vast space. He loved that abandon in her. It was a gift. The way she surrendered even as she came at him for her own piece of the action, gripping his face in her hands, using her thighs to ride him.

When he bent his knees and flexed his hips to withdraw, to renter, to do it again and again, bouncing her back into the padding, they were both vocal, incoherently; a conversation like the combat in their bodies: taking, giving, striking, receiving.

"Can you come this way?" He had her shoulders pinned to the wall, his hands under her thighs.

"I want to."

He groaned. "I know you do. Use your hand."

She used her eyes first; it was almost the end of him. Swapped heavy lids for a wide clear focus, aimed directly at him. He'd never been so grateful for being shortsighted. No barrier between their gazes, nothing hidden, everything given. How had he lived so long without knowing was this?

"Jack." She might've said more, her mouth opening, her breath short, but his control was shot. He pushed her hand aside and got a thumb to her clit and sent her shaking and crying into her release, taking his own in tight, hard thrusts and spilling into her heat.

They might have slept on the mat after that, but he knew Barney would be unhappy about this and he didn't want to actively annoy the man.

A week with Derelie and he still felt that lost, found, patched sensation. It couldn't be this easy to fall into something this good. If he had to thank an experiment for that, he would. But the questionnaire didn't give any hints of what you were supposed to do if you got beyond intimacy. That had to be what this was. An overwhelming desire not to be parted from her, to know she was near, to hear her voice and see her smile. To know he could touch her in the most casual way and understand her in the most solemn. To feel in the core of his being that his own happiness was brought to life by hers.

He didn't know what to do about feeling that way. What to call it except love.

It was a sucker punch, and he'd voluntarily walk into that blow repeatedly.

He'd have liked to have found a more romantic way, a more considered way to declare it, but it happened in the pet food section of the market.

The woman was young, colored pieces in her hair, skintight athletic wear. "Are you Jackson Haley? You're him, aren't you?" She had a voice for shouting at kids across a football field. "Oh, I'm such a fan."

"Thank you." He said it softly, hoping to encourage her to turn it down a notch; they were attracting attention, an older couple had stopped to watch.

"You have a cat." He had a tuna-and-rice concoction in his hand. "How precious. I'd have taken you for a dog person. Can I take a selfie with you?" She rummaged in her bag. "No one will believe it. Jackson Haley buying cat food. Me and Jackson Haley."

"I, ah, really, I'm in a hurry."

His special fan had her cell phone. There was a time when he'd reacted badly to people pulling unseen items from bags in front of him, but this would be a social media hit inside five minutes and that always made the *Courier*'s marketing team happy, and since he hadn't delivered on the love experiment story yet, this was a goodwill gesture.

"Come on. My name is Ginny." She pushed alongside him, leaned in. "Put your arm around me and say pizza." She took a shot, checked it. "No good. Try again." She lifted her cell.

"Hi. Can I take that photo for you?" Sweet rescue. Derelie had a basketful of fruit and vegetables she put down at her feet and a proprietorial look in her eye.

Ginny bristled and threw an arm across Jack to block Derelie. "Whoever you are, you can wait your turn."

He should've stepped away but he was frozen food, looking at Derelie, trying to thaw. "She's my—" What? More than a colleague, more than a friend. "Derelie is the woman I love."

Ginny tugged on his arm. "I just want a photo for the laugh. I don't want to steal you. You're not that famous or that good looking."

He let Ginny under his arm again. He smiled for her selfie, but he was looking at the woman he loved the whole time and the amused expression on her face made him antsy.

"She just wanted a photo," Derelie said, watching Ginny leave.

"That's what you took from that fiasco."

"Interesting hair, needs her eyes tested. You *are* that good looking."

He was coming unstuck here in front of the Whiskas and the Fancy Feast. "Derelie."

She turned to face him and stepped closer. "I'm the woman you love."

"I'm desperately sorry that got said here, now, like that." He was a writer, a broadcaster, and he'd fumbled the most important declaration of his life.

"I'm not."

He put his fingers under his glasses to rub the bridge of his nose. "It should've been said when we were alone and I was holding you and looking into your spooky eyes and you'd know I meant it."

"Instead I get the cat food special backdrop, two for one deal."

He was mortified. "You came to bail me out." You could slice him, dice him, puree him into cat food.

"Shucks. It was nothing."

He'd never known how much he needed rescuing until Derelie and her questions opened up his life, until he thought about the meaning behind the Oscar Mayer jingle and why it had stuck around in his earworm collection all this time. Christ, he couldn't be this lucky to be loved by her.

He picked up the basket, added the cat food. "Let's get out of here."

They held hands on the way home, like they'd done all weekend. It was childish, like the jingle, like being a grown man but aching to be loved. No one had held his hand for a very long time; he'd never wanted to hold anyone's hand. He didn't want to let Derelie's go. He held it while he pressed her up against his apartment door, with Martha yowling and pawing the door on the other side. He held it while he kissed her, whispered into her mouth words that'd sounded so bumbled, so loudly wrongly declared and so right at the same time.

"I love you."

"It's a cliché, and Jackson Haley doesn't do clichés."

She had the edge here. The power to make him bleed. "It's a fact and I'm the defender of truth."

There was a loud thump from inside the apartment. Derelie's eyes were stars and planets and all their mysteries and logic, but maybe too distant for him to reach, until she said, "I love you too."

Chapter Twenty-One

Jack said he loved her in a million ways to go with the words whispered into her skin, and Derelie said it back, thrilled and terrified, her insides twirling about like an excited puppy discovering its tail for the first time. She'd been the cool one in the pet food section, but now she might wet herself with excitement if she wasn't careful.

This was real. There was no way to misinterpret the way Jack looked at her, touched her, found a way for her to practice yoga under the stars.

"I want you to meet my parents." She said it before she'd thought that through. It was a big deal. He might not be into that. She had no desire to meet his. "If you want, and I mean on the phone." Home was a day's travel away and they hadn't made it inside his apartment.

"Only if we get in before Martha punches a way out."

Judging from the complaints, Martha was one pissed pussycat. As soon as Jack cracked the door she tried to push her way out. He used the grocery bag as a shin level shield and scooped her up with one hand so Derelie could get in without the cat getting out.

"You know how to spoil a moment," Jack said, holding a purring Martha dangling in outstretched arms. "Drama queen. How am I supposed to convince Derelie to move in if you're going to carry on like you're possessed?"

"Did you just ask me to move in with you?"

"Technically, I asked Martha to quit being a hellcat so you don't run a mile when I ask you to move in." He stooped to put Martha to the floor. "How do you feel about moving in?"

"You mean more than a few hangers in your closet?"

"I mean half the closet."

His place was bigger than her shoebox and in a better neighborhood and it had Martha. This was a bigger deal than waving to her parents on FaceTime.

"My hellcat and I would love to have you here, if you can put up with us."

The hellcat had knocked over the bag of groceries and was head and front paws inside it, butt up, shaggy britches to the fore and tail waving a question mark.

"I get that it might be too soon and it might not be what you want, but you're here nearly every night, so I thought it made sense."

"I need to think about it." It's what a rational, sensible adult who grew up in a town called Orderly would say. This was all so new and fast.

Jack rescued the groceries, and she said, "Yes."

He double-blinked. "Yes?"

Adrenaline-fueled enthusiasm deserted her in one wild drop, but it was still, yes. "I need to sit down." She planted herself on his couch. She was in love with Jack. She'd been in love with him since question seventeen when he talked about his granddad. It's just that she hadn't known what to call this feeling that made her want to cleave to his side.

"What if it wears off?" she said. "This fizzy thing I feel about you."

"It's not wearing off for a long time. Not for me." He sat beside her, but was astute enough not to touch her. If he touched her she might cry. "Because it's strong. Because you showed me what was missing in my life by filling it. Because everything I am is richer for being with you."

Pretty words. Easy to say for someone who made a life working with them.

"I've had a shitty week, Derelie. My Keepsafe story is falling apart. It's hundreds and hundreds of hours of work, thousands of dollars invested by the *Courier* in time and other costs. A week like this, I'd have been living at the church, taking any fight Barney would let me have, begging every favor to get in the pit. But I knew you were here waiting for me, and the last thing I wanted to do was feel pain."

What he'd done was wrap her in his arms and ask about her day, to tease her about her morning hair and strategize about their staggered arrival at the office.

"It's still yes, the biggest, loudest yes, but my head is spinning."

He took her hand and brought it to his chest. "There's no hurry. We're not on a deadline. I wanted you to know where I was with this. No second-guessing. I want to be with you."

She turned her body into his, still a puppy wanting to sniff him all over, wriggle into his hands, to revel in this moment. "When did you know you loved me?" She rubbed her hands over his shoulders, slid her knee over his thighs and watched his eyes behind his frames go bright.

"You knocked me sideways the day we met." When he'd thought she was a cub reporter on an internship. "You sassed the heck out of me and I didn't expect it. Kept thinking about you." Was it any one answer to any one question or the way she still sassed him? He took his glasses off and set them aside, dragged her closer, a hand on her thigh, an arm around her back, interlocking them. "But I knew I was in deep with you—" he kissed the side of her mouth "—when you changed the kitty litter when I was off chasing bad guys."

"Ahh."

He took the rest of that complaint by kissing it away and weathering the thump she aimed at his chest without flinching. He kissed her so well, so intently, mounting a thorough investigation of her mouth that she climbed over him, and humor turned to need and need to hands under clothing, and it was some time later they were interrupted by Martha, squeaky dragon between her teeth, jumping onto the arm of the couch.

Jack took Martha's dragon and tossed it into the bedroom. He didn't look at the cat as she tore after it, he held Derelie tight to him. "I don't know when I fell in love with you. You crept up on me, but I know that's what I'm feeling and it just gets better, because you feel it too."

She could forgive him for the kitty litter quip after that. "What about at work?" It was difficult pretending Jack didn't mean more to her than a colleague. "Phil told me not to fuck anyone." Artie was anyone. "Or to keep it a secret if I did."

Martha was back with the dragon. Jack threw it again. "We don't owe the *Courier* our private lives."

She stared after Martha, the cat who played fetch. "I don't want to give Phil any extra reason to think I can't do my job."

"He doesn't think that."

She sighed. It sure felt like it. He'd either shot down or been uninspired about every story she'd proposed in the editorial meetings.

Martha was back with the toy. Jack ignored her, though from the couch arm she batted at his arm. "Madden is a smart man. He didn't promote you because he thought you'd fail. I don't think you'll fail. You're the only one of us who's worried about that."

"You're biased." Surprisingly, delightfully one eyed about her.

"No bias in journalism." Jack mock threw Martha's dragon, but she was too clever to chase nothing, one up on Ernest and something Derelie still had to learn. "Once upon a time, at least." He threw the dragon for real and Martha chased it all the harder for having been denied, fur padded feet sliding on the hardwood, tail pointing straight up with a curl at the tip.

"Have you ever been in love before?" That should've been an experiment question. The toy had gotten wedged between Jack's dresser and the wall and Martha was having trouble reaching it, trying one paw then the other, different angles of attack, flattening herself out on the floor.

"Only with ideas. You?"

It was a good answer. "If I'd have known you would want to be with me, I'd have been obsessed with you." As obsessed as a cat with a squeaky toy.

"You should call home while I'm in the mood to let you."

"Let me?"

He ran a finger inside her shirt and under her bra strap and snapped it against her skin. Oh, gosh. She could call home later. She took his hand and brought it to her breast. He squeezed, his other hand pressing down on her tailbone so she could feel exactly what mood he was in. They were almost lip-locked again when Martha reappeared on the couch arm.

"Marah. Merrow. Yip." She was dragon-less and not happy. "Marah."

"About moving in," Jack said, looking at Martha. "Did I mention I own a cat who's a boner killer? You can have the whole closet. I only need a hanger or two."

"I like the way you're thinking. I am a dog person, after all."

"I taught her to fetch just for you."

"No lying in journalism."

He shrugged. "How about gross exaggerations?"

"In my limited experienced that gets more eyeballs."

"Go call your mom before I eyeball you into bed."

She stole one more kiss and climbed off Jack's lap, looking around for her purse.

"Derelie." Cell in hand, she looked back at Jack. "I'm in love with you." Never going to get tired of hearing that, whether it was in the pet food aisle, or on the street, or in his arms. "But maybe do some buttons up before you call home."

She was in love with Jackson Haley and it made her dizzy enough to forget she was half-dressed. Buttons done, hair brushed and tied back, she called home.

"Mom."

"Hi, honey. How was your week? Are you at your friend's place again?" She got all silly saying the word *friend*, rolling her eyes and grinning.

"His name is Jack."

"Can he hear us?"

"I can," Jack said from his place beside her on the couch.

"Well, that's not fair," Mom said, before Derelie angled her cell so Jack was in the picture too. "Oh, look. Hello there, Jack, I'm Karen."

"Hello, Karen, nice to meet you. Your daughter is a very special person."

"Oh, she is, she is. I told her she'd make friends in the city, but she hasn't mentioned you—"

"Mom."

"Okay, okay. Is that, what is that?"

"Yip, yip." It was Martha walking across their laps in front of the screen.

"Nosy cat, sorry." Jack said, lifting Martha away. "I'll take her and leave you so you can talk." *But not about me*, he mouthed over his shoulder as he carried Martha into the kitchen.

"Bye, Jack, nice to meet—has he gone?" Mom watched for her to nod. "He has a cat. He's very cute with the glasses and the shoulders." She made a "the fish was *this* big" gesture, her face was out of the shot for a second, and Derelie got a glimpse of kitchen cupboards. "Where did you meet?"

"At work, he's a colleague. You've read him. Jackson Haley."

"Oh. The one who does the, with the, I see. He's very accomplished." *Accomplished* was the word Mom used when she was impressed but also suspicious. "Is it serious, you and Jack?"

She nodded. She wasn't ready to tell Mom she was in love; it was such tender knowledge. She could hear Jack in the kitchen running water, banging about. "It's serious. He asked me to move in with him."

"Oh, honey." Mom put her hand to her throat. "Do you love him?"

Another nod. Mom could smell a lie in a raindrop and see one in an eyebrow. "I do. It's only new, but I do love him."

Mom blinked fast; there'd be tears. "Do you think he's the one?"

Maybe. Yes, she so wanted Jack to be her one. "Like you and Dad."

"Two days, that's all it took for us." There was the eye wipe. "We had a weekend together and I just knew."

"Dad said it took two months." This was an old family argument.

Mom shook her head. "Stupid man, slow waking up to the truth. You email me some more about you and Jack because you've been holding out and I want to know everything."

"Don't make me into town gossip, okay?" It was one good reason for not sharing.

"Not till you tell me I can."

As close to a promise she'd get. "Is Ernest there?"

"Here he is." The screen showed Ernest looking the

other way, tongue lolling. Mom tried to get in front of him. "Ernie, it's Derelie, here's your girl," but Ernest kept moving out of her way, panting and wagging. Mom's face came back on screen. "Oh, honey, he's just a dog that doesn't understand technology."

He had forgotten her.

"You go cry on Jack's lovely big shoulders about that."

"Mom."

"He needs to see you ugly cry sooner rather than later, you know."

Derelie spent the night alternatively in Jack's arms laughing at Martha pushing one of his shoes around the room with her face buried in it, and sharing increasingly heart-melting kisses.

He almost saw her ugly cry the next day. At the editorial meeting, Phil tore into her about the *Tribune* getting the scoop on the country's biggest divorce scandal. The *Courier* lost a substantial amount of traffic over the weekend by not being on that story, and that was her fault.

"Why didn't we have that story?"

She'd had no idea it was even in the wind. "I—"

"What did we lead with?"

"Movie stars and sick kids."

"I know that. I'm asking why we weren't on the story everyone else had a bead on?"

Not everyone, just the Trib. "I'm—"

"Sorry?" Phil barked. "Sorry doesn't run a newspaper."

Sorry didn't begin to cover what she felt. "I suspect it was given as an exclusive."

Phil slapped a hand on the table, and she flinched. "I'm fucking sure it was. Why wasn't it our exclusive?"

She couldn't look at Jack's face, but he had a grip on his cell that spoke of cracked glass. Now she was sorry she'd finished a sentence, sorry she was caught looking like she didn't know her job, sorry Phil had gone for her in front of everyone. It wasn't personal. The same thing happened to others, but that didn't mean it didn't sting.

Jack didn't fare much better. "We need to run the Keepsafe story this week or I'm calling it over," Phil said.

Jack put his phone on the table. "It's not there yet."

"Face it, Haley. It's not the story you wanted it to be. Get it there or move on." Phil spun his chair to zone in on Derelie again. "Where's the love experiment?"

Oh shit. It wasn't done because they'd both been busy and since Keepsafe wasn't finalized, Derelie hadn't gotten in Jack's face for his part. "It's—"

"Fuck," said Phil, glaring at her and Jack in turn. "Don't care. I'm over it. Drop it."

"Altogether?" she said. It was going to make a cute story. She'd done her part and even had a staff photographer take candid workplace pics of them that weren't as revealing as the ones Barney had taken. Dropping it altogether was a waste, marketing would be pissed off. But the only story Jack cared about was Keepsafe, so dropping it was for the best.

"For future reference that's what drop it means, Honeywell. Dogs get it, shouldn't be hard for you."

Oh. She tucked her head down, to hide how insulted and embarrassed that made her feel.

Jack stood, but it was Spinoza who said, "Enough, Madden. What's biting your hairy ass?"

Phil blew out a stream of angry air. "I don't know if you people get it, but keeping this paper in print is like pushing shit uphill. The runoff is filthy and smells of failure and it doesn't wash out. Every time we miss a major story or overspend or screw up, it's another reason for advertisers to desert and our owner to fold the whole thing into an online edition, and you know what that means—less of fucking everything and everyone."

"We get it. No reason to be such a bastard," said Jack.

Phil stood, turning to Jack. "Are you saying Honeywell shouldn't be in this room? Can't take the heat?" She held her breath because shouting at them to stop was a bad idea, and if Jack came out in her defense it would only demonstrate she'd needed it.

"I'm saying it's not helpful if you're going to abuse us."

She let the breath go and hoped everyone was too focused on Phil to notice.

"You think I'm going to keep our jobs alive being a nice guy? Fuck off, Haley." Phil went for the door. "Any of you can't take the rough with the smooth, do us all a favor like Shona did and take a hike."

There was silence when Phil left, until Jack, who'd managed to defend her without calling attention to their relationship and without decking Phil, said, "Cliché count?"

"Five," she said when she realized no one else was going to answer. "Can't take the heat. Pushing shit uphill. Do us all a favor. Rough with the smooth and take a hike."

"Six," Jack said. She'd missed one. What was it?

Spinoza laughed. "Hairy ass?" There was a general chuckle at that and chairs got pushed back as people moved about.

"It's a more accurate description than nice guy," said Jack.

And that was enough to sustain her through the rest of the day, a dental appointment, working back and missing yoga, but by the time Jack got home she'd lost the ability to keep it together. He only just got through the door and she was in his arms, gulping in the cinnamon clove scent of him, holding back sobs, holding on to the solidity of him when everything else felt slippery. She could so easily lose this job, lose her way in the city, lose her place in Jack's life.

He squeezed her tight. "The day was made of stone, huh."

It was made of shards so sharp and lumps so heavy, she was struggling to see a clear path forward. "I screwed up."

"Yeah, you did."

Oh God, even Jack thought she was a giant, pulsing, in-over-her-head cliché. She shifted to pull away but he locked her against him.

"And it'll happen again. It's the business. You have to be ready for the hit, know how to roll with it and recover quickly."

"What if I can't learn how to do that?"

"Why would you say that?"

Because right now it felt like too much and just when she was feeling more at home in the city.

She didn't get a chance to respond. Jack backed her

to the couch and sat her down, going to one knee in front of her. "You know why I didn't take Madden's head off today? It's not because I've learned patience, it's because you truly didn't need me to."

"But I couldn't get a sentence out. I was a stammering mess." And even if she had managed to talk like a normal person, she didn't have anything to say that Phil wanted to hear. She'd failed to get the story of the day and to have the love experiment ready to run.

Jack cupped her cheek. "He was talking at you, not to you. It wouldn't have mattered what you said, he'd already lost his temper. He's done it to all of us. It's not personal. Next time he does it and you don't have the answers he wants, don't let it fluster you, wait it out."

"How many screwups do I get before he wants me out? There were more qualified people than me."

"Madden didn't offer you the job out of charity." He sat beside her and took her hands in his. "Quit hijacking yourself."

She leaned her head on his shoulder. "What if I'd just wanted a good cry?"

Jack grunted. "I screwed up. You wanted comfort and I gave you a pep rally. I'm the one out of my depth. We're going to need a sign, headline type, so I know when you want a lover, not a workmate. Blink three times, ring a bell. Straight out tell me to shut up."

"We don't need a sign." He'd given her exactly what she needed. He'd treated her like a professional, a colleague, and tears weren't a useful workplace strategy. "You got it right. I wanted to feel sorry for myself. I needed to hear what you said."

"I got it right?" He shook his head. "It was an accident."

"No, it wasn't. You do right by me, Jackson Haley, and I think you'll know what to do if I just need a good cry."

"Too much faith in me. I'm a rank amateur at this being in love thing."

Martha came out from the kitchen, merrowed, and went back into the kitchen.

"I got home just before you. Haven't fed her." Home—she'd called Jack's place home. It was time to give notice on her shoebox, because she wanted to live with a man who had no difficulty telling her he loved her or giving her a pep talk or being concerned he was getting it right. "You're rolling with the being in love thing. But how are you going to roll with Keepsafe?"

"Marah," Martha said from the kitchen. She made it sound so much like hurry they both laughed.

Jack stood and drew her upright with him. "I'm going to take Bob Bix down. The deeper we dig, the more victims we find. It's gross mismanagement, but I need to prove it was deliberate fraud and not an administrative mistake that can be corrected. It's a story either way, but unless I get proof, it's not the takedown I want it to be. I need more time."

He looked less certain than he sounded, and Phil had kept telling Jack he was out of time. "Anything I can do to help?"

He took his glasses off and tossed them on his desk. He was done with talking about work. He caught her face between both hands. They'd never formally done the four-minute staring part of the experiment. They'd done deep eye contact naked and entwined, both of them finding a heady pulse beat in each other's eyes. They'd done it sated and replete, telling stories that deserved the closest audience, but they'd never done it like this. Tired, hungry, after a day of stone, both of them disappointed at work, still trying to figure out what the rules for being in love were, with a demanding cat, merrowing and marhahing in the next room.

Jack looked into her spooky pale eyes and without words told her he admired her, wanted her, desired her, cared for her, loved her. He told her he was surprised and hopeful and concerned and tentative. That he didn't want to break this new and lovely thing they were and was worried he wouldn't know how to protect it. That he'd been lonely before they'd met, but never understood it, that he was grateful for the experiment that'd brought them together and helped him to see he could make a new home with her.

She looked into Jack's brilliant blue eyes and told him without words he was the smartest, sexiest person she'd ever met, that no matter where she looked she wouldn't find anyone she wanted to be with more, to share her life with more. She told him she was less afraid with him by her side, that she was more comfortable in her own skin, that she craved his hands and his lips and his body because it fitted to hers, excited hers. That she was a girl fresh off the farm and he had the stink of the city in his blood, but that when they were together they were sunshine and birdsong, all the things she needed to be happy.

She looked into Jack's brilliant blue eyes and saw that it didn't matter if she screwed up at work, or ugly cried or argued with him, or was too bloated to want sex, or had bad hair or put on weight, or got irritated at women who propositioned him in markets. He was the one for her. She looked into Jack's eyes and her own filled with tears, because the feelings inside her had to find a way out or she'd explode.

He brushed a thumb across her cheek. "I'm not sure about these. Do they come from today or did I make you cry?"

She'd made herself cry, but in a good way. "Happy tears." They spilled plentifully now, a stream of emotion.

He angled his head and repeated the words "happy tears" as if that was a foreign concept. "You're sure?" He brushed another away.

"I'm the one crying them."

"I've got two suggestions. I kiss those tears out of you or I sing the wiener song until all you feel is blinding rage."

She chose the kisses. She'd always choose the kisses.

Chapter Twenty-Two

Jack was all talk. He'd told Derelie he didn't want to put a fist into Madden's face when the guy went for her in the morning editorial meetings, but that was a fat, slimy toad of a lie. He wanted to knock Madden's teeth in. He'd told Derelie she didn't need to be defended and that was a shiny truth. She'd learn to manage their boss, but it didn't mean Jack enjoyed witnessing Madden's daily power trip.

Amongst the next day's proposed lead stories was the teacher's union strike and a cancer breakthrough. There was a piece on a shootout on the South Side, plus a story about a human head found in a bag in a Chinatown parking lot. Jack's own story was on fraudulent bank accounts and how seniors were being ripped off by marketing schemes that skirted the law.

"What's lifestyle got?" Madden said to Derelie. He'd left her till last as usual, when everyone was keen to get out of the meeting and on with the day.

"Feature on the new penguin exhibit at the Lincoln Zoo and the annual firefighter's charity calendar shoot," she said.

"That's the best you've got for the day? Oiled up, half-naked firefighters and fucking penguins."

"You don't like firefighters or penguins?" said Spinoza. He made a "what gives?" gesture when Madden gave him a death glare. Spin had faced Madden's ire earlier about a Cubs story Madden thought was soft on the team's management.

"The new penguin exhibit cost millions and we're the first to cover it," Derelie said. "We're exclusive on the firefighters too. We'll have video of the shoot, plus a reader zoo pass giveaway."

"And?" Madden barked.

Jack wanted to find a fucking penguin and have a half-naked firefighter stuff it up Madden's ass. Forcing a neutral expression to stay on his face made his jaw ache, but Derelie took Madden's belligerence in her stride.

Last night he'd almost messed up with her and when she finally did show him tears, he felt like his skin had been rubbed away and he was nothing more than raw meat and electrical impulses. Tears in Derelie's eyes made him feel broken in a way no fight did. He had no idea what he'd do if he ever caused them and it wasn't like he'd been easy to get along with so far.

"There's no and, Phil," she said. "They're two great stories on top of the regular features and syndicated news. If the firefighters don't hit the top viewed stories list, I'll eat my pencil."

Spinoza offered Derelie a high five and Jack unclenched his teeth. Madden was last to laugh. "I'll sharpen it for you," he said, but there was no menace in his response, and Derelie wore a nailed-it smile Jack wanted badly to kiss.

He watched her across the table, laughing with Spin, and wondered how much this secrecy added to the thrill of her. Would he be less inspired to find a way to get her alone if it wasn't a challenge? That was like asking if he preferred his right eye to his left—it was more shortsighted but he didn't need it any less. He needed Derelie in a way that knocked his breath out.

They both dawdled. It'd become a habit, creating a way to be the last two out of the room. It wasn't smart. Derelie fiddled with her notepad and he scrolled messages absently on his screen, surreptitiously aware of every movement she made, until they had the room to themselves and he could give himself over to her.

She tapped her pencil on her bottom lip. "Can you get lead poisoning if you eat a pencil?" The question was innocuous enough if overheard; the way she dragged the pencil over her lips not so much. His body read it as pornographic.

"That depends on whether you're personally oiling any firefighters." His gut tightened at the thought of that.

"I wasn't planning on it." She came around the table toward him, trailing a finger along its surface making it too easy to imagine that finger running over his body. "But if you think it would make a better story…"

He met her at the top of the table. "You're the story. The front page, the number one read."

"Is that yes to getting my hands on firefighter pecs?"

She was high on her victory with Madden; he was blitzed on the cheeky glint in her eyes. "It's yes to whatever you want." Impossible to imagine denying her anything.

"You say the nicest things."

There was no privacy in this room with its glass walls. He dropped the volume on his voice. "I want to kiss you. I want to back you into a wall and get my hands under your skirt." That was the nicest thing he could think of in the moment.

"It's because of the penguins, right?"

It was because she'd had a win, one of what he trusted would be many; because she was his experiment and the result of them was nothing he'd ever expected. "It's because you turn me on."

She waved a hand and looked at the ceiling tiles, affecting boredom, but rosy-cheeked with mischief. "You told me that at breakfast."

"You're tired of hearing it?"

That hand in motion flirted with landing on his chest. They were already standing too close for colleagues. He wanted that touch and leaned toward her.

"Haley, the boss is looking for you."

Jack jerked back as if Spinoza's words were jabs.

"Huh, what did I interrupt?" Spin came into the room. "You jumped like I goosed you, Haley."

"Jack's giving me tips on how to deal with Phil," Derelie said, dodging like a pro boxer.

Spin's hand clapped across Jack's shoulder. "Ah, that's what he's giving you."

Derelie met Spin's disbelief with an award-winning sigh. "Phil's intimidating when I've only got penguins to throw at him."

"You could take his eye out with a well-aimed pencil," Spin said, slapping down on Jack's shoulder a second time.

Shit, he didn't buy any of this as innocent. "I wasn't advocating violence," Jack said. Of all the people to suspect something was going on, he and Derelie had to be flashing like neon for Spin to notice. But he could be trusted not to gossip.

"Advocating, that's a big word for a jock like me."

That didn't mean it wouldn't be painful, and Derelie's concern about being found out was in her angled brows. He bit off a crack about ten dollar words. He was a bastard for not being able to keep his thoughts off Derelie long enough to keep her safe from rumors.

"Guess that means Jack's being hands-on with his advice, Honeywell?"

She folded her arms. "Hands-on? That'd be a hackneyed word, wouldn't it, Spin?"

Spin grinned at her, backing off with both hands up. "It would be a none-of-my-business word." He left the room laughing, but caught the middle finger Jack gave him before the corridor swallowed him up.

"Oh no," she said.

"That was my fault." Jack hated this sneaking around, resented the double standard that would brand him a stud and Derelie a career slut. "Spin won't say anything."

"It's as much my fault. I liked the wall idea."

He twitched to touch her face. "I'll see you at home."

He turned to leave, but she stepped into him, pressed her body into his back, a brief blaze of heat rooting him to the spot, the unexpected weight of her hands flattened on his ribs making him groan at the contact and the way it hotwired him.

"I hate having to be a secret," she whispered. He tried to turn to take hold of her, but she had better survival instincts. "Later."

She walked around him to leave the room first, the cocky swagger in her stride at odds with the sheen in her eyes. It swelled his chest to know she was as affected by him as he was by her. But he had to play this smarter for her sake. Tonight he'd show her what she meant to him. It would be the calm before the drama of the Keepsafe story running.

He tracked Madden to Roscoe's office on the executive floor, knocked to interrupt the two of them arguing a point of law. Roscoe looked grateful for the disruption. "Come in, Jack."

Roscoe had two drafts of the Keepsafe story in front of him. The one where Bix went to jail for fraud and the one where he presided over gross incompetence.

"Fucking lawyers," Madden said, as Jack took the seat beside him.

"You don't have it, Jack," said Roscoe. "There's not enough here to tie this up as fraud and not simply straight mismanagement. It'll get us done for libel."

"We'll run with the incompetence leadership mismanagement angle," said Madden. "It's enough to get Bix fired."

"But not jailed," said Jack. "And that's what I want."

"Odd fact for your digestion—the *Courier* isn't run on what you want, Haley."

"You've almost got enough, Jack." Roscoe ignoring

Madden gave him hope. But almost wasn't going to get him page one above the fold and before the scroll.

Madden stood. "We're going with the mismanagement story. Runs Friday."

"Why are you pushing for Friday?" Jack said, looking at Roscoe for any clues to why Madden had a deadline hard-on over this one. This was the first time Madden had pushed for a specific end date to an investigation. "This is a national story now and we're the only ones on it." That was a big win for the *Courier*, something Madden was normally all over to champion.

"Had enough of it. Gone on too long."

"It's a great story," said Roscoe, and Jack could've hugged him. If the lawyer thought he could pull this off, Madden would back down. They'd been in a similar position a dozen times before. Roscoe was generally the cautious one.

"The moon landing was a great story. JKF's assassination was a great story. Watergate, OJ's trial, that baby down the damn well in Texas, Princess Diana's funeral, Hurricane Katrina, Obama's inauguration, Bin Laden's death, those Chilean miners trapped for months, Edward Snowden, Hillary Clinton, Peggy Whitson's record number of days in space. There are great stories breaking every day. Great stories about penguins and oily firefighters and celebrities divorcing their fucking underpants. I've had enough. You're done, Jack. I'm calling it."

The temptation to stare at Madden with his mouth open was too good to refuse. Roscoe started to say something soothing and Jack jumped in with, "A week. Give me another week."

"What difference is a week going to make?"

"My inside source needs time to find what I need."

Madden slapped his hands over his skull. "You're out of fucking time."

On his feet, Jack lost his head. "Fuck you, Madden. I can bring the fraud story in."

"Fuck you twice as hard, Jack—you got two days, or I'm sending the mismanagement angle to print." Madden looked at Roscoe. "Clear it to run." He walked out leaving Jack with an uncomfortable feeling that there was some other agenda at play.

"What was that?"

Roscoe cracked his knuckles. "I don't know. More ornery than usual. He's under a lot of pressure on costs. What was the thing about underpants?"

"It's not the same news business it was."

"If it bleeds it leads, if it roars it scores, if it snoozes you lose it. That's still the same."

"But now the truth matters less than whether the story is entertaining. Whether the dress is black and blue or white and gold. We're competing for readers with Pokémon, Netflix binges and Pornhub."

"It was white and gold," said Roscoe. "Nearly got divorced over that. I see your point. We can still make Bob Bix bleed if you bring in the fraud story by Thursday night's deadline. I love the idea of that crook getting what he deserves. Jack, you gonna let celebrity underpants take your column inches?"

Henri Costa had gone cold. He wasn't answering, email, phone or text. Without another source Jack was sunk. Almost all the victims defrauded by Noakes and Whelan had been promised recompense. Someone inside Keepsafe knew the *Courier* was investigating and was trying to neutralize the story. They'd succeed unless Jack could join the dots. He now knew of fifty other doctors scattered around the country who had higher than average levels of claims denied. But he couldn't connect them to Bix or each other like he'd been able to do with Noakes and Whelan, to prove a conspiracy.

He stood to leave. He couldn't see another way forward with this. "No paper ever got sued for penguin stories." There was no legal risk in running the mismanagement angle either. Maybe that was Madden's game. Playing it safe. Making sure costs were contained.

"No penguin story ever righted a wrong. I can't believe you're going to give up on this."

"I'm trying to roll with it." If rolling with it felt like being pummeled by an avalanche, buried with no clear path to the light. It's what he'd told Derelie she'd have to learn to do. Time to suck it up.

"I'll hold off clearing this story Phil wants till the last minute."

That would give him hours, not days, but he'd take what he could get.

"It could be worse, Jack."

He stopped in the doorway to look back at Roscoe. "Yeah, we could both be unemployed."

He spent the rest of the day with Berkelow trying to track down Henri Costa or someone inside Keepsafe who was close to him, without tipping them off to what Henri had been doing. According to Keepsafe HR, Henri was on a leave of absence. According to the guy who had the internal extension one digit higher than Henri's and sat in the cubicle next to him, Henri was simply missing.

"This is bad," said Berkelow. "Like head in a bag in a Chinatown parking lot bad."

She'd said what Jack was worried about, and by the time he'd filed the next day's story on a grain supply antitrust conspiracy, Derelie had left a string of messages.

Oiling firefighters is exhausting work. Who knew?

By oiling firefighters, I totally mean yoga.

By yoga I mean I sat on the couch with Martha and now my legs are on strike.

Also we're out of groceries.

Bring pizza.

"You're smiling." Berkelow rested her elbows on the partition between their desks. "Is that Henri?" The dark circles under her eyes were a matched set to the ones Jack sported.

It was the one thing better than hearing from Henri. "No."

She sagged. "We're not going to get the fraud story, are we?"

He shut his computer down. There was nothing more he could do tonight. He had a date with a deep-dish pizza. "We're not going to give up till the last minute."

"Barbra Shenker called. They got their money from Keepsafe. It's going to change their lives. She said to thank you."

But millions of other victims wouldn't get the same attention. "Go home, Berkelow."

"You know, before I worked with you I thought you were a manipulation. Someone the *Courier* created because you looked good on a billboard and you've got a good voice for broadcast. You made it look easy to get the headlines."

"And now?" He wasn't sure he wanted to know, but a manipulation had gotten him the woman who was marooned on the island of his couch starving for pizza, so he was more open to the discussion than he might've been.

"I want to be you when I grow up, Haley."

Berkelow was about the same age he'd been when he started in the newsroom, back when print was indisputably king. "Are you trying to make me feel old?" She laughed, but didn't issue a correction. "Be careful what you wish for." He'd never wished ill for Henri Costa, but it was looking increasingly like the man was in trouble.

By the time he got home, the notion that he'd encouraged Henri to put his livelihood if not his life at risk and Madden's uncharacteristic lack of support had ground down on him. The pizzeria messed up his order, a road closure with a police blockade meant he had to walk the long way home and he had a shouting match on the phone standing on the street outside his apartment.

Madden said, "I had a call from Bob Bix's lawyer today. Told me he'd sue for reputation damage if you didn't stop sniffing around."

"And you told him we don't take our instruction from third parties."

"We're running the mismanagement angle."

"Bix is a shark and you're going to let him get away with it."

"You're going to let him get away with it, Jack. You're so sure Bix is crooked, prove it."

"I need more time."

"It runs Friday."

Madden disconnected, leaving Jack to shout obscenities to dead air. By the time he got inside the apartment, the pizza was cold and his temper was boiling. Months of work, endangering Henri, and the best he'd been able to achieve was a story about an internal company screwup that would be buried in the business pages and probably still get them sued for reputational damage.

"Oh, pizza. What did you get?" Derelie got off the couch and relieved him of the box.

"Does it matter?" Martha wouldn't stop circling him, making a racket. "You couldn't fucking feed her?" He scooped Martha up and carried her into the kitchen. Her bowl was empty. He dropped the cat to the floor, picked up the bowl and dumped a tin of ocean fish fillet into it. Martha sniffed the bowl and then lay down beside it.

"She's not hungry."

"I can see that." At least she'd shut up.

"That would be because I fed her. What happened?"

What could he say? Derelie kicked ass today and he'd failed. "It's all falling apart. Madden just called to say Keepsafe threatened to sue. Bix is going to get away with defrauding millions of policyholders."

"Your big story is dead?"

"That'll leave plenty of room for your clickbait."

Derelie sucked in a breath. He looked at her properly for the first time. She was still wearing her work clothing, but barefoot, her hair coming undone. She'd been slogging long hours under considerable pressure and it showed on her face. He was pissed off with Madden, with Henri, with himself and he'd taken it out on her. *Fuck.*

"You need church."

He put his hands to the back of his neck, tension stored there making it rigid.

"Seriously, Jack, call Barney. Do whatever it is you do when you want to burn the world down, but don't take it out on me."

He took a step toward her and stopped. He wasn't fit to be in the same room with her. "I'll go." Barney would set him up. A fistfight was exactly what he needed.

She moved aside and he went to grab his gym bag. When he came back she was standing uncertainly in the living room, tracking his movements in a way that made him want to claw his eyes out. "You should go home."

He got out the door without Martha realizing he was leaving. He got to the bottom of the stairs before he understood he didn't want to get smacked around and what he did want he'd need a miracle for: more time, a new lead on Keepsafe, Derelie's forgiveness. There was a lesson he hadn't learned as a child; he was learning it again as an adult. If you wanted people to stick around you needed to be easy to get along with.

She was waiting for him when he eased back inside the apartment. Still barefoot, still rumpled from the day, still on edge. She wouldn't have wanted to run into him on the stairs or waiting for a cab. She was beautiful and clever and generous and he felt the loss of her already in the drag on his spine and the weight of his head.

He kept his back to the door, kept half the room between them. "I don't want to fight. I'll stay out of your way."

"I'm glad you came back."

"I don't want you to go." The words were out even as he knew they were redundant. She would go because he'd finally shown her the side of him that was ugly, the side he'd tried to hide by avoiding the experiment and then cheating it. The part of him that was too hard to love.

"I don't want to go home."

"What do you want? Maybe you could shout at me. Go crazy, I deserve it." And then she'd leave him and he'd regret it forever.

"I don't want to shout at you. You already feel bad enough. I'm hungry, I'm warming the pizza."

She wanted pizza? That didn't make sense. He put his bag down, but stayed where he was. His phone rang and he let it go through to his message bank. Nothing was more urgent than trying to understand this.

"The best part of my day was watching you kick ass with Madden, knowing you wanted to be in my arms, and your texts. Everything else was shitty."

She lowered her eyes and smiled. He could smell the pizza and his stomach growled. Martha sauntered in, sprawled in the patch of floor between them and proceeded to clean her face like she did after she'd eaten.

Derelie shrugged. "She was still hungry."

Martha would vomit later and he'd have to clean up after her. There was no one to clean up after him. "You should take the pizza with you."

"Why would I…oh, Jack." Derelie stepped over Martha and put her hands to his chest. "You had a bad day, you lost your temper and stomped around. No one got hurt. I'm not going to stop loving you because you act like a dick sometimes."

Had he not had the door at his back he'd have been on the floor. His whole life had taught him people close to you would turn away if you were difficult.

"You don't mean that."

She brought her hands up to his shoulders. "I knew you could be a dick before I let you see me naked."

"You're not leaving me."

"Over feeding Martha? Think I'll stay."

It wasn't about Martha. Why didn't she see that?

"Question. Would you rather stand with your back against the door or eat pizza?" She took his hand. "Answer." She waited and, when he didn't respond, said, "The answer, for a lifetime of kisses and staring into each other's eyes, is—pizza."

He let her lead him into the kitchen, put a plate in front of him and served him a slice of pie. When Martha started yakking, he followed her around the apartment, watched her vomit up chunks of undigested slop then cleaned up after her. He didn't check his phone until he'd given Derelie a ration of kisses, and stared into her eyes for the sheer amazement that she'd stayed.

When he did, it was to discover Henri Costa was in New York, he had what Jack needed and he wanted to meet.

Chapter Twenty-Three

Derelie spent the night alone in Jack's bed because Martha abandoned the bedroom to sleep on the empty pizza box and Jack took the last flight out to New York to chase his story.

He wasn't around to see her firefighters duke it out with her penguins for top spot in the most-read list. Phil was. He sent an email, two words: Good job. It made her buzz with pride. Not long ago she'd have printed that out and taped it to the wall above her bed, but she hadn't slept in her own bed for weeks and didn't intend to start again.

After work she went back to her apartment to pick up mail and her brown boots, and to search for a missing blue glove. She needed to give notice. She couldn't find the glove. Why did she always seem to lose only the left hand ones?

Would you rather lose one glove of each pair you buy or witness your lover blow his cool once in a while? She'd choose a frosty left hand for all of winter in preference to missing out on any time with Jack, even when he was coiled tight enough to snap.

The only thing that worried her was how he'd reacted after their spat. As if a cold pizza and an argument was a much bigger deal, as if it had been enough for her to pack a bag and leave. He'd been quiet afterward, withdrawn but not distant, if his make-it-up-to-her kisses were anything to go by. It was something to talk about when he got home.

A very dead peace lily hit the trash but the job of completely emptying the refrigerator could wait—she had time to make the late yoga class and no fear of running into God's gift to yoga since she no longer cared what he thought, was slightly embarrassed she ever had.

Back at Jack's place with Martha and a tub of frozen mango yogurt she'd earned by virtuous sweat and life-affirming contortion, she sat on the couch and checked the time. An hour until the print deadline. She itched to call Jack, but he hadn't responded to texts and he was obviously busy and she didn't want to be that girlfriend who was annoying.

Calling home was a useful distraction.

"Has he seen you ugly cry yet?" Mom asked.

"No, but we had our first argument as a couple last night."

"Oh, you have to have those, honey."

"I know." Mom and Dad had argued about dumb things all her life, like who moved the car, whose turn it was to unstack the dishwasher, but she knew they were happy together. "He's uptight about a big story and a tough deadline and he got delayed coming home and the pizza was cold and Martha was being annoying, so he thought I hadn't fed her and he got angry with me."

"And you told him right where he could put that tantrum."

"I did, but he already knew. He went out for a minute to cool off and when he got back it was as if he was frightened about how I'd react."

"How did you react?"

"Hugged him and gave him pizza. He didn't have a great family life, left on his own a lot. His parents are surgeons and he always came second to their careers. I guess he thought he didn't deserve to be forgiven."

Saying that aloud made it obvious. Jack reacted as if he genuinely thought she'd leave him over a blowup that had nothing to do with how they felt about each other.

"You okay, honey?" You couldn't hide in silence on FaceTime.

She wished Jack was here now and she could explain to him that knowing how insecure he was about them hurt more than his clickbait crack. "I only now realized how much Jack deserves to be loved and how little he understands that." And how much she would love him to make up for what he'd missed out on.

They talked about Jack's shoulders and forearms next, in detail, and she got news from home and neither of them mentioned Ernest, and it was easier not to be sad about him forgetting her when the call ended, because Martha had made a surprise attack on her abandoned bowl of frozen yogurt and Derelie made the surprise discovery that cats get brain freeze.

Martha's tongue darted out and she took a bunch of quick licks of the melting yogurt before Derelie could snatch the bowl away. Martha's mouth opened, her pink tongue stuck out and she stayed that way, her head cocked, her eyes wide, her ears flattened as her big body made like furry iceberg.

"That'll teach you." Derelie could hardly get the words out for laughing. Ernest loved ice cream, but he'd never suffered brain freeze. "You're a freak, Martha."

Martha came back to life, retracting her tongue, passing a paw over her mouth in disgust and retreating to a place of safety under Jack's desk, where she gave Derelie narrow-eyed, cruel-hearted, "you'll get yours" looks.

As if on cue her cell rang—the ringtone she'd installed for Jack. Not quite the Oscar Mayer jingle, but a close approximation. He didn't know about it yet. He'd pretend to be annoyed. "Hey, where are you?"

"I'm standing behind a pillar at the Plaza watching Bob Bix and a dozen of the other doctors we suspect of being crooked drinking top-shelf liquor and patting each other on the back."

"It's like when we watched Bix have dinner with Noakes and Whelan."

"They're here too."

"You're going to get your proof, but oh my God, Jack. Can you make the deadline?"

"No, but I've got enough to convince Madden to give me until Monday. I talked him into pulling the mismanagement story. I'll have to spend the weekend working on this. I'm going to get Bix. I'm going to get all of them."

"I'm so happy for you."

"I have to cut out. I'll be back tomorrow morning."

"I love you." She'd tell him till he believed it in his bones.

He made a sound that told him she'd taken him by surprise. "You're sure it's not just part of a fucked up experiment?"

"If it is, I'm your forever lab rat."

The next sound he made might as well have been the audio that went with brain freeze. "Last night—"

"If you apologize again I'll get mad at you." He would hear in her voice she was joking.

"The way I feel about you scares the hell out of me."

"That's what all the lab rats say. Tell me you love me and go catch the bad guys."

He told her he loved her in a tone deep with emotion, crackling with heat and wicked with the promise of one crazy good reunion.

He didn't make Friday's editorial meeting but she sensed the moment he arrived in the office. She had no legitimate excuse to go to him and he didn't spend long at his desk, disappearing into meeting rooms with Phil and the lawyer. It was difficult to concentrate on her own work.

"I guess you'd already know about Haley's scoop, some fraud story," said Eunice, mid-afternoon.

"What did you hear?" Oh yeah, she needed to work on her nonchalance. Almost leaping across the workstation partition at Eunice didn't help with the "what's it to me" attitude she was meant to be projecting.

"Was in the elevator with Berkelow and one of the lawyers. Sounded big. Why are you smiling like that? It's creepy."

Derelie rolled her lips to get rid of the overly enthusiastic smile. "Everyone loves a scoop."

"Not if it pushes your own story off the front page."

What did it mean if frolicking penguins or oily firemen could push a genuine news story off the front page and out of prime website real estate? It wasn't the day to ruminate on that. There was green tea to reject in favor of coffee, because she'd never really enjoyed it, and deadlines to meet.

And on the way to the break room there was Jack, appearing unexpectedly at the end of the corridor, on his way back from where she was going, with a steaming cup in his hand. He looked distracted, eyes down on his cell screen. There was no one else around, though the noise of the office was their soundtrack, and not a lot but hot coffee stopping her from running to meet him and throwing herself in his arms.

She slowed her stride and let him draw closer, until they were almost at the point of passing each other. He looked up to check his progress and broke into a smile that squeezed her heart. That sudden joy was for her, a visual echo of what her own face must be doing. Another two steps each and they were face to face, but the corridor was no longer empty, people behind Jack, laughter behind her.

He pocketed his cell and shifted his cup to the hand farthest from her, his eyes up briefly to whoever was going to interrupt them. "Anything interesting happen in the editorial meeting?"

Everything interesting happened here, in a service corridor that led to rooms where people did ordinary, everyday, unmemorable things. They used the bathroom, they washed their hands, and dithered over clothing, hair, teeth and makeup because nothing rang, beeped or screamed for attention there. They poured coffee and searched for the cookies that were plentiful this morning when their willpower was stronger but gone now when they were desperate for a pick-me-up.

This corridor was for slices of downtime, for essential pit stops and stalling like her breath did. Everything in her body went on high alert because Jack was here, stealing her attention, robbing her of the willpower to walk on, close enough to touch, to smell the sweet cloves from his smokes, but wired to detonate her career in ways neither of them wanted.

"Nothing interesting happened." Except her whole life was somehow rammed into this stuttering moment where the office, the job, the city, her decision to build a bigger life, fell away and there was nothing but what she could be with Jack.

That laughter was right behind her now and the mailroom trolley was lumbering its way toward Jack.

"Good to know," he said, weight shifting as he moved to pass by, his arm brushing hers, the back of his hand grazing over the back of hers, eyes warm behind their frames licking softly over her face and then going blank to meet the world again. She turned her hand and he did too, their fingertips glancing before he stepped clear.

Derelie reeled in his wake, looking at the floor to hide her expression. Anyone could tell she was love struck.

From behind, "Hi, Jack."

"Tomas, Samar." Jack's voice, strong with a side of amusement.

From in front, "Did you drop something?"

Eyes up on the mailroom guy. "A button, I thought." She patted her shirtfront. "No, no. It's fine." She stepped around the trolley and went to the break room, face hot and blood hotter.

When she got back to her desk there was a text from Jack. You're the headline in my heart.

She responded, Derelie Loves Jack. Verily, merrily. No clickbait. She put hearts at both ends of the phrases.

He came back with, Sub head: Jack Can't Believe His Luck.

And then she got an email from Phil. See me.

She knew her way to Phil's office well now. Knew to wait in his doorway until he motioned for her to enter. Knew not to bother sitting in one of his guest chairs because it was more efficient not to.

He motioned; she stepped inside his glass-walled office. "Do the love story with Artie Chan."

"Ah, okay. I almost have it with Jack." Almost, nearly, maybe. She grimaced. They were words she'd tried to eliminate from her vocabulary when dealing with Phil, because they were hesitant and cautious, and the only word Phil wanted to hear was *yes* and its variations—got it, exclusive, most clickable.

Phil looked up from his screen. He didn't look annoyed. "I should never have pushed Haley on that. It was a dick move. Don't bother him about it. I'm sorry I wasted your time. Start again with Artie. Get video. Get marketing involved."

The signal to noise ratio in what Phil, a man of as few words as possible, said, fixed her to the spot in close to the same way she'd been a magnet stuck on Jack in the corridor. "Did you—?"

"Yeah, don't get used to it. Apologies give me gas."

"I'll do the love experiment with Artie."

"And don't…" Phil made a crude gesture for what he didn't want her doing with Artie. "Now get out."

Phil was never going to be her favorite person, but he'd given her a chance and there was no malice behind his brusqueness. She knew who he was now, a big old porch dog, lots of bark, would growl at you if you got out of line, best left alone to do what he enjoyed, snooze in the sun, only Phil's version of snoozing was putting out a daily newspaper. If you respected him, waited for the right moment, he'd roll over and let you pat his belly, and so long as you didn't sleep with him, he'd be as loyal a friend as you could ever need.

And despite her affection for Martha, Derelie had always been a dog person.

Chapter Twenty-Four

Walt Disney was fired from a newspaper for lacking imagination. Henry Ford went broke trying to sell cars. Van Gogh only sold one painting during his lifetime. Albert Einstein was a miserable student, but famous for his genius.

Bob Bix would become infamous overnight for ripping off millions of honest American accident victims when Jack's story ran.

Two hours before press time, Sunday night, and Roscoe couldn't stop grinning. "Keepsafe will still come at us, but we're ready. Eh, it'll mostly be posturing." He rubbed his hands together. Legal posturing was *Friday Night Football* for Roscoe. "You have the whole money trail direct to Bix's own pocket. He'll be jobless by lunchtime."

"We'll need the next day's follow-up story, and what do we do about your source?" asked Madden. "Is he profile potential?"

Henri Costa had a rough week since that last meet up. His supervisor discovered the same statistical problem Henri had first picked up on and brought to Jack, but instead of being in Bix's pocket and a threat as

Henri feared, he'd enabled Henri to get access to the information Jack needed. All Henri wanted now was his old, secure, not very exciting job in a company that treated policyholders fairly.

"No. He's keen to stick to his anonymity." Madden grunted, and Jack understood why; whistleblower stories made good copy. "But we've got a dozen juicy case studies with victims that will make Bix and his cronies look like the pieces of shit they are."

"Right, we're done then." Madden pointed at Jack. "Get some sleep, you've got a long day Monday."

Another one, but this time he'd be telling the story, not working on it. Breakfast radio, newsbreaks during the day and a TV spot in the evening.

"The case studies are Berkelow's work." He wanted to make sure she got credit for her contribution.

Madden acknowledged that with a nod, and ten minutes later Jack was on the street making his way home. He needed to iron a week's worth of shirts. He needed to drop into bed and not fall asleep while Derelie was talking to him. He was still unsure what he'd done to earn her forgiveness and acceptance. It gave him emotional vertigo every time she said she loved him, and she'd said it often since the night he'd been foul with her, but instead of being reassuring, it made him uncomfortable, like he was part of an experiment that could only end in creating a disease, not finding a cure.

He was tired; that was all it was. Focused. Had to be. There'd be time after the story ran to talk it through.

Martha was full of complaints when he eased in the door, standing on her hind legs to paw at him, but there was food in her bowl and fresh water, plus clean litter, so what was her deal? Apart from being left in the apartment alone.

He chucked her under the chin. "Life not going your way, huh?"

If she could understand more than his tone of voice and roll her eyes, she would've. Instead she dug a claw into his thigh, and like any half-decent assault and battery artist, she bolted to the other side of the room with revenge and blood on her paws.

He swatted at the sting. "Take it up with your lawyer."

That's when he saw the note taped to one of his screens. Derelie had gone to catch a late yoga class, and since he didn't tell her what time he expected to be home that was nothing to be concerned by. Except he felt her not being here was a gap, an activity not ticked off on his to do list, a detail forgotten, a point not expanded on. She'd created a hearth outside work he'd never truly known before.

He stood in his apartment and noted the changes in it since she'd arrived with stolen property and her determination to get the story of him. It was tidy, for one thing. Work was confined to his desk and his bookcase instead of being spread everywhere.

Every surface in the kitchen was functioning as a kitchen, not an extension of his workplace. His doing. There were flowers on the table by the door, cheap and cheerful, there was a pot of something that smelled piney in the bathroom where there was an extra toothbrush in the holder and assorted girl things. Her doing. The ironing board was behind a door, there was a bright throw rug that didn't belong to him over the back of the couch and a pillow that matched it. He'd never have bought a throw rug or a pillow. He'd never have cleaned up for himself, but because she was there, it was the obvious thing to do—make it a home, not a destination he used to do more of what he did in the office: to sleep, eat, wash and leave a cat.

Who'd have guessed thirty-six questions would lead to a different angle on life?

Derelie arrived while he was starching collars and cuffs. He made a grab for Martha before she could go for the door.

"Hello, Heartbeat of the City, Defender of the People," Derelie said, dropping her bag on the floor. She wore her yoga pants and a zip-up sweatshirt. Her hair was both damp and frizzy and her skin flushed, freckles standing out. She had chipped nail polish and a red breakout on her chin. She wore her aligner. She was head to toe wonderful. "It's nice to see you awake."

Martha paddled her paws, so he put her down and she flopped over at his feet in a pose Derelie called carpet. "Hello, Reporter of Stories People Love to Read. It's always nice to see you."

She raised a brow. "If the clickbait fits."

"I've come to accept that clickbait has its value." He meant her to understand that as an apology for his vicious clickbait crack the other night.

She put one sneaker-covered foot on its toe and rolled her knee inward, cocking her head to the side and bringing her shoulder up. Five-year-old girl. Unforgivably cute. "Aw, Dinkus, you say the sweetest things."

He wasn't thinking about being sweet in return.

She straightened. Nothing girlish about the predatory way she looked him over or the reaction it caused. Not a tired bone in his body now. "I'm all sweaty."

"I like you sweaty." He liked the salt tang in her skin, the earthy funk. He liked peeling her out of her tight pants.

"My mama taught me never to interrupt a man with a domestic appliance in his hand."

The iron was hissing and steaming on its stand; the hothouse was them, inspecting, inciting each other. He bent and jerked the power cord from the point in the wall. "I'm done."

She played with the tag on her zipper. "Are you propositioning me?"

"Inviting." On his way to instructing, invading, adoring. Sunday nights she always called her mom. "Phone home, ET." Family before pleasure.

She rumbled in her bag for her cell, fingers to the screen. "'Busy tonight. Having fun. Call you later. Smiley face.'" She tossed the cell on the couch and undid her zipper. "Busy with you. Having fun with you."

"I want to show you I'm sorry for the other night."

The zipper top hit the couch. Martha got up and went to sit on it. The tank Derelie wore underneath was sweat-stained. "I've got ironing you can do if you want to show me how sorry you are."

"I see—the way to your forgiveness is the application of domestic order."

"I like the way you say domestic order." She pulled her tank off and dropped it on the floor.

He didn't let her say anything much in English after that, kept her mouth busy and her body in motion and later, tangled in the sheet and dozing in his arms, she accepted his apology. Before he left in the morning, he checked the *Courier* website for the Keepsafe story and ironed two of her dresses, a shirt and a skirt to cement the deal.

It was nearly midday before he got through promotional responsibilities and made it into the office. An hour later while he was still clearing messages, the photographer he'd had on stakeout outside Keepsafe's headquarter got a shot of Bix exiting the building with a cardboard box. They were the first news site to run it, with a caption suggesting what the company's press release later confirmed.

As a result of the discovery of the criminal intent to defraud Keepsafe policyholders, the board had removed CEO Robert Bix from his role, suspended the services of a number of consultant doctors, naming Noakes and Whelan, and launched an internal investigation. The chairman promised to cooperate with the police and regulators and see all victims were compensated.

The press release didn't mention that it was Jack's story that landed Bix and his cardboard box on the sidewalk or that the *Courier*'s investigation was what would bring justice to all the families like the Shenkers. But it didn't have to. Syndicated, partner and rival media organizations were all talking about it. Jack had an email from the *Courier*'s owner congratulating him on the story, and he was ready to file the follow-up and go shave again so he was fit for evening television.

The next few days played out the same way. Another piece of the story would come to light and Jack would write it up and go talk about it on TV and radio. In the market one night with Derelie, he was approached by a man who insisted on shaking his hand. He was a Keepsafe policyholder and grateful for the exposé.

By the end of the week, there was nothing more to say about Keepsafe or Bob Bix, who'd been formally charged, and Jack was running on cloves, coffee and adrenaline when Madden called him up to Roscoe's office.

"Come in," Roscoe said. He wore a somber expression, which made Jack grimace. He could do without being sued again.

"How bad is it?"

"Sit down, Haley," said Madden.

That bad. "What are they saying?" He took a seat.

Roscoe came out from behind his desk to close the door. "That's not why we're here. Go on, Phil."

A lawyer, an editor-in-chief and an investigative reporter sit down in a room with a closed door... "What's going on?" There was a staff meeting in half an hour—whatever this was, it was going to go down quickly.

Madden stared at the pile of folders on Roscoe's desk. "We're shifting from broadsheet to tabloid and dropping the Saturday edition. We're going subscription on the website. That's what I'm telling people at five."

A heads-up. It accounted for the door, but not for Roscoe's presence. "What does that mean for the business pages?" Less space, more of a shift to running stories online.

"We didn't save enough money from the voluntary layoffs. I need to make more changes to staffing."

Goddamn, Madden was going to ask him to single out reporters who'd lose their jobs. He could do his own dirty work. "Don't ask me to—"

"The *Courier* isn't in the investigative reporting business any longer."

Jack would have laughed, but Roscoe wouldn't look at him and Madden's eye contact was bouncing around. "Any longer?"

"You no longer have a job here, Jack."

He let those words hit his chest, glance off. They didn't make sense.

"We'll do straight business news, companies reporting, but we don't have the resources for the big investigative stories anymore."

"Resources?" Why did he feel flatfooted, out of breath?

"It's not just your salary, it's the other expenses you need to do what you do. It's not the direction the owner wants the paper to take."

He was standing, body realizing the blow before his brain caught up with the impact. "You're firing me."

"Laying you off."

"You're doing this now, on top of Keepsafe?" On the back of his words and face and voice being everywhere for the *Courier* this week. After months of work to bring the paper a leading story he knew earned more from newsstands and sent webstats up, made money for the paper, built its credibility.

"I'm sorry, Jack. It wasn't an easy decision. I knew you'd start up on something else and we won't have the space for it." He had two new story leads in his messages, two potential Keepsafe stories in the making.

"This is about real estate."

"It's about the high cost of investigative reporting."

The legal costs. If he wasn't employed by the paper,

there was a chance he could be held personally liable. This would ruin him professionally, not to mention financially.

"You knew you were going to do this." It explained why Madden pushed the deadline so hard. He looked at Roscoe. "I need my own lawyer."

Roscoe motioned him to sit and it felt like defeat when he did. "It's a layoff, Jack, it's happening across the whole industry. You don't have an unfair dismissal case against the *Courier*."

"But Keepsafe can come after me personally."

Roscoe looked at Madden. "I'm talking to the owner about that."

"Which means what?"

"I don't know. I'm trying to convince them it's in their interest not to fuck you around."

He heard what Roscoe didn't say—*if you fight this dismissal, you're on your own with any suits*. Jesus Christ. "When?"

"Today," said Madden. "You get the usual severance and entitlements owing."

He earned enough to afford to rent his apartment, to live in the city, to have some savings, but that would mean nothing if he needed to fight Keepsafe, if he couldn't get another job. The last time another news organization had tried to poach him was years ago. No one was employing, the whole industry was in contraction. He was fucked and he hadn't seen it coming.

"I'm sorry, Jack. If I thought you'd want to stay on and write straight business news, I'd have offered it."

"But you can get a cadet do that, use more wire service syndicated news." Fill the *Courier* with infotainment, which was cheap to produce. His reporting career might be over; he could be washed up before he even hit middle age.

"It is what it is. I can't change what's happening to the industry."

Jack took his tobacco pack out of his suit pocket and rolled a smoke, and no one stopped him. "You're going to announce this with the other changes."

"Yes. I have a favor to ask of you."

After the insult, after the humiliation in a week that was built for triumph, Madden was going to ask him to front the staff meeting, to show he was taking his exit gracefully. He didn't need to be an investigative reporter—ex-investigative reporter—to know that. It was going to give him an ulcer.

He blew a stream of smoke over Madden's head. "You want me to be at the meeting."

"I want to give you a decent send-off."

He took another drag on the cigarette and then raised his brows at Roscoe, who'd produced a small silver ashtray, like the removable ones in cars. "My wife would kill me if she knew I still smoked," he said.

"Your wife already knows." Jack didn't have to be an ex-investigative reporter to know that.

He didn't have a lot of choice in this. If he skipped the staff meeting, he'd have to make his own announcement as he said goodbye to people. He didn't want to leave without wishing the remaining team well. He didn't like the idea of explaining this and dealing with the shock a dozen times, and Madden was banking on that, and on the fact it looked better for him to have Jack in the room as an ally when the hit landed.

"I'll be there. I'll be…nice." His only chance of getting another job in the industry might depend on how he was seen to react to this. No one wanted to employ an angry man.

Madden stood, as did Roscoe. Jack was last to his feet. He was weary to his sinews and synapses and his stomach was a bound fist. He'd planned to take Derelie to Elaine's as a surprise tonight, as a celebration. It'd be more like a wake.

A few minutes later, after a savagely uncomfortable elevator ride where no one spoke and or made eye contact, they were on the main floor, and Jack listened while Madden announced the *Courier*'s new direction and rang the bell on the end of his career with the paper. There were gasps. The stoic Berkelow cried. Spinoza was vocal in his disapproval and made Madden squirm. It took less than forty minutes from the time Roscoe closed his door to the applause that signaled Jack's redundancy.

In the sea of people milling around, some like the older reporters, stunned and concerned about the longevity of their own jobs, others blithely ignorant it could be them on unemployment next week, he looked for Derelie. The office divide between the mostly print and website reporters and the mostly online-only writers still existed, at least for now. She stood with her team, face creased with concern, eyes down. This was a win for her. It was her time to shine. She was in the right place, at the right time, and she didn't need to keep secrets anymore.

From all sides, his name was called. He only wanted to hear one voice.

"Excuse me a moment."

He had to ignore the press around him, honest expressions of outrage and shock, well-wishes, and offers to buy him a drink. He'd take those offers—he needed to get plastered. He pushed through the throng, fixed on the north star of Derelie, her own people hovering like satellites around her, the mood different on this side of the office, excitement and opportunity in orbit instead of gutted hopes and fear.

The satellites scattered in his wake and Derelie looked up, her lips pressing into a thin line balanced between anger and distress, her pale eyes a wet reflection of all his ambitions shaken loose and set adrift.

Chapter Twenty-Five

People parted like pins bowled over, eager to get out of Jack's roll across the office. No one sure what to say to him or why he was headed this way. He'd looked tired this morning; now his face was ashen, even while he moved with single-minded determination. Derelie ached to throw her arms around him and hug him if only to make herself feel better.

No doubt he'd come to formally say goodbye, to keep up appearances. No amount of ocean breaths helped. She needed to look away so she could school her features and act professionally, but it was impossible not to watch him advance on her as if she was the high score and he was gunning for her.

She'd looked for him over workstations and around shoulders and heads while Phil had been speaking, wondering if he'd interject, if he'd put up a fight for his beloved business pages. She thought she'd misheard when Phil said that as a result of the changes, the *Courier* would no longer have the space or resources for investigative reporting.

That's when a tangible ripple spread across the floor, sharp brains interpreting the news ahead of Phil's words. She'd already teared up before he announced that after an illustrious career and one hell of a week, Jack would be leaving. Phil said praiseworthy things about Jack, but they tumbled over her in a haze of confusion. How could the company do this to him? Use him for his talents so obviously and then discard him so blatantly?

Now he stood right in front of her, his chest rising and falling with obvious stress he was consciously controlling. "How are you feeling about secrets?" he said, voice strong despite how crushed he must feel.

"I, ah." What was he really asking? She hardly cared, took a step forward the same time as he did, conscious of the gasps of surprise around them and not giving a damn.

"Excellent." He put his hand behind her neck as she tilted her face up, hands going to his ribs. "You won't mind me doing this."

He touched his lips to hers, pulled back, smiled, and when she wrapped her arms around him, he angled his head and kissed her in a way there was no mistaking. They weren't colleagues dealing with bad news or workmates saying goodbye. Jack brought her closer and lifted her off the floor. They kissed like lovers in the middle of the *Courier*'s newsroom, making out while a whole floor of reporters watched.

And cheered like they were at Wrigley Field, eating wieners.

Jack lowered her to the floor and they broke off, foreheads pressed together, breathing erratic. The only thing that could make this more romantic would be if he carried her out of here.

"Want me to carry you out of here?"

"Dammit, you're going to make me cry and I have dry cleaning and my gym bag." This wasn't that scene from *An Officer and a Gentleman*, Mom's favorite movie. "Let's get out of here."

He released her and she fled to her desk. She heard him tell people to settle down, go back to work while they still had jobs, and half-blind with emotion, she ran straight into Eunice.

"You and Jack." Eunice was steamed. Derelie did a grimace, nod combination. "Jackson Haley, who you said was boring and what else I can't remember, but it wasn't 'I'm sucking face with the guy.' You lied."

"I, ah, omitted." A ten dollar word, felt so much less incriminating.

"You sucked face with him."

There really was no dodging this. "I plan to continue sucking face with him." Never mind other body parts.

"Duh." Eunice grabbed her shoulders. "That was so hot."

And now her life didn't need to revolve around a secret, but that privilege had come at Jack's expense. "I need to go."

"I need to do the love experiment," Eunice said, which was so "I'll have what's she's having," they both laughed.

Derelie looped her purse over her shoulder, picked up the dry cleaning and her gym bag, and made her way back to Jack. He was surrounded again, but only a slice of his attention was on the people around him. He held out a hand and then noted she had no easy way to take it. She was about to give him the gym bag so they each had a spare hand, but he bent and grasped her under her knees and to great shouts of surprise, he lifted her.

She wanted to hide her face in his neck like Debra Winger in her flannel shirt did to Richard Gere in his dress whites, and at the same time she wished she had her cell ready to record this. Mom would never believe it. Bags and baggage in her lap, arms around Jack's neck, she tuned the stares out as he carried her across the office, accepted his suit coat dumped in her lap by Annie and smiled at Spinoza, who held an elevator for them.

"Way to go," Spin said, which made her laugh. He'd echoed a line from the movie. "Expecting you at Donovan's. Kelly has opened a tab in Madden's name."

"We'll be there," Jack said.

Spin reached inside and pressed the ground floor button and the doors closed.

"You can put me down." It was peak elevator use time.

"I could." But Jack made no attempt to do it, and when the doors opened two floors later to admit people he stared them down and they stayed right where they were. The second time it stopped he said, "Next car," and Derelie was so choked up she had to do a Debra Winger and bury her face in his neck where his tense breathing was more apparent.

At street level, he did put her and her baggage down in a remote corner of the foyer where they could be undisturbed by the stream of people leaving the building. Derelie watched Jack try to keep it together by staying focused. He answered a call and spoke sparingly, another and thanked whoever it was for their concern. To a third he said, "I'm unemployed, like a lot of reporters. I have zero income, rent to make and a cat to feed." He let the next call go with the words "My father. Proof bad news travels fast. He can wait" and then he turned his ringer off.

"When did you know?" The thought that he'd known and kept this from her was a live fuse of fear sparking through her.

"It doesn't matter. I'm out."

She wanted to come at that question again, but now was not the time.

He turned his screen so she could see his social feed. "The official word is my skillset is not aligned with the *Courier*'s strategy going forward. Fucking corporate speak."

The next message that followed was Spin's:

Jackson Haley has been martyred for the crime of journalism.

That got a wry smile out of Jack, and they watched as a dozen more messages like that appeared. Meanwhile, his cell was blowing up, little envelopes and message counts multiplying on his screen: emails, texts, calls.

He closed his eyes, a hand to his forehead. "I have no idea how to respond."

He refreshed his feed and another series of messages appeared.

Jackson Haley's firing heralds dying days of serious journalism.

Who defends our city now? RIP Jack Haley's career.

Courier without Jackson Haley. Courier without truth in reporting.

Please won't somebody give Jack Haley a new job.

Jack Haley out. Journalism's death knell.

Courier dumps Jackson Haley to become more digitally focused.

Bob Bix would still be ripping off Americans without Jackson Haley. What now?

It was an outpouring of shock, anger and grief. Derelie recognized the social handles of colleagues, who were risking Phil's wrath by posting about their discontent. Annie tweeted:

Vale investigative reporting. No one did it like Jackson Haley.

Derelie touched Jack's arm. "Maybe you don't have to say anything."

He looked stunned as his cell continued to light up, not that it was all supportive. Amongst the messages of distress there were the victory cries.

Good decision by the Courier to exit scaremonger Jackson Haley.

The Courier steps up. No more of Haley's lies.

Doomsday reporter Haley out. City sighs with relief.

Jackson Haley on the scrapheap. Toss out the junk.

Haley is a prick. Great decision to shut him down.

To this last one Spin replied, May you never feel the prick of injustice. You're on your own now.

Jack shook his head, turned the phone off and slipped it in his pocket. "I never wanted to be the story." He reached for her and she went willingly into his arms. She didn't know if he simply wanted to go home or to join the others at Donovan's. She didn't know how best to support him except to stand by him. In the pocket of her jacket, her own cell had been vibrating like crazy, receiving some of the same feeds.

"What do you want to do now?"

"Get very drunk." He tipped her chin up. "Is that okay with you?"

It was better than him going to church and chasing a black eye or worse.

"I was going to take you to dinner tonight to celebrate." He dropped his arms from around her and heaved a breath. "Fuck." And that answered the question. He didn't know about this until today.

"We've got plenty of time for that." She opened her mouth to say more, but he was staring off into the distance, lost. She tugged his arm. "It's going to be okay, Jack. You'll get another job." Of course he would— he probably had offers already in his messages. This was awful, but nothing was going to keep Jack down. "Come on, let's get you drunk."

He gave a grunt of assent, and together they went out to the sidewalk and headed toward the bar. They got one block and a man in dark suit dodged in front of them. "Jackson Haley, I just heard. I'm appalled. I'd like to help." He handed Jack a card, said, "Call me," and walked on.

Jack stared at the card, an expression of disbelief. "Who was that?" she asked.

He handed her the card. "Ambulance chaser."

So not someone he knew, not a job offer. Kingston, Biddle, Alfredo and Low, Labor and Employment Law. "A lawyer came up to you on the street and handed you his card because he thinks he can help you."

"He can't." Jack took the card out of her hand, crushed it and pitched it toward a trashcan. It missed and the wave of passing footsteps blew it out onto the road, where a bus with his face on it ran over it.

"Jesus Christ," he said.

The bus sat there in traffic and Derelie willed it to move, to evaporate, to be taken by aliens, anything but sit there rumbling, mocking them. It was unfathomably hurtful that Jack would go from savior to needing to be saved in the space of a day. That this morning the *Courier* wanted his face everywhere and tonight they had no role for him to play.

She pressed her face into his arm. "I'm so sorry this is happening to you."

He looked at the bus long and hard while it spewed diesel fumes and half the city pushed around them. "I can be fucking grateful there'll be no more of that."

They didn't walk on till the bus passed, till Jack smoked a cigarette, and by the time they got to Dono-

van's Bar it was jammed with *Courier* employees who
let up a rowdy cheer when they came in. The whole
editorial team was here. So was Phil, sitting awkwardly
alone at the bar. Someone put a drink in Jack's hand.
Annie had packed Jack's desk and brought the contents
in a box and the irony of that, in the same week as Bix
and his sad box had been all over the *Courier*'s pages,
made Derelie want to take the contents of Jack's desk
and shove them one by one up Phil's ass. She hoped
there was a really enormous stapler in that damn box.

Monday morning she'd sit in an editorial meeting
with Phil and there'd be no Jack sitting opposite, studiously ignoring her. There'd be no Jack to flirt with
as the meeting ended or pass in corridors, hands grazing, eyes greedy and glancing. There'd be no Jack to
play wait five and follow with as she arrived at work,
and no one to check in with about what time she was
leaving for the night. There'd be no Jack, full stop, in
her work life and there was no way not to be deeply
saddened by that, or by what that meant for the profession she'd chosen as her own, for the paper she'd
moved across the state to work for.

She stood with Jack while Spin jumped on a chair
and led a rousing toast.

"This week two titans of the city lost their jobs.
One was a crook, a thief and a weasel. His name was
Bob Bix, and our own Jack Haley brought him down.
The other was a good guy, the best, a journalist and
a hero." There was a huge cheer, and Derelie tucked
herself under Jack's arm. Let everyone see what he
meant to her on the night where the celebration was
so bittersweet.

"Bix will go to prison. Jack will go on to defend the city for someone who appreciates what he does." Another cheer. "This is a sad day for the *Courier*, for journalism. I might only be a sports writer—" that got a chuckle "—and robots are already taking over parts of my job, but I can't help thinking this is a sad day for the whole city. Tomorrow, people are less protected from fraud, corruption, and here's a ten dollar word for you, malfeasance—it means doing wrong, you knuckleheads—than they were today." Spin raised his glass and the room followed. "To Jackson Haley, the Heartbeat of the City."

Jack dropped his chin, closed his eyes as the response rang out. His body was taut. Derelie could feel muscles flexing and shifting though he was standing still, not something the one drink he'd had helped.

"I have to say something," he said, and pulled away, going to the chair Spin stood on and replacing him.

It took a while for the applause and shouts of Jack's name to die down before he could speak. "It's true what they say, you don't know what you've got till it's gone. Spin might only write about athletes who've gotten their jockstraps in a twist, but he's right—journalism is changing; the rules, the way it's consumed, how we produce it. Anyone with a social feed can break a story. Facts are less important than emotion, and the news that's cheap to serve up is more entertaining than it is enlightening."

Someone heckled, "You won't believe how we used to write the news," aping a headline style that was popular online. There was laughter, but it wasn't a happy sound.

Jack went on. "We've entered the clickbait age and long-form, thought-provoking journalism is an endangered species. We're saying too long, didn't read. That made me a dinosaur even before today, but like the velociraptor, I didn't see it coming."

"Meteor takes out journalism, live at five!" another wit shouted. That got a hearty laugh, but it was black humor.

"I'm out, but you all have a job to do. Bring the city its news in the best, most comprehensive and engaging way you can. I may be off the payroll, but I'm not off the clock." He paused and the room held its breath. "I lost my job, but I won the love of a great journalist and wonderful woman."

He tipped his chin up to look for her in the crowd and smiled at the hoots and cheers. If he'd glimpsed her face he'd have seen it glistening with the tears she'd wanted to shed earlier. *I love you, Jack Haley, in your darkest hour, in the moment your dream died and your worst fear came true, I love you all the more.*

"I'll be reading you." Jack didn't have a glass, but one was passed to him and he raised it. "To writing the news."

There was a chorus of "To writing the news" as people bent their elbows to drink.

"Hear, Hear."

"To the news."

She wiped her face and looked around. She wasn't the only one to feel this moment as something bigger than what'd happened to Jack, but she was the only one who'd live closely with its consequences both at work and at home.

Before she could make her way to Jack, Eunice appeared at her side. "You need to check your cell."

"I saw some of the chatter on Jack's."

"You need to see this." Eunice shoved her own cell in front of Derelie's face and there it was, her *An Officer and a Gentleman* moment. Jack sweeping her off her feet in one slick move and stalking across the newsroom, as people scrambled to get out of his way or stood back applauding. She looked surprised and delighted, Jack looked strong and fierce; together they looked like true romance and whoever made this had captioned it *Swoon.*

"Oh my God." Yes, she knew everyone had seen this go down, it was really no surprise to learn there was video and that it was well shot, but it was wild to see it in replay, to know she could have her own copy to keep.

"That's not the OMG part." Eunice took her cell back and switched apps, turned the screen so Derelie could see. "You're trending."

"Oh."

"You and Jack are a meme."

"My."

"You made the evening TV news."

"God."

"Nine months from now Derelie will be the most popular baby name for girls."

"No!"

Eunice laughed. "Your five minutes of fame have arrived."

Her face was on fire. "My mom will have seen this." Everyone back home would be talking about it.

"That's what you're worried about?"

"Apart from Jack—" and how drunk he might get tonight and how angry he might be tomorrow "—what should I be worried about?"

"What our editor-in-chief wants to do with it."

Now her issue was less about getting to Jack than getting to Phil. She thanked Eunice and made her way to the bar where she'd last seen Phil. He was still there, beer in front of him, drinking with his back to a room full of people who worked for him and didn't want to acknowledge him. It had to have taken courage to show up. She slipped onto the stool beside him. This was where she and Jack had first tried to get to know each other, two bar stools, a questionnaire. Nothing about that awkward, stilted exchange, where she'd almost kneed him in the manhood, would've lead her to believe they'd be a viral feel-good news story now.

Phil glanced at her when she sat down. "You did get the story." Not the way anyone had envisaged. She shrugged and he laughed into his beer. "A fucking love experiment and it worked."

She needed to say what she came over here for. "You can't use the video."

"Two of the *Courier*'s employees, filmed on the paper's premises. I told you to get visuals. I think I can use it."

"Jack wasn't a *Courier* employee when it was filmed and I don't give my permission." It wasn't a strong argument. It would take more effort than she knew how to muster to remove that footage from the internet. It was public property now, but it wasn't the way Jack would want to be remembered.

Phil checked her over. "Tougher than you look, Honeywell."

"What exactly is tough meant to look like?" Like Jack's source who'd acted to right a wrong, despite being afraid, like Phil's booming porch dog bark, like Jack standing on a chair trying to help others make sense of what had happened to him. Surely tough came in a variety pack to account for all the ways life could beat you down and force you to get back up again. Sick, disadvantaged, disabled, minority, poor. Sometimes tough was fighting for justice, sometimes it was trying to live a bigger life, sometimes it was getting out of bed in the morning.

"Right now it looks like my most junior section editor ready to fight me for what she believes in."

She'd take that.

"We won't run the tape, but I still want the story."

"I can't write it without Jack." And Jack's last story for the *Courier* wasn't going to be something he never wanted to do.

"Sure you can, you're tough. You'll find a way." Her way would be to write the story with Artie Chan like they'd agreed and then sell it to Phil as his only option and double-dare him to fire her for it.

"Why, Phil?" He knew she wasn't asking why he wanted the story.

"The work Jack does is complex, takes time, and it's bitterly contested by the people accused. The *Courier* doesn't have the budget for that anymore. There are only a handful of media companies that do. This wasn't personal, and I agree with Jack and Spin and everyone here, it's a sad day for journalism. And the timing fucking sucked. Just don't you go telling anyone I said that."

Courageous of him to admit that. "I kinda hate you right now." And kind of respected him too.

Phil turned back to face the bottles lining the bar. "I kinda hate me too."

But the man she loved was standing behind her frowning. She swiveled her stool and he put a hand to her shoulder and stopped her knees with his thigh. Had someone shown him the video?

He bent so he could whisper in her ear. "Is Madden bothering you?"

She brought her hand to his face. "Not anymore."

"I'm sorry about the video. I wasn't thinking clearly."

She stood and he was so close she was pressed against him. "I'm not." He shook his head. She drew a heart over his heart and ran an arrow through it. "Jack loves Derelie." And he'd declared it for all to see.

He caught her hand in his. "Jack should've asked if Derelie wanted that kind of attention. Jack knows better."

"Jack had other things on his mind."

He kissed the back of her hand. "Still."

"Still want to get drunk?"

A quick headshake. "I'd like to find a back exit and leave quickly without a fuss."

There was no back entrance and they didn't get out of there quickly, and there was a fuss. Too many people who wanted to wish Jack well, to laugh about the video and pledge to stay in touch. He spent a few minutes with Phil and they shook hands. The contents of his box—mostly books, no stapler—went in her gym bag, and eventually they made it out to the sidewalk.

The city was breathing easier now, less people around, traffic moving freely. Derelie answered a text from Mom, one of dozens clogging her inbox, with a yes, that did happen, and a promise to call later, and then she took Jack's hand as they walked home and tried to be what he needed when he'd lost the thing that he cared about the most.

Chapter Twenty-Six

Jack got drunk on slowly heating rage and a cold six-pack on his own couch, staring at the TV and not seeing it. Derelie hung in there with him, but Martha had a better sense of his mood and cleared out, going to the bedroom and not reappearing.

Holding back his anger and taking the high road in public had seemed like the smart thing to do, but he was all out of fucks about appearances now. When Derelie quit on him and went to bed, he stayed where he was, hot discomfort in his body, jangled thoughts that wouldn't line up in any direction but shot off down contradictory side alleys.

He'd get a new job quickly. He wouldn't find a role anything like what he'd had. They didn't exist anymore. The *Courier* would give him sterling recommendations. Being fired by the *Courier* would scare anyone else off employing him. Particularly if he was trailing legal trouble. He was going to need more beer, more everything alcoholic and more cigarette papers. Everything would be fine because this was a watershed moment. He'd look back and realize it was a jumping off point for something better, like a shift to television.

What was this crap he was watching, some superhero shit? Superheroes didn't wear capes, they were average people like Henri Costa.

This was the end of his career, and if he wanted to keep living in the city he'd need to take the first job that came along. He could learn to write more entertaining stories. He'd rather lose a hand than write lifestyle. Most digital newsrooms wouldn't know what to do with him. He didn't have enough savings; he should've tried for a bigger-paying TV gig years ago. This was just the push he needed. He'd have to give up the apartment in a month, two, three at the most. Much as it would be humiliating, his parents would loan him money. He'd never ask them for money. He'd never give them the satisfaction.

He should go to bed, but he wasn't tired. He lit a smoke, ashed in an empty bottle. Derelie believed in him, she loved him. Derelie loved Jackson Haley, investigative reporter, but when he was Jackson Haley on unemployment, she wouldn't love him half as much and he wouldn't deserve her love. Her career was taking off and his was over. A has-been. Part of the way things used to be in a world that valued distraction more than truth. He'd drag her down and she was nobody's footnote.

She'd leave him.

She'd be right to leave him.

He should let her go before what they'd had was poisoned.

He couldn't get his thoughts to line up in any rational order, so he drank, smoked and seethed until he was tired enough to sleep, and when he woke there was a pillow under his head and a bright throw rug over his legs and the stench of eggs cooking that made him gag.

Derelie stood over him with a glass of green evil in her hand. "Hangover cure."

He rubbed his eyes. His glasses were somewhere. "What's in it?"

"My dad's patented recipe, best you don't know."

He drank it, as foul tasting as it was smelling, and then stumbled to the bathroom to shower. He couldn't eat the food she plated; his stomach too unsettled. He gave monosyllabic answers to her cheery questions. The more she cared, the more he got annoyed by her unfailing calm until he was disgusted with himself.

While Derelie puttered around the kitchen he sat at his desk and returned his father's call. His mood was dark enough for it.

There was a windy static sound. Dad was on the golf course. He switched to speaker to try to hear better. "What happened, Jack? You pissed off the wrong person?"

The whole industry was pissed off. "Victim of disruption." Which was the truth, but it didn't help his situation.

"What are you going to do?"

"Get a new job."

"I'd have thought you'd use this opportunity to change direction before you're too old to catch up. I don't know if that's even possible now."

"You know, the robots are coming for surgeons too."

"Always with a line. Glib and smug, Jack. I'd hoped you'd turn out a better man."

"You've made that consistently clear."

"A child choosing the wrong friends is one thing. A man choosing to squander his life and talents on spurious pursuits is unforgivable."

He rubbed his forehead. "What did you want, Dad?"

"Are you drinking?"

"Suffering."

"Doping?"

"No."

"Still smoking, I imagine."

"I'm a lost cause."

"Are you suicidal?"

He almost laughed. If he was, last person he'd tell was his father. "No."

There were voices. "It's my tee time. Whatever you're going to do, don't wallow."

The connection went dead and Jack tossed his phone on the desk and pressed his knuckles into a throbbing spot over his left eye. He'd have to live through a similar conversation with his mother. It was possible she'd be less sympathetic but at least she'd be pleased the vulgar billboards would come down.

"That didn't sound good?" Derelie said tentatively, coming into the room.

"About as well as I expected." Careless to let her to hear that.

She put her hands to his shoulders, a gentle touch, as if she feared rejection. She had good instincts.

"Fun is not an efficient use of Dad's time."

"My dad would take you to Barrow's Bar and drink with you till you both felt sick and then take you camping till you could no longer stand how bad you both smelled. It's his remedy for any trouble."

"I like his style."

She nuzzled the top of his head. "Can I do anything for you that doesn't involve making you feel sicker?"

He gave one of her hands a squeeze. "Go out, go shopping, go do whatever it was you used to do. I'm not fit to be around."

It was a relief when she cleared out. He tried to sleep and couldn't. Spent the rest of the morning at his desk, with Martha at his feet, responding to messages, meeting outrage with pragmatism and being worn down by the need to put on a good show, and smoking, numbing his tongue, not caring that it stank up the apartment, teetering between giddy hope and dizzy despair. The only clarity was knowing he needed to get on top of this while he was being talked about, hit on every potential employer he could think of and make them a proposition they couldn't refuse, including two new exposés he could deliver.

That's how the day passed. Derelie dragged him out to a picnic on Sunday and made it impossible for him to brood.

"It's okay," she said, when he snapped at her for no good reason. "I know you're not angry with me."

"It's not okay." There was supposed to be more to that sentence. A supporting clause. He just didn't have it. All that came out of his mouth was smoky cloves. It was as if all the words he knew how to manufacture for a blank page in clear type, or a half a dozen minutes of airtime had dried up.

All he could do was murmur his apology and accept the grace of her kisses.

Monday morning, he wandered around the apartment, missing Derelie, not able to settle, confusing Martha, who kept waiting by his desk with a look that said "what's going on, slacker, get to work." In the afternoon, he made phone call after phone call, failing to get through to Roscoe to get clarity on whether the *Courier* would support him in legal action, setting up coffee dates and drinks and filling his week with meetings. It felt like business as usual on Tuesday—he shaved, put on a suit, left home with Derelie and went to work on finding work.

It wasn't until Friday that he let his lack of success get to him. Roscoe was dodging his calls and letting his emails go unanswered. At every meeting, he heard outrage, concern and support, but no one was hiring, at least in Chicago. The one job that was available was a corporate position. He'd write press releases and case studies for a construction company's website, and prepare presentations and annual shareholder statements. The role paid less than what he'd earned at the *Courier* and it was the kind of work that would rust his brain and drain his will to live. There were better qualified candidates already on the shortlist.

But it was either that or look for work in other cities.

He needed to talk to Derelie about it. He'd have to find words.

He stood in front of the cat food at the market and checked prices for the first time. Derelie had moved on with the cart. Martha might need to go on a diet, less sashimi broth and more three for five dollar fish deals.

Out on the street, it was chilly and the wind was dirty and hard, tugging at his glasses, getting into

Derelie's hair and yanking pieces of it out of her twist. They were almost home when it happened.

A man shouted his name, a hand stopped his shoulder, a fist caught him on the jaw, snapping his head back. Jack dropped the groceries to defend himself, taking another punch that knocked his glasses off and blocking a third with his forearm. People scurried around them and Derelie shrieked, "Stop, stop!"

His assailant came at him again. Heavier, angrier. "You shit, Haley. You shit."

"Hit me again, I'll put you on the ground." The guy swung and Jack dodged, caught his fist and spun him, forcing his bent arm up his back. "Whatever you think I did to you wasn't intentional."

"Keepsafe. She'll never leave me now."

The guy struggled, but Jack kept him pinned. "What?"

"My fucking slut of a wife was finally going to leave me, but now I'm getting a payout, she'll never go. She'll want half of it, you shit, you fucking shit."

Jack let go abruptly and pushed the man. "Stay away from me." Even when he won justice it was wrong by some people. Thinking the episode done, he made the mistake of looking for Derelie, because the guy went for her.

"He hurt me, I'll hurt you!" the man screamed, lunging toward Derelie.

Jack got there first blocking him, shielding Derelie, getting his hands to the man's shoulders and shoving him hard enough he stumbled and went down on the sidewalk. He got up quickly and shaped up again, but suddenly aware of the crowd that'd gathered he turned and ran off.

Derelie's hands were on Jack's back, her face pressed into his shoulders. He could feel her shaking. "It's over. You're safe." He moved to take her into his arms. All the wind-whipped color in her face had fled and her eyes were large with shock.

She put her hands over her face and stifled a sob. Their groceries were all over the sidewalk: eggs broken, fruit bruised, vegetables trampled, but it was Derelie he was worried about. Her safety was compromised because she was with him.

"It's over, baby. He's gone." He wrapped his arms around her and felt her shuddering sigh before her hands were everywhere.

"He hit you." She took his chin and moved his head. She smoothed a hand over his jaw. "A stranger on the street hit you."

He caught her hands. "I'm fine, but the bastard smashed my glasses and trashed our groceries."

"Over Keepsafe, because his wife wasn't going to leave him. That's unbelievable. Oh, Jack." She was shaking, but not from fear—she was furious.

That night in bed, Derelie clung to him as if she was broken, as if the violence had undone her affair with the city in a way that was permanently damaging. He should've done a better job of comforting her, but he didn't trust the promises he could make would be what she'd need to hear. He no longer had anything to offer her. He had no control over how people reacted to his public profile. No job, no money, no place in a city that'd taken everything he had to give and thrown it in his face. He couldn't even prevent her from being attacked for being at his side.

A week later his precarious future began a death spiral. He interviewed poorly for the corporate job. Not enthusiastic enough about the role, the recruiter said. He also had a letter from Keepsafe's lawyers notifying him of their intention to sue, and still no response from Roscoe.

Derelie compounded his problems by announcing she was letting her apartment go.

She said it casually, as if it was nothing, while she dangled a shoelace for Martha to play with. "I'm almost all here anyway."

"You can't."

She took her eyes off Martha and got claws in her hand. "Ouch, Martha, no fair."

"We can't both be homeless."

She swabbed her hand with a tissue. "What do you mean?"

"I can't keep this place."

"I'll share the rent, that's no problem."

It would help, but it wasn't the point. "Derelie, I can't hold on to this place without an income."

She came to sit beside him on the couch. "Okay, so we find something cheaper a little farther out that works for both of us."

Farther out was New York, Los Angeles, Philly, Dallas, Frisco, Washington, Atlanta, anywhere he might find another reporting job. "I'm going to have to look for work in other cities."

"Other cities. Oh." She took that in. Her hand would be stinging, three torn blood lines decorating it. "I've never lived anywhere outside of the state. It would be a new adventure."

"You'd leave the *Courier* to follow me?"

She blinked; it was the tiniest moment of hesitation, but it was everything.

He stood, needing a little distance from her, because now that they were here, it was time to stop deluding himself, time to recognize the fight for what it was and up the violence. "Don't give up your place."

"We work this out together, Jack. You and me, we're together."

They were together because of an experiment and all the conditions for success had changed. If they stayed together they'd be a new experiment. One where they had no jobs, no home, no financial security. One where Derelie's life was compromised because Jack's had been beaten to a pulp in a street fight and there was no guarantee he'd recover. She would see it and she would leave him, but not until her faith in him ground her down to nothing.

There was only one humane way to do this. Quickly.

"We can't be together anymore."

"It makes sense that you get settled first. We could both squeeze into my shoebox for a while."

"Honeywell, we're done."

She reacted to the way he used her name, eyes narrowing. "What are you doing, Haley?"

"I'm calling this over."

"What do you mean by over?"

"It's a two dollar word."

"No, no, no, no." She stood and flung her hand out, the surprise of that sending Martha jogging into the bedroom. "You don't get to push me away because you've had a setback."

"It's not a setback." It was a natural disaster. "I don't know how long it's going to take to find another job. I don't know where I'll need to move to. Keepsafe is suing me for reputation damage. If the *Courier* doesn't support me, they will have me in court for years, no employer is going to want to touch me, and I'll be bankrupt with legal fees. Meanwhile, you get attacked in the street for the crime of being with me."

"But we'll work it out."

"There's no we."

"But—"

"You're not in Orderly now." Derelie flinched, but it didn't stop him. "Life isn't neat and things don't just work out because you want them to." Thousands of Keepsafe victims almost didn't get justice.

"And all that adds up to you not loving me anymore."

It was because he loved her. "Your career is only just taking off. You need to stay at the *Courier* and cement it. You don't need me."

"You think I value my career ahead of you?"

"You should."

"Because you value yours ahead of me."

This was his moment to hesitate. He saw it, like he could see a punch coming through an opponent's change of weight. A woman choosing to squander her life and talents by tying herself to deadweight was unforgivable. And he couldn't let Derelie make that mistake.

"Yes." It was a lie because the chances of rebuilding his career were slim, and because he loved this woman with tears glittering in her pale, otherworldly eyes, with a generous heart he was willfully breaking.

She backed up, shaking her head.

"You've always known that about me. You knew it before you ever asked me a question, before you wanted me to kiss you. My job is who I am. I live to chase a story. My first love is a great headline. My identity is in my dinkus."

"No, Jack, no. That's an excuse. That's you pushing me away because you're having a hard time right now. Because you've never had people to stand by you."

He didn't want her standing by to watch him flail, be defeated. She would leave in increments, a thousand cuts, it was better to concentrate on one fatal wound. "It's me telling you we're over."

"You love me. I know you do."

Some truths he would always defend, and this was one of them. "I love you. I always will."

Her shoulders sagged with relief. "Then we—"

"It's not enough."

"Loving you is first for me. It's top of the tree, that bright star to the left of loving my family. Everything else comes second."

There was a moment in every fight where you knew you could turn it, deliver a crushing blow, win. This was the moment of no return for him and Derelie. The love experiment was bad science. A manipulation that didn't allow for changing circumstances. There was no happy ending here.

"Not for me."

She backed up again and sat. Her hands shook and her face contorted, but she would not give in to sobbing in front of him. He stayed where he was half a room away, a whole different lifetime only glimpsed, now exploded into sharp pieces of pain, regret and loneliness. Before Derelie he didn't know agony like this existed.

She put her hand on the throw rug, bunched at the end of the couch. "You want me to leave?" She'd take the concept of home with her.

"It's better that way."

She watched him, closely enough to see his self-inflicted injuries. "There are so many things I can fight you over, but not letting me love you enough isn't one of them. What will you do?"

Hope his heart continued to pump, hope his chest didn't cave in and his knees held him upright. "Work the phones. Hit the road."

"What about Martha?"

He'd have to give her up too, at least until he found a place to land. "Would you take her for me?"

Derelie glanced toward the bedroom, to where only this morning they'd woken, legs tangled, lips following. She stood, cutting though skin, tissue, muscle, bone when she turned her eyes on him. "I'm sorry, Jack. I'm a dog person."

"We'd never have made it," he said, hands reaching behind him for the edge of his desk, his forced humor as destructive to him as her cool acceptance.

"Just as well we broke up. I'll pack a bag. Let me know when you're going to be out and I'll come back for the rest of my stuff and leave my key."

This was how it had to be.

She went to the bathroom, then the bedroom, and he followed her movements through the sound of her opening and closing drawers and closet doors, a zipper, a clip, the sound of a suitcase wheel on his hardwood floor.

She rebuffed his help. She worked efficiently, calmly, and in no time packed most of her stuff to go and rolled her case over to the door.

He shut Martha in the bedroom. "Let me carry that downstairs for you."

She kept her back to him, hand to the door handle. "I'll take the elevator."

"I'll walk you out." He wanted one last look at her face, one last chance to hold her.

"Please don't do that." Her voice shook, her breathing was messed up.

Ah fuck. "Derelie."

"I have one last question."

Martha pawed the bedroom door. Questions were the beginning of them. Fitting a question ended them. "Anything."

"Was it real, you and me, us, being in love, or did you just get carried away by the moment and decide to sweep me off my feet for the headline?"

It was the challenge of her, the depth, the quick sweet intimacy and the promise of what they could've become had things been different.

"It was real, but things have changed."

Martha switched from pawing to heaving her body against the door. Derelie turned the front door handle and tipped her bag onto its wheels. "The only thing that's changed is that I discovered you're a coward."

She rolled her bag into the corridor at the same time as Martha forced the bedroom door open and shot toward freedom. Jack grabbed one back leg, earning an angry yowl, and swept Martha into his arms.

When he looked up, Derelie was pulling the door closed behind her. "Goodbye, Jack. Good luck finding what you're looking for."

He didn't find it in the ball of frustrated fur in his arms, or at his desk, or in the number of calls he made and emails he sent. He didn't find it in bed, where he had trouble sleeping alone, or the bottles he tried to drown himself in. Martha sensed his self-destructive mood and stayed clear of him. He flew out to New York and did a round of coffee meetings and planned the same for Washington, but with the suit hanging over his head, he was too hot to touch.

He'd had an email from Roscoe with a curt I'll get back to you when I know something. Madden said he had nothing to add. Jack couldn't wait much longer to find his own legal counsel.

He hung out a writer-for-hire shingle, built a website and found its contact page flooded with spam and conspiracy theorists who wanted him to donate his time to their particular search for justice. For the want of a way to get paid, he could write about secret societies in control of the world, cults who could predict the end of the world, or shape-shifting extraterrestrial reptilian humanoids who wanted to eat the world.

He read Derelie's daily stories and saw the future of journalism in her words. He watched their Swoon video on endless loop like it would help him make sense of his life. The wonder in her smile, the laughter in her eyes. He remembered Barney's images as well. In them he was the alien. A different man who looked at ease. Then after his longest absence from the Church of the Cocked Fist, he requested a fight and got put on the schedule.

"Thought I'd see you sooner than this, Haley," Barney said, when he arrived. "A month since you lost that job. Why now?"

"Does it matter?" It always mattered to Barney, and it wasn't about losing his job. "I lost her."

"Put her down and don't know where? Not likely. She left you? No." Barney laughed. "You pushed her out."

Jack looked around the old garage. It was buzzing with men juiced up on adrenaline, looking for action, resolution, momentary oblivion. "I just want a fight." To be in a place he could use his anger and not have to be careful about it. "I did it for her."

"In my admittedly limited experience, women do not like it when men make decisions for them."

"My life is unraveling, Barney. I'm being sued. The *Courier* is dodging responsibility; no other media company is going to employ me while that's a factor. I can freelance, but it's not going to keep me afloat. I'm the wrong fit for a corporate job, don't have the right attitude, and in another month, I'll need to get out of the city. Her career is just starting to take off. Why would I want to drag her though all of my muck?"

"Maybe because she loved you."

He shook his head. "No." Love needed sunlight, fresh air and birdsong. The part of him that wasn't built from congealed anger and frustration was constructed of regret over Derelie, but not because he'd made her leave, because making her leave had been essential. "This shit storm would kill anyone's love."

"Never took you for a coward."

Barney could call it whatever he wanted. Derelie had tried to goad him with the same insult. He'd have been a coward to hold on to her and drag her down, wreck her own chances to star.

"I'm here to fight."

"Your whole life is a fight, Haley. You need to learn how to ask for help."

"You want me to quit?"

"That would be your problem. Everything through the frame of right and wrong, winners and losers. You're all black or all white and you don't see the gray."

"I see it. I don't like it." The cruelty, treachery and falsehood that hid in the gray zone could be more deadly than the evil you could see clearly. He'd spent his career going after the shadows and hitting them with a spotlight.

"It's in the gray, that's where you find real love. In the spaces between whatever shit storm passes for life. It's easy to be in love when it's sunny. It's easy to abandon it when it's thundering. What's not easy is holding on to it through the ordinary times in between. You had that with your girl. She had that with you. You're dumb as a sack of dicks if you don't know it, and I don't know if I'm going to give you a fight."

What the old priest knew about love was warped by religion and distorted again by how his church betrayed him. "I'm on the schedule."

"My schedule, my rules. Your stubborn heart gets to fight when I say so."

"You know I can go stand on Michigan Avenue and get hit without trying." Pick a more dangerous suburb like Chatham or Gage Park and that was more certain.

"I know it."

"So put me in the pit where it's safer."

"What's the fucking lesson?"

"Resilience." He'd need it to get to the other side of this mess.

Barney gave him a once-over and walked away without a comment.

Jack didn't get a fight that night or the next, and all that served to do was make him lose hold of his temper. He'd have taken on a brick wall bare knuckled and not cared about the damage to his hands. He thought about Ryan and Alvarez and all the men he'd been in the pit with, all the lessons he'd learned: kindness, patience, humility, generosity. They meant nothing.

On the third night, he confronted Barney. "What the fuck do you want from me?"

Barney left off tying another fighter's laces and motioned to an assistant to take over. "Not about what I want."

"Christ, then put me in the pit."

"No one gets to hit anyone without knowing why they want to do it."

"You won't like anything I have to say." He hadn't so far, and Jack had tried a variety of lessons out on the ex-priest.

"Stalemate then." Barney turned away.

"I am full of rage I can't put anywhere." That made the other man stop, but not turn to face Jack. "I want to hurt someone. I want them to hurt me. I'm already hurt.

I gave everything I had to give and it wasn't enough. I don't have a place in the world anymore. I'm numb, paralyzed. I want to be fury, let it burn through me so I can feel something again."

Barney didn't walk away. Derelie only walked away because he gave her no choice. She'd stood by him till he failed her by insulting her generosity, cutting her out, rejecting a chance with her to be a bystander in his own crumbling life. He couldn't be at the church without thinking about her, look into the pit without remembering what they'd done together there—laughed, learned each other, loved.

"I should never have told her to go. I should've been more careful with her. I love her. I can barely function without thinking of her. She taught me to want a life outside of the one I've been living, but I know I've done the best thing for her. I want her back and I can't have her, I miss her when I breathe and I'm dead inside."

"You keep talking, Haley." Barney turned, yanked on the towel around his neck. "Because finally you're making sense."

"She is not in the gray. She is the light and she's bright enough for both of us, but I didn't understand that. I thought it was a trick with mirrors, a party favor, bad freaking science, not something that was real enough to last. I didn't believe enough in her, in us, so I quit on her. I quit. The only mystery I've ever quit on was the one person who saw through me."

"What's your lesson, Jack?"

It was a confession and a prayer. "Accepting love."

He got his fight, with an opponent bigger, meaner, and owning his anger, when it was too late to have discovered it wasn't what he wanted. And he got hurt—a cut cheek, a smashed nose that was close enough to broken to call it that, both his eyes would be black. He hurt back, wildly, brutally, and the fight didn't end till he was on his knees unable to stand without help. He wouldn't make this mistake again. He'd fight for what was most important.

Barney came to him as he was cleaning up. "I want to talk to you about work."

He popped a couple of ibuprofen and washed them down with water. "Go ahead."

"Freelance. How does that go?"

"I come up with a story—" dear God, his face hurt "—and try to sell it into a newsroom."

"They buy it, so that's how you get paid."

"That's right. The issue is writing something they want to buy."

"What if someone else was willing to pay you for writing stories the papers didn't want to publish? What if you were the publisher?"

"You're talking about a sponsor."

"More like a benefactor."

Privately funded journalism. He'd heard of it. There weren't a lot of writers doing it. "What are you thinking?"

"That there's a way to keep you in Chicago and pay you to do what you do."

Jack worked his jaw. "The work I do is risky, complex, and not even the big media companies have an appetite for the trouble it can cause, legal trouble."

"Yeah, but I got that covered too."

"You've got it covered? A broke-down old priest who runs a shady fight club?"

Barney laughed. "A broke-down old priest who's fucking well enough connected in this city to front a high-profile group of concerned citizens, men and women in business and the law, in government and industry, who know the value of the truth, believe in social justice and are prepared to pay for it. We never forgot what you did for the church, shined a light on the foulness and forced things to change. This city needs what you do, Jack, and there are enough of us who think so to put you back to work and keep you there."

Jack manipulated his jaw again and one ear cleared. "You tell me this now."

"Been waiting for you to ask for help, Jack. You're a stubborn bastard. Figured you'd walk through my door weeks ago. Figured when you didn't, maybe you'd decided to give up the fight."

"You can find a way to fund me to keep reporting?" He was having trouble piecing this together. Private funding would allow him to chase story leads. He could freelance and publish on his own website, use his other media contacts to drive readers to his stories, build a list of subscribers. It could work. It could fail miserably, but it was worth a shot.

"I'm only a broke-down old priest who runs a shady fight club, but you had to wonder how I keep managing to do that. First thing we do is get you clear of any legal trouble."

They talked the details out. Barney's lawyer—another man Jack had met in the ring, Abdullah Khan—would remind the *Courier* about their obligations. It felt remarkable to know he had people in his corner.

"And Derelie?"

He should've guessed Barney would remember her name. She'd been in Jack's corner too. He just had to come up with a way to ask her to come back and be there again.

Chapter Twenty-Seven

Would you rather be a romance meme or break your hand hitting a punching bag? As far as Derelie was concerned, yoga was dead to her, dog and cat people had no common ground, and bring on the bandages.

Bring on the love for Artie Chan too. He was easy to fall for. He was intelligent and humble and quick-witted. He had a sense of humor that made you instantly warm to him. He wasn't reticent or difficult or moody disguised as complex like a certain other person Derelie had tried the love experiment with.

Like that other person, Artie's family had been upset when he dumped medicine for journalism, but they'd adapted, got with the program, loved and respected his choices.

"It was the fluids thing," Artie had said. "I couldn't handle the blood and pus and poop, you don't want to know what else. I feel a little sick if I have to say the word—" he'd shuddered "—viscera."

They'd laughed, trading answers, sharing information joyfully. Around the time Artie said he sang opera badly in the shower but K-pop in his car, Derelie thought it was a tragedy he was single. When he said the greatest achievement of his life was not murdering his annoying baby sister, and blushed when admitting his relationship with his mother was very close, she wanted to hug him. Artie hadn't met the right girl yet because once he did he'd have to pry her off with his cold, dead hands. Artie liked a good cliché and he knew a lot of ten dollar words and he knew Derelie was pissed off.

It wasn't so easy to learn how to deal with a punching bag, but it made her feel better. Despite the aching arms, abs and a stiff neck, it felt fantastic to whack something, to go full-on Wonder Woman does Supergirl on a leather wiener. Violence was an antidote to being humiliated and having your heart broken, who knew?

Well, the whole newsroom, that's who.

And that was her own fault. If she'd said no to that newsroom kiss, if she hadn't practically fallen into Jack's arms in front of everyone, she wouldn't have had to explain that they were no longer together. Not that she'd explained in words so much as action. She showed up to work tired and worn, took her first sick day when a stress headache got the better of her and generally acted like she had a thorn in her paw.

When Phil asked how Jack was getting on, she might as well have stabbed a sharpened pencil in his throat by telling him exactly what he could do with that question. She told him if he was so concerned he could call Jack himself and that she had no idea since her skillset had not been aligned with his strategy going forward and he'd dumped her a month ago.

Way to take your private life to work. You go, girl.

And that was humiliating too.

But it would pass. She knew it. Mom kept reminding her of it. Phil brushed her apology away as if he'd expected to get grief from her, Eunice brought her good coffee, Spin insisted on patting her on the back in a "we're on the same team" manner every time they crossed paths, and Annie Berkelow invited her to lunch and neither of them mentioned Jack. And the only thing she could do to feel better was take it out on a punching bag, enjoy her new friendships and write up her story with Artie.

Relaxed and friendly where Jack was intense, fun where Jack was reserved, ambitious but not to a fault, and secure in his choices where Jack was conflicted. Artie was the control group. He proved the experiment worked, that thirty-six questions answered honestly and an unnerving stare-off contest could create intimacy.

But they weren't enough to make you fall in love.

They both wrote their impressions from the exercise, and the story was scheduled to appear, while Derelie learned the basics of throwing a punch at the gym, Spin taught her how to drink beer like a pro journalist and lunch with Annie became a regular thing.

She bought a new plant for the window ledge in her shoebox apartment and remembered how to grocery shop for one. The city seemed louder, dirtier, faster, though that couldn't be real. There were no more or less stars in the sky than there had been when she was with Jack, it's just that he'd stopped her from feeling the need to note their absence.

She didn't call Jack. He didn't text her. His name

got taken off the internal email and messenger systems. Stories he'd written were slowly on their way to a digital archive and his dinkus no longer appeared anywhere.

There was little satisfaction that hers did.

None of that made it easier to forget how alive she'd felt when Jack's guard had come crashing down, when he'd teased her, made her laugh, let her into his life and shown he cared for her. At night, she hugged the red pillow she'd bought for his couch as if that might make not having his arms to fall into, his lips to tempt her feel less tragic. That pillow soaked up tears as well, not over Jack, over the fact Ernest had most definitely forgotten her forever.

That was the lie she told herself.

It didn't help.

On top of it all, she missed cuddling Martha.

She could only be grateful she hadn't given Jack her ugly tears, because he wouldn't have known what to do with them.

She fitted in the city now, knew its rhythm and grind, felt secure at work despite regretting she could be a news headline. "Ten Easy Ways to be a Loser at Love." Her heart might hurt, but that's what living a bigger life was about: operating beyond your comfort zone, stretching yourself and overcoming obstacles, buying nice clothes, thinking outside the box, dumping yoga because you really hated the peaceful resistance of it, having straight teeth and not needing your aligner anymore, eating all the ice cream in the world and feeling sorry for yourself.

The one thing she was proud of was that nothing

about losing Jack made her want to tuck her tail under, ditch the city and head for the familiarity of home. She was home, even if it was less cozy, less exciting than it had been when it included Jack.

And that was her new normal until her email delivered an unexpected story. It was headlined: You Won't Believe What Happened When I Did a Love Experiment.

That made her want put to her fledgling punching skills to use. You couldn't get on with getting over a person if he was going to show up suddenly in your inbox.

She didn't have to read it.

But he'd clickbaited her.

It started:

Recently I had an epiphany. It happened fittingly at church and it hit me like a power-packed right cross.

She knew what that meant. Jack had been putting his fists to use.

It will seem like a small thing when I tell you about it. It seems ridiculous when you know my life's work has been about helping others who had no voice to help themselves.

The bastard had written this ready to drop into a feature again. The last time he'd done that, she'd met his Jesus jeans and Martha. She'd surprised him into answering questions and they'd kissed without pretending it wasn't for the sheer pleasure of it. But she'd asked him a final question and he'd answered it. He didn't love her, and what she'd thought was real was a lie and there was nothing more to say.

My name is Jackson Haley. I'm an investigative reporter. I like to ask questions and hunt for the answers. I'm owned by a large, rambunctious, freedom-seeking cat. I'm addicted to clove cigarettes. They're going to kill me and I'm trying to give them up. I'm currently unemployed and as a consequence of not knowing how to be loved, I lost the love of my life.

Except maybe that. She was helpless not to read on.

It started with an experiment and considerable masculine posturing. The idea was to test out a questionnaire designed to develop intimacy. The theory being that thirty-six questions could kickstart a relationship and lead to love. I wasn't a willing participant.

Since I spend my time writing about crime, nefarious practices and wrongdoing, call me a cynic about love. My partner in this exercise called me other names, some not suitable to print, and she was right. She was also generous and clever and wise and heroic and, Jesus toast, I was attracted to her from the moment we met, falling for her by question two (Would you like to be famous?) and in love with her by question five (When did you last sing to yourself?).

And by the time we talked about our greatest hopes and fears, she was in love with me.

We answered thirty-six questions, looked deeply into each other's eyes and had an emotional reaction, and then we strayed outside the boundaries of the lab to kiss, and it was chemical, and the rest as they say is swoon.

[Insert swoon meme visual, gif or video link here]

Apart from that editorial instruction, which was presumptuous and so very Jack, Derelie was unshakably engaged in the story, eyeballs locked, attention loaded.

But then I messed it up. I ran into some career challenges, in that my career fell off a cliff and I was too much of a man, which is to say, stupid, to ask for help. I became the guy who makes decisions for other people on the basis of what works best for himself. I told the love of my life she was better off without me and I put conditions on how I loved her in return.

As you might imagine, she had little incentive not to agree with my ugly stubborn heart and moved out of my life without a backward glance. Told you she was smart.

I didn't know a home until she was in my life, and no one told me the immensity of that would rock my world. I cratered it by asking her to leave.

It took thirty-six questions to find her and only one to let her go.

Oh, Jack.

Maybe we weren't meant to be. She is a dog person, after all. She has no reason to give me a second chance.

I'll admit I'm rattled. That's how I felt when faced with the experiment. I didn't think I had much other than my work that would interest anyone else. I didn't want to share the details of my life in case they proved a disappointment. I didn't have anything to lose then, and still reluctance was the foot I led with. I have a whole new vision of what my life could be now, and rattled is too simple a word to express how that makes me feel. My crisis of the heart is more terrifying than my career crisis ever could be.

I'm not usually a quitter. In fact, I've had more than five minutes of fame based on fighting for people who've been disadvantaged. This time I'm fighting for me. I've got a question to ask this wonderful woman, and depending on what she says I might get a second chance at love.

What? It ended there. A cliffhanger. There had to be more. She scrolled and there was nothing until his email signature, above which was the line:

You Won't Believe What Happens When She Meets Him at Their Picnic Spot in the Park Today at Five. (Text Y/N to confirm.)

She stared at the screen. She wasn't meeting him in the park today. She wasn't cutting out early so he could pull this elaborate stunt. She didn't fight for Jack because it wasn't her job to teach him how to be loved. He had to want what she could give or she would burn herself out on him.

He was a cat person. He'd dumped her, insulted her, made a fool of her. It'd been fun while it lasted, but all good things come to a clichéd end and no amount of being clever and cute could make her forget that. Besides, she was busy. She wasn't open to being manipulated like this. Clickbait while you were at your desk looking at a screen was one thing, exploring it in real life made no sense.

It was safer, more considered to stay right where she was.

And if she'd followed that advice she'd still be in Orderly, home of the white squirrel, and the *Orderly Daily Mail*, where the most exciting thing that'd happened to her was a drunken entanglement with a barbwire fence and a sordid affair with a probably married salesman.

She picked up her phone, opened Jack's number, typed in one letter and pressed Send.

An hour later she walked into the park with no idea what to say if Jack asked her to come back to him, because not only had he been quick and brutal in ending their relationship, if he was going to move to New York or Washington or the moon, it made no sense to follow him when she was doing well in Chicago. She couldn't trust him enough for that.

She'd only texted Y because she wanted to see him again, wish him luck without the anger of their parting. Kiss him one last time in memory of the way his kisses had made her feel.

But then the dog happened.

Jack stood under their tree in the park with a dog that looked a lot like Ernest. A tan and white hound who took one look at her and nearly pulled Jack's arm off trying to get to her and then almost pushed her over when he did.

He jumped and squirmed and whined and licked and wriggled and put his paws and his back all over her, shedding fur and slobbering. It couldn't be. She grabbed his collar to check his tag, and he smashed his nose under her chin, making her bite her tongue. It was Ernest, all the way from Orderly, and he did remember her. He remembered her so damn hard he stung her shins with his whipping tail.

She pressed her face into his coat. "What are you doing here, Ernie?" He barked when she said his name. "Did you miss me, boy? I missed you so much. I thought you forgot me. I thought you didn't love me anymore." That was met with more excited whining and a big wet lick to her cheek. "You're such a good boy. My good boy."

She looked up to see what her other boy was doing while her hands were full of Ernest's ecstasy.

Jack kept a respectable distance, stood watching, wearing jeans and a white business shirt with the collar undone, with his hands in the pockets of his beaten leather coat. He wore a new pair of glasses that would've made him look as Old Hollywood glamorous as the last pair had if his face wasn't scraped and his eyes weren't sunk in dark bruises.

That was evidence of his epiphany at the Church of the Cocked Fist.

And Ernest was proof he'd been to Orderly, found out where she grew up and met her parents. That couldn't have gone well. It was possible the black eyes didn't come from church.

"You met my parents?"

"They said to say hello." She motioned to his eyes and he said, "Courtesy of St. Longinus. Your dad thought it was bad form to hit a guy who was already hurt."

She almost smiled at that. She almost did an Ernest and rushed Jack, slobbered all over him. "Why is Ernest here?" Ernest barked and slumped against her, his head lolling on her thigh.

"Because I'm a coward and I could use all the help I can get."

"You're using my dog as leverage." And her insult as a peace offering. Jack wasn't a coward, but he might not have a tolerance for love.

He took a couple of steps toward her and put his hand to Ernest's head. "I tried using my cat and that got me nowhere."

She shouldn't want Jack to be touching her instead of her dog. "I appreciate you bringing Ernest and writing another installment of the love experiment story, but it's all too late. I did the experiment with Artie."

He blinked hard, his head jerking up. "Did you fall in love with him in thirty-six questions?"

"You don't get to ask that." He took that with a sharp nod. "You can read the story with everyone else next week. Why am I here, Jack?"

"Because I have a last question for you and I wanted to get the conditions right before I asked it. It's not perfect, but there are trees and some early stars, and you can pretend not to hear the city. I think Ernest scared all the birds away, but he's here at least and I'm staking my reputation as an investigative reporter on him being part of your perfect day."

Jack's question was going to shake her safety and challenge her caution. Her limbic system was on red alert, breaking news all over her body, fear and desire and excitement and anger and pleasure and wanting, so much wanting.

"I love you. I didn't stop loving you when I pushed you away. I didn't understand how much you could ask of love, how much you could receive."

His question was going to wreck her in a way his story had made her resolve fray.

"I quit on us because I was afraid to lean on you and forgot the first thing I learned about you."

That she was a rookie and not cut out for the "if it bleeds, it leads" of journalism. That she was too green for the rough and tough, an imposter in the city.

"Your strength."

She looked down at Ernest, at Jack's hand resting on his head. He'd made her feel small and worthless when he pushed her away. He made hope tremble in her now.

"From the first day you stood up for yourself and the love experiment, I knew you had grit, and look at what you've done since then."

Professionally, she'd kicked ass. She put her hand on Ernest's back. Personally, she'd been cut back, sold out. "I lost you."

"No, you didn't." Jack slid his fingers over hers. Ernest used their movements to lie at their feet. "I had to find myself before I could keep you."

"What does that mean?" Other than the terrifying painful, expectant thudding of her heart.

"I'm staying in the city. I've found a way to keep working and the *Courier* is going to defend me from Keepsafe."

"I'm glad," and she didn't disguise it, letting him see her smile. "But I didn't love you for the work you did or your face on the TV, or the money you have in the bank."

"I didn't understand that. No one has ever loved me for being me. I thought I was doing the right thing for you. I wanted you to shine. I didn't want you to be a footnote in anyone's life."

She put her hand to the collar of Jack's coat. If he was wearing a tag she'd check it. She'd want to read on it that his name was Jackson Haley and his home was with Derelie Honeywell and anyone who found him should return him to her immediately. There'd be a reward.

"Ask your question." She already had her answer. Yes, she loved him. Yes, she'd come back to him. Yes, to Ernest and Martha, and working life out together.

"Will you do a new experiment with me?"

She tugged on his collar till he brought his face close, and he pulled her into his body heat. Their eyes locked. His said he missed her, he needed her, he loved her and her answer terrified him.

"On one condition."

"Name it." He kissed those words against her temple and it would be too easy to forget what she had to say, except they'd be nothing together without it.

"Trust me to love you."

He let go a long-held sigh. Held for minutes, days, weeks, years. "My most perfect day is the one where Derelie Honeywell agrees to be with me while I work out who Jackson Haley is when he's in love, where we never stop asking questions and giving answers, where we disagree as thoroughly as we make up." He put a hand to her hair and smoothed it. "Derelie Honeywell, will you do the love experiment with me for the rest of our lives?"

A lifetime of investigating each other, a lifetime of moments too good to look away from, too interesting not to share, repeat and share again. Every metric through the roof and no buyouts. A lifetime of cats and dogs and hugs and kisses and making each other laugh and cry, no matter where they lived or worked. This was Jack embracing his whole life. This was Derelie's big adventure, her new place in the wider world.

"Yes. Yes." Front page exclusive, hold the presses, add the visuals, assign a URL, load the page. "Yes."

Stars in each other's skies, sunlight on each other's hopes and dreams, passion pure like birdsong, love as clean as fresh air and laughter like an overexcited hound.

Who knew you could get to love in thirty-six questions and grab it forever with one more?

You'll never believe what happens when two estranged lovers meet in the park, but it was swoonworthy clickbait and hard news wrapped together, and they lived happily ever after.

* * * * *

About the Thirty-Six Questions

The thirty-six questions that can make you fall in love with anyone (according to the *New York Times*) began life as an appendix in an academic paper by psychologist Arthur Aron and others in 1997 called *The Experimental Generation of Interpersonal Closeness: A Procedure and Some Preliminary Findings*.

Participants were told to work their way through the questions in order, each answering all thirty-six questions, over a period of an hour. Six months later, two of the original participants were married to each other.

Others who've recorded their experiences with the thirty-six questions included a four-minute session of staring into their partner's eyes without speaking. It's colloquially known as a stare off.

The original paper included the following instruction from the authors:

"This is a study of interpersonal closeness, and your task, which we think will be quite enjoyable, is to simply get close to your partner."

If you're brave enough to try it—good luck.

It might not lead to love, but there are worse ways to get to know someone.

Set One

1. Given the choice of anyone in the world, whom would you want as a dinner guest?

2. Would you like to be famous? In what way?

3. Before making a telephone call, do you ever rehearse what you are going to say? Why?

4. What would constitute a "perfect" day for you?

5. When did you last sing to yourself? To someone else?

6. If you were able to live to the age of ninety and retain either the mind or body of a thirty-year-old for the last sixty years of your life, which would you want?

7. Do you have a secret hunch about how you will die?

8. Name three things you and your partner appear to have in common.

9. For what in your life do you feel most grateful?

10. If you could change anything about the way you were raised, what would it be?

11. Take four minutes and tell your partner your life story in as much detail as possible.

12. If you could wake up tomorrow having gained any one quality or ability, what would it be?

Set Two

1. If a crystal ball could tell you the truth about yourself, your life, the future or anything else, what would you want to know?

2. Is there something that you've dreamed of doing for a long time? Why haven't you done it?

3. What is the greatest accomplishment of your life?

4. What do you value most in a friendship?

5. What is your most treasured memory?

6. What is your most terrible memory?

7. If you knew that in one year you would die suddenly, would you change anything about the way you are now living? Why?

8. What does friendship mean to you?

9. What roles do love and affection play in your life?

10. Alternate sharing something you consider a positive characteristic of your partner. Share a total of five items.

11. How close and warm is your family? Do you feel your childhood was happier than most other people's?

12. How do you feel about your relationship with your mother?

Set Three

1. Make three true "we" statements each. For instance, "We are both in this room feeling..."

2. Complete this sentence: "I wish I had someone with whom I could share..."

3. If you were going to become a close friend with your partner, please share what would be important for him or her to know.

4. Tell your partner what you like about them; be very honest this time, saying things that you might not say to someone you've just met.

5. Share with your partner an embarrassing moment in your life.

6. When did you last cry in front of another person? By yourself?

7. Tell your partner something that you like about them already.

8. What, if anything, is too serious to be joked about?

9. If you were to die this evening with no opportunity to communicate with anyone, what would you

most regret not having told someone? Why haven't you told them yet?

10. Your house, containing everything you own, catches fire. After saving your loved ones and pets, you have time to safely make a final dash to save any one item. What would it be? Why?

11. Of all the people in your family, whose death would you find most disturbing? Why?

12. Share a personal problem and ask your partner's advice on how he or she might handle it. Also, ask your partner to reflect back to you how you seem to be feeling about the problem you have chosen.

If you'd like to find out more about the thirty-six questions you can read The Experimental Generation of Interpersonal Closeness: A Procedure and Some Preliminary Findings *here:* http://journals.sagepub.com/doi/pdf/10.1177/0146167297234003

Now Available from Carina Press and Ainslie Paton

A master jewel thief meets his match in a daring romance of love and larceny.

Read on for an excerpt from Hoodwinked Hearts

Gorgeous. Cleve Jones toggled the control and adjusted the camera hidden in Greville's Auction House eleven thousand miles away in Geneva. From his villa in Ubud on the island of Bali, he now had a clearer view of the hunk of rock known as the Sweet Celestia, and it was an even more brilliant stone than he'd been led to expect.

It would make a fine asset to his patron's collection of priceless possessions, and in another few hours, when this publicity circus event shut down and the auction house was closed for the night, it would be his. And very shortly after that, there'd be a large sum of money that would more than cover the expense of this heist, deposited in an untraceable Cayman Islands bank account that Cleve just so happened to have the unique iris recognition for.

All that and he'd not bothered to put on a shirt, or shoes.

Funny how these things worked out.

Professor Donald Harp had always said Cleve had the talent to become the kind of man who didn't roll out of bed in the morning for less than a few multi-million, but Cleve had never quite believed it.

He was a kid from nowhere with nothing but a gift for persuasion, who'd bluffed his way into Harvard by impersonating a member of a distant branch of the famous Kennedy family. He'd surprised himself by getting as far as Professor Harp's Ancient History class and was happily soaking up the privileged Ivy League atmosphere and the flirty smiles of the gold class babes while he waited for his fake tuition payment to start stinking, and the moment where he'd go from living in his car to hoping it would start so he could make a clean getaway.

The professor had sniffed him out quicker than he could say Alexander the Great loved his horse Bucephalus, and instead of turning him over to the authorities—and a no doubt shamefully long stint in an incarceration facility not of his choosing—had offered Cleve a deal.

The professor was in need of an apprentice, and since Cleve was in need of a regular diet that didn't come from dumpster diving, a roof over his head, and a way to channel his talent for deception that ensured he stayed on the right side of a jail cell, they shook on it.

He'd always thought the trade-off of security for nefarious deeds would eventually lead to a Greek tragedy. He was no student of history, but he listened to police scanners and read court transcripts and true crime novels, and happy endings were a myth.

He'd been right, but not in the way he'd imagined.

And now, ten years after the death of his mentor, that made him a man who genuinely didn't bother getting out of bed for less than a few million, except for the odd occasion when the temptation to stay between the sheets was worth its own weight in another kind of gold, the kind shaped like a desirable woman.

It'd been an annoyingly long time since he'd forgotten about work and spent the day in bed.

"Oi, she's a bit of all right."

It was a shame Brandon Bartley hadn't decided on a lie in. It was a shame Brandon Bartley was a thing in Cleve's life at all.

"Sweet Celestia is the largest vivid pink diamond in the world—she is more than a bit of all right."

It was a shame Brandon Bartley was still breathing. The man has shown such promise as a thief, but turned out he was just a common garden-variety bagman, useful for collecting the rent as it were. Not at all what Cleve was looking for, because Cleve was looking for a partner to share the load, to go for even bigger paydays, in exactly the same way the professor chose him.

The problem was he was simply awful at picking the right accomplices. Brandon was his fourth not-rotten-enough-in-the-right-way apple.

"Hah, not the rock, mate." Brandon tipped his chin at the screen. "The dolly bird."

Cleve had been aware of the movement in the room on screen. The photographer's assistants bustling about while the gum-chewing photographer herself barked orders, the furniture being moved in, the PR flak furiously typing on his cell, and the girl.

"'Ard up like you bin, gov, fought you'd be all ova vat."

Cleve took a deep breath, thought happy thoughts,

like not dropping his aitches, and the deep tissue massage he'd have after he knew Sweet Celestia was his. Like hoping Brandon got another job offer.

Of course he was aware of the girl. He hadn't had the delicious feel of a girl's skin under his hands for months, and that girl was more than a dolly bird; she was genuinely beautiful, slender and steely strong like a ballerina, with clouds of almost-white hair and Elizabeth Taylor eyes.

But she also wasn't much more than a walking manicure. Her job was to hold Sweet Celestia in her buffed and polished hands, adding warmth to cold perfection while the stone was captured in digital glory.

The girl, whose name was Melody Solo, wasn't famous. She'd had all the usual physical attributes: height, slim form, barely enough curves to count, and a symmetrical face, as well as the relevant career milestones—beauty pageant, catalog, catwalk, magazine fashion layout—to her name. But she'd been chosen for this job because she was no doubt cheap and available and looked a lot like the famous model she was replacing at the last moment.

It was Cleve's job to know these things, just like he knew the photographer's assistant with the ginger hair was having an affair with the PR flack, and the dresser, Katerina, was soon to launch her own label, and the guard with the cauliflower ears liked to bake, so yes, he'd noticed the girl, and she was indeed a bit of all right.

Given the chance, he'd stay in bed for her.

But she was eleven thousand miles away and within the next hour would be irrelevant.

She was also silly as a box full of kittens. She tittered, she fluttered her lashes, she had trouble walking in the jewel-encrusted shoes she wore. He might wrinkle a sheet for her because he was, after all, hard up, but he would most definitely kick her out of bed in the morning. He had no tolerance for silly—tried it, not to his taste. He'd apparently been ruined for silly for all time by the professor's daughter.

On the screen, Annie swallowed her gum and the redhead positioned Melody on the chaise lounge as if she was a bendable Barbie.

The professor's daughter was two years younger than him, sixteen going on juvenile delinquent when they met. Half her hair was dyed burnt orange and the other half of her head was shaved and later adorned with a tattoo of two crossed bones. It was a joke, skull and crossbones, and Cleve had loved her for that alone. She had a pierced tongue, a savage wit, a healthy disrespect for authority, and her favorite shoes were steel-capped boots. She'd been expelled from more schools than Cleve had bothered to bluff his way into, and she was the hottest, wildest, smartest woman he'd ever kissed.

The professor forbade him to talk to her. "It's very simple. If you speak to her, I will turn you in. If you touch her, you die," he'd said, with the same student-friendly tone he used to say, "Of course you can have an extension on that paper."

A decade later Cleve had never quite recovered from his first love. Neither the high of risking his life to fall in love with her, nor the devastating low of losing her, raising the earth to find her, and coming up with nothing but empty whispers. She was a ghost, but the memory of her magnificence had stayed with him.

When a score went bad, you cleaned up, covered your tracks and moved on. He'd never quite been able to move on from Aria Harp and doubted he ever would.

Don't miss Hoodwinked Hearts *by Ainslie Paton.*
Available now wherever
Carina Press ebooks are sold.

www.CarinaPress.com

Acknowledgments

To the BTA crew. We did it again. Thank you, as always.

About the Author

Ainslie Paton always wanted to write stories to make people smile, but the need to eat, accumulate books, and have bedclothes to read under was ever present. She sold out, and worked as a flack, a suit, and a creative, impersonating business leaders, rabble-rousers and politicians, and making words happen for companies, governments, causes, conditions, high-profile CEOs, low-profile celebs, and the occasional misguided royal.

She still does that. She also writes for love, and so she can buy shoes and the good cat food.

More here: www.ainsliepaton.com.au and on Twitter @AinsliePaton.

Get 4 FREE REWARDS!

We'll send you 2 FREE Books plus 2 FREE Mystery Gifts.

Harlequin® Desire books feature heroes who have it all: wealth, status, incredible good looks... everything but the right woman.

FREE Value Over $20

Get 4 FREE REWARDS!

We'll send you 2 FREE Books plus 2 FREE Mystery Gifts.

Harlequin Presents® books feature a sensational and sophisticated world of international romance where sinfully tempting heroes ignite passion.

FREE
Value Over
$20

YES! Please send me 2 FREE Harlequin Presents® novels and my 2 FREE gifts (gifts are worth about $10 retail). After receiving them, if I don't wish to receive any more books, I can return the shipping statement marked "cancel." If I don't cancel, I will receive 6 brand-new novels every month and be billed just $4.55 each for the regular-print edition or $5.55 each for the larger-print edition in the U.S., or $5.49 each for the regular-print edition or $5.99 each for the larger-print edition in Canada. That's a savings of at least 11% off the cover price! It's quite a bargain! Shipping and handling is just 50¢ per book in the U.S. and 75¢ per book in Canada.* I understand that accepting the 2 free books and gifts places me under no obligation to buy anything. I can always return a shipment and cancel at any time. The free books and gifts are mine to keep no matter what I decide.

Choose one: ☐ **Harlequin Presents®**
Regular-Print
(106/306 HDN GMYX)

☐ **Harlequin Presents®**
Larger-Print
(176/376 HDN GMYX)

Name (please print)

Address   Apt. #

City   State/Province   Zip/Postal Code

Mail to the Reader Service:
IN U.S.A.: P.O. Box 1341, Buffalo, NY 14240-8531
IN CANADA: P.O. Box 603, Fort Erie, Ontario L2A 5X3

Want to try 2 free books from another series! Call 1-800-873-8635 or visit www.ReaderService.com.

---

*Terms and prices subject to change without notice. Prices do not include sales taxes, which will be charged (if applicable) based on your state or country of residence. Canadian residents will be charged applicable taxes. Offer not valid in Quebec. This offer is limited to one order per household. Books received may not be as shown. Not valid for current subscribers to Harlequin Presents books. All orders subject to approval. Credit or debit balances in a customer's account(s) may be offset by any other outstanding balance owed by or to the customer. Please allow 4 to 6 weeks for delivery. Offer available while quantities last.

Your Privacy—The Reader Service is committed to protecting your privacy. Our Privacy Policy is available online at www.ReaderService.com or upon request from the Reader Service. We make a portion of our mailing list available to reputable third parties that offer products we believe may interest you. If you prefer that we not exchange your name with third parties, or if you wish to clarify or modify your communication preferences, please visit us at www.ReaderService.com/consumerschoice or write to us at Reader Service Preference Service, P.O. Box 9062, Buffalo, NY 14240-9062. Include your complete name and address.

HP19R

Get 4 FREE REWARDS!

We'll send you 2 FREE Books <u>plus</u> 2 FREE Mystery Gifts.

Harlequin® Special Edition books feature heroines finding the balance between their work life and personal life on the way to finding true love.

FREE
Value Over
$20

YES! Please send me 2 FREE Harlequin® Special Edition novels and my 2 FREE gifts (gifts are worth about $10 retail). After receiving them, if I don't wish to receive any more books, I can return the shipping statement marked "cancel." If I don't cancel, I will receive 6 brand-new novels every month and be billed just $4.99 per book in the U.S. or $5.74 per book in Canada. That's a savings of at least 12% off the cover price! It's quite a bargain! Shipping and handling is just 50¢ per book in the U.S. and 75¢ per book in Canada.* I understand that accepting the 2 free books and gifts places me under no obligation to buy anything. I can always return a shipment and cancel at any time. The free books and gifts are mine to keep no matter what I decide.

235/335 HDN GMY2

Name (please print)

Address   Apt. #

City   State/Province   Zip/Postal Code

Mail to the Reader Service:
IN U.S.A.: P.O. Box 1341, Buffalo, NY 14240-8531
IN CANADA: P.O. Box 603, Fort Erie, Ontario L2A 5X3

Want to try 2 free books from another series? Call 1-800-873-8635 or visit www.ReaderService.com.

Get 4 FREE REWARDS!

We'll send you 2 FREE Books plus 2 FREE Mystery Gifts.

FREE Value Over **$20**

Both the **Romance** and **Suspense** collections feature compelling novels written by many of today's best-selling authors.

YES! Please send me 2 FREE novels from the Essential Romance or Essential Suspense Collection and my 2 FREE gifts (gifts are worth about $10 retail). After receiving them, if I don't wish to receive any more books, I can return the shipping statement marked "cancel." If I don't cancel, I will receive 4 brand-new novels every month and be billed just $6.74 each in the U.S. or $7.24 each in Canada. That's a savings of at least 16% off the cover price. It's quite a bargain! Shipping and handling is just 50¢ per book in the U.S. and 75¢ per book in Canada.* I understand that accepting the 2 free books and gifts places me under no obligation to buy anything. I can always return a shipment and cancel at any time. The free books and gifts are mine to keep no matter what I decide.

Choose one: ☐ **Essential Romance**
(194/394 MDN GMY7)

☐ **Essential Suspense**
(191/391 MDN GMY7)

Name (please print)

Address   Apt. #

City   State/Province   Zip/Postal Code

Mail to the **Reader Service:**
IN U.S.A.: P.O. Box 1341, Buffalo, NY 14240-8531
IN CANADA: P.O. Box 603, Fort Erie, Ontario L2A 5X3

Want to try 2 free books from another series? Call 1-800-873-8635 or visit www.ReaderService.com.

Get 4 FREE REWARDS!

We'll send you 2 FREE Books plus 2 FREE Mystery Gifts.

Harlequin® Romance Larger-Print books feature uplifting escapes that will warm your heart with the ultimate feel-good tales.

FREE Value Over **$20**

Wedding the Greek Billionaire
Rebecca Winters

Her Festive Flirtation
Therese Beharrie
